A
PRAYER
FOR
TRAVELERS

A
PRAYER
FOR
TRAVELERS

RUCHIKA TOMAR

RIVERHEAD BOOKS

NEW YORK

2019

RIVERHEAD BOOKS
An imprint of Penguin Random House LLC
penguinrandomhouse.com

Copyright © 2019 by Ruchika Tomar
Penguin supports copyright. Copyright fuels creativity, encourages
diverse voices, promotes free speech, and creates a vibrant culture. Thank you
for buying an authorized edition of this book and for complying with copyright
laws by not reproducing, **scanning**, or distributing any part of it in any form
without permission. You are supporting writers and allowing
Penguin to continue to publish books for every reader.

Library of Congress Cataloging-in-Publication Data

Names: Tomar, Ruchika, author.
Title: A prayer for travelers : a novel / Ruchika Tomar.
Description: New York : Riverhead Books, 2019.
Identifiers: LCCN 2018050220 (print) | LCCN 2018051765 (ebook) |
ISBN 9780525537038 (ebook) | ISBN 9780525537014 (hardcover) |
ISBN 9780593084489 (international edition)
Classification: LCC PS3620.O474 (ebook) |
LCC PS3620.O474 P73 2019 (print) | DDC 813/.6—dc23
LC record available at https://lccn.loc.gov/2018050220

Printed in the United States of America
1   3   5   7   9   10   8   6   4   2

Book design by Meighan Cavanaugh

A
PRAYER
FOR
TRAVELERS

31

I drove to the Crossroads with the windows rolled down, the radio off, scanning the flat, packed earth in the glare of afternoon light, the land broken up by clumps of creosote and rabbitbrush. I was hoping to see Penny walking on the shoulder of the road heading in my direction. I drove so slowly it would be impossible to miss her. When I saw her figure, tall and milktea pale, her long black hair nearly to her hips, I would pull over and unlock the passenger door. I would make room for her on the bench seat while she chronicled the saga of the delayed bus, the careless excuse Flaca had given when she hadn't shown up to give Penny a ride. When she was finished, we would wait in silence for the reality of the previous day to dawn. She would reach across the seat and we would embrace each other gently, needing to feel the other whole. She would tuck her chin in the dip of my shoulder, careful to avoid the bruises covering the right side of my face. I would say her name.

Instead a car horn sounded and a battered Trans Am shot out from behind, flying past, taillights flashing red at the corner a half mile down the road. I watched the car turn off and disappear. For the rest of the drive I considered what I would say to Penny when she finally answered her door, the nature of rebuke to deliver. *Answer your fucking phone!* I was prepared to resume the role of surly outcast, if only to stir her incautious charm.

At the entrance to the Crossroads, two young girls stood a few feet apart, tossing a big red ball between them. It was the cheap plastic of the swap meet, certain to deflate within a day. Countless other balls lay flattened like the vibrant, molted skins of mythical creatures in weed-strewn backyards all over Pomoc. The taller girl wore her black hair in pigtails and looked up when I drove past. In another week they would both be back in school. The careless feeling of summer was almost gone.

I pulled down the narrow lane to Penny's neat white mobile home, the pot of bee balm still flowering on the ledge. I took the stairs two at a time and banged on the door, straining my ear for the familiar sound of Penny's television or the slight, high-pitched yip from the new puppy. But Penny always slept in a deep, comatose oblivion, impossible to rouse.

"Penny!" Pounding on the door with the side of my fist.

I had, on occasion, slept over; I woke early to the sound of the workers running down the stairs of their units in their steel-toe boots, calling to each other across the east side of the park; I had pulled back Penny's gauzy bedroom curtains to watch them walk down the drive. Now I left the front door to walk around the rear of the unit, crouching down to peer through the sliver of Penny's bedroom window where the curtains met the sill. If a neighbor chose this moment to look outside, they would have cause to be alarmed—but Pomoc was still at work, the men tossing bags of ice down the chute at the plant, sweating under yellow construction hats all over the county, the women assembling circuit boards at the electronic manufacturing plant in Noe. Through the window, I could just make out the edge of

Penny's rumpled bed and a twist of white sheets, but not whether Penny was still inside, lying in them. I rapped on the glass, waiting for some response.

It was the bright afternoon hour of small shadows, my reflection liminal on the glass, vanishing and reappearing with a tilt of my chin. I returned to the front of the mobile home, the light sparkling on the antennas of parked cars, gleaming off a doublewide's stripped metal siding. I hesitated at the front door. *Go home.* If it wasn't for the unanswered voicemails, the sandman, Lamb—maybe I could have. But Penny was a reliable waitress, punctual to a fault, and with each passing second it felt increasingly necessary to see her, to test our shelter. To bear each other's witness.

Under the pot of bee balm on the ledge, I felt for Penny's spare key. *Let it just be her inside.* Not Penny and a half-naked stranger, or worse, just the stranger. The sandman lurking in the hallway, primed for his revenge.

I slid the key in the door and the lock popped open, the knob turning easily in my hand. Inside the old television sat mute, the screen staring blankly, an eerie, vacant hush swallowing the room. I walked straight back to her bedroom. Her bed was empty, the sheets pushed back to reveal an impression in the mattress where she had slept curled toward the wall. I ran my hand in the hollow her body left. The sheets were cool.

I grabbed the tangled covers and shook them out, a hard object falling, making solid contact with the floor. I dropped to my hands and knees, inhaling dust bunnies to reach the familiar glint of her phone under the bed. I pocketed it, climbing to my feet again. I called softly for the dog, checking behind the door, inside the hamper— anywhere a small, scared animal might think to hide. I retraced my steps to the hall to check the coat closet and the bathroom, flinging aside her shower curtain: empty, empty. Penny could have walked to the general store, caught a ride to the diner—but where was the puppy? In the kitchen the counters were clear; no dog food or water bowl, no toys. Not even the milk crate she had used to carry him home.

Returning to the front room, I considered the dwindling options. The dog wasn't behind the couch or the television, not curled under the serape throw folded neatly over a chair. If the dog had gotten sick, she could have hitched a ride to the vet. But Penny wouldn't forget her phone. On the mirrored table, an assortment of silver gum wrappers had been folded into a flock of origami cranes. I squashed one with my thumb. Any moment the front door would fly open, and Penny's low voice would arch across the room in surprise. She would stamp her feet on the threshold. She would carry the newborn pup in her hands, drowsy and soft as velvet. She would ask why I was here.

I flopped on the couch to wait. Nothing happened.

Eventually I got up again and wandered into the kitchen, opening the fridge. A bottle of ketchup, a carton of eggs. A takeout container from the diner. I picked an apple off the top shelf to bite into the fruit, cold and wet against my teeth. In the freezer were several empty ice trays and the old coffee can. A couple weeks earlier I had stood in this exact same spot watching Penny flip pancakes on the stove. I had taken the coffee can down to brew a pot, only to have her set her spatula aside and cover my hands with her own. Penny, who could talk and talk, hadn't said a word. She simply took the can away and replaced it in the door. At the time, I understood it to hold something precious or peculiar—ashes, the flat frozen corpse of a pet fish, some embarrassing boundary our friendship had yet to cross.

I took the can down again now, holding the apple between my teeth, brushing loose coffee grounds from the lid before peeling it away. It was packed tightly with rolls of cash, each bundle tied off with a rubber band. I reached for one of the rolls and unwound the rubber, the feel of textured paper underneath my fingertips. I took all the rolls out and stacked them on the counter; twenties, all of them. There was nothing else inside. After staring at them awhile, I replaced the money in the coffee can and shut the freezer door. On the handle, a rust-colored smudge that flaked when I touched it. My heart began to sink.

I pulled Penny's phone from my pocket and tried powering it on, looking around the kitchen as if a power cord might appear, or Penny, some useful explanation. But the phone was dead. I tried to remember if I could ever recall Penny with two phones, if this could have been a duplicate. The sick feeling grew, the omniscient gray vapor rolling low and sinister through the halls.

The truth is, I knew when she didn't show up to work. I knew when she didn't answer her phone. I didn't know where she was, or what might have happened, but I knew something was wrong. I knew, and yet it had taken me hours to arrive. The mobile home was silent, the entire community still. At long last I heard my own blood rushing in my ears, steady as a storm.

2

Lamb's daughter was tall, her hair the color of rosewood. A pale, square chin and a wide mouth, a jagged-edged mole above the right lip like a scar. She stood on the perimeter of the emergency room in Tehacama where her own mother died twelve years before. She was dressed in dirty jeans and a ratty coat, a baby tied to her chest with a cotton sling.

Later, a hospital janitor pushing a mop bucket of filthy water would say the girl seemed distracted, impatient. She was overheard asking a man in the next seat for the time. The baby cried and the sound was lost amid the wail of an ambulance just pulling up, a cacophony of voices melding English to Spanish, back to English again. The crying stopped and started again, hours passed; nothing matters. When the girl's name was finally called she walked into a wide adjoining room divided only by paper screens.

Later, when the nurse rolled her cart in, the girl was sitting on the exam table with one leg folded underneath her, the other swinging back and forth. The baby had fallen asleep on her breast. The nurse straightened one of the girl's pale arms, tracing blue-green veins like rivers underneath smooth, unbroken skin. The girl didn't seem like a junkie, at least not in any obvious way. But twenty minutes later the nurse returned to find the baby alone, lying on the exam table's creased paper, quiet as you please, mouthing an expired driver's license. The nurse called the police and the police called a second number and several hours later an older man with a long angular face and black hair walked in from the cold. He was unknown to any of the parties involved and showed his identification to the uniforms guarding the child. He had driven three hours just to get there.

No, he told the officers. He had not seen his daughter in many years. He did not know where she was living.

They gave him the child, promising someone would call to follow up. The long-faced man took me home and built a cradle out of the lodgepole pine he'd been saving to make a desk. When I grew older, he told me I was his granddaughter. He told me my name was Cale.

He had a first name he never liked, last name Lambert. The boys in school called him Lamb, a lark because he was anything but. He was more like a tree grown bent from the earth, weathered and sound. Every day he went to work at Cesar's ice plant forty miles down the freeway. It began as a high school job: six dollars an hour to catch bags of ice at the bottom of the assembly chute and stack them on pallets for delivery. After three months came a promotion; in another six, he ran the floor.

Before Trixie, before Wolf, I was his only shadow. At two, already queerly distinct from the daughter he had lost. Brunette and yellow-eyed like one of the coydogs they bred on the mountain. In all the important ways, I was of him. I wore his socks, five sizes too large, and drank the dregs of his coffee from the cups left carelessly unattended throughout the house. In the evenings, when he retired to the front room to read the paper, I crawled into his lap to tuck my head under his grizzled chin, comforted by the smell of pine tar soap and Marlboro Reds, the clean, faded scent of laundry detergent on the breast of his checkered shirts.

At three and four and five, I asked for dogs. I had a pathological desire for warm animal bodies to kiss. Does this signify some kind of loss, a lack of attention on the guardian's part, an absence of love freely given? I don't know. I wanted to love something and know what it meant to grow it. I wanted to put my love on places and things that didn't mind. I had gotten to know about farms, where cows and pigs and dogs lived. These were things Pomoc would never have, lives that could never happen. Oh, you might buy a pot-bellied from the breeder in Nixon, but it's hard to keep fat things happy in the summer heat.

Our house was simple, one of the few in Pomoc with a second story. The floors had been stripped and remained unfinished; the stairs creaked and the taps ran cold for a long while before growing warm. In the front room stood the old blue couch where Lamb read his paper, the Paiute rug Wolf slept on those nights the temperatures dropped low enough to frost the saltbush. One summer we built bookshelves into the wall from harvested trunks of birch. When the panels had all been fitted together, we stacked our treasure there: Lamb's collection of dog-eared textbooks from two years at state college, my own assortment of dime-store paperbacks like snapshots from phases I'd outgrown—mysteries, romances, slow and sprawling biographies of famously short men.

Lamb's room, and his daughter's, was on the second floor, cool in the winter and the early hours of morning. I woke alone in her twin bed across a wide window overlooking the land. The room carried echoes from its previous owner: two black scuffmarks by the closet door where a full-length mirror hung, delicate pencil marks on the doorjamb where she grew taller and taller, until she stopped growing and had me. I lay in bed for hours imagining the million cruel ways she moved about the room, the smell of her hair as she stepped out of the white-tiled bath, even the shape and feel of her hands.

Across the hall, Lamb's bedroom had been modified for a widower. He kept the dresser polished to show a thick, wide scar in the wood and a black-and-white portrait of Catherine with her short, dark curls pinned up. The glass plate that held her jewelry had been packed and stowed, along with all her blouses and coats. In the attic were boxes of photo albums: the fresh-faced couple with dusty shoes, clasping hands in front of Pyramid Lake; the newborn baby swaddled in cloth; a wide-eyed toddler slick and gleaming in a tub. Later photographs showed a surly, cinnamon-haired daughter in corduroy trousers, clinging to Lamb in a dry field. I studied these photos to gauge Lamb's happiness and compare it with our own. Did he already know then, that he held the wrong daughter by the hand? Had the largest, most generous part of him always been waiting for me?

If family is nothing but the accumulation of routine among two or more people, here was ours: Lamb cut the thick pine table in the center of the kitchen himself, along with four spindle back chairs to match. We sat in the same pair every meal, though the others were hardly occupied. It was the only time he showed blatant affection to the dogs, dropping a piece of meat into each of their bowls, rubbing a grateful furry head.

After Lamb retired for the night, I stayed up washing our dishes in the sink, the kitchen window facing our rocky yard, the grade of pebbled soil and milkweed rising gradually into mountain. I lingered over the soapy plates and glasses, waiting for coyotes to emerge along the back ridge. They scavenged for small dogs, an unlucky cat, their bright eyes bobbing as they ran. The way they paced the fences, raising their snouts to howl.

5

Penny hung out with the same girls since elementary school. I remembered them as they were on the playground: sweet Luz; severe Flaca; Lourdes the petite, mercurial math genius. In high school they met every morning on the brush-covered knoll in front of the administration building, haughty and dispassionate in their tight jeans, constantly reapplying layers of glittery lip gloss. Penny was the obvious beauty among them, all long hair and dark eyes, the kind of mouth that could never successfully be made demure. Boys waylaid her in the halls with their coughs and dip-legged swaggers, leaning their hands against her locker as if they could box her in. I assumed she was the girls' ringleader, the bad influence, the reason they were always in the bathrooms smoking slims or joints with their polished nails flashing.

Late spring my senior year, when the desert snowberry and golden suncups were blooming on the hill above the classroom, and the promise of freedom was mounting in the halls, I went in to use the girls' bathroom. They were all there inside. I took my time washing my hands, then stood dripping for full minutes, waiting for Luz to notice she was blocking the paper towels. She was telling them all a story, using her hands to draw dramatic shapes in the air. When she saw me, she dropped her hands to her hips, trying to decide whether or not to be annoyed. I still wore shyness then, I didn't know it wouldn't be long in shedding, that I would molt my timidity in stages like the collared lizards racing across the desert, leaving pieces of themselves behind on the sand.

Penny sat on one of the sinks and leaned back against the tiles, studying me. She had painted her lips a new, bright fuchsia. I didn't understand why they were still here. Lourdes had skipped the first grade, and Flaca had been held back in the fourth. Though Penny was a year older than me, she had ditched the entire spring quarter the previous year for reasons that remained elusive to Vista High's most interrogative gossips. During this sabbatical, she was spotted slinging plates at Jake's diner and flirting with Trigger Casey at his father's corner store while the crew roamed the aisles, lifting bags of chips and bottles of beer. One afternoon I had run into her alone, picking through the dusty thrift store bookshelves. When she saw me, she had flushed red and straightened immediately as if reproached, stalking past me to the registers with her hands full of decade-old glossies. Now in a few weeks we would all graduate together. I doubted any of them knew my name.

I should have stepped away from the sinks and dried my hands on my shorts, letting them be. But I had been invisible for so long, I was starting to wonder if I still had a fleshly outline, a concrete human shape. I was struggling to find the right thing to say, and a reason to say it. Penny held her cigarette at a rakish angle, narrowing her eyes at me in the smoke. Finally she reached over, pushing Luz on the side of the head.

"Move, pinche," she said.

3

Lamb took me to the Blue Creek Casino and Eagles Bay, the Lucky Grand, the Golden Bear and East River Mills. There still existed, in those early days, a palpable space between the second father I made him into and the bachelor he used to be. Early winter mornings, when it was cold enough for our breath to fog the air, we packed into Lamb's truck for the long drive and watched the land dip and surge across the miles, breaching under a wide, glassy sky.

I slept away the day, my head bumping gently against the window, and opened my eyes to fading dusk. How the first sight of sparkling lights outside a passenger window could transfix a lonely girl. We stood in the check-in line for casino motels, still wearing crisp January air on our cheeks and collars. I clung to the three outer fingers of Lamb's calloused hand, ignoring the discriminating glances of older men and women. Who would bring a child to a place reserved for adult things, adult sins? I could have told them. *Someone who has nowhere else to put her.*

I trailed Lamb across smoke-tinged rooms, treading elaborately patterned carpets, the wood tables polished as jewels. The underbellies of these casinos were cold and drafty basements, cheap carpeting buckling under card tables ringed with beer-glazed men, raucous and wild. A furtive society, balm to the desert's sand-worn lifers, those souls grousing eternally between earth and sun. Oh, yes—the west takes care of its own in these small, forgotten towns. We build in us still those cursed dreams of gold.

At the East River, with a pale, gibbous moon hanging high, we arrived weary. We checked in after midnight to two twin beds, side by side. In the middle of the night, I woke to the sound of a heavy latch falling into place. In the next bed the sheets were mussed, empty. Lamb was gone. I pushed aside my own scratchy sheets and climbed out of bed. I looked for him in the bathroom and the closet, as if a grown man might play games in the dark, as if he might hide himself away like a parcel. I stole into the cold hall still muddled with sleep, wearing only a T-shirt.

I took a few steps down the hall and nearly collided with an odd, dark stranger rounding the corner. He wore a high, round collar and diagonal tie, a long frock coat. He walked on without a stumble or excuse, striding, his hands tucked behind his back. Lamb's word for a friend you meet in old places, a man you should never follow: s-p-e-c-t-e-r. The ghost brought me up short. I could have ridden the elevator down to the gaming floor and run across the carpet of players, screaming for Lamb, for rescue. They'd kick us out, which wouldn't bother Lamb a bit. But he would feel he had made an error, bringing a child on one of his peculiar tours to some place where I might do little and participate in less. I was meant to spend my time amusing myself in the café with ice cream sundaes or watching the television in the room—luxuries exotic when compared with our home, which held only books, and each other. These trips felt like running, but what were we running to?

I returned to the doorway of our room and sat on the floor to wait.

An hour passed, maybe two. When Lamb manifested at the end of the hall, his expression was warm and loose, his eyes bright with the far-away look of someone who had visited a freedom and wished to remain there. He saw his impolitely dressed gargoyle in the doorway and bent to lift her. I didn't have to ask. He packed his bag and then my own. An hour later, ours was the only truck heading west on the two-lane, zooming past the other cars that took fast shape in the dark, emerging from nothing and disappearing just as fast, headlights fading gently into night.

32

The police station was an old timber-front at the end of a long, sloping road, a lingering reminder of Pomoc's coal mining days. Scattered along the western ridge were the town's other relics: the three-sided frame of a gutted firehouse half a mile past; the rusted, hollowed-out caboose from the railway depot standing in a field of weeds; the tracks long since foraged for lumber. Only a few steps inside the station the feeling of history began to dissolve. The smell of wood shavings from recent construction, the stale remains of a burger lunch. The first and only time I'd been inside was ten years earlier: Lamb determined to talk his way out of a ticket for a broken taillight, and I still small enough to be made coy by the aged spirit of the place; the mold in the wood, dust particles floating by a front-facing window. A gray-haired patrolman stationed at the front desk had broken into laughter at the sight of Lamb, then Lamb followed suit, the two men clasping each other's hands and shoulders, reminiscing a shared boyhood I would never know.

There was no one at the front desk now. The entire reception area was covered by a heavy plastic tarpaulin, the station in the midst of painful repair, flailing helplessly toward modernization. The pole chairs in the waiting area had been replaced by four rows of molded orange seats bolted into the floor and another dense, filmy tarp hung over the doorway, obscuring what lay beyond. On the floor, gray dust lay mottled in the fading light.

Beyond the tarp, I heard a phone ring. I pushed aside the plastic sheeting and followed a man's short, muffled laugh down the length of a cramped hallway, past several plywood doors painted white, unisex signposts nailed into the wood. The hall widened into a large room furnished with six wide desks, three set close on either end. The south wall was lined with metal shelves buttressing cardboard boxes and ancient computer monitors, a wild tangle of multicolored cords and wires, a coffeepot giving off the burnt, acrid scent of recent use, a stack of Styrofoam cups and stirrers.

The room's only occupant was a young, lanky cop I didn't know, his buzzcut bleached platinum, eyebrows still dark and spiky. A part-time townie from one of the census-designated places surrounding Pomoc, waking each morning to dress in the dark, climbing into his car to travel fifteen to forty-five down a two-lane to clip on a badge for a town that wasn't really his. He glanced up briefly from his call, then again, in a way that recalled to me the ugly cut above my eye, the bruise an imprecise crescent moon around my right temple, spilling onto my cheek. I hesitated, but his call was winding down, and when he hung up he reached over to turn on the small silver radio on his desk, fiddling with the knob to filter out the sound. Staticky AC/DC filled the space between us.

"I called earlier," I said. The room had the poor acoustics of old timber. "I spoke to a woman on the phone. I'm worried about a friend of mine."

"Yeah?"

"She didn't come in to work today. I went to her place and she wasn't there."

His touch on the radio dial: refining, meticulous, coaxing a hatched insect to fly.

"She doesn't miss work," I continued. "The woman I spoke to earlier on the phone told me I could come. I could file a report."

"That number gets rerouted to county."

"So?"

"I don't know what she said to you. She's a secretary." He chinned in my direction. "What happened to your face?"

I could feel the perspiration gathering underneath my arms, the back of my neck. "The woman on the phone said it didn't matter how long she's been gone. I could just fill one out."

"Your friend takes a day off work, you don't fill out a report. Maybe she went shopping."

His fingers dropped from the radio knob. He looked up at me again, his eyes a cool sandstone assessing the marks on my face, the nervy energy I knew I was giving off, the jitter I had been feeling ever since my fingers closed around Penny's cellphone. I took a deep breath.

"I'd really like to talk to someone."

"You're talking to me."

"No, I want to file a report." The building with its tarpaulins and dust. A structure in disarray, the feeling of things that had already gone too far.

The cop was watching me more carefully now, a curious expression on his face.

"Give it a day," he said.

6

In the evenings after work, Lamb drove by the house and laid on the horn until I emerged, streaking barefoot across the drive. Cesar sat up front with Lamb, a worker between them in the jump. I clambered onto the truck bed where laborers were crowded thigh to thigh, laughing at the sight of me.

"¡Ay, cuidado mija!"

"¡Niña loca!"

One of the workers grabbed my wrist, hauling me up. I pressed baby hands onto their denim-covered knees, scrambling for a seat. What I mean to say is, from a young age, I have known men's hands on my person. Brothers and fathers and sons pulling me to sit on a lap, squishing me into too-small spaces between them. Permitting me to crush my nose against their T-shirts, trace their varied arms—light as teak, dark as dravite—sniff their necks damp with sweat and sweet cologne, liberally reapplied after quitting time. For their wives maybe, or for each other.

Then Lamb peeled down the road, a parachute of dirt billowing from our back tires. Dusk bathed Pomoc in ginger light, softening all her edges. Even the turquoise hour motel on the corner appeared an oasis, a cool aquamarine. We drove by the swap meet, the proprietors breaking down wire stalls of spandex tops and plastic toys, twelve distinct candy scents of rollerball perfume. In front of Lupe's grocery someone had hung a piñata in the shape of a donkey, his flame-colored tail fluttering in the breeze.

The Crossroads was in the center of the *palo*, the mobile homes arranged in blocks of four connected by several narrow lanes, each unit augmented by a slim asphalt yard. Before the truck came to a stop the men dropped the hitch, jumping off one by one, rapping their knuckles across the truck's flank before dispersing into the maze. Cesar lingered to finish his conversation with Lamb; their friendship forged in the early days of the plant when Cesar still worked the ice chute beside the men, braced by years of success and failure: two wives buried, one child lost, another eventually found. Four weeks after Cesar laid his wife to rest, his house was boxed up and tagged for sale, the furniture carted off. He returned to the Crossroads by choice with a card table and a La-Z-Boy recliner, one coffeepot for the black stuff, a second to boil hot dogs in.

After they finished talking, Cesar came around the truck bed and swung me into his arms, my sneakers knocking his hips and thighs. He buckled me into the front seat and let me grasp two of his gnarled fingers—to prefer him, as I did, whenever Lamb was cross, obstinate, oblivious, all gradients of Lamb's residual bachelordom that flared during a day spent in the rough company of men. Only when Cesar was gone could Lamb begin the slow process of recalibrating to guardianship. He glanced over several times on the drive, as if just discovering the small, strange stowaway in his passenger seat, gold eyes affixed to his coarse and ropy largeness.

Remember me. Be my family.

How he must have felt, to be handed a child so long after that part of his life was through.

33

I walked out of the police station into the haze of late afternoon. The smell of smoke hung low on the air, another brush fire late in the season. I stood by the truck feeling damp heat gather at the center of my back. Any other day, Penny would be waiting at home for the last vestige of afternoon to wilt before starting off for work, making her way through the Crossroads in her waitress sneakers, heading in the direction of the long road parallel to the park's entrance. She would veer right, past the first sooty bus stop, heading straight toward the *palo*'s dusk hustle. To make short work of cutting across town, she might wait at the second bus stop on El Cerro and catch the number 36 express line, riding five quick stops to Main, or cross catty-corner to the panadería for a coffee and a roll, chatting with Maria until Flaca emerged from the back room and offered her a ride. Penny would wait for Flaca to step around the counter before brushing the flour from Flaca's clothes, tugging her ponytail, pinching her arm, dodging to avoid the other girl's swat. Finally they would walk outside and climb into Flaca's car for the short drive across the *palo*, arriving in the diner's parking lot under the glorious blue evening already unfurled.

In the midst of scribbling down an order, I would hear Penny slamming the car door outside, jogging up the porch steps in her sneakers. At the delicate tinkling of the gold bell above the diner's door, I would look up to catch her slipping inside, pink-cheeked, sweat gathering at the edges of her temples, her long hair swept up into a gravity-defying topknot, shooting a grin before she disappeared into the back room to set her purse onto a shelf, picking her apron off the hook to wrap the long strings twice around her slender waist, yanking them tight.

Leaving the station now, I pulled out of the lot to follow her trajectory, passing the bus as it turned down View to Fortuna, hanging a left on Main, the buzzcut cop's voice echoing behind. *Give it a day.* I was hoping for a happy accident: stumbling upon Penny in the diner's back room; she was studying next week's schedule with her canted squint, taking down her hair to brush it out with her fingers before bringing it around her shoulder to methodically plait a long, thick braid. *Give it a day,* the cop said. But he didn't have the image of her empty bed seared into his mind, the coffee can full of cash.

I pulled up to the diner, a few cars dotting the lot. The porch's fresh coat of white paint caught in the sun. In another hour someone would come outside to empty the ashtrays between the Adirondack chairs and plug in the Christmas lights that sparkled around the railing in all seasons, luring truckers and townies both. I spotted Jake's rolled-shouldered shape moving in the window, lumbering between the booths. A Junior, Jake was his father's namesake and reluctant heir. The diner remained their grand linoleum kingdom despite Jr.'s well-documented scorn for serving. If Penny had called, if she was on her way now, Jake wouldn't be running plates. Still I climbed out of the truck and stepped carefully up the stairs, waiting until Jake turned his back to ease open the door and slip past the counter. The back room was cool and quiet. The three-part sink had been emptied of dishes and an array of aluminum blender cups dripped on the rack, signaling a busy lunch. A stock delivery had recently arrived, the boxes piled high against the shelves. The massive walk-in freezer gave off its eerie low hum. Above Jake's desk I pulled down a stack of dusty phone books, the newest still two years old. Of all the girls, I figured Lourdes was the most likely to be home. I flipped through the white pages to the letter *H* and ran my finger down the list of names. Thirteen listings for Hernandez, all of them men. I dialed the first number listed. A child answered on the first ring.

"¿Dime?"

"Hola, ¿puedo hablar con Lourdes Hernandez?"

The receiver crashed back into its cradle, the dial tone flat and steady in my ear. I dialed another number, letting it ring endlessly before I was forced to hang up. Two more calls, both wrong numbers. I bypassed several answering machines, a disconnected phone line bleating in angry protest. Others rang on, too, their owners still punching out time cards in towns near and far, stripping off their coveralls, readying themselves for the drive home. The next number I dialed rang twice before a woman answered, listening to my request without comment. She set the phone down on a desk or table, my own voice echoing back to me. A moment later the phone was picked up again.

"¿Quién es?" A new voice, young enough.

"Lourdes?"

"Who's this?"

"Cale—we went to school together. At Vista. Also before." I imagined her on the other end of the line, a moon-shaped face with dimples, the Monroe piercing above her thin lips. In her silence I could hear the TV in the background, the new baby crying.

"Am I supposed to know you?"

I rolled my eyes to the ceiling, a spider web of fine cracks in the plaster. "You do know me," I said. "It's about Penny? I work with her at the diner."

"So?"

"So she didn't show up for work last night. No one's heard from her. I didn't know who else to call. Maybe you know where she could be?"

"Nope." She clipped it, but her voice eased up a degree.

"You don't have any idea?"

"How am I supposed to know? I don't even see her anymore. I'm at the college now."

"I heard," I said. "That's great. I just—"

"I had a baby," Lourdes continued, "we wanted to. What did Penny say?"

"About what?" I asked. "I was just wondering if—"

"She thinks it's too soon. I know. But I can do both. I'm transferring to a real college in a year or two. You watch. We're getting married as soon as we save up. No one wants to marry Penny now, so she's jealous of people who can."

"Lourdes? I really just called because Penny didn't come to work. I used the spare key at her place. She wasn't there. I found her cellphone. You know what I mean? She doesn't miss work, not ever."

"Which Kate are you, anyway? The one with the freckles? The Chinese girl?"

"No, that's—it's *Cale*. Could you call her parents?"

"Cale. Overalls, right? Geskin's geometry II? Flaca stole his grade book once. Didn't help her. I think I do remember you. You got a B. So quiet, I thought you were smarter than that."

"Lourdes!"

"What?" A snort. "He wouldn't know."

"How can you be sure?"

"Her father? Are you serious?"

"What about her mom?" I said, remembering the short, squat woman waiting in the elementary school parking lot after third grade open house. Two long dark braids, a sweatshirt, flat sandals, leaning on the hood of the station wagon that took Penny home. A woman made memorable for how unlike Penny she seemed, how rarely she appeared.

"Her *mom*? Are you crazy? Her mom moved away ages ago. Wyoming someplace. Colorado." In the background, the baby crying again. "Anyway, I don't even have her number."

"Let me give you mine, in case you hear from her."

"No way. Ask Flaca," she said, her voice already receding from the phone.

"I don't have her number, either. Can you give it to me?" I ripped the schedule off the bulletin board, pushpins pinging on the floor. I scanned the desk for a pen. "Lourdes?"

She had already hung up.

7

I sat up reading in bed, a fan balanced on the lip of the dresser blowing air across my bare legs. Wolf lay curled alongside me on the mattress, panting. Already this dry, steady June heat was responsible for suffocating Pomoc's oldest working postwoman in her bed; the radio warned against leaving children alone in the car. I sucked down a Coke and fished an ice cube out of the glass for Wolf, yelping when his sharp-toothed enthusiasm pierced flesh. *You're going to lose a finger someday, feeding him ice like that.* On the edges of every subsequent page, an abstract crimson smear.

I walked across the hall to Lamb's bathroom for a Band-Aid and froze with my hand outstretched toward the medicine cabinet. In the sink, a thick splatter of blood clung wetly to the porcelain. Taken alone, it signified nothing more than an accident with a razor, a deeply bitten tongue. Only at lunch, I hadn't noticed any cuts on Lamb's cheek, he hadn't complained of a split anything. He drank his coffee too hot and too strong, then pushed back from the table to smoke a cigarette alone on the porch.

In the medicine cabinet I upset a tube of toothpaste, a box of cinnamon toothpicks, cuticle scissors, a bottle of rubbing alcohol. No Band-Aids, no styptic pencil. But behind a new bar of soap were two missile-shaped suckers on the bottom shelf. Fentanyl, the name all the girls at Vista learned when Lisa Jo Baker went to visit her sick grandmother in Vegas and returned in an anesthetic cloud, stumbling down the halls in her cork espadrilles. In the small wastebasket under the sink were more crumpled tissues stuck together with blood; a bouquet of soft, speckled paper roses.

I was in the habit of regularly inventorying Lamb: his occasional restlessness, his aches and sprains, the accumulative gray peppering his hair, the smoker's cough that seemed to exist alongside him in perpetuity, as Lamb-like as his green cans of shaving cream and black cotton socks sold five-for-ten at the drugstore on Main. Now I left the bathroom and walked to my bedroom and shut the door, kicked off my slippers, and stretched out on the bed. I closed my eyes. Only when I woke hours later did I understand I had slept. The room was warm and foggy and there was a vague foreboding in the air, like a slow and dangerous animal had broken into the house and was even now moving up the stairs. I strained to hear Lamb's familiar downstairs sounds: the scrape of a chair pushed back, a cup being placed on a counter, the opening and closing of the icebox when he stole a slice of cheese.

I forced myself to go downstairs. The rooms were empty and the back door was open to the screen. The world outside was a deep, vibrant navy. Wolf was splayed on the back porch with his hind legs illuminated in a pool of light. I spotted Lamb in his white shirt pulling weeds at the top of the grade and resisted the urge to run out into the middle of the yard and scream. He would have made me climb the grade. Instead I went back inside to make a pot of coffee. When it was done I turned off all the lights, so he had no choice but to pack it all in. It still took him thirty minutes and when he pushed open the screen door he looked foul, foul. For the first time in my life, I didn't care.

"Sit down," I said.

34

The second time I went to the station, I parked down the dirt road from the police station and hiked up along the rocky shoulder, a fine, bone-colored dust clinging to my boots. The front desk was still vacant, trapped under its filmy shroud. I pushed aside the tarps to the back office, following the sound of voices. The buzzcut cop was leaning at the edge of his desk, talking to a tall, trim older man in profile—his rigid posture still familiar, the thick, dark hair curling over his ears. The uniform I remembered was long gone, replaced by a light collared shirt and dark jeans, a shield clipped to his belt.

Buzzcut cop glanced over, his expression turning sour. "You're back."

"I want to file a report."

"Friend skipped work yesterday," Buzzcut explained to the older man. "Forgot to call."

"My friend's missing." I paused, studying the other man. "You're Ava's daddy, aren't you?"

"Call him Sheriff," Buzzcut said.

From the middle of the floor I had a sense the older man was trying to place me, to figure out if I was someone he should know.

"Do you remember a fat boy named Dallas?" I asked him.

He gave a half-smile. "Where was this?"

"Career day. You gave him the baton from your duty belt. He broke a desk with it."

His face softened, tempering the ten years between then and now. "I do remember that."

If there is something to be said for daughters, this was it. Guilt, our familiarity with the form and how to play it. It would be impossible for him to recall, under any other circumstance, the lone hour he spent in his daughter's classroom a decade earlier; the messy-haired tomboy sitting Indian-style on the floor among other children, her skinned knee flush against his daughter's own. He squinted, mining the depths of memory. He was just a brash cop then, dangling a pair of handcuffs in front of twenty-six puppy faces, sermonizing on the dangers of drunk driving ten years before we would earn the address.

"Please," I said.

The buzzcut cop was watching our exchange closely. He stuck a hand in his pocket, jangling loose change. "Boss? I'm going for smokes."

The sheriff reached out a hand to stay him, motioning in the direction of an open door at the end of the room, behind the rows of desks.

"Wait in there," he said. "Five minutes."

On the windowsill of the sheriff's office was a photograph of a younger, better behaved Ava: her neat, brunette bob, a smattering of freckles across a pert nose. I stood awkwardly in the room studying the photograph and the row of plaques arranged behind it, snapshots of the sheriff in banquet halls with other suited blues, shaking hands with Carson's silver-haired chief. Just outside the door, Sheriff Fischer and the buzzcut cop were still speaking to each other in hushed tones.

When Fischer finally came in he took his seat, gesturing across his desk for me to do the same. I sank into a chair bucketed from wear, trying not to think of all the others who must have sat there year after year, the kind of news they had come to deliver. Up close, the sheriff wore his age in the shallow bows around his mouth, the delicate feathering around his eyes, an almost imperceptible quality of fatigue. But we had all grown older, made adjustments. In the last two years of high school even Ava had transformed, shedding her cop's-daughter naïveté in a surprising second coming as an inky-eyed goth. What happened to some girls between the fourth and twelfth grades, and not others? I had never experienced this blossoming; I spent every lunch hour eating a sandwich on the low stone planter in front of school, watching mohawked boys in black trench coats make out with girls on the knoll, until one day Ava appeared among them. Our own shared past reduced to the occasional smile Ava flashed down the halls in my direction, her incisors filed to predatory dimension.

"So you're friends with my daughter," the sheriff said.

"I was." I hesitated. "More so in grade school."

He smiled. "You don't have to explain."

"Sheriff—"

"Just Fischer, all right?"

"I'm worried about a friend of mine. She didn't show up to work yesterday. She never misses. I went by her place."

"You knocked. Looked in the windows?"

"I know where she keeps the spare key. I went inside."

"And?"

"She wasn't there. I found her cellphone."

"Could she have gone out for some milk, something like that?"

"No. She takes her phone with her."

"What about a purse?"

"I didn't see one."

"But she usually wears one."

"Yes. Sometimes."

"You girls," he made a motion with his hand, encompassing us both. "How old are you?"

"She's nineteen. Listen, I don't know what he told you—"

"He didn't tell me anything." Fischer cut it with a smile. "Look, sometimes this happens. People take off, dry out a little. They come back when they're ready."

I stared at Fischer across the desk. He touched his cheek just below his eye. I realized he was miming the bruise under my own. "What happened here?"

"I just want to file a report." I heard how loud my voice sounded, filling up the room. His smile underwent a slow demise.

"Of course. If that's what you want."

He rolled his chair in closer to the desk, keeping an eye on me as he rifled through a drawer, pulling a sheet of paper free and sliding it across the desk. I took a pen from the cup on his desk, uncapped it. Stared at the black bold type of the form. MISSING PERSONS RE-PORT. I hesitated, putting pen to paper.

"If I fill this out right now, and she comes back, what happens?"

"Nothing."

REPORT TYPE (circle one): RUNAWAY VOLUNTARY MISSING ADULT LOST DEPENDENT ADULT UNKNOWN CIRCUM-STANCES CATASTROPHE STRANGER ABDUCTION SUSPI-CIOUS CIRCUMSTANCES PARENTAL/FAMILY ABDUCTION

Catastrophe. My pen hovered above the word. I circled UN-
KNOWN CIRCUMSTANCES and moved on. Under REPORTING
PARTY I wrote my name. I printed all my answers carefully, recalling
handwriting lessons from school: HAIR COLOR (black), EYE
COLOR (brown), LAST KNOWN RESIDENCE (the Crossroads),
IDENTIFYING MARKS (mole on right cheek), JEWELRY (none).
There were other questions—a surprising number—I couldn't answer:
CLOTHING LAST WORN ( ) POSSIBLE DESTINATIONS ( ). My
pen hovered over LIFESTYLE ( ). I wrote it in. (Waitress).

Fischer was watching me carefully. When I set down the pen he
took the form, reviewing my answers.

"When was the last time you saw her?"

"I'm not overreacting. We went to school together. We work together down at Jake's."

"Last time you saw her?"

"I dropped her off the day before yesterday, we . . ." I felt the cold,
wet paper towels Penny wiped across my throat in the gas station bathroom, the red water dripping down my shirt. "We went for a drive."

"A drive to where?"

"What?"

"Where were you driving to?"

"Just around. We were bored. We wanted to drive."

"You girls drinking?"

"No."

"Take anything else? You smoke?"

"No, nothing."

"Is that when you got your—" He waved at the right side of my
face.

I should have been prepared for the question. I should have identified all the pertinent details that were safe enough to share and sifted
them carefully from the others. But if I'd thought long enough about
all the questions I might be asked, I wouldn't have come at all.

"Okay," he said. "So you're just driving around, the two of you,
going nowhere, not drinking or getting high, not doing anything you
ought to have gotten pulled over for, and then—"

"That's not it, really. I—"

"No argument? Any reason you think she could be avoiding you?"

"No." I realized I was clutching the edges of the chair, and let go.
"I left her at her place and haven't heard from her since."

"When was that? What time?"

I lifted my hair above my head, then let it down. The room had
grown exponentially warmer. I glanced over my shoulder; he had shut
the door to his office when he came in. Why hadn't I noticed? Now he
picked up the form and scanned over my answers again. I opened my
mouth slightly and tried taking small breaths through it.

"Cale. I'm saying that right? What time did you drop her off?"

"I don't know."

"Give me a range, would you? Morning, afternoon?"

A reasonable question, a fair one. Still, a salty taste began filling my
mouth. The room was actually hot; a pressure was building steadily in
my ears. I could feel my body tighten against the impulse to return to
that night. How to explain that time had broken apart, that it would
not come back together again?

"I can't—" I stood up, but the look he gave made me swallow. I sat
down again. I crossed my legs, a single booted foot twitching. Fischer
was still watching me with eyes the color of toffee, the quality of

liquid. I could feel them moving over my face and neck, I balled my hands into fists.

He looked at the sheet again. "Penelope . . ."

"Penélope Miguela Reyes. Penny."

"Does she have a boyfriend?"

"No."

"Did you reach out to her parents?"

"They're not close. She doesn't live with them. But her friends—there are a couple girls. I don't know their numbers, but they might know. I can give you their names."

I reached for the form again and turned it over, tried printing them out. The pen was slippery now, difficult to grip. Christina Pilar Cruz. Lourdes Hernandez. Mariana Lucia Perez. "They're in the *palo*. Can you find them?"

"If we need to. Suppose you want to tell me how you got that eye? You don't seem like the fighting type."

I licked my lips. "How would you know?"

He smiled. "I've been doing this a long time."

"Penny and I didn't fight."

"You mentioned her phone. Where is it now?"

I stood up again, reaching into my back pocket to hand it over. He took it, closing his fingers around mine, checking my eyes for permission. He moved his thumb, slowly, inching it over my knuckles. First left, then right. An easy, simple thing. I swallowed carefully.

"I want you to try to relax a little."

"No, it's just—"

"Relax. Close your eyes."

His thumb, slow. Left again. Circling the bone.

"Good. Keep them closed. Okay? Take a deep breath. That's it. You're with your friend again. You girls went out for a drive. You're on your way back home. What time of day is it? What does it look like outside?"

I was sinking, the ground falling away.

"Everything is dark," I said.

8

Forty miles outside of Pomoc in a town called Cajon, big enough for a real grocery store, a hair salon, and a tumbledown movie theater playing a tired roster of five films already forgotten by the rest of the world, the baby-faced doctor stood in the middle of a handsome office, crushing my small hand inside his clammy palm. I stared at his tie, then him for confirmation.

"Yes, parrots," he said, then withdrew to settle behind the kind of desk Lamb would never make, a gleaming, ostentatious cherrywood spectacle. On the wall behind the doctor's head hung an impressive display of diplomas from colleges in New York and California. I took a seat in the empty chair next to Lamb. What kind of man would go live in so many beautiful places, only to return here?

"As I was telling Mr. Lambert earlier . . . in these situations, it's always a good idea to have someone to talk to. A friend."

"She doesn't have friends," Lamb said. "She doesn't like people."

"That's not true," I said, but I heard the plaintiveness in my voice, and swallowed it.

The baby-faced doctor spread his hands as if to stay us. Despite their supple quality they were large, masculine. In an instant I imagined them wrapped around my neck. It was the heat of the room, the summer, the feeling of everything pressing in. Yet the air-conditioning was pumping audibly, and Lamb appeared comfortable enough in his long-sleeved chambray. I was the only one suddenly and persistently burning. Three times that week I had woken up in the middle of the night slick with sweat, moisture gathered underneath my breasts and in the creases of my arms and legs, my hair a damp tangle at the base of my neck. I dreamt of oranges floating on a pool.

"Isn't there anyone else you might feel comfortable discussing your grandfather's condition with?" His voice was gentle now, attempting kindness. I wanted to return it, but the word *grandfather* lay on the desk between us like one of the gophers Wolf caught on the grade, still punctured and mewling. It suggested a different type of man, the kind who kept caramels in his pocket for children.

"My *grandfather* still refuses to discuss his condition with me. My *grandfather* still smokes a pack a day. Did he tell you that?"

"Cale," Lamb said testily, staring straight ahead. "Don't be a shit."

The doctor nodded. "Disease can be hardest on the ones we love. I'd be happy to recommend someone, a therapist I know very well."

"Hah!" I glanced at Lamb. "He would never see a shrink."

"I meant for you, actually. Or what if you both went, together?"

In the quiet room, the clock ticked behind us.

"Cale . . . as your grandfather's physician, my job is to advise patients to seek the most effective course of treatment possible. What I can't do, unfortunately, is force a patient to follow my recommendations. And without Mr. Lambert's consent, I'm afraid I'm not at liberty to discuss the particulars. But I can assure you we've reviewed a variety of treatment options—"

"You're an oncologist, aren't you?"

The doctor paused, his hands in midair.

"It's on the door," I said.

"Yes."

"And it's on the forms in the waiting room."

He said nothing.

"Have you ever had a patient refuse to say the word? To tell his family he's sick? To discuss it?"

The baby-faced doctor looked pained and there was a quick, commensurate sting behind my own eyes. Beside me, Lamb didn't move. I looked down, studying my boots and the rich low-pile blue carpet woven with threads of gold. It was possible to distinguish the tight metallic strands, glinting under the lights. Maybe the doctor was right—maybe Lamb was—to place their faith in a myriad of rainbow-colored pills, to trust in the fine margin of milligrams, transfusions, a syringe, a scalpel, some opaque potion hung by a nurse from an IV pole. Maybe a rich place like this could unravel time.

"How can we even afford you?" I finally asked.

"You're too young to understand," Lamb said. "But the life insurance will hold you, if it comes to that."

For a moment, the room was quiet again.

"Fuck you," I said.

9

Pomoc entered the season of lazy feeling, men and women wearing T-shirts with lake-shaped patterns of moisture on their backs, schoolboys setting off firecrackers every afternoon, the tang of sulfur lingering for hours. I escaped periodically to the diner, where I stood hovering over the cashier's desk, waiting for Rena to swoop out of the back room with her short ponytail pulled high, a pencil stuck behind one ear, directing me with short, stubby fingers to one of the booths where I might read undisturbed for an hour or more. Today the tables were empty, the booths, too. I walked up to the counter, a handful of regulars clogging the stools: ancient, crepe-skinned Tyrone Young, who would never die; Elvin Eckles, notorious for wandering up and down Main Street naked in the middle of the night, save for a pair of briefs and his headlamp; and a pair of heavyset truckers, presumably just passing through, whose gaze flickered between their yolky plates and Penny, leaning cross-armed against the counter, watching all the men eat their eggs with a withering expression I didn't want to know anything about.

"Where's Rena?" I asked her. I had seen her only once since school ended, standing in front of a display of candy bars at the drugstore, paralyzed by indecision. I knew Penny usually worked the overnight

shifts, the trucker-heavy times when tips were better. Afternoons belonged to Rena and the slow, sad girl I didn't know, who wore rubber
hospital shoes that squeaked on the linoleum floor.

"Are you going to stand there all day waiting for her?"

"She lets me take a booth."

"It's just me today. If you want to eat, you have to join the rest of us."

She knew it was enough to send me away, but I had nowhere else to
go. I took one of the empty stools, setting my book next to the place
setting. She passed me a sticky menu, chinning at it.

"What's this one about?"

"Aliens," I said. "Where is everyone today?"

"Too hot for them. You want your sundae?"

I scanned the menu as if I didn't already know it by heart. Hearing
her say it out loud, the sundae sounded childish, indulgent. It sounded
exactly like what it was.

"Basket of fries. A Coke."

"No sundae?"

"Not right now."

She leaned back to repeat the order at the cook's window, then
disappeared down the counter, returning to set down the soda. She
reached for my book before I could stop her and flipped it over. "A
searing, kaleidoscopic portrait of the valiance of men amid the haunt-
ing decimation of war," she read, amused. But in all the times I saw
her around school with her friends, it couldn't have escaped her attention that I didn't have any.

"You can borrow it when I'm done," I said.

"Actually, I can barely read. That's why it's lucky I'm so pretty." She
batted her eyelashes. Then, dropping the act, nodded at all the men on
the stools, pretending to be focused on the game. "They'd believe it."

Just then one of the truckers waved to her from the other end of the counter. I opened the book and tried to make sense of the same sentence over and over again, but I couldn't concentrate. Eventually Penny returned, toting the fries and a bottle of ketchup. The fans above us were oscillating too slowly.

"Say there were aliens," she said. "What do you think they'd do?"

"What do you mean?"

"I mean I've been working doubles every day since Rena's gone," Penny said, tilting her head meaningfully down the counter. Next to me, old Ty Young was staring glaze-eyed at the salt and pepper shakers between our plates, his mouth slightly parted, his napkin crumpled in the remains of his tomato soup. Elvin Eckles slurped his coffee. The truckers were talking among themselves at the end of the bar, the one closest to us sending the occasional hopeful look Penny's way. "Give me something," Penny said.

I picked up a fry, still too hot to eat. How did other people make small talk? I had nothing to say that wasn't about this strange and persistent heat, the way Pomoc felt unbearable in it, the way I did, too. "I don't know. I guess they'd want to go to Vegas, like everybody else."

"Wow," Penny said. "All those books. This is the best she can do."

"Where *is* Rena?" It was the only thing I really wanted to know.

"Her husband got hit by a car." The look on her face reminded me of Penny in the high school bathroom, the girl with the hooded eyes.

"Are you serious?" I took a long pull on my Coke. "That's awful," I said.

"Is it?" Penny sighed. "I don't know. She was always stealing my tips. Now we get to hire someone else. What are you doing these days?"

"Me?"

"What, you don't need a job? You're in here all the time."

"I just—what about your friends?"

"Please. They've got better things to do. No offense."

"Aren't there a bunch of other people who want to waitress here?"

"Everyone is old or so weird. Have you seen the other girl who works here, Clara? She's even weirder than you." Penny pulled a napkin out of the dispenser and laid it on the counter, clicking the pen from her apron. She pushed them both toward me. "Just write down your cell. I'll have Jake call you."

"I don't have a cellphone."

Penny studied me seriously for a moment, as if I were the alien from the book that didn't exist, sprung to life. "Incredible," she said.

"Can I ask why'd you ditch that quarter at Vista last year?"

"Why do you think?"

I picked up the pen. "I'm not sure. I thought you wanted to graduate with them."

"Them?" Penny cocked an eyebrow.

"Your friends?"

She seemed to consider this, nodding slowly. She wasn't going to tell me either way, I realized. I set the pen down. We stared at each other awhile.

"Jake will be here in an hour," she said finally. "Just stay right there."

10

I drove to the animal shelter and walked up and down the rows of dogs baying to be let out, desert dogs used to streaking across dry land and climbing wild. The first time I passed the cage the dog was sulking in the back corner, shoulders drawn down as if she might be able to disappear. She was a mutt but I recognized a pit terrier's triangular head, the sinewy muscles bunched under her short coat. She wore the bright pink collar they put on the biters like an obnoxious next-day souvenir from a rave. On my second pass I asked them to unlock the cage.

At the sound of the key in the lock, she gathered herself into a tense pillar and growled. The information sheet next to her cage didn't provide a name or age, the reason she had been left behind. They dragged her out, forcing her to sit down.

"Eleanor?" I asked her. "Louisa? Maya? Sacagawea? Muriel? Tomoe?"

The dog stood up, turned a circle, and sat down again with her back to me, facing the wall. Appalled by human beings, the inanity of our affairs.

"Trixie," I said.

On the ride home she was quiet, sniffing herself first, then the truck; staring at Pomoc as we passed as if waking up from a long dream. When we arrived, Lamb was sitting in his chair reading the newspaper. Wolf ran up to the porch screen from outside, furious, pressing his nose into the net, barking up a storm. Lamb glanced at us, briefly. It was the same with the waitressing job, my backtalk, the new dog. I was floating things out, carving out the shape of a new permissibility. There were a number of things I could not say: *I will take this and this and this. I will need things. This dog will be here if you cannot.*

Lamb shook out the newspaper and cleared his throat, turning his attention back to the page. That was all.

35

There were three names listed under Cruz in the phone book, but I didn't bother trying any of them. *Ask Flaca.* If Lourdes had been hostile to my call, Flaca, I knew, would hang up the minute she heard my name. I had always considered Penny their favorite; she was always the most admired in school, the one other girls strove to emulate. But Flaca was their backbone, the mainstay, the friend who dispensed favors and counsel. I decided to look for her in the one place I knew she would eventually be forced to return.

It was already dark when I left the diner, but I could have found my way to the *palo* blindfolded, even with all light stripped away. The Cruzes' panadería was a flamingo pink storefront at the southernmost corner of a petite arc of businesses that included, among other things, a smoke shop and a laundromat. I parked the truck and climbed out as the barber was closing up for the night, unplugging the red and blue helix in the window, locking the door, rolling a hatched metal gate over the glass. He locked it, rattling the grille to make sure it was secured. Only the bakery stayed open late enough for workers returning from Sparks and Tehacama to drop off their lunch pails and tool kits at home, hunt their children from varied backyards, and corral them to the bakery for tortas and Cokes. As I walked to the entrance, a large blue van pulled up to the curb, unloading a dozen women in identical pressed white uniforms. These women were Pomoc's illusionists, soon to be ferried out to office buildings and casinos and hospitals in southern cities, armed only with plastic bottles and brooms to toil unseen, tasked with erasing our collective past. I followed them inside and lingered near the wall opposite a glass case full of pan dulces tucked into neat, full rows. The women placed orders for tacos de piña, puerquitos, and coffee strong enough to power them through the evening into the pardoning dawn. Behind a small screen that separated her from customers, Maria's short, corpulent figure bent to the glass case, shaking out one paper bag after another.

When I was a child, Lamb had brought me here so often that Maria often emerged from behind her veil-like screen. She clasped me against her supple bulk, flattening dexterous, flour-dusted fingers across my eyebrows and down the dark tails of my schoolgirl plaits, humoring Lamb with his awkward gringo patois while checking for my growth spurt that never seemed to arrive. Even after all these years her face was still full, a few strands of silver in her high, tight bun catching in the light. When the last of the uniformed women left, I unlatched myself from the wall and stepped up to the counter, searching Maria's expression for some sense of recognition, an acknowledgment of the pigtailed tomboy who loved her. She nodded at me through the screen. "¿Qué quieres?"

"Is Christina here?"

"No." Her reply was sharp, as if this was a question she'd been asked too often. Flaca's business was growing, and it wasn't hard to guess how many others might have shown up in recent months, seeking a dispensary.

"I just want to talk to her."

"¿Quieres comprar algo?"

"I used to come here." I held out my hand flat at my chest, indicating a child's height. "This tall, overalls. I came with my grandfather. We sat over there." I pointed to the corner table, the hard plastic chairs. She shrugged.

"You don't remember me?" My voice sounded more desperate than I intended. What if I split my hair in braids again, if Lamb were beside me, if I clung to his rough hand the way I had then? Instead I pointed to a row of pink conchas behind the glass, as if nostalgia might stir Lamb's dwindling appetite. "Cuatro, por favor."

She reached for a pastry box and laid the conchas down like sleeping children. I paid and on my way out, held the door for a father shepherding inside twin girls, the pair of them in light-up princess sneakers and vague, kittenish smiles. Outside, I stopped at the truck and slid the pastry box on the hood to fish the keys out of my pocket when out of the corner of my eye, I saw a mouse dart out from underneath a nearby car, scurrying along the side of the building to the dumpsters crowding the small back alley. Lamb and I had wandered there more than once to discard our trash, and I knew at the end of the alley lay the bakery's kitchen where, during any weekday lull, Maria could be found chatting with any number of family members who cycled through to mix dough and answer the phone, transcribing elaborate cake orders. I settled the pastry box in the passenger seat of the truck before shutting the door and picking my way into the dark passage, edging past the dumpsters. Halfway down I could make out a square of light on the brick wall opposite, the top half of the kitchen's Dutch door pushed open, giving off a backdraft of heat. I peeked in past the tall, silver rolling racks of pastries pulled away from the wall, the working counters covered with bags of yeast, mixing bowls, rows of sweet breads cooling on wire racks. A fan in the corner of the room rattled as it worked, its face pushed up toward the ceiling to keep from blowing flour into powdered mist. A slim girl, her back turned to me, pulled open the top door of an oven, sliding a baking tray inside. She shut it and moved to lean over the fan, shaking out the bottom of the tank top that clung to her, a red bandanna tying back her hair.

"Flaca," I called her name softly. She made no movement to signal she heard, but a moment later, a familiar pair of hard, dark eyes pinned mine. She crossed the room and reached for the Dutch door, her face already forming a scowl. I took a step back, one foot into the dirt. A voice called out something indecipherable from the other room.

"Nadie, Mama," Flaca called back. She jutted her chin at me. "What do you want?"

"I need to talk to you."

"Me? About what?"

"What else? Penny."

Flaca studied me with an expression I didn't know how to read. She pushed the door open wider for me to catch, but once inside reached for me so quickly I didn't have time to pull away. She caught my jaw in her firm grip, moving my face back and forth carefully in the light as if it were a ruby or disaster, something to be appraised. Her breath tickled my chin. This, the closest we had ever been to each other, even as girls.

"Penny didn't do this," she said flatly.

"God. Of course not."

Flaca released me, moving away. It was twenty degrees hotter inside the kitchen, and the skin on my arms began to take on a thin sheen. The room smelled overwhelmingly sweet, the pastries baking in the double oven. I followed her back to the counter where she picked up a silver sifter, shaking powdered sugar over a rack of wedding cookies.

"Dime. You pissed someone off."

"That's not what I came to talk about."

"Oh? What does *Cale* want to talk about?" She set down the sifter and lifted the tray, sliding it onto one of the rolling racks.

"Penny never showed up to work last night," I spoke to her back. "Maybe you'd know where she is."

"I have no idea."

"But you're always together."

"So are you," she said, turning to shoot me a look. "Lately."

"Flaca, I went to her place. She didn't answer. I used the spare. She wasn't there but she left her cellphone behind. You don't think that's weird?"

"That Penny forgot her phone?"

"She didn't forget it. And she hasn't come back, not that I know of."

"Where is it now?"

"What?"

"Her phone, Cale."

I hesitated. All the drops Penny was making for her, the business Flaca would lose if Penny didn't have it on her. There was no good way to deliver the news.

"I might have given it to the police."

"What!"

"I'm sorry! That's why I'm here."

Flaca rubbed her face, smearing flour down her cheeks. The bandanna pulling back her hair brought her features into stark focus; the angle of her cheeks and chin, her nose a degree too sharp. I longed for Flaca's mother to emerge from the front of the shop, to see mother and daughter standing side by side and compare their faces and hands, to ask how some things could be passed down so easily from one to another while other familial aspects were entirely betrayed.

"I didn't know what else to do. Maybe it could help? I have a feeling—"

"A *feeling*!"

"Something could be wrong."

"And what are the cops going to do?"

"Help find her?"

Flaca laughed. In all the time we had been in school together, I couldn't recall the sound. I had never heard it, or I had heard it too often; it had dissolved into the childhood soundtrack of playground sounds along with the recess bell, the squeak of swing sets, the rhythmic whip of jump ropes slapping the blacktop. It cracked her face wide open, making her appear less birdlike, revealing a pliable warmth: a secret she had kept hidden inside herself all this time.

"You can't help it, can you?"

"They're probably going to call you," I said.

"The cops aren't going to do shit."

"How do you know?"

"I *know*."

I met her eyes. "If they don't, who will?"

"Relax. Penny's fine. If she went somewhere, she's already back and pissed you went through her shit."

"Where could she go? She doesn't have a car."

"She can get a ride."

"You're the one who gives her rides!"

"I'm not the only one." She said it pointedly, something in it I was supposed to extract.

"Fine. Okay? Say she got a ride. Why hasn't she come back yet?"

She looked heavenward, as if the answer was soon to arrive. "You don't understand. She thinks she's like you. But we're not anything like you."

"What's so wrong with me, anyway?"

"For one thing, you're dumb about things you never had to know about."

I realized we were standing at a cross angle from one another, that I had one hand on my hip, that she had both on hers. I wanted to drop my hand, to tell her where I'd found Penny's phone, and how, the rolls of cash in the freezer, what they might mean. If Penny was here, she would have trusted Flaca enough to tell her about the desert and the sand-colored man, everything. If we were going to traffic in secrets, Flaca's could rival us all. Flaca was surveying the pastries on the counters, a curious expression growing on her face, as if they were bizarre, diminutive creatures struggling toward life.

"What is it?"

"How long has it been?" Flaca asked.

"Since she's been gone? I don't know. She was supposed to be on shift the night before last. What time is it now?"

"Almost eight. So what is that? Two days? Three?"

I didn't answer. She looked up, finally seeing me. The wheels in her mind, I could tell, were beginning to turn.

"You have an idea. Someplace she could be."

"No," she said. "But maybe I can find out."

11

The other waitress, Clara, was awkward but gentle. A small woman, elflike in stature, wispy platinum hair trimmed into a bob. In another life she was a nurse. I had no idea when that career began or ended but I imagined all manner of possibilities: a patient dying on the table, a lost child, an affair. The only token remaining from her previous identity was those pragmatic, rubber-soled shoes, their mouseish echo trailing behind her on the waxed floors. The things Penny disliked about her were not eccentricities so much as personality traits that, when compiled, revealed a sensitivity, a tendency toward artistry. Clara remained quiet for hours, speaking only to request the music be lowered a degree, a piece of silverware polished a second time. Her requests were exacting, startling in a voice so gently delivered. Her singularity contributed to the diner's familial quality. Jake's was a place where a plate of scrambled eggs and a Monte Cristo might overshadow other problems, other lives.

Junior arrived early every morning, bull-shaped and perpetually vexed, and stayed long enough to collect receipts and the previous evening's deposit. The rest he left to us. Besides Rico and Benoit, the other short-order cook, it was a space ruled entirely by women. So maybe this is why the men came. Maybe we made the diner feel like a bosom, a warm lap. Maybe we made it feel like home.

By now I could walk from one end of the diner to the other with my eyes closed, the blueprint etched firmly in my mind. In the front of the diner were six square Formica tables; behind them, a long counter wrapped around the kitchen like a grin. The second stool over had a rip in the tobacco-colored vinyl, the fourth worn so shiny it would split any day. All the stools squeaked when turned. To the left of the counter, a faint indentation remained in the floor where a wall once partitioned the space. I stood in the ghost of that room and imagined a family moving inside; what they talked about, how they spoke. Beneath four east-facing windows, a coveted row of booths overlooked a patch of tangled juniper bush.

During the week, Penny worked the overnight shift and our paths crossed in the morning hours. I arrived at ten and propped the front door to air the sharp odor of bleach. Penny counted tips while I tied my apron and checked stock. Luz and Flaca arrived together and smoked cigarettes on the porch, waiting for Penny to finish. When I saw them now, Luz chinned at me, but Flaca still tracked me with her eyes. I wondered what they did together so early in the morning, before the bars were open, Pomoc's list of diversions were few. There was only one kind of business I could imagine, and I was fairly certain it was one in which they were all developing a stake.

By the afternoon, when the sun seared the windows and the patrons skittered like wise animals seeking cool dark shelter, I walked onto the porch to smoke one cigarette after another, scanning the road for the next car that might turn off, white or blue or green, a minivan, a truck, a man, a couple. Here was the hour Lamb would return to our empty house; now he would open the fridge for a slice of cheese, now he would pour a cup of coffee into his favorite striped mug, smoke a cigarette, take his pills, read a book in the front room, then pull weeds in the yard. If I wasn't there to call him to the table, would he eat his dinner just the same? It was as if I'd forgotten all the years between his old family and new, the hundreds of evenings he must have stood alone in front of a fridge or a bed or a mirror, evaluating how to proceed.

I counted the hours until dusk began to eat the light, her ravenous rose glow. I wiped down countertops and stacked dirty plates, refilled salt shakers and ketchup bottles, stocked napkins and paper-covered straws. Rico slipped out of the kitchen after sunset, squatting in the back alley with a cigarette clamped between his teeth, staring at shadows in the dirt. When he returned I poured him a cup of coffee and watched him shake little blue pills out of the Ziploc bag Penny hid underneath the register every Monday morning before she left work. He crushed one under the back of a spoon and cut the line off the prep sink, bending his face to vacuum up the powder with a rolled dollar bill. After years of moving through the same small town with the same tired faces, we all knew the tweakers, potheads, and pipe fiends; who might get high for fun and who needed a bump to get by—and who they called for their supply. In all that time, I had never known Penny to deal. It was Flaca with the reputation; Flaca in the girls' bathroom at Vista, angling her sharp, lean figure over some blitzed-out cheerleader by the sinks. So if Rico was getting drugs from Penny, Rico was actually getting his drugs from Flaca. For the most part, Pomoc's chain of supply wasn't of particular interest. It was just all those years I spent carefully watching, the habit slow to leave me.

By night the diner cooled off under the fans. Rico returned to his post behind the cook's window. I went outside to plug in the Christmas lights, their diminutive bulbs twinkling in the window. The promise of Rico's food once again lured peckish townies from their homes;

they creaked over to the diner in rattling cars; they sat at the counter, where they could catch sight of Rico's white shirt moving behind the stove, his battle-scarred hands plating their meatloaf year after year, in all manner of heartbreak and joy. They made small talk, watching me roll forks and knives in paper napkins. They asked for pie.

I came to recognize the cross-country truckers winding along the same routes, again and again. These men tipped their hats and ate fast, then lingered over their last cup of coffee. I imagined other lives for them, wives and babies and dogs somewhere, awaiting their return. Some nights I left before Penny arrived, driving home under a sky the impermeable color of spilled ink. I let myself into our shuttered home. The dogs slunk from the shadows to greet me in the hall, wagging cautious, loyal tails. I stroked their solemn heads, feeding them each a square of cheese. Their parting signal was a whisper, a kiss on the ear, a clap of my hands to send them off. I listened to them racing upstairs, the squeak of Lamb's bedroom door. They settled at the foot of his bed like sentinels against the night, shielding him against all manner of danger we could not yet know.

12

On the weekend, Penny and I arrived early to meet a shipment of stock, then loitered behind the counter, waiting for the weekend crowd of families and their sticky-handed children, groups of sulky friends still hungover from a night at one of the *palo* bars. Penny leaned back against the counter and twisted her hair, still wet from a shower, into a bun on the top of her head. She dug into the wide pockets of her apron and scattered a number of bobby pins onto the counter; a compact, a squashed stick of gum, a slim tube of mascara. Once she secured her bun, she flipped open the mirror and examined her high cheekbones before reaching for the mascara, parting her lips to ink her lashes. When she finished she screwed the cap back on, arching an eyebrow in my direction. "Want some?"

"No," I said. We were both keeping one eye on the door as if bracing for a mob, but the parking lot was barren. Pomoc dreamed on.

"I have my whole makeup kit in the back," Penny said.

"No way."

"Just a little makeover? You're pretty, actually, it's your clothes. You're very committed to this Ponyboy look."

I shot her a dark look, surprised when it muted her into silence. We stared out the window side by side, waiting for a car. After a while she flipped open the lid on the sundae tray and picked at the chopped peanuts. Ate a few. Dug for a handful and threw them at me.

"Penny—" I ducked, but she was already reaching for more. She shot them hard and fast, the spray bouncing off my bare arm.

"You're going to clean those up!"

"Cale, come *on*! I'm bored. You're a loner, so I'm going to tell you how this works, okay? When people spend a lot of time together, they get to talking. They tell each other things, even when I'm not asking you a direct question like *Cale, where did you put the pineapple sauce?* Or *Cale, how was your week?*"

"You hired me!"

She chucked another handful of nuts in my direction. "Temporary insanity."

"Ugh." I untied my apron and tugged my shirt free from of my shorts, shaking out peanut bits. "I hate you."

"Liar." Penny wiped her forehead with the back of her wrist, a brusque, elegant motion, already familiar. The fans were going, just pushing the hot air around. I moved down the counter to pour myself a cup of coffee. I poured a second cup for her and slid it down. She caught it, sighed.

"My week was lame," she said. "Tips were shitty. Every week here is lame." She paused. "I should have just hired Luz. But she's so dumb."

"Then why do you hang out with her?"

She shrugged. "She came with Flaca. They were a package deal."

"What do you guys do together all the time?"

"Nothing. Hang out."

I dug deep inside my shirt to fish a peanut out of my bra and tossed it on the floor. "You've been friends forever, right?"

"It feels that way."

We both heard the car turning into the gravel lot and turned to look. It was a woman in an ancient teal two-door. We watched her climb out; pink pajama bottoms, a loose T-shirt hanging over a large bosom. One of those cottage cheese and cantaloupe ladies, her hair pressed in curls.

"What are you doing after work?" Penny asked.

"Nothing," I said.

"Well, I'm going to Rena's."

"Are you asking me to go with you?"

"If you want."

"Is this the kind of thing you'd do with Luz and Flaca?"

"No, we make tamales and listen to mariachi."

"Funny."

"I am, actually. But you . . . who knows? I've been meaning to ask. ¿De dónde son tus ojos? ¿Eres india? ¿Dominicana?" She took an exaggerated step back, squinting. "Wait. Don't tell me. ¿Egipcia?"

The woman was walking toward us now. I watched her get closer and closer until she disappeared under the low stair.

"Your guess is as good as mine."

I didn't have to look over to know Penny was pursing her lips, flattening them; the thing she did when she didn't know what to say. She picked up a rag from the counter and wiped the rings under our coffee cups. The front door opened, the woman huffing in.

"Listen," Penny said finally. "I haven't seen Rena since her husband got hit by the car. It'll be depressing. Better if I bring someone."

"Why don't you take Luz or Flaca?"

"Are you obsessed?"

The woman watching, waiting for us to finish.

"I'm asking you," Penny said.

"I didn't think you and Rena were friends."

Penny grabbed a menu off the stack and smiled at me, flashing teeth.

"I'm not really anyone's friend," she said.

Penny didn't have a car, so I drove. The truck was unbearable in the heat, the vinyl seats sticking to the bottom of our thighs. For the first few minutes I gripped and released the steering wheel by turns, the plastic leaving a welt across the center of my palm. Main Street was empty, the heat keeping the townies locked inside. The diner had received only stragglers all day; occasional regulars arrived, looking wilted, their expressions pained from having made the journey. They placed incongruous orders for egg whites and lemon pie, afraid to consume.

I rolled down the windows, a bead of sweat trickling between my breasts. We came to a red light, both of us reaching for cigarettes.

"How were you going to get there if I hadn't agreed to come?" I lit up, passing her the lighter.

"Why do you think I invited you?"

"Penny. You're not really so mean."

She arched an eyebrow in my direction. When the light turned green, I drove.

"What about you?" she said, flicking her ash out the window. "You could be a serial killer for all we know. So quiet; never a peep in school."

"I used to raise my hand in class all the time. I liked to read. It was the first thing Lamb taught me. When he was at work I used to practice all day so I could show him how much better I was when he got home. I read out loud when I was alone in the house; I made it a game to see how fast I could go. Then I'd volunteer to read in class. I'd speed read so fast no one could understand the words. I don't know what I thought. Maybe they'd think I was cool."

"Smartass."

"Right. They thought I was showing off. It was just something I could do. After reading one day we lined up outside for an assembly. Dusty Cowan started kicking me from behind."

"Dusty Cowan's dumb as rocks," Penny murmured.

"I tried pretending nothing was happening, but he kept doing it. I fell and skinned my knee. Dusty wouldn't stop, and Allan Grimes was standing behind Dusty—"

"Oh," Penny said.

"They stomped me pretty good." I took my right hand off the steering wheel and held it up. The ring finger twisted at the first phalange, the pinky finger bent at the tip. She glanced away quickly, back to the road. For a while neither of us said anything, just watched the town roll by. It was the most I'd said to anyone in a long time, even Lamb. So maybe I'd made the same mistake as him then—as Cesar and Trixie, too—I'd shifted so far away from myself in defense of one problem, not realizing how I might harden, creating another.

"If I can't get a ride I usually walk," Penny said finally, breaking the silence. "Hitch a ride. I figure it out."

"I thought you had a car in school?"

"Everyone needs to total a car once in their life. Pull up over there, will you?" Penny gestured to the convenience store approaching on our right. I pulled into the lot and idled while Penny jumped out and disappeared inside. An empty maroon sedan was parked off to the side, a season of dust accumulated on the windows. Yet for all the times I'd stopped here, I could swear I'd never seen it before. These days everything felt singular: the strained silence at home; the long

afternoons at the diner; the strange sensation of driving with someone in the next seat who wasn't Trixie, who panted loudly, refusing to
stick her head out the window like other dogs.

A few minutes later Penny emerged from the store carrying a six-
pack of beer and a bag of licorice. She climbed in and set the cans
between her legs. I pulled onto the road slowly, hoping to prompt
Penny into offering directions, since I'd never been to Rena's house
before. But Penny sat up on her knees, twisting around in her seat to
reach the storage space behind the bench, a string of red licorice hanging from her teeth, investigating the finds: a gallon of water, a tire
iron, Lamb's heavy winter gloves, Trixie's favorite warm blanket,
which she pulled back over the seat to show me, brushing uselessly at
the short, golden hairs stuck in the weave.

"You have a dog," Penny said.

Rena lived on the opposite side of town, in flat land. Penny pointed
out a sequence of directions that circumvented the shortcut through
the *palo*. I got the sense she wanted to avoid it altogether, maybe in the
same way I did when Lamb and I took long drives out to Tehacama or
Washoe, any place far enough away that Pomoc began to feel like the
tiniest pebble in a boot I had walked on for miles, irksome but forget-
table. Since the development of the *palo* businesses ten years before, the
dusty roads skirting the perimeter of town had fallen into disrepair. The
brittlebrush grew over into the lane, the sharp, woody stems snapping
at our tires. Had it really been a decade since I drove by the abandoned
burnt-out house behind the road, that mythic signpost from our childhood? The legend, passed around every Halloween since the first grade,
was of a lover's quarrel: a man so angry about his wife's affair that he

poured gasoline on her nightgown, lit a match, and watched her burn. Our neighbor Jackson had a car repair by the old lumberyard, and Lamb brought us out this way several times a year. Every time we drove by the blackened frame, I laid a child's palm flat against the glass, a mournful greeting to the spirit trapped inside. Only now did I see how unlikely the story was to be true, how strange it was that I never asked Lamb about the house or the rumors behind it. I felt Penny tracking my attention on the house in the rearview, but she didn't say a word. Maybe she had nothing to add. We had grown up alongside each other all these years, separate, but in proximate reach; we heard all the same stories, had the same townie markers and points of reference. Yet how different our lives were. How much, ultimately, was still the same.

After several miles the road ran out near the aging water tower and I cut speed. Penny gestured up another dirt road, clicking her long nails against the glass when she meant for me to turn. We bumped up a small hill and turned into a stretch of gravel ending in a cluster of homes set close enough together that a neighbor could hear every word a person spoke to a dog or child outside, and half of any argument carrying on inside. The sun was beginning its vermilion stretch into the horizon, the air just beginning to cool.

I parked in front of the plain single-story home, a slatback rocking chair and pallet rack of firewood crowding the porch. Rena emerged from the screen door, a hand shading her eyes from the sun. She squinted at us in the truck, struggling to make us out in the glare. I unbuckled my seat belt, hesitating.

"You did tell her we were coming, didn't you?"

Penny pulled the beer into her lap. The look she gave me, largely unconcerned.

"Kind of," she said.

38

I didn't want to go to the waiting room, but I didn't know where else to go, either. The fourth floor of the hospital was ice cold, the long hall between the elevator and the oncology department a beige plank under fluorescent light. Somewhere in this hospital Catherine had died, and with her a part of Lamb I could only imagine: a hazy silhouette cobbled together from old photographs and Cesar's anecdotes of their past exploits; the soft, faraway expression Lamb wore late summer evenings before bed. Those nights it was as if, though his body remained in the house with me, something less substantial slipped away, deserting our life together for a realm of happier memories.

At the end of the hall I ducked into the women's restroom, avoiding the mirrors. I bent over a sink and turned on the tap, splashing my face, letting the water drip in the sink. Impossible, in this place, not to see my own reflection and wonder how closely it resembled Catherine's and her daughter's, not to feel an eerie pull toward the fifth floor where both women had been born, or the first, where Catherine's daughter had returned just long enough to deposit something unwanted. I cupped my hands under the tap and drank from it, tasting metals.

I stopped outside the bathrooms at the pay phones. I had left my wallet in Lamb's room, but I patted my pockets and came up with two quarters, a nickel and Sheriff Fischer's card folded in half. I picked up the phone and tucked the receiver in my chin to smoothe out the card, dialing the first number printed. Fischer's voice came over the line.

"It's you," I said, pleasantly surprised. The mechanized telephone operator interrupted us, drowning his response. I had only five minutes to speak.

"Who?" Fischer asked.

"It's Cale Lambert. I came in yesterday."

"Cale. How can I help you?"

"I'm calling to see if there's any news about Penny?"

"Your friend, right? An officer called one of the names you wrote down, Christina Cruz."

"Flaca."

"Right. Hasn't seen your friend and has no idea where she might be. If she doesn't turn up in a couple days, we'll put out some feelers."

"Feelers! What about—"

The door to the men's bathroom swung open and two young boys went streaking down the hall, shrieking in play. An older man followed a moment later, looking sheepish.

"Where are you, a circus?"

"The hospital in Tehacama. I'm on a pay phone. I don't have much time."

"You get into another fight?"

"No, nothing like that." I laid my head against the wall, closing my eyes. *Please don't let Flaca be right.* Why did I think Fischer would be any help? Because I used to split ham sandwiches with his daughter in grade school? Because if Ava ever went missing, I thought he'd do more than *put out feelers*? I didn't know the first thing about him. But

I recalled the feeling of his hand on mine, the pressure of his thumb circling my knuckle.

"She's already been gone for three days."

"Feel free to check in anytime."

I looked down the hall at the sad, scuffed floor, the stark blank walls. In the corridor was some desperate feeling obscured in normal life. Bodies laid on gurneys on floor after floor, all human mystery stripped away.

"Listen," I heard myself say, "there's something I didn't tell you. When I was in her house, I saw something in the kitchen. It could have been blood. Also, last week—it didn't mean anything to me at the time. She mentioned she was afraid of someone."

I waited, hearing only silence. I wondered if we'd already been cut off.

"Cale." Fischer returned to the line, my name now a curt syllable. "I don't think you want to start making things up."

"Some guy had been into the diner a few days in a row," I continued, "someone she'd never seen before. She told me he was giving her the creeps." I squeezed my eyes shut. How easily the lie came, how naturally it was made. The way it could, in so many ways, be true. Hadn't Penny voiced similar fears herself, of trespass, of danger? *Someone got broken into the other day.*

"I have a hard time believing you wouldn't have shared that when you were sitting in my office."

"I was upset. I've been having trouble—"

"You told me she took her purse with her."

"No, I said she only carried a purse sometimes."

"Did she describe this imaginary man to you?"

"Why would she leave her house without her phone?"

I could hear his breathing, the exasperation in it.

"Lying to me would be the worst thing you could do."

"You don't know what Penny really looks like. When guys see her . . ." But I was starting to hear what I was actually saying, to imagine it. I pressed my back flat against the hospital wall, my entire body flushing warm, the metallic taste of the sink water returning to my mouth. My lungs felt like a paper bag someone was crumpling in their palm, a man pushing his knee between my ribs. Did Fischer know the worst thing a person could do? I let go of the phone and bent over, hands on my knees, another wave of nausea rolling. I could still hear Fischer's voice emanating from the receiver, dangling on its cord, but I didn't retrieve it. Let Fischer consider the kinds of men who might take an interest in a beautiful girl, the kinds of things they might do to get her. Let Fischer speak into the dead space, waiting for a reply that never comes.

13

I still couldn't tell if Rena wanted to see us, even after we were all standing together on the porch. If Penny and I shared a psychic catalog of Pomoc's minor landmarks—the burned-out house, the old rail station, the western sloping mountain—we also carried a directory of its most familiar faces, Rena's chief among them. The longest-working waitress at Jake's, she was linked eternally in our minds with Charlie, her high school sweetheart, a darkly bearded, bifocaled trucker. Together since high school, they had produced two rangy sons who could have been twins, but weren't. Just now it seemed Rena was the double, an impostor of herself out of context from the diner. Her denim clam diggers and baggy T-shirt lacked the definition of a tightly wound apron at her waist; her limp, unwashed hair translated none of the swift efficiency of her high waitress ponytail cleaved by a No. 2 pencil, the pull tightening the southward trickle of her jowls, a face puddling together in middle age. Up close, her eyes were pink, rubbed raw. When she saw the beer, she held open the screen door.

We passed through a hallway decorated with family portraits, the centerpiece a sixteen-by-twenty inch frame of her husband in a fluorescent trucker's hat and camouflage hunting jacket, the sons in matching pants and vests, Rena a petite anchor at the end. The hall opened into a large, comfortable living room, a tattered couch I imagined Rena's sons throwing themselves on after school still in their sneakers. It was a house any of the boys' friends would be welcome to stay in for a night, or a week. Rena expected all young people to genuinely like her, if only for the beer she bought them. Just now the house felt conspicuously empty; the boys bailing to a friend's house, the movies, anything to eject themselves from the pall.

In the kitchen, a chair had been pulled out from the rear of the large oak table, a half-drunk cup of coffee and a crumpled pack of Winstons next to a saucer full of crushed butts. Without needing to be asked, Penny set the six-pack down on the table, twisting off cans for me and Rena, then another for herself. I popped the tab, the aluminum still cool to the touch. Rena brushed past us to resume her seat by the window. She reached inside her baggy shirt and pulled an orange prescription bottle from her bra. She shook it, several pills rattling around in the plastic, before setting it down on the table.

"We need more of these," she said.

Penny picked it up, squinting at the label. "Oxy? What else did they give him?"

"Not much. Said to have him come back next week. How am I even supposed to get him to the hospital? The casts are as big as he is."

"I'll get them for you. What else?"

I took a sip of my watery beer, nearly flat already, and set the can down on the table amid a growing sense of unease.

Rena reached for her cigarettes, lit one with a shaky hand. "I don't know."

"Are you sleeping? You need something to help?"

Why don't you just bring her a menu? But Rena didn't seem to be picking up on Penny's suggestion. She uncapped the prescription bottle and shook three remaining pills into her palm, tucking one inside her cheek. For several moments the conversation stalled, Rena dissolving into her own mind.

"When can you bring them?" she asked suddenly.

"Tomorrow," Penny said. "I'll come back."

Rena looked up at me across the table, as if only just noticing I was there. "How's the job?"

I felt like I was lagging a beat behind the both of them, trying to sort through the vagaries of their conversation, how I managed to find myself mired in it.

"Good," I said. "It's nice to have something else to think about. Learning the small things."

"Like what?" Penny asked, a little dry. "Cleaning the shake maker, or talking to humans?"

"I had that job for twenty-three years. Longer than either of you have been alive." Rena paused, took a drink of her beer. She set down the can and tucked another pill inside her cheek. We waited. "Are you even twenty-one?"

"Eighteen soon," I said.

"Penny? What are you? Twenty-one, twenty-two?"

"Ew," Penny said.

"You're not careful, trouble'll age you. Sucks the meat clean off the bone."

I shook my beer, surprised to find it nearly empty. Penny twisted off another can from the six-pack and handed it over without a word. Ever the artful supplier.

"I loved that job," Rena said and set the last pill on the table next to the empty prescription bottle. "You know that? Got me out of here."

She looped a finger alongside her head. "People come in, tell you their problems. They asked for me."

"I asked for you," I said. Penny kicked me under the table. "I'm sure Jake will take you back when you're ready."

"How am I going to do that? I've got a busted-up man in there. No. I'm done-done. Stick a fork in me. Isn't that what the kids say?" She crushed her cigarette in the saucer and turned to Penny. "How long?"

"Tomorrow. I'll bring something to help you sleep. Okay?"

Rena nodded, and after a while her mood seemed to be level, or the pills in her cheek had begun to dissolve. She stood up and grabbed the crumpled pack of cigarettes off the table. "Come on. Cale, you've never met him."

"Oh," I said, because I had actually run into Rena's husband plenty, in the way that places home to only a few hundred bodies seemed to promote encounter. He was one of several hulking figures around town in whose direction I'd vaguely smiled, waiting patiently behind his long diesel cabs blocked the pumps. It was definitely Charlie I'd seen at the gas station a few months earlier, piling a mound of Slim Jims and chocolate bars on the counter for the clerk to ring up, then adding several bottles of poppers at the last minute, glancing around the gas station to meet my eyes.

Rena was already moving toward the hall, expecting us to follow. Penny stood, too, and started after her. I wanted to excuse myself and sneak out, but for what? To hurry home to another prolonged evening with Lamb, the two of us steeped in our silent resentments with only the dogs to keep score? I forced myself to follow Penny across the living room and down another hallway to a bedroom door Rena threw open, flipping on the lights.

The room was painted a milky beige and the blinds were drawn, the space above a sturdy dresser embellished by an assemblage of decorative wooden archery targets. On a bed that took up half the room, Charlie's immense body recalled the sleeping giant in Lamb's readings of Jack and the Beanstalk. He was fast asleep in a kink of sheets, his mouth agape, emitting a low puff and wheeze. Either Charlie was bigger than I remembered, or it was his round gut, exposed by the T-shirt riding up his chest, that made him appear more substantial. He wore the tight white briefs of a little boy, and I looked away from their obvious bulge to the tops of his soft, pale thighs visible above two solid casts enclosing both legs. His left arm lay crooked across his chest in a sling; a pattern of berry-colored contusions stippled his other fleshy arm. Penny was studying him with clinical remove.

Rena came forward and began to pull at the sheets twisted around his casts. I was afraid the movement would disturb him, that he would wake startled and find us gawking, but he snored on. When she finished, Rena sank down on the corner of the mattress by his plastered heel and lit another cigarette. She was looking at him as if he were a Christmas tree or a wheelbarrow, something familiar but inexplicably out of place. On the other side of the bed, a club chair had been arranged with several pillows and a blanket. On the nightstand was a tumbler of water, another prescription bottle.

"The doctors say he'll never drive a rig again." Rena flicked her ash onto the carpet.

"Maybe he will," I said, unable to help it.

For a while, none of us said anything. Beside me, Penny shifted her weight from one foot to another and started to say something, trailing off as Rena's cigarette began to bob, the cherry dipping dangerously close to her knee. Penny grabbed Rena by the shoulder as she began to nod off. I didn't want to think about how many of Charlie's pills were making it to him, which one of them might need them more.

"What?" Rena jerked away, sitting up.

"Maybe you'd better lie down," I said. A second later, Rena's eyes were closing again. I picked the cigarette out from between Rena's fingers, watching her body weight fall incrementally closer toward Penny, until Penny was grasping Rena under her arms, struggling to keep her up. Rena grunted but didn't pull away.

"A little help!"

I took a drag on Rena's cigarette. When Rena was just about to slip off the bed, I reached over and grabbed her ankles. Penny pulled toward the head of the mattress, and I heaved, both of us ignoring Rena's grumbling until we had her laid out next to Charlie. She was still precariously close to the edge.

"If she turns over she's going to fall off," I said. I looked around for somewhere to put out the cigarette, and, finding none, pressed the filter more tightly between my lips. We rolled Rena over as best we could. Penny stretched an arm to drape over Charlie's bulk, and I lifted one leg, angling it over his casts. When we were done, we took a step back, surveying our work. It looked as if we'd just stumbled upon them; a long-married couple in repose.

Outside, the air smelled sweet, wet pinyon bark and loosened earth. It had cooled slightly, and a light mist was clinging to the hood of the truck. We had missed a delicate shower, a light summer rain. The beers provided the evening a flexible quality. I bent my face to an opaque sky. Penny stood by, watching me carefully.

"Maybe I should drive," she said.

I didn't answer. I gathered myself and walked around the truck, unlocking the doors. I waited for her to climb in and buckle up, flipping on the lights. We idled in the driveway for a few moments, Penny still scrutinizing me from the shadows.

"I told you it would be depressing," she said.

"That's not what I'm trying to figure out."

Somewhere between Rena's kitchen and climbing into the truck, Penny had let her hair down. It hung down impossibly heavy and black, brushing her elbows. She turned to the window, hiding her face. "Elvin ran into her at the hospital, high as a kite. I knew she'd want pills."

I was sure Rena hadn't moved from where we'd placed her, curled around her husband. Still I worried she might somehow be watching us from a window, wondering why we lingered. I turned on the radio, letting the sound fill the space between us, and pulled out of the drive. The headlights were weak against the growing dark, illuminating only a small pool of dirt and brush, but there was only one way back to the *palo* and I knew it by feel alone.

When we were almost to the center of town, Penny turned down the radio. "You're mad now?"

"Where do you live?"

"I don't want to go home."

"I can drop you somewhere else."

"I don't want to be dropped off anywhere."

I turned the radio back up. We drove the straight route back through the *palo*, passing the turquoise hour motel. Beyond the narrow crosshatch of streets lay the rest of town, but few options within it. The diner was the only place that stayed open late besides the *palo* bars, which wouldn't serve us unless Penny charmed a bartender. In

Golan, fifteen miles down the interstate, there was the all-night Tex-aco and the strip club that I had visited in the disordered days after finding Lamb's blood in the sink, driving the highways past familiar landmarks and interstate drive-thrus until the warning light lit up on my dash and I veered off the exit to the path dead-ending at the gas station, the Fat Trap marquee next door spelling out an eternal special on beers and wings, a lavender-pink light seeping from its shuttered windows. I almost suggested it, because we could get in and they would serve us. Plenty of girls from Vista began dancing there after graduation; we saw them around town in good jeans and expensive hair. Curious, I had expected some barrel-chested bouncer at the door, but it was only Eric from school with his long blond ponytail and an ill-fitting black suit, still *the new guy* three years after landing in Pomoc. The Trap was dark and icebox cold inside, truckers slitting their eyes underneath their ball caps. Onstage, Kate Enders from freshman biology was twisting around the pole in wobbly clear heels, her soft body moving languorously off-beat to a decades-old rock track, the lingering smell of tanning salons and fruit body spray on the girls walking by, trailing their acrylics on the bar.

"Let's just go to your place," Penny said now, still staring out the window.

"I never have friends over."

"That's because you've never had any friends," Penny said.

It was possible I'd hurt her feelings, that Penny had feelings, that they were vulnerable like everyone else's. But in all the time I had known her, she had always seemed immune. We were heading for the sparse lights of Main Street, and I was sifting through memories of our childhood, trying to recall how often I had ever seen Penny alone, without Luz or Flaca or Lourdes in tow. I wanted to ask about them again—how Lourdes seemed to disappear after graduation while Luz came and went; how strange it was not to see them all together anymore, when some part of me had assumed we would all go on seeing each other forever, that nothing would ever change. But maybe it was only school that had brought the girls together in the first place; maybe their bonds had begun to fray.

The road we followed was bordered by that same endless gravel on both sides, clumps of bitterbrush overgrown in the road, their poky stems in the headlights like the legs of so many spiders. Penny was quiet the rest of the drive. Where else could I have taken her? Really, there was nowhere else to go.

14

At home, Wolf was lying on the porch in the dark. He climbed to his feet at the sight of Penny, curling back his lip to snarl. A mystery, where Wolf learned this distrust of strangers; from birth he had been showered with affection, though Lamb's attempts at behavioral training were always scrupulously ignored. I laid a hand on the back of Wolf's neck, feeling the vibration under his fur. He stood down but shook my hand free of him, annoyed by my interference, the fracturing of our silent pact against outsiders in our home. I held his collar and let Penny in ahead of the dog. Lamb was in the front room, reading in his chair. His glasses were perched at the edge of his nose, his profile a degree more sharp each day. Trixie raised her head from the floor and wagged a drowsy tail once, twice. At the sight of Lamb, Penny tucked her hair behind an ear, a nervy gesture I'd never seen before.

"Lamb, this is Penny. I work with her at the diner."

"I know who you are," Lamb said to her, closing his book around a finger so as not to lose his place. "Your father runs the nursery in Noe."

"That's right."

"You're surprised."

"I'm surprised anyone knows him," Penny said.

"We were visiting a friend," I interrupted. "I forgot to call."

Lamb didn't bother to look at me. To Penny he said, "If you're spending the night, you can use the phone in the kitchen to let your parents know you're here."

"Oh, I moved out a long time ago. There's no one waiting up."

"You must have been in Cale's grade?"

"The year above. But I'm almost twenty."

"We're going to bed now," I said, grabbing Penny's arm to pull her along. A protective measure or punishment, I couldn't tell, just an overwhelming need to separate them, to remove Penny from the private world I shared with Lamb. If I expected Lamb to express some measure of surprise at my retreat, I was disappointed. He just met my eyes briefly and looked away, returning his attention to his book. After the blood in the sink and our combative, strained visits with the baby-faced doctor, maybe there was nothing left we could do to surprise each other.

I showed Penny up the stairs, leading her down the hall to my bedroom. I tried to see the space as she might: a fair-sized room with a small oak desk, a bookcase overcrowded with paperbacks, a narrow dresser painted white, the frayed oval rug Wolf considered his own. I went to the bureau and pulled out a couple of T-shirts, tossing one to her. She caught it, still studying the room.

"You have two dogs," she said.

I began to undress, pulling my shirt over my head. Penny followed suit, not shy about shucking the jeans from her long, tanned legs or baring her breasts. By comparison, my slender figure must have reminded her of a child's. I pulled back the sheets on my bed. It was only a double, but I was used to waking up in the middle of the night with Trixie like deadweight at the foot of the bed, or Wolf with his heavy, selfish sprawl pushing me to the corner of the mattress. Penny was a more considerate companion. She tucked herself into the far side of the mattress, her dark hair covering the pillow, and drew the sheet up to her chin, curling toward the wall. After I climbed in, she pushed a leg out behind her, resting her toes, inexplicably cold, against the side of my calf to warm them. I lay flat on my back, staring at the ceiling joists I'd slept under since childhood, one of them a shade lighter than the others; a raw, pinkish hue. Sap, bleeding into the heartwood.

"Where are your real parents?" Penny asked.

"I don't know."

"And Lamb is—"

"Her father."

I waited for the other questions, the ones I least liked answering. But she seemed to be considering how to proceed, or she had already closed her eyes. A few minutes later I turned off the light and lay back down.

"Do you ever wonder where she is?"

"I used to." Our voices depressed to whispers in the dark.

"You just stopped?"

"I made myself think about something else. I started reading. I got through all of Lamb's books, and then there was the library, the thrift store."

Penny curled her toes to dig into my calf.

"Since when do you mess with pills?" I asked.

"Does it matter?"

"You brought me along. It's hardly a secret now."

"It's Flaca. You know that. I just help out sometimes."

"Why? You never did before."

"We're not in school anymore, are we? Business picked up. I see Rico all the time; one day she just asked me to pass his along. Then Rico's brother came by. Rena found out. Some extra cash here and there."

"You don't mind?"

"Why would I? Waitressing isn't enough."

"To get a car?"

"A car," she said, her voice softer by degrees. "I don't care about a car."

"Then what?"

"I want to get out of here."

"And go where?"

"It doesn't matter. You think about it, too. I know you do."

"I don't," I said, surprised. But I tried to imagine it for her: Penny somewhere else, Penny anywhere but where I'd known her. All of Pomoc, a capsule of time and place. I started to say something, but stopped. Her breath had begun to deepen beside me. I heard Lamb climbing the stairs, the dogs' collars tinkling as they followed behind. But in the middle of the night, I startled awake. I could tell by the quality of darkness pushing into the room and the profound hush that hours had passed. Some noise must have roused me, Penny shifting beside me in the bed, her unfamiliar weight enough to trigger unconscious alarm. When I resettled in the quiet, I realized the sound of Penny's deep breathing was gone. I reached across the mattress to make sure she was still there. My fingers met her low, warm back, her reassuring solid form.

"Penny?"

She didn't answer, but I knew she was awake, too, I could feel it. She had been awake for some time. I rolled away and closed my eyes, meaning to afford her some privacy; to distance myself in slumber. Only sleep never came. We lay beside each other for hours, silent in the dead of night, each of us barely breathing.

17

The brush fires bloomed on the mountain like California poppies, burning steadily through the night. I woke with the smell of smoke in my hair, on my pillow, a lingering trace of cinder on the laundry I loaded into the washing machine. After darkness fell, Lamb and I took our cold drinks out on the porch. The blaze was close enough that we could hear the dry brush snap and crackle. We nursed the smoke in our lungs. Trixie followed us onto the porch and settled down, only to rise a few moments later, circling, whining at our knees, pushing her snout into the screen to be let back inside. The fires made both the dogs nervous, but Trixie was beginning to rely on Wolf to spot her guard. Wolf had been banished from the porch altogether for his incessant howling, as if indignation alone could beat the fires back; his persistence, year after year, undeterred by spectacular lack of outcome. Whatever his shortcomings, at least Wolf managed to communicate.

Lamb struck a match in the dark, the small flare illuminating the edge of his rough jaw, his thick, calloused fingers as they shook out the flame. His profile, day by day, was whittling down to the essential, and his expressions were becoming more spare along with it. He ran a finger unconsciously along the length of his shirt collar buttoned high, the movement revealing an inch of raw, singed flesh.

"How does it feel?" I asked.

This heat lingering in the creases of our elbows, behind knees.

"The radiation," I said.

"I know what you mean."

"But you keep at it." I reached forward, picking up his pack of cigarettes. I dropped my voice several registers and spread it out, his syrup drawl. "Quittin' ain't spittin'."

In the dark, the movement from the whites of his eyes.

"Jackson saw tracks by his hose," he said.

"Where?"

"Didn't I just say?"

It was the same every year; the fires smoking coyotes and mountain lions out from their dens. They stole into our yards, prowling the cool dark spaces of garages and sheds, stretching themselves to fit underneath the bodies of cars.

"You'd do best to keep the dogs inside," he said.

"I know," I said. "The dogs listen."

He coughed, a car backfiring in mud. When he finished he took another sip of tea, ice clinking against the glass. Nearby, a cluster of dry brush popped. Since childhood it had seemed like a game, watching the fires advance every season—how far down they would come, how much they would burn. Why Lamb still watched, I didn't know. Maybe there was a sense he could protect the house through his surveillance, though he knew better. The expression on his face when neighbors hosed down their fences and roofs, the recognition of futility.

"Remember when you listened?" he asked.

"Maybe that's been my problem," I said. "I always listened."

In the distance the choppers were ticking in against the dark. Several minutes later, twin sabers of light crested the mountain, piercing the haze. The sound grew louder until we could just make them out, two small tin cans bobbing atop the flames. In daylight we would have been able to make out the shape of men in the cockpit, but they were invisible now. They released their buckets one after another, water flaring down in slender galactic streams.

Lamb climbed to his feet, grinding out his cigarette on the railing. The screen door snapped shut behind him. I waited for his kitchen sounds to fade before reaching for the matches left behind on his chair. Trixie nosed my knee, her black eyes shimmering in the dark. She turned back to the screen door and whimpered.

The helicopters banked right, circling for a moment before chopping away. In half an hour they would return again, dropping water all night until the flames hissed to ash. After crushing out one cigarette, I smoked another, then a third, and a fourth, until the pack was empty and there was a raw, caustic feeling in my chest, until I could imagine how it might be for him, my lungs a pulsing, upper body sore. By the time I stood up the fire was sputtering low to the ground. I held the door open for Trixie and followed her up the stairs. At the top of the staircase she paused, deliberating which end of the hall to choose. She wanted to leave me for Lamb, I knew. I turned to my room, surprised to hear Trixie trailing behind. She leapt onto my bed in one graceful movement, stepping her paws up and down. I pulled back the sheets to join her. Did she wonder which one of us she might rely on in her waning years, to feed her, brush her coat, wash her paws? All of us, just survivalists in the end.

When I lay down she arranged herself peculiarly, curling herself on top of the pillows in a sinuous, furred corona around my head. In the middle of the night she nudged me awake, whispering elaborate mongrel confidences in my ear.

15

It had been years since I'd driven through the Crossroads, but the park was largely unchanged. I drove with Penny through a dense hive of mobile homes connected by narrow tar lanes, a smattering of cars parked under aluminum awnings. I found myself looking for Cesar's cream-colored sedan among them, even though I knew it was gone, along with the rest of him, to a lively retirement community in Florida Bay. The photos he sent us every Christmas were not of his new wife or the white-sand beaches or the majestic Everglades, but a small, sunlit corner of his room where he tended a collection of potted cacti and smoky quartz, the postcards we sent him of the dry, desert landscape taped up on his wall—everything he couldn't quite leave behind. In the Crossroads his doublewide suffered under new ownership, the siding repainted a lurid salmon pink.

Penny directed me to a neat white single in the center of the park. I followed her up a wobbling exterior staircase to the landing, a pot of scarlet bee balm flowering on the ledge in tubular clusters. A surprise, until I remembered her father and his nursery, the prospect of a hereditary green thumb. She lifted the pot and removed a key from the water dish, disturbing a pallid butterfly that hovered nearby, waiting for us to get lost.

"Want to play a game?" Penny opened the door, shooting a mischievous look over her shoulder. "I say a word, and you say the first thing that comes to mind."

"No." I followed her inside and bent to untie my boots, adding them to the assortment of shoes lined up by the door: well-worn sneakers and high-heeled mules, a pair of leopard slingbacks and over-the-knee boots, one large, mud-caked set of Timberlands much too big to be hers. Some remnant from the mechanic boyfriend, her father, the brother I hadn't met.

"Ready? The first word is your favorite. *Book*."

"No," I said again, wandering through her front room, noting a short futon hidden under a pile of knit blankets; a chipped full-length mirror set across two columns of textbooks to create a makeshift table; a small television in the corner, its rabbit ears twisted askew. Penny walked down the hall toward her bedroom, peeling off her clothes as she went. She dropped her jeans on the floor amid other items previously discarded: a short skirt, pair of cutoff shorts. A lace bra hung from the corner of a mirror, a thong dangled from the bedpost. She rooted around in her bureau before pulling out a strappy tank and a pair of shorts. When she finished dressing she collapsed backward onto the bed, patting the mattress next to her. I took a seat and lay back by degrees, until our heads were nearly touching. We stared at the popcorn ceiling. A bell-shaped water stain fanned out from the joint between two panels, a winter leak of rainwater or snow.

"Just try being fun, Cale. You might like it."

"Maybe I'm not in the mood," I said.

"If we all waited to be in the right mood for something," she said, "we would all be in bed. *Book*."

"*Library*."

"Table."

"Salt."

"College."

"Why is that a word?" I propped myself up on the bed and studied her carefully; the unblemished skin, her wide, generous mouth. She rolled her eyes.

"Did Lamb talk to you?"

"No."

I lay back down. "Liar."

"Cale—"

"My turn. *Stab*." I didn't need to look to know she was rolling her eyes again.

"Spear."

"Starship."

"Mars."

"Whale."

"Lourdes."

"Lourdes?"

"She's pregnant. And commuting to college, doing all this math stuff. It's hard being a genius." She poked me with a sharp finger. "*Mother*," she said.

I waited. For a word, a feeling. If we lay there for any longer, I would fall asleep.

"Cale. He just wants you to have a plan. That's all Lamb said, about college. *I don't think she has any kind of plan.*"

"Because he has so many?"

"For what you're going to do. Going to be."

"Do you have one?"

"Well, I thought you would. Don't you know what you want to be when you grow up?"

An astronaut, a librarian, a teacher. Thoughtless answers collected from a contented child whenever an answer was required. The future, beyond Pomoc, beyond Lamb, was always obscure.

"What's it like to live by yourself?" I asked Penny.

"I have all the closet space."

"That's it?"

"What else is there to say?"

"You don't like it," I said.

"I do and I don't."

"You could get a roommate."

"Oh, Cale."

"What?"

"That wouldn't work right now."

"Why not?"

She turned her head on the bed, the look she gave me was soft, pregnant with something I had yet to fully grasp.

"It just wouldn't," she said.

21

For two days no one ventured into the diner at all. Steering wheels were too hot to touch, the idea of traveling the length of a street for a drink or a meal, unimaginable. Here was the hour a truck might crunch into a fender at the corner of Juniper and Spruce, when a customer might refuse his meal and bellow for a manager, when a vexed waitress might hurl a stack of plates to the floor. Rico and I took turns standing on a small, wobbling table underneath the largest oscillating fan. I leaned into the cold case until the edges of the ice cream buckets began to soften and drip.

At sunset I propped open the screen door and wandered onto the porch, picking up a half-smoked cigarette on the armrest of one of the Adirondack chairs. I lipped it but didn't bother looking for a light. My chest still ached from smoking all of Lamb's cigarettes the week before, and I didn't want to think about how he managed a pack a day. I had an image of the black tar gumming up his lungs, his body's pitiless revenge.

In the distance a narrow shape was moving down the road. I tracked it until it became a thin blue bike, its rider bent low over the handlebars, weighted by the burden of a heavy pack. I waited for the rider to pass, but the figure slowed in front of the turnout, hooking a left into the diner's lot, leaning up on the pedals near Rico's van. I recognized the tight, high set of his shoulders as he climbed off his bike and rolled it to the porch, an unmistakable long blond ponytail when he turned to wipe his chin on his shoulder. It was Eric from school, from the Fat Trap, the evening I hoped he'd already forgotten. He climbed the porch steps and stopped the bike in front of my outstretched legs.

"Do you mind?"

"If that gets stolen," I said, letting him pass, "we're not responsible."

Eric leaned the bike against the railing, removing his helmet. The top of his hair was mussed, and a drop of sweat clung to the curve above his lip. I must have been staring, he wiped it with his hand. I led him inside to a booth near the window and brought him a menu. Rico had returned from his break and was bent low in the cook's window, squinting to ID our first customer of the day. I stared, too, trying to remember something about Eric I liked. My reaction to him was always knee-jerk, a defense against all the qualities we shared. Eric, too, had spent countless high school lunch hours sitting alone, tucked in an unoccupied corner of campus, picking at a sandwich he had no desire to eat. Up close now I saw a severity around his mouth, but his eyes were the remarkable, irregular gray of lace jasper. He turned the menu over on the table.

"I'll get the burger plate, rare. Bring me one of those butterscotch milkshakes. Extra whip. Come sit with me."

"Me?"

He looked around as if to emphasize the empty restaurant. "Why not? I hate to eat alone."

Then you should have brought a friend. But I placed his order with Rico at the window and busied myself with his shake, trying to remember what else I knew about him. Sophomore biology, he had sat in the back of the room and never raised his hand. But who did? The past two summers he seemed to come out of his shell. I saw him with the construction crew on the highway laying tar, chumming with the other men in orange vests and yellow hats. Now there was the Trap job, too. When Rico slid the order through the pickup window, I brought it to Eric and slid into the seat across from him, keeping an eye on the parking lot through the window.

Eric took a straw from the dispenser and slid it from its paper sheath, crumpling the wrapper between wide, long fingers, a half-moon of dirt embedded deep under a short fingernail. He salted his fries and pushed the plate toward me. I took one, holding it gingerly while it burned through my fingers. I tried to think of something to say. I was getting better at it, but I never knew where to begin. *You're a loner, so let me tell you how this works, okay?*

"How long have you been working here?" Eric asked.

"Couple months now."

"You get this job after I saw you at the Trap?" A long strand of his hair had come loose from his ponytail. He shook it away from his face. "I never thought I'd see you there."

"I was just taking a drive," I said, feeling my face flush. "I don't know why I went inside."

"Nothing like a nice long drive to the Trap." He was looking at me curiously now, expecting me to say more. But I didn't want to go into the peculiarity of the summer, Lamb, my growing listlessness, the fog that came and went.

"I thought you might be looking for work." He took a bite of his burger.

I shifted in my seat. "No." Out the window, still no cars. "I was just bored."

"I hate to think of you bored. Needing excitement."

Did I dislike him solely for his solitariness, his exclusion, the ways he reminded me of myself? Or was there something else, some reason why—despite his relatively good looks, the mystery he managed to cultivate by dropping into town from some Midwest cornfield—he never managed to make friends or keep a girlfriend longer than a couple of months? That shifty, eager grin spread across his face again, the one that, I remembered now, always made him seem like a creep.

"I can get you an audition," he said. "You can practice your routine on me."

I slid to the edge of the booth, gripping the edge of the table. "I've got to get back to work."

"Stay a minute." He held out a hand to keep me.

"Have you ever tried just not—"

"What?"

"Not being, you know, quite so direct."

"That's right," he said. "You're subtle. I knew it when you walked into the Trap by yourself. What were you looking for in there, the library?"

I stood up, pushing away his hand, but he grabbed my wrist—a tight, firm squeeze before releasing. He was watching me with those cool eyes, a grim smile.

"Trap's not good enough for you?"

"It's fine," I said. "It's great."

"What is it then? The bike's just temporary."

"What?"

"I'm saving up for a 450 on lift, a real cherry red screamer. Trap's helping me pay for it."

"Eric. I didn't mean—"

"You could ask that other girl who works here. Trap's not too good for her."

"Clara?"

Eric smirked. "Not Clara. The hot one."

"Penny?" For the second time that summer, I felt like I'd taken a wrong turn and ended up in the middle of a conversation I was never meant to have. Of course Eric knew Penny from high school—the construction crew were regulars here, piling into the diner early weekday mornings. He would see Penny all the time; she would bring him his eggs. Now Eric was pretending to be absorbed by his meal, dragging a limp fry through the ketchup.

"She took me up on the offer."

"I'll bet."

"She came in for an audition. Couldn't get the job."

The flush in my cheeks spread to my chest. It was his smirk, the way he had looked at me outside the Fat Trap, the way he was looking at me again now. As if he already knew everything about me; Penny, too. As if we were, somehow, all of us the same.

"I saw the girl they had dancing at the Trap," I said. "If Penny wanted a job there, you'd be begging her to take it."

"Nope. Manager didn't want her stealing his customers. But it's all right. I'm thinking about opening my own club. Me and him have been talking about it. He's going to help me get a loan."

"So Penny stealing customers for what?" I laughed. "Our Sunday brunch striptease?"

"You really don't have any idea. She walks around like she's headlining for the Golden Horseshoe. Penny and her friend, that girl skinny."

"Flaca?"

"At the Texaco at like three, four, five in the morning, filling up or something."

"How do you know what goes on at the Texaco at four in the morning?"

He gave me a pointed look. "Even you know what goes on at the Texaco. The first time I saw them it made sense, right? The skinny one sells her pills, sure. Now Penny does, too. That's smart. But they must have seen how easy the other girls made their money. I saw her leave with a guy more than once."

I grabbed his empty glass off the table, to refill it or throw it at him, I wasn't sure. It *did* make sense for Flaca to sell to the truckers at the Texaco, the girls who worked the truckers, too. Those girls weren't careerists, not the same way as the women milling the block at the hour motel, their faces grown more severe every year. The girls at the Texaco were mothers and girlfriends with day jobs whose checks came too late or too short; the extra baby formula, the surprise hospital bill. I heard girls whispering about it in the locker room at school, buzzed girlfriends bent over plates of cheese fries at the diner after the *palo* bars had closed. *We already sleep with guys for free. What's the difference?* If Penny was going to the Texaco to sell pills, it wouldn't have been such a leap.

"You asked Penny out sometime and it didn't take, is that it? She didn't give you the time of day."

"What do you bet she charges? Those other girls are trolls. She could double their make, easy."

"How would you know? I'm sure you don't get up to anything yourself. I'm sure you're just an honest observer."

"Fuck no." He smiled again, his lips shiny with grease from the burger. He sensed it, pulling a handful of napkins from the dispenser and wiping his mouth, his hands; ringing the napkin around one finger at a time. "What do you think Jake'll do when he finds out? Maybe he already knows."

"You should leave."

"You change your mind about the Trap, just come down. When I get my club, we could use a girl like you. I'm going to have all sorts; big girls, small girls, hot girls. Nerds like you." He threw his napkin on his plate and leaned back, crossing his arms above his head in a long stretch. He was lean but looked strong; he had grown wiry from the construction work, his chest stretched against the thin cotton shirt in a way I was sure I was meant to notice. I got up and walked across the empty diner and into the back room. I stayed there for a long time, leaning against the sink, until I heard the bell over the front door chime, the muted clatter on the porch as he gathered his bike and bumped it down the stairs.

There were only two coffee cups in the sink from the slow day; one of them was stained with Penny's rose-colored lipstick around the rim. I opened the dishwasher and began re-racking plates. I was thinking about the outsized Timberlands by Penny's front door. But Penny usually worked overnights at the diner, waiting tables for tips.

Penny doesn't work every night. Penny doesn't always waitress the whole night through.

16

The kitchenette was the most orderly space in Penny's home; a small dish rack, a toaster, a petite coffeemaker, the counters wiped spotless. When Penny opened the fridge I recognized one of the diner's white take-out boxes, a carton of eggs, a lone grapefruit. I watched her move around the kitchen and tried to imagine her here every day alone, shaking cereal into a bowl, waiting for the electric kettle to sing. She pulled a box of pancake mix from the cupboard.

"Grab those eggs for me?"

I took them and cracked two into a bowl, whisking with a fork. "What are your neighbors like?"

"Bunch of old people, mostly." She rolled her wrist, oil sliding in the pan. I poured the eggs into her bowl of flour; she added butter, baking powder, chocolate chips.

"Did your mom make pancakes when you were small?"

"Never," she said, ladling the mix into the pan.

While we waited, I studied all the clutter on her fridge door. An old photograph of Penny as a fierce-looking child in red tulle; a birth announcement for Lourdes' baby boy stuck under the laminate magnet of a cross; a plastic letter *P* magnet securing a short grocery list (apples, Oreos); a work schedule hastily inked on a diner napkin underneath a magnetic *R*. I lifted the *M* to read the scrap of paper torn from county classifieds: *6 wk old Timber Wolf X GSD puppies, female & male avail, agouti, blk, sble $200–$900. (775) 457-6789.* I turned it over. No date listed, nothing to indicate how old the ad might be.

"You're not thinking of getting a dog here?"

"Why not?"

"Wouldn't you want more space?" Though there were plenty of dogs at the Crossroads; I heard them barking from inside screened windows, saw them tied to hitches with a leash, sunning themselves by dry bowls.

"Everyone has dogs. You have dogs."

"I know, but they can be such a pain. What if you ended up with one like Wolf?"

She laughed, flipping the pancake onto the plate. "I'd give him to you."

"You work so much. When are you going to find time to walk a dog three times a day?"

"You know what time I get home from Jake's? Someone got broken into a few weeks ago. Stole their television." She shrugged, pouring more batter into the pan. Had I embarrassed her? I was only thinking of the cool, untouchable Penny from high school, a Penny whose proficiencies didn't extend to caretaking. But that image was already losing its fixed shape, yielding a complexity I was still learning to maneuver. She was still sharp and airy—but also warm, funny, playful, cruel. Like all the best people I had ever known, she enjoyed pancakes in the afternoon. She glanced in my direction, narrowing her eyes. "I don't want to borrow Wolf," she said.

I flipped up the lid of her coffeemaker, dumping the soggy filter in the trash. I checked the freezer, where Lamb kept our grounds, and took out the coffee can, cold to the touch. Penny set down her spatula on the counter and pulled it out of my hands. I watched her replace it in the freezer, shutting the door. She looked away, cutting any chance of discussion. "In the cupboard," she said.

I looked in a few, discovering rows of spices, sugar, a variety of boxed teas: orange clove, cinnamon, lemon, mint. I took down a fragrant bag of grounds and leveled several spoons in the machine's catch. We carried our plates to the mirrored table and took seats on the futon. Penny turned on the small TV, flipping the channels until finally settling on a rerun of *I Love Lucy*. It was the episode Lucy and Ethel volunteered to duet a Cole Porter song for a variety show, surprising each other by showing up in the same elaborate, gauzy dress. I stopped short of asking Penny if she'd already seen it, too. Something in the way she set the remote down on the armrest signaled the comforting gesture of routine. Penny had come home from a hundred overnight shifts at the diner to unwind on the futon with a black-and-white rerun and a meal. *If you're ever in a jam, here I am.* Ethel Mertz snapped her fingers onstage, holding focus in the frothy gown. *If you're ever in a mess, S.O.S.*

Sitting side by side, it felt like we were grown, like we, too, shared years of fused history between us. In a way, we did. Penny's posture, leaning over her plate, and her rabid attention to the show, was already affectionately familiar. I felt somehow sure that, despite their closeness, she'd never shared this particular intimacy with Luz or Flaca or Lourdes. They had spent their entire childhoods dressing alike, passing notes, sharing secrets—but I couldn't imagine any of them sitting still while Penny indulged in an afternoon of singular preference—any of them letting Penny be Penny, outside of who they all had to be, together.

"You're right," I said to her then. "I never had any friends, not really. I never wanted to pay too much attention to anyone, because what if that meant Lamb would stop paying attention to me? But I know that's not how parents work. That's not how you lose them."

"You can lose them all sorts of ways," she said distractedly, her attention still absorbed by the television. When the show ended, Penny handed me the remote—her good humor, unlike my own, always so easily restored. I flipped through channels while Penny stood up and disappeared into the other room. I knew she would return with a board game, a deck of cards, one of the magazines she was always browsing through, the book of magic tricks we had checked out from the library the day before. She emerged a few minutes later carrying a slender box, one of the thousand-piece puzzles she'd purchased from the thrift. I groaned at the sight of it. We had already spent three sweltering afternoons trying to finish the last one she'd bought, only to discover a quarter of the pieces were missing. Still, when she turned one of the boxes over on the floor, I climbed down from the couch to sit beside her, studying Florence's romantic cityscape portrayed on the lid. I had little patience for the task, I could never manage to assemble more than a single uniform corner of sky before losing interest. Only Penny had the scrupulous eye of an architect, the ability to see, by handling only a few obscure pieces, how to forge the path toward a viable, coherent world. I envied her this, but I could begrudge her nothing.

"You definitely need a guard dog," I said. "What if someone broke in and stole your puzzles?"

She arched an eyebrow in my direction.

"I am getting a dog," she said. "And I'm making you come with me."

"Oh, fine," I said. And because I had already hurt her feelings, I skipped the obligatory jokes about Carr, our townie disdain for any CDP whose desolation surpassed Pomoc's own. Nor did I mention the strange, nebulous feeling that had begun to surround us, which I couldn't yet begin to parse. The night before, alone in my bedroom, I felt it creeping in as I tried to fall asleep—a bleak, overwhelming sadness; despair—but the next morning I woke up and forced myself downstairs. I made omelets for the dogs. I let them out in the backyard, stepping barefoot off the porch onto dew-dampened earth, winding up a tennis ball for them to catch. So many things seemed to be floating by the edges of that summer; I felt them brushing past. I had yet to ask Penny about her own mother, the pot of flowers on her landing, her greatest living fear. There would still be time to ask tomorrow. We would walk through this summer side by side. We would blossom, we would swagger. Everything, I knew, would be fine.

22

The next day the heat broke, and there were no new brush fires on the mountain. The dogs remained on the porch through dusk, licking the fading smell of soot from their coats and paws. I remained poised for a gentle rain to wash away the dust that lingered, the shower that would leave the desert as soft and open as a peach. I woke up in the middle of the night, clammy with perspiration. I climbed out of bed to turn on the lamp, pulling down my damp underwear, expecting to find it soaked with blood. Yet nothing bodily had changed. I was only sweating again, a heat that came seemingly from nowhere and built steadily along the base of my spine.

Somewhere in the night, Eric was driving down the highway out of town, heading toward Golan's Texaco. Here was a sandpapered boy from the cornfields of Illinois who had formed a crush on a beautiful waitress he would never have. Maybe he had spoken to her before; maybe she had turned him down. Maybe he never tried. Who knew better than I, how a lonely mind could construct invisible towers, how quickly they could fall? A boy who can't get the girl he wants drives to the whore place and uses another. I imagined their fucking: a painted face used hard against his truck's back fender for fifteen minutes. I stripped off my clothes and the sheets from the mattress, bundling them into a pile in the corner of the room.

There would be no simple way to bring it all up with Penny. It had to be done with patience: the finesse required to dig splinters from Wolf's swollen paws, dodging his bared teeth, the instinctive animal wisdom of self-protection. Talks like this could lengthen into long labyrinths of theory and conjecture; they were like cake between girls, something to savor.

I grabbed a clean T-shirt and went down the hall to the bathroom, taking a quick shower in the dark. On the way back to my room I paused in the hall. There was a thin bar of light coming from underneath Lamb's bedroom door, a tacky, wet cough that no longer bore any similarity to the habitual throat-clearing I used to know. He had been avoiding me, securing himself behind books and buttoned collars, his cinched belt, his age-worn brash. In the quiet of night, the truth was laid bare. Before I could change my mind I crossed the hall to his bedroom door and turned the knob.

Lamb was propped up in bed by a cluster of pillows, his nightshirt baggy around his winnowing frame. His features, behind his wire-rimmed glasses, appeared hawkish in the lamplight. There was a book lying open on the mattress beside him, a prop meant to divert attention from his resting. He peered at me over his spectacles, all at once an old man. We said nothing to each other. I walked past him into his bathroom, bracing against the possibility of more blood in the sink. But there was no blood now. On the bottom row of his medicine cabinet was a new box of fentanyl suckers. I brought one back to Lamb. I sat on the edge of the mattress, the sucker dangling between my fingertips like fruit too ripe to claim. But I had asked nothing of him all summer long; hadn't I practiced wanting less? He coughed again, a rasping, guttural sound. I steeled myself against the strain of his body on the mattress.

The less concern for Lamb I chose to display, the more comfortable Lamb seemed to feel. It would have been easier to issue a contract extolling my precise loyalties: *I, Cale Lambert, do solemnly swear to avoid any emotion pertaining to your wasting. I will not be a daughter, a child, a girl. I will pretend you are not my everything.* Yet in order to succeed, to leach myself of all pity, I would lose something essential. So I would double myself, I would sever: two hearts, one body. My fine twin unwrapped for Lamb his fentanyl sucker, her murky sister twisting on the wire. *I will leave him if he takes it, I will pretend this isn't real.* The gloom girl materialized in secret, categorizing Lamb's decline on the pages of a waitress pad at the diner downtown: the last time Lamb ate dinner (Thursday); Lamb's expression toward cornflakes in a bowl (apathy); the last time Lamb set his wide, warm palm on the crown of my head (April); the frequency with which Lamb appeared as the person I used to know (nil).

Amid his growing inattention, all new freedoms were mine to steal. I could escape this modest home like either of those two mothers, dead and disappeared, but all I wanted to do was stay with Lamb, Lamb, Lamb.

My Siamese set the fentanyl on the nightstand, and walked away.

40

The Texaco was like any other gas station, with rows of motor oil and packaged cakes and sticky buns on display, glass refrigerators stocked with sodas and beer, cigarettes and thirty-seven varieties of chewing gum up front, the grisly bathrooms in a small stucco outhouse ten yards behind the building. The Texaco's distinction lay in the small pancake house attached through a short hall, consisting of one flat gas griddle and a handful of cramped acrylic tables. The quality of the food was, even by trucker standards, low. Every year a rumor circulated that it would close, yet it survived on the drips of business accumulated between shadowy meetings, pickups and drop-offs, pills and girls. As a child, whenever Lamb stopped at the Texaco, I feigned a need for crackers or pop, only to pass through the aisles of candy and kneel at the glass door connecting the two businesses, trying to spy on the large, hardscrabble men who occupied the tables and the varied and listless women that came and went. Sometimes they made eye contact through the glass and smiled. Mostly they stared straight through.

I was older now, I should have been the wiser. I arrived in the evening lull preceding the late-night surge of girls. They came after midnight, like jackrabbits and kit foxes venturing across the scrub to feed.

The Texaco was their last stop of the evening, the restaurant's tight quarters discouraging loiterers. At least the room smelled of coffee. Two men sat at a small table, their heads bent toward one another under harsh light. One of them was older, skinny with a thinning pate, dressed in a striped nylon windbreaker that it was much too warm for. The other man was big boned, caramel skinned, a hangdog face that made him appear, when he looked up, like a sorrowful witness to bygone tragedy. It could also have been the sight of me that left him disheartened: a whippet-slim girl with messy hair in jeans and a tank top, no makeup, a stitched bruise.

I took a seat by the window and tried to imagine Penny doing the same; Penny ordering a soda, pushing her long hair out of her face, preparing to massage dull egos. After a moment the men returned to their conversation. The restaurant was too small, their murmurs floated by. I could have tried to make out what they were saying, but I was distracted, imagining the type of man who would pick up a girl the same way he picked up a tube of toothpaste or a cup of coffee, the inconsequence paid to trivial objects. Eventually the regular waitress, an immortal spirit in a hairnet and flesh-colored compression hose, stopped by with her pad. I ordered a Coke. When she brought it, I sucked it down so fast I felt my brain freeze, then asked for another. I had no distinct plan, no clever strategy. *That's all Lamb said. I don't think she has any kind of plan.* It seemed too late to acknowledge this new understanding of myself, feeble in a way Penny would never be. When the girls came, I would ask them how often they saw her, the last time Penny was here, who she might have left with. The caffeine was constricting my attention to pinpricks. At the other table, the men finished their meal and rose to stand. They dug in their pockets for crumpled bills and littered them across the table. As they passed by, the man with the hangdog face slowed, trailing a beefy hand on the back of the opposite chair.

"You waiting for someone?"

I kept my eyes down and drew a heart in the condensation on my glass, the side they couldn't see.

"No," I said.

"I don't think I've seen you here before. How about you?" The man turned to his companion before retraining his attention on me. "Why don't you come with us?"

"I'm fine here." I tried a smile, and felt it falter.

"Are you?" When I didn't move, "You know what happens when you get picky?"

I looked up then, examining the scruff on his cheeks, the fold of skin underneath his chin, his cheerless expression. If this man had ever tried to pick up Penny, I wanted a sign, some divine clairvoyance. But how would I know who Penny might choose to leave with, when the entire reason I was here was that I didn't know Penny at all? He set a heavy hand flat on the table, a thick, strong hand capable of breaking a glass, an arm, a person. He wanted me to know.

"You skip meals," he said. "You don't eat."

I looked up at him. "Maybe I'd rather starve."

Big Bones looked, briefly, murderous. The skinny man, working a toothpick in his mouth, pulled on his friend's shoulder. "Forget her," he told him. After a beat, his friend relented, turning away. I watched them go, listening to their heavy footsteps fade through the short hall into the Texaco. A minute later they were outside, their voices low through the glass.

Somewhat cheered, I ordered a stack of pancakes to keep the hairnet waitress at bay, but when they arrived I watched the pendant of butter

melt on their surface. Sometime later, a pair of burly truckers came in
and took seats by the window, skimming their attention over my table.
It was impossible to know if they were the ones I needed to talk to, the
vague, formless enigma who would know where Penny had gone.

"Something wrong with the food?" This voice was familiar. I
twisted around in my seat to find Fischer standing there, holding himself stiff, his anger palpable. The truckers glanced over, too, trying to
gauge Fischer's purpose. In his jeans and collared shirt, he could have
been anyone: a boss, a father, a spurned date. He came around the
table and took the empty seat without asking, motioning to the old
waitress. When she came by, he handed her a folded twenty.

"Eat up," he said to me. "Because you're leaving now."

"You can't do that. You can't make me leave."

He flashed a thin smile. He was Ava's daddy no longer, the jovial
cop playing a classroom of innocents. "Where do I begin?" Fischer
asked. "Should I explain to you all the things I can make you do?"

"I'm free to eat wherever I please."

"Yet you're not touching your food."

"Maybe I'm working up an appetite."

"There's an officer parked outside by the back fence. He's not in his
station car, so you might have missed him when you came in, unless
you knew where to look. He's been watching you sit at this window for
the past hour. Neither one of us can figure out why you're here."

My mouth felt dry. I resisted the urge to reach for my soda. "What's
he doing watching me? Shouldn't he be looking for Penny?"

"He isn't here for you. He's on patrol. This place gets busy at night,
a certain type of crowd. But you knew that. From what I've heard,
your friend was a regular."

"Who told you that?"

"A better question is, why didn't you? You say your friend vanished into thin air. You didn't think to mention how she makes her money?"

Vanished. It was worse than *missing*, a word retaining the feel of something temporarily mislaid—a shoe, a lock—an object soon to be rediscovered.

"She's a waitress," I said.

"And?"

"Before Lamb was a manager at the ice plant, he'd drive up to Washoe every weekend with the guys. They painted houses, remodeled bathrooms." I tried one of Penny's careless shrugs, a roll of one shoulder, like working back a kink. "It's called supplementing your income."

The truckers were staring openly now. Fischer, too. I was having difficulty meeting his eyes. I dropped my attention to his mouth, the creases on either side that must have come from laughter, the repetition of it, though I could hardly imagine it now. The heavy, swollen center of his lower lip like a drop of milk not yet wiped away.

"The problem with opening yourself up to risk," Fischer said quietly, "is that it's impossible to know what kind of trouble you're inviting until it's too late. Your friend had to know that. You ought to, too. You're doing the same thing, just by coming here."

"You're saying she made her bed."

"No. I didn't say that."

I glanced over at the truckers, who looked away. What I wanted to say, but didn't know how—who decided these rules in the first place, the kind of danger risk must follow?

"I have to know she's okay."

He sat back in his chair. I could feel his eyes roving over my face, my bruise, the doctor's knotted stitches poking from my brow. The waitress returned with Fischer's change and left it on the table. He laid his hand over the money but stopped short of collecting it.

"I want you to promise me you won't come here again," he said. "You won't interfere. Can we make a deal? And I'll do everything I can to find her."

"You're supposed to be doing that anyway."

"I'm making you a promise."

"Why?"

"You think I do this for my health? Let's say you're right—your friend didn't skip town. I prefer one missing girl to two."

I felt tired then, weary. A part of me wanted to be transported back to the hospital and Lamb. I didn't believe Penny would just skip town. But she had probably done all sorts of things she'd never bothered to tell me, things I hadn't known to ask. The clock on the wall read ten to midnight. Soon the girls would come. Fischer stood up, tucking the change in his wallet, replacing his chair. He motioned for me to follow. "Come on."

"No."

"Cale."

"I'm sorry. I can't."

Fischer came around the table and leaned so close I could smell the cedarwood on his skin, a muted but distinct soap. The scent would be there in the creases of his arms, the panel of cotton lying flush across his chest, the island-shaped nook behind his ear. He was close enough that when he spoke I could feel his breath on my cheek. He laid a warm, wide hand on the back of my shoulder, rubbed his thumb up and down the base of my neck. My ears flushed red, a white-hot feeling shooting straight down to my gut. The men at the other table were staring again.

"You're going to get up right now," Fischer said.

23

Penny knocked on the door late morning, breathless, having hitched a ride from the early cook to the local road, walking the rest of the way. She wore her hair in a long braid over one shoulder, her cheeks flushed, the fine hairs curling up around her forehead.

"Hi," she said, her voice on the porch like a star. I let her in and we walked back to the kitchen. She took a seat at the table and poured herself a cup of coffee, tucking a leg underneath her on the chair. I had taken down Lamb's tray of pills on the kitchen counter and lined up the vials. She helped herself to the plate of bacon Lamb had left on the table, watching me shake out his pills and count them back into their containers one by one. It was gratifying to see someone eat so casually, as if only for the pleasure of the activity. If Lamb was here I would point to Penny as a model of appetite and vitality. *Do you see? This is how it's done!*

She waited for me to finish counting, to replace the tray in the cupboard behind an old bag of flour, as Lamb had. When I was done I took a seat at the table. She picked up another piece of bacon, watching me with those deep, dark eyes that could swallow the whole world. "Cale," she said, "¿qué haces?"

"Lamb forgot to take his medicine two days in a row."

"Maybe he didn't forget."

"Penny."

"Cale. What can you do about it?"

Behind the house came the sound of dirt bikes revving up; they would peel up and down the desert until after dark.

"I don't know," I finally said.

"It's a beautiful day," she said, glancing out at the yard, the sound of the bikes. "Have you been outside yet?"

"I don't care."

"I do." She was looking out the window, her gaze spanning our rocky yard, the scrub-strewn grade sloping upward to the fence, the mountain behind it. "When was the last time you went up there?"

"The mountain? Not since I was a kid. Ten years."

"So let's go."

"Ugh. No way."

"Yes way, Cale. All you want to do is count pills. We'll trade off, okay? One thing I want to do, then one thing for you."

"All we ever do is what you want." Until I said it out loud, I didn't realize it was true. All this time I must have been cataloging our moments together, sorting them into recognizable piles. Mine, hers, mine, hers. For her part, Penny seemed largely unconcerned.

"I just have better ideas," she said.

The air was finally clean again, still cool in pockets of shade. I carried a stepstool from the house across the yard. The dogs walked with us, nudging our legs, eager to know our plans. Wolf trotted ahead, then stopped to look back, wanting to make certain we would follow. Penny was more comfortable with them now, grazing Trixie's ear with her fingertips. We climbed the grade first, a pebbled, weedy ridge, our sneakers slipping on the ascent. As a child, the grade itself had been a challenge, producing countless scabbed knees and elbows. One particularly rough tumble resulted in a sprained ankle, another, a busted chin. If Lamb hadn't encouraged it, I would have avoided the mountain altogether. But the land beyond our fence, like the vacant expanse between those lost casinos, was a place Lamb shed his gruff and forgot himself to pleasure. When I finally mastered climbing the grade, Lamb would jump the fence first, then lift me over, his arms made sinewy from years of hauling ice. Once my sneakers touched down on the other side of the mountain, I tore away from him, hunting off trail for wild penstemon and wily lizards, overturning rocks and digging through weeds, poking into the dark, secret spaces between boulders, where scorpions might hide from the sun. Yet I never went so far that I couldn't see the speck of his work shirt in the distance. Even then I knew, if we were ever to lose each other, which one of us would be the better off. One of us already knew how to be alone.

I was relieved to find that the grade had become, with age, much easier work. Once we made it to the top, I set the stool in the corner of our fence and hauled myself up to straddle the ledge, balancing on the flat, narrow precipice, toes dangling. For a moment my old, childish hesitation returned. Then I pushed off, dropping to the ground. A second later, Penny pulled herself up and over the fence, landing next to me. Wolf and Trixie barked furiously from the other side, distressed at our vanishing.

From the window in our kitchen, as Penny would have seen it first, the mountain must have looked like an extension of our property, as much ours as any tangled weed. But on this side of the fence, that illusion collapsed. We were standing in the midst of the mountain's wild expanse; miles of tightly pebbled earth and sparse brush, an incline of swale grass, dry weeds, and boulders stretched toward a cerulean sky. I bent down and dug my hands into the dirt, letting the fine ochre dust sift through my fingers. Though Penny had been the one to suggest the hike, she was waiting for me to begin. Only now I realized how inappropriately we were dressed in our shorts and tank tops, how we had neglected to bring any of the essentials—sunscreen, hats, water, food. In the ten years that had passed since I last set foot on the mountain, I had forgotten everything I once knew. It was too late to go back. I started off, Penny in tow.

Hikers had cut switchbacks in various ascents over the mountain; some trails were overgrown, others still clear enough to maneuver. For a long time we didn't speak, bent on creating distance between the house and ourselves. The small rocks of the trail crunched underfoot; I could feel them sticking in the tread of my sneakers. I scanned the ground, too dry to preserve tracks. A few feet from the trail I spied the furred tapers of coyote scat. After a half mile, I stopped to catch my breath. Penny twisted her hair into a pile on the top of her head, her cheeks flushed pink once more. Trying to find her footing over a small formation of rocks, she stumbled and shot out a hand for balance. I grabbed it, steadying her. We had come high enough that when we looked back we could see down into the yard, Wolf a small hunkered shape in the center of it. Even from a distance I could tell he was still tracking us, his body tense. I waved, setting him barking again, the sound a faint echo down below.

"What do you think he's saying?" Penny asked.

Already I regretted not bringing water. My mouth felt full of sand.

"Pissed you ate all the bacon," I said. But I wondered if Wolf, who spent years patrolling our borders, knew something about the mountain that even I did not.

The cool air was slowly burning off, the sun moving directly overhead. Somehow we'd switched places; now I was following Penny up a scrabble of rocks. As the incline grew steep, I could feel the rosy heat of sunburn bloom on my arms and legs. Every now and then a slight breeze fluttered by, desperately welcome. I bent to snap a poppy from its stem and handed it to Penny. She tucked it behind her ear. After several yards she snapped off another flower, folding the stem into her braid. We were high up now. I slowed to maneuver over a steep slope, the sound of dirt bikes long since faded. If one of us was to slip, it would take the other climbing all the way back down to get help. I recalled my earlier conversation with Lamb, the mountain lions roused from their dens, dislocated by the recent fires. Those that didn't steal into backyards would climb higher still, seeking the coverage of unburnt brush. I stepped over a patch of chaparral and a small lizard shot past my foot, green and purple skin stippled in the light. Penny pulled a hairband from her wrist and handed it back to me. I pulled my hair into a high ponytail and felt cool for a few minutes before the tops of my ears began to burn.

Thirty yards ahead to the right was a large, flat boulder grouped near several others. I called out to Penny and we adjusted our trajectory, heading for the outcrop. I reached the boulder first and climbed on. Penny climbed up next to me, lifting her braid from the back of her neck. I lay back and settled my bones against the rough surface, the rock's stored heat toasting my back and hips. I imagined all the mountain's wildlife that had roamed by and done the same. Penny stretched back, too, and we stared up at the bright, impossible blue sky, unbroken by a single cloud. When she spoke her voice emerged disembodied, as if originating from within the natural world surrounding us.

"Did you know there's a tribe of women living near Russia somewhere, camping on a sliver of ice all year round, just helping the reindeer get around?"

"That sounds cold," I said. But then I laughed, picturing it, squeezing my eyes shut. I saw sunbursts through my eyelids. I had a sense I was falling, though I knew I hadn't moved at all. I forced myself to open my eyes again. "Where did you read that?"

"In a magazine. You want to be warm? There are places you can climb real volcanoes. There are women who do that."

"I've never even seen the ocean," I said. But I had read about it, the way it had been described in the best book of fifth grade: *The sea is smooth. It is a flat stone without any scratches.* Penny raised her arms to the sky, moving them like waves above us.

"Okay," I said. "Let's do it. We'll live on the water, hunt sharks, sew blankets out of kelp. If we're going to sail, we'll need a boat."

"Getting the boat isn't the problem," she said, as if we'd already discussed this many times. "The problem is you're not serious. At some point you have to stop reading, and start doing."

"Do I?" I was silent for a long time. "Do you think maybe there are some people who just aren't meant to do things?"

"No. There are just people who are scared, and people who aren't."

It was getting too hot on the rock. I had to shift onto my side to avoid searing my back. But I didn't want to leave; I wanted to stay, I wished all our problems were like a boat we had already learned to sail in our hypothetical, fantastic future. There would never be a better time to ask.

"Penny. Do you remember the new guy from school?"

"Who's that?"

"Eric," I said. "Long blond ponytail. He always sat by himself in the quad at lunch. He works at the Trap now."

"What about him?"

"He came in to Jake's yesterday. He said you went by the Trap last month. That he'd seen you at the Texaco."

"So?"

"Penny." I sat up too fast, the blood rushing to my head. I could see all the way down the mountain to our speck of yard, the winding road that led down the hill to town. But I could no longer make out the dogs. They had abandoned their watch, retreating to the shade of the porch. Penny remained perfectly still, eyes closed, her impeccable features composed, her hands folded on her stomach. I grabbed her sneakered foot, shook it.

"What, Cale."

"Is it true?"

"What do you think?" She didn't bother opening her eyes.

"Are you selling pills down there? Or what?"

"Does it matter?"

I couldn't tell if she was serious. Taking that risk, trafficking in probabilities. But that wasn't what she meant. *Does it matter to you?* A part of me, annoyed she would even ask. "I care that you could get arrested. Or worse. What if—"

Penny sat up on the rock and one of the poppies fell from her hair onto the boulder. She began to pull the burrs from her socks. I reached for the flower, its petals already wilted.

"Do you know these guys?"

"They're all the same, Cale."

"Was it Flaca's idea?"

She gave me a wry look. "It's been every girl's idea, forever."

I threw the wilted poppy at her. She raised her hands in mock protest. "What's your problem? You want to come with me?"

I could tell she was trying to lighten the mood. She still didn't really want to talk about it.

"I just want you to be more scared of some things," I said. I hesitated, meeting her eyes. "Do you want me to come with you?"

She sobered a little. "No."

"Then are you sure you know what you're doing?"

"Not at all," she said.

We started off again. We had only been climbing for a few minutes when Penny grabbed me, digging her long nails into my forearm. I cried out, trying to pull away.

"Snake," she whispered.

I froze, scanning the ground. It took a moment to decipher the long tawny body and chocolate markings from the brush and gravel, already slithering off toward the shade of a rock. She waited for it to disappear before loosening her hold. When I looked down I discovered five crescent-shaped indentations in my flesh, the mark closest to my wrist beading red. She looked pale, glancing guiltily at the damage.

"It's just a gopher snake," I said. My arm was throbbing. "Are you okay?"

She nodded in the direction we had been going, indicating I should go ahead. I started to walk, Penny sticking so close behind I could hear her breathing; feel her tense at every sound. I should have suggested we turn around, but for some reason I'd become desperate to finish what we started, to exert our power, if nowhere else, over this single achievable goal. And although I was still worried about what she was doing at the Texaco—on some level, I understood not wanting to talk about it, not knowing how to feel—I was hurt she couldn't, didn't want to discuss it.

It took another half hour to reach the peak, and when we finally arrived I searched for the absolute highest point, the apex so clearly defined from my bedroom window. From where we stood, it all looked the same. Still we walked around, admiring the view. Penny stopped at a western-facing vista and propped her leg on one of the small boulders lining the crest, holding up her hand to shield her eyes. I had to smile at the picture she made. She could have been any of those infamous conquistadors from the paintings in our middle school history books: Hernán Cortés surveying the spoils of combat, Pizarro conquering the Incas. Only our kingdom amounted to gradations of rock, the sprawl of dirt and char, a cluster of streamlined roads intersecting at the junction. Penny glanced over her shoulder, smiling too when she saw my face, already expecting to be let in on the joke. If anyone could turn a battleground of rivals into willing subjects, it would have been her. I gestured to Pomoc stretched out below. I told her about the photos I remembered from history class, her unconscious mimicry. I lifted my imaginary skirts to bend in mock curtsy.

"Your spoils, m'lady."

Penny turned to look again, adjusting her perspective.

"Ours," she said.

41

Outside the Texaco, Fischer kept tight hold of my arm above the elbow, steering me past the gas pumps and the outdoor bathrooms. We passed a dark car near the dumpsters, nearly indiscernible in the shadows. Fischer made a terse gesture in its direction; the car returned no indication that we'd been seen. I squinted in the dim light, but beyond a vague human outline, I couldn't make out anyone behind the wheel. Two long freight cabs were parked in a T by the diesel pumps. Otherwise the lot was empty. Fischer guided me toward a black sedan parked on the gravel and folded me into the passenger seat, waiting until I was buckled in before slamming it shut. The car's interior was cool and quiet, a discreet maple air freshener on the dash. I could detect Fischer's scent underneath it, too. I tried the door, the sound like a hollow metal latch straining. Fischer came around the driver's side and climbed in, starting the engine.

"Child locked," he said. "For adults who act like children."

He drove with one hand on the wheel, the other resting between us. I tried to imagine the hours he must have spent traveling back and forth to county, the freedoms he allowed himself when he was all alone, the music he played, if he ever relaxed enough to sing along. The only sound now was the car's tires over the uneven roads, our

headlights filtering the dark, but the silhouette of the road was enough
to orient me. Even Pomoc's vacant stretches of gravel were recognizable, the rabbitbrush in the headlights.

"How did you get to the gas station?" he asked me.

"I caught a ride."

"You make that a habit, hopping in cars with strangers?"

"You're a stranger." I could still feel his thumb sliding up and down
my neck. "Did you get a chance to talk to Penny's other friends?"

Fischer didn't take his eyes off the road. "How does your grandfather get you to drop something once you've got your teeth in it?"

"If it was Ava who took off, would you drop it?"

"What makes you think she hasn't?" We came to a stoplight, the
eerie red glow accentuating his high forehead, a bump on the bridge
of his nose healed from a break, his flexible mouth. "She's taken off
before. Forgets to call. Drives her mother crazy."

"But not you."

"Of course me, too. But I know where to find her, and when she's
ready, she always comes back home." He glanced over. "What about
you? You ever forget to call Lambert?"

The signal changed, the car's interior filling with emerald light as
we passed under before dissipating into pitch, as if there was an invisible tether attached to the front of the sedan, pulling us deeper into
night.

"No one really forgets," I said.

I realized we were heading toward the mountain, though I hadn't
provided Fischer with any directions. He turned the sedan at the end
of the hill and we began to climb.

"How do you know where I live?"

"I know a lot of things."

"Look, I don't need—" But what was it that I didn't need? An escort. A cop who thought he could protect girls who weren't like his daughter from turning into her. I hesitated, the story of the sand-colored man on the tip of my tongue, as if the strange intimacy created by the darkness, and the evening spent in each other's company, necessitated confession. Fischer pulled the sedan into our driveway and we sat for a moment, the engine idling. There was a dog's sharp bark from the backyard, then another. Wolf, testing my proximity, the range of his guard. I reached over and hit the radio, a booming, dynamic voice kicking over the stadium's roar—"*bottom of the eighth lad-ies and gentle-men, Rodriguez at bat showing no signs of mercy, we're looking at the ab-so-lute*"—I hit the button again, plunging us into silence. I thought I saw Fischer smile, but then it was gone, a trick of the headlights. I was beginning to sense how alone we were, sitting side by side in the dark. I tensed at the sound of a chamber falling, but it was just the doors unlocking. I felt my own confusion, the thorny shape of it. A part of me, disappointed.

"Don't forget," he said as I climbed out of the car. "You'll leave it to me."

I stood on the drive and watched the sedan ease down the hill, slipping back into night.

24

The dogs were in Carr. I blew cigarette smoke out the window into the hot air rushing by, watching the road get eaten up by our tires. Penny fiddled with the radio. For a few minutes Chuck Berry bopped in the dash before crackling into static. I hooked a finger under my bra and pulled it away from my skin for a moment of relief. Yet we were well past the hottest hour of the afternoon. The sun had nowhere left to go but down.

"We should see the exit soon, don't you think?"

"I don't know." Penny shrugged. "I've never been."

"What?" I straightened behind the wheel. "Penny, you said you had."

"No," she said, fiddling with the radio some more, "I said I'd been to Corken and Jasper. What's the difference? All these shitty places are the same."

"You said you'd been to Carr." I heard the accusation in my voice, residual angst from the morning waiting tables. Ms. Potter, the prim elementary-school teacher who wore her harlequin eyeglasses on a beaded chain, had come in requesting a booth and three runny eggs. When I brought them to her, she sent them back, snapping her laminated menu back and forth like a fan. *I can't even look at them, runny as all that!* Finally she'd nibbled at a stack of buttered toast and left a plate full of crumbs, no tip. Penny had taken the previous night off; I was careful not to ask her how she spent it. Tonight Clara would work the overnight shift alone.

"Do you want to check your phone?"

"You just stay on this until you get on the interstate, then take the 210 all the way out. That's what the lady said."

But for how long? We had already been driving an hour. It took an hour and a half to get from Pomoc to Sparks, half that to get from Pomoc to Jasper or Noe. The way people talked about Carr, it had always sounded close by, too. The sky was beginning to bleed coral and tangerine, swaths of violet in the cirrus. Dusk, lowering onto us. We drove on, watching the chaparral fly by, spasmodic radio activity filling in the silence. After twenty minutes I spotted our connection to the 210, and we took a long, arching off-ramp depositing us onto a local two-lane freeway, the cars thinning out. It felt like a narrowing, funneling us toward our destination.

"Do you know I took acting classes in Tehacama once, at the community college?" Penny asked. Both of us, watching the cars going by.

"No." I glanced over. "Actually, maybe I heard you wanted to be an actress."

"Can you see it?"

"Of course," I said, but the longer I thought about it, the more difficult it was to conceive, Penny trying on all those different personalities like dresses, as if she were not already so impossibly, indisputably herself. "Weren't you in the school play?"

"They made me a cheerleader. An extra. Four lines. And you had that part at the end, what was it? Something serious. I was in fifth grade, so you must have been—"

"A librarian? I don't remember," I said, but I was beginning to. Lamb's dubious expression when I had asked to buy a navy blue skirt to play the part.

"A curator! You were the museum curator at the end."

"That's right," I said, but I was also watching the highway signs that had begun to drop away, just sprawling desert and clumps of creosote for miles, though the mountains were still visible in the distance, like colossal watchmen guarding the horizon. By the road, short blond weeds covered patches of ground, their prickly burrs turned up to the deepening sky. We had yet to find the second exit, and I was beginning to realize that when it grew dark, the rural highway would lack any of the intermittent lights of the interstate in Pomoc, whose exits we knew by heart. Finally I saw a sign approaching in the distance and began to slow. The pole had suffered a clash with some vehicle larger than itself, bending it askew, the words half obscured in slant. Penny rolled down her window as we approached.

"I can't make it out. Jenson Ave.?"

"Maybe we should call," I said, slowing further, looking for a turnout, somewhere to pull over. Penny dug into her bag for her phone and held it in the air to search for a signal, as if it were a face mirror and she was examining her angles. She dialed, transferring the call to speaker. The phone rang loudly before a woman answered, the kind of scratchy voice that belonged to a life lived between drags.

"Hi," Penny said, "I called earlier, about the dogs? We're trying to find you now, but I think we might have gone too far. Are you past the Jenson exit?"

"You want Pasco," the voice said. "Keep going. When you get close, turn right at the fork."

"But how much farther is Pasco?" I asked. The sky seemed to be dimming too quickly, but it was only the lack of streetlamps that made it seem so, the unfamiliar roads, the way pockets of shadow seemed to deepen and spread. I looked up from the road back to Penny. She was still studying the phone, pressing a button to illuminate the screen.

"We lost her," she said.

Ten exits past Jenson, or thirty miles that felt like sixty, the sky was darkening still.

Penny pointed at the windshield, the outline of a ghostly moon.

"We should have started out earlier," I said.

"But you didn't get off work any earlier. Anyway, I'm hungry now. Where do you think these people eat?"

"There was a Burger Barn back there."

"That was thirty miles ago," she said.

"Really?"

"The sign said *No gas next forty miles*. We must have gone most of that."

I hesitated. "Maybe we should turn around."

There was another exit approaching, but I couldn't make it out. Penny leaned forward and slapped the dashboard with a flat palm, triumphant.

"That's it. Pasco, two miles."

"Okay. But how are we ever going to find our way back?"

"Just turn around. Easy."

I nodded, but I was beginning to feel, as we coasted the off-ramp onto a dirt road, that we had already gone too far. There was no sign to indicate what lay ahead in either direction. I looked down the road to the left and saw nothing but shadows. I took a right; our tires already pointed that way. We drove for several minutes in silence, seeing nothing except for an occasional, indistinct silhouette in the distance, that, driving closer, became a boulder, a tumbleweed. I turned on the headlights, illuminating a small pool of gravel ahead.

"There's nothing here," Penny said. "I think this is the wrong way." The interior of the cab lit up by the light of her phone. "I still don't have any service. Is this a two-lane?"

"I'm not sure I'm on a road at all," I said, and the uncomfortable feeling grew. "What if we run into another car?"

We saw it at the same time, flashing by the window. I braked too hard, and Penny threw her hand on the dash. It was a wooden pole hammered into the ground, a street sign handwritten with white paint. If it had been difficult to read signs in the failing light, it was nearly impossible now.

"Whoa," Penny said. I took my foot off the brake, and we inched along by degrees. More street signs marked the dirt lane at odd intervals, the writing indistinguishable in the growing dark. The road narrowed, then a slim white edge grew in the dark as we came closer, until it became a porch, then a house, and another, the houses spaced far apart, all of them shuttered and dark. I felt struck by a thought too terrible to consider. What if we weren't really heading toward dogs at all? What if Penny had brought me along for another reason entirely, the way she'd taken me to Rena's, and the husky voice on the phone was just another customer waiting for pills, a setup for some lonely Texaco regular who asked Penny to bring a friend? I flashed the truck's brights, illuminating the shape of an old metal mailbox in front of one of the houses, its red flag raised to signal a pickup. The next house we passed had a similar mailbox, the same raised flag. I took it as a sign of civilization that a postal worker was still coming by, unless no one had ever bothered to lower these flags and there were still letters trapped inside these mailboxes, like messages cast hopelessly into bottles, never to reach shore. Penny unbuckled her seat belt and scooted forward with her hands on the dash, pointing ahead where the road split in two.

"That's it," she said. "The woman said turn right at the fork."

I took the turn, the path running rough, the truck pitching from side to side over chunks of gravel. I understood it now, the expression on a townie's face when someone mentioned Carr, the precise degree of isolation they were calling to mind. I kept the brights on, which made everything both better and worse, illuminating the immediate swath of gravel before us, plunging everything else into sharp contrast, sacrificed to the darkness. At least we finally knew we were headed the right way.

A moment later Penny tapped on the passenger window to get my attention, and I turned down a long empty lane into a hamlet of trailers that made the Crossroads seem like a bustling social enterprise. I slowed the truck to a crawl and parked in front of a long peach trailer in lot six, the number listed in the advertisement. Half of me hoped the raspy-voiced woman had already split and we would have no choice but to turn around and drive home. We climbed out of the truck, our boots crunching on the gravel. A collection of ceramic wind chimes strung up between two trailers snapped in the sharp breeze, making frenetic music. The wind felt stronger across Carr's flat land without the mountains to offer shelter.

Penny rapped on the trailer door. A gooseneck lamp lit up in the window, followed by a tall woman answering the door, rail thin, her smile wide enough to reveal a dark hole where an eyetooth was missing, her chin and cheeks bumpy with raw scabs. I recalled the billboard we passed on the interstate, a pair of ashen feet sticking out of a covered gurney, the morgue's hangtag from one big toe spelling out

METADONES MUERTAS in white block letters, a 1-800 number printed across the bottom. I prayed Penny wouldn't offer any of her own wares.

"Thought you got lost," the woman said. It was the same scratchy voice as on the phone.

"We did, and then we found you. I'm Penny, this is Cale."

The woman looked us over. I smiled. We followed her into a small trailer overwhelmed with the smell of wet dogs, urine, the fading aroma of buttered popcorn. To the right was a cramped kitchen, a foldout table set against the far wall. In the middle of the room a futon had been turned around so that its wide back formed one make-shift panel of an octagonal exercise pen. Inside the enclosure, several black and tan puppies lolled around on the floor, each about the size of a man's shoe. They didn't look much like wolfdogs, but who was I to diagnose origin? An adult shepherd brushed past and I reached for him instinctively, my fingers sticking in his thick, matted fur. I thought he'd snap at my hand, but he just fixed me with a weary look as he continued on his way to the water bowl by the fridge, bending his head to drink. After he had his fill, he settled down on the lino-leum, lowering himself with visible effort. Sore in the hips, getting on in age.

"That's Hank," the woman said, noticing my attention. She stepped over the pen and Penny followed suit, both of them reaching for the puppies. I hung back, not trusting myself to get too close without bringing another dog home. One of the puppies, gold around his nose and tail, raised his head and gamboled over to Penny, who knelt on the carpet to meet him. He set his front paws on her knee and yipped.

"We were going to get Hank fixed, in the beginning," the woman said. "Lord, my son raised hell. *You're not taking his balls, Mom, you don't know what it's like.*" She rolled her eyes. "We let the neighbor's bitch get at him and sold the puppies. I swore it was the last time. But Hank likes being a father, even if it's a lot of work for me. My son promised to help out, but they never do. You all have kids?"

"No." Penny was scratching the masked puppy behind the ear. His diminutive tail wagged in response. "No kids."

"I always wanted twins," the woman continued. "I saw those commercials when I was a little girl, you know, the Doublemint twins? But I had my son instead. My husband worked eighteen years over at the air force base. Twenty-five and they give you a real pension. Every time I went by the hangar I could see how they were living. Coffee cups everywhere, hydraulic on the mat. You become a mother, you don't get any say. They've got people to clean up, he said. Eighteen years and he gets his boots wet coming down a ladder. He only ever got well enough to hunt pussy after that. If he can get another family, why can't Hank?" She laughed, a sound so coarse I wondered if it didn't hurt her doing it. She was watching Penny cuddling the cinnamon-colored runt, making cooing noises low in her throat. "I'd let that little one go for two-fifty. The black and the fawn are three each. Where'd you come in from?"

"Pomoc," I said. "I don't think we realized how far the drive was. We probably shouldn't stay too long."

Penny's new friend wandered off to a patch of newspaper and raised a stubby leg, a dark spot of water spreading underneath him. The black puppy came over to investigate, biting the runt on the nose.

"I'll take the black one," Penny said. She dug in the pocket of her shorts and pulled out a wad of cash, counting off five twenties too many, and folded the wad into the woman's open palm. We still didn't know her name, even though we'd told her ours.

"Let me get you a box," the woman said, excusing herself. "You picked some trouble."

She disappeared down the hall, and I tried not to notice one of the other puppies scrabbling at the baby gate, yipping in my direction. Would Lamb understand if I brought another puppy home now, how all the world's remainders shared a responsibility to stick together?

Before I let the thought go too far, the throaty, deafening sound of an engine filled the air, swelling louder and louder, fracturing all rational thought. I felt the vibrations in my skull and covered my ears, certain that whatever vehicle it belonged to was going to run the trailer right through. When I thought the noise would swallow us, the engine cut. Penny picked up the puppy again, nuzzling him underneath her neck. I stifled an urge to remind her that the animal licking her throat had just recently rolled in its own piss. She didn't seem to mind. A door slammed outside, a pair of booted footsteps heavy on the stairs. The front door yanked open and a medium-sized man with sand-colored hair walked through the door, carrying several bags of groceries. I could just make out the red and blue dots of a loaf of Wonder bread through the plastic. He took in Penny right away, eating her up with his eyes. She stiffened a degree, the animal sniffing her chin.

"Hey," he said. His resemblance to the woman was betrayed by his heart-shaped face, the pointy chin. Here was the prodigal son, staunch opponent of neutered dogs. He looked only a little older than us, a slim margin of years that placed him on an island of neighboring experience, a murky horizon I sensed but couldn't touch. He was still staring at Penny with the frank, intrusive interest she inspired in all manner of men: hoary diner regulars, truckers pumping gas, high school boys angling the wide stance of their legs in her direction. What simple power her beauty had to arrest. Would she ever try to temper her appeal underneath a baggy sweater or ugly clothes, a pair of oversized glasses? As if it might make any difference.

The man turned his attention to me, his eyes an unnerving cobalt blue. I looked away, to the puppies still penned in, to Penny standing in their midst, cradling the black puppy in her arms. The litter had come to gather at her feet, sitting on their haunches like rambunctious schoolchildren called to attention, tilting their faces toward her sun. Surely there had been more than four of them once? Surely they could understand what had to happen now?

The woman reemerged from the hall, carrying an empty milk crate. She handed it to me. Her son moved away, beginning to unload groceries in the kitchen. If she noticed he had returned, she didn't pay him any mind. I could still feel his attention trailing Penny as she stepped over the gate. I held the crate out to her and she settled the dog inside, our eyes briefly meeting. How do you explain the unique physiology of girlhood friendships, the telepathy formed fast and fierce between hometown strangers?

"We should go," I said to the woman. "Is there a better way to get back to the 210?"

"There isn't any 210 here," the man spoke up from the kitchen. But the woman interrupted, cutting him off.

"When you get out of here go left, drive down a ways. You'll find it. You want a little towel for him? I hate this part, I'm not ashamed to say it. Just hold on," she held up her hand to stay us, hurrying back down the hall.

"The 10 turns into the 210 at Norman," the man continued, watching us from the kitchen. He smoothed one of the plastic bags flat against his chest, pressing out the air, his eyes shifting back and forth between us. When it was thin as paper he began to fold the plastic into fourths. "You should turn right out of here, there's a small off-road path that loops back to the 10. It's faster that way, but the ramp's tough to make."

"Thanks," I said. "I guess we took the long way. It's impossible to get a signal out here. We got lucky and headed the right way."

"Don't need a signal," he said, flashing a strange smile that seemed to be testing something in the air. "You just need to know where you're going. Everyone around here does. Where are you girls from?"

Penny skittered her eyes over mine. He was watching us closely now, following her gaze. She took the crate from me and balanced it on her hip. "Tehacama," she said, and I was glad the woman wasn't around for the lie.

"Service isn't much better there. I weld for Mentco. We do all the cell towers. Our parents did fine without them. You ask me, we'll keep doing fine. I'm out in Tehacama sometimes. Where do you girls work?"

"We actually have to start heading back," I said. Penny inched closer to the door.

"I'll follow you out."

"Oh, that's okay. We'll be fine," I said.

The man came out of the kitchen. He was wearing an expression on his face I wasn't sure how to read; his lower jaw tightening, as if there was something there he was missing—a wad of chew, some gum. "You girls aren't really from Tehacama," he said.

"Does it matter?" Penny asked. It came out a degree too sharp, her patience spent. The distance we had already traveled, how far we had yet to go.

"It does when I ask you."

"And who are you?" she asked.

"You don't know. You don't have any idea."

Penny shrugged. "I know this place feels like the *Twilight Zone*."

"I was going to do you girls the favor."

"We don't need your favors." Penny said, her hand already on the door. "Do we?"

Outside the night was packed like tight black wool, the wind picking up. The gravel crunched under our boots on the way to the truck. Penny cooed to the puppy in a nonsensical language I had not previously thought her capable of. She climbed in and set the box between her feet on the floor of the cab. There was no choice now but to use the brights. When I turned them on the ground in front of us sprang to life in all its minutiae, the rabbitbrush leaves reflecting like small, strange dinosaur parts in the light. Only when we had locked the doors and had our seat belts on did I look down at the small animal peeking out of the milk carton, his black eyes glinting in the dark.

We were turning left out of the lot when I heard the sound behind us, the squeaking hinges of a door. In the rearview mirror the man was running out down the front steps of the trailer toward a hulking 4x4 parked in the corner of the lot. There was nothing in his hands.

I tried to form Penny's name in my mouth, my tongue lifting and falling, over several seconds, to form a consonant, a vowel. Penny twisted around in her seat to get a better look. When he started the engine it was the same monstrous sound, loud and guttural, that had engulfed the park earlier. It wasn't until he switched on the lights that we could finally see it: one of those modified zombie off-roaders on lifts, custom headlights, a full light cage strapped to the hood. He flipped on the cage and our rearview was flooded with light so bright that our skin became translucent. One of us let out a cry, and even I couldn't tell the difference between us. He switched off the cage again, and we were made blind, spots floating in our field of vision.

"Maybe he forgot something at the store." My voice was lost somewhere in the cab.

"Drive," Penny said. Her voice more clear than I'd ever heard it. "Go now."

29

"Cale?" The baby-faced doctor stood up behind his massive desk, squinting across the room. Lamb was somewhere down the hall with his fat, redheaded nurse. Every time this place managed to feel like the captain's quarters in a luxury cruise ship: the gold-thread carpet and desktop hourglass, his diplomas framed on the wall. The fentanyl I stole from Lamb's bathroom slithered through my system, making everything cotton candy soft. I laid my head against the doorjamb, trying my best not to puddle into the carpet.

I had snuck into the house sometime after midnight, feeling my way up the stairs in the dark. For hours I lay curled in bed, twitching at every creak of the house settling, the wind whistling outside, the dogs' nails clicking on the hardwood floors. Finally, after dawn, I heard the front door slam, Lamb leaving for his doctor's appointment alone. I crawled out of bed to the hall and picked up the phone to dial Penny's number, listening to it ring. But when the time came to leave a message, I couldn't decide what to say. Maybe we both needed a day alone to repair. Maybe I ought to preserve my words, my limbs, my parts, my wits.

"Come here," the doctor said. "What happened to you?"

I walked to him on unsteady legs, conscious of his attention. He came around his desk and stopped me, closing his cool, spongy hands around my arms. He palpated my neck and shoulders, probing the sides of my chest. He pressed a tender spot under my breast and I cried out, gulping air. This close, I could make out a small spattering of sunspots along his forehead and the top of one cheek. He was not as young as I imagined, though it was his displeasure aging him now. His censure, like Lamb's, nearly too much to bear.

"Stand up straight."

"I *am*."

"What did you take?"

"Nothing. One of Lamb's suckers."

"You can't do this right now. You understand? Talk to someone, I don't know. But this—"

"I know."

"Do you?" He lifted my chin with a finger, manifesting a penlight from the deep pocket of his coat. I had already seen my reflection in Lamb's bathroom mirror. My right eye was swollen to a discolored slit, a deep gash bisected the brow, a nasty purple stain mottling the top right quadrant of my face. The doctor probed the fragile orbital bone.

"When did this happen?"

"Last night." My voice like something left out in the sun to dry.

He clicked off the penlight. "There's nothing to do for those ribs but to take it easy. You're lucky nothing's broken. If you waited any longer I might not have been able to sew you up."

"Can't I see him first?"

The look on his face, enough to shame me. "He hasn't seen you?"

"I got home late."

He shook his head, moving away from me to his desk. He pulled out a drawer and slammed it shut, then another. I waited while he found what he was looking for, hauling out a tiered white box. He pulled out a pair of gloves, gauze, swabs, sterile packages of tweezers, clamps, suture thread. He ripped open an alcohol swab. "Don't move."

"Aren't you going to numb the—"

He tapped a cotton swab against the tight corner of my eyelid to relax. I felt the first prick and realized I was gripping a fistful of his coat. In ten minutes it was done. I forced myself to let go. He snapped off his gloves, discarded the trash.

"Ice gently. Don't touch. Come back in five days, I'll take the stitches out. The bruising will take a couple weeks."

"Where is he now?"

"Down the hall, room seven. And Cale—"

"I know." I missed his hands, clinical but tender. I was in the market for healing, the long-term kind. I wanted to crawl under his desk and hide. "How long, do you think?"

"We just took his blood. You can go back now."

"I mean, how long do you think he has?"

The doctor had moved away to the other end of his desk. He opened a drawer, uncapped a pen. He was scribbling something on a notepad. I was grateful for his distraction, that he wasn't a witness to the coveting all over my face, oozing from every pore.

"Never as long as we would like," he said.

At the end of the long hall, I pressed my ear against the door of room seven. No noise came from the other side, though a phone rang distantly from the doctor's waiting room, a receptionist's murmured tones. I felt for the doorknob and let myself in. Lamb sat on the edge of the exam table wearing only a cotton gown. His legs were a star-tling paper white, leanly muscled still, his knees two angular fists of bone. I had never seen these legs, I could swear it. We had lived years together in intimate proximity, yet here was a brand-new part of him I had forgotten to love. Lamb's head was bent, his palms turned to the sky, as if waiting to receive a benediction. But Lamb didn't pray, at least not that I was aware. When he looked up I watched it all bloom and wither on his face, taking in my cuts and bruises, my violation of his trust. His cheek twitched. I tried to hold myself apart; Maria from the panadería behind her mesh screen.

"What did you do?"

I grabbed one of his warm, supplicant hands in my own. He squeezed it hard enough to crush my bones to dust. *I'm here*, he meant, or *fuck you.*

Since finding Lamb's blood in the sink, I had been afraid—not that his illness was a contagion meant to seep into my life, but that it wouldn't; that this obscure malignance was Lamb's own, meant to alter him in some way I could never know, leaving me distinctly alone. He was still examining me closely, as if beyond the bruises, he was only beginning to notice an erosion of my character, a slipperiness, a willingness to distract from my own failures and turn them back into his own. I had been an honest child, I could only hope it would come full circle again. But how could Lamb be anything but impressed by my ingenuity, my ability to devolve so seamlessly in concert with life's disappointments?

He was still holding my hand; I pulled on it to straighten his arm, revealing a pinprick in the crook where the nurse had taken his blood. He hadn't let her bandage it. A few times when I was a child, they had tried to draw mine. Terrified of the needle, I screamed until Lamb rolled up his own sleeve to offer his veins instead, as if we might be so close as to be interchangeable, as if even a spinning centrifuge couldn't tell the difference between us.

He squeezed my hand again, gentler now. This, the first time we had touched in months. Since childhood there had been the natural widening of physical boundaries between us, the long-dispensed habit of crawling into his lap, the comfort of being rocked to sleep. But I had always kept his gnarled hands for myself. I tucked my knuckles inside his palm, still a sheltering nest.

Maybe the bruises reminded him I was fallible; maybe he was beginning to doubt my ability to survive without him. Maybe I was, too. Either way, one of us was softening, leaning toward the other in apology. And although I always thought it was Lamb who needed to bend, I suspect now that it was me. This entire time, I've been the one who needed to change.

25

When my vision finally cleared, the sand-colored man's zombie was still in the rearview mirror, the sound of the throaty engine revving up. I turned left out of the trailer lot, following a barely perceptible curve in the dirt. It was impossible to make out where the path ended and the rest of the desert began. I drove down what I hoped was the center, my heart hammering in my chest. Penny kept one hand steady on the side of the milk carton, watching her side mirror. A moment later the zombie fell into the lane behind us, engine thrumming. His cage lights were so high they flooded our mirrors but offered little transparency to our measure of road.

"You've never met him before, have you?"

"Cale! Can't you drive any faster?"

I gassed the truck, speeding up, creating a wide cushion of space between our cars. We drove tense in our seats for a mile, maybe two. I imagined the raspy-voiced woman in the trailer addressing her only son. *Maybe you'd better help those girls find the highway after all.* Because the zombie was only tailing us to the on-ramp to make sure we didn't get lost. I repeated it to myself, willing it to be true. Then the truck revved again, the man throttling the engine to close the gap between us in an instant, the 4x4 zooming so close its grille disappeared in the rearview. Penny screamed. I white-knuckled the wheel, bracing for impact.

"What's he doing?" I glanced at the mileage on the truck, then back to the road, trying to remember how long we'd driven from the exit to the trailer in the first place. Five miles? Seven? Was this the way we came? If there was a sign for the highway, I was afraid we would miss it now.

The man tapped his horn, once, twice, making us jump in our seats. Penny grabbed my arm, her fingers pressing into the crescent-shaped wounds she'd left earlier on the mountain, still healing. She must have remembered it or decided I needed both hands on the wheel, because she let go. I pressed my foot on the gas and took us up to sixty. It felt like the gravel was flying by.

"Go faster." Penny twisted again in her seat to peer out the back window.

"I can't see anything! If we go any faster, we could crash into some-one coming." But if we didn't speed up, if the zombie clipped our bum-per, we would fly off-road into the gravel and whatever waited for us there: a ditch, a cluster of rocks, a tree. I stepped on the gas again, thinking of Lamb's wife, her sharp turn on the mountain's curve all those years ago. I didn't need any help conjuring the image of a fatal car crash, our necks snapping in our seats. The zombie dropped back again, bouncing on his suspension. At any second he could close the distance between us. He was toying with us, enjoying the 4x4's mon-strous advantage over our truck, all of it a game to him. The snare drum of his engine echoed behind us as we drove, the modified ex-haust mounting and falling. The brights helped a little, pushing back a few more feet of darkness, revealing more of the same pebbled earth and brush, clusters of rock, the occasional gleam from beer cans and broken glass bottles near the road. Beyond the jerky, roving cushion of our headlights, the night swallowed all.

A small boulder the size of a basketball appeared in the headlights, coming too fast to avoid. It clipped our bumper and rolled underneath the truck, followed by a series of loud thumps and metallic screeches. Penny was saying something I couldn't hear. I prayed the rock wasn't sharp enough to rip out a brake cord. The puppy began a low and steady growl from the floorboard of the truck, a surprisingly full snarl for such a tiny body.

"Shhh," Penny said, her voice tight. She lowered a hand to stroke the animal behind the ears. "It's okay."

In the rearview the zombie loomed up again, sweeping right to left and back again, zigzagging like a crab. If we fell back, he would clip us for sure.

"Where's your phone?"

She rustled for it, tossing lipstick and compact into the console. The light brightened the cab. "Still no service."

"Are you sure?"

She threw it at me. I jerked the wheel, the phone clattering against the console.

"Are you crazy!"

"Go *faster*!"

"Fuck you!"

Another cluster of rocks appeared ahead and I jerked the wheel, sending Penny slamming into the passenger door. The zombie followed our erratic path with distressing ease. But if we were patient, he would tire of his stupid game; he would drop back and change direction, he would turn around, leaving us shaken but alive. The off-roader zagged abruptly from behind, roaring up alongside. The sound was deafening.

"Don't look!" I screamed it, but we both did. He had his window down and was yelling, gesturing wildly. *Pull over.* Fat chance.

"Drive *faster!*"

"I can't drive any faster! We're going to fly out of the fucking windshield!"

The zombie veered left and there was the long, high-pitched whine of metal kissing metal. Penny screamed, the puppy snarls interspersed with short, baby barks. The man was hollering, too, not making any sense. *Fucking bitch. Cunt. Pull over. Pull over.*

My heart was threatening to burst out of my chest. Where were those red and blue police sirens when you needed them or, at the very least, another car? If I slammed the brakes, would we spin out? Crash? Would the truck flip? I could already imagine the windshield shattering into sharp, sparkling sand. Any minute now, and we would fly.

He swerved the zombie close again. I took a deep breath and jerked the wheel sharply to the left, slamming on the brakes. The zombie shot past but the Ford shuddered, the sound of gears screeching against each other in all the wrong ways as we began to spin, the truck picking up momentum, whipping around so fast my hands flew off the wheel. Penny was still screaming; I was screaming, too. The entire truck *tilting, tilting, tilting,* a centimeter more and we would flip, a shower of rocks pinging at the undercarriage. I felt a wave of nausea and swallowed hard. Something thumped—*God, not the dog, please*—time stretched taffy-like and snapped back, the tires slamming on the dirt so hard our bodies bounced, the seat belt cutting into my neck, the puppy yelping. We came to a hard stop amid a smell of burning metal and rubber. A cloud of sand was settling around us, a delicate crystal rain.

In the low light Penny's cheeks looked wet. She stared straight ahead as if in shock. The puppy had stopped growling. It no longer made any sound at all. I would not look down. *If we turn around and start first, he will let us go.* I tried the gear. It was stuck. I wiggled the shift. Penny reached for my hand, her palm hot and clammy on my own. I shook her hand away.

"Cale?"

"Shut up!"

I wiggled the gear until I was able to push it into park, fumbling with the keys, killing the engine. I felt as if I had run a mile, five miles, ten. I waited a beat. Turned the keys again.

"Cale. What are you doing?"

"Shut up!"

I jiggled the shift again, slamming my foot on the brake. The deafening sound from the other engine was gone. It was possible he'd already turned around and left. The third time I turned the keys the engine coughed, turned over, coughed again. Then a hum.

"Yes!" I looked over at Penny, triumphant, expecting her to crow. She was popping the lock on her door, pushing it open to the dark.

"Penny!" Something white hot expanded in my chest, filling my throat. I grabbed at her wildly, yanking strands of black hair, wrenching her head back before she pulled away. "Stop!"

I saw it then. The zombie, stopped several yards away. It was hard to tell against the white lights, but I couldn't make out the shape of a man behind the wheel. I fumbled with my own seat belt and pushed open the door, surprised to be out of the car and flying around the bed of the Ford, head pounding and chest aching, the headlights from both cars casting a sphere of light before we were pushing into dark. I could just make out Penny's legs up ahead, scissoring against the dark, her hair whipping behind her as she ran. Who knew she could move so fast?

"Penny!"

He came out of nowhere, powerful legs and feet pounding into the dirt, bursting out of the night like a linebacker. I felt the heavy animal crash of muscle and bone before we both slammed into the ground, the air knocked out of my chest. The back of my head hit gravel, once, twice—a blinding white light, the reverberations of impact in my skull and teeth. A heavy hand closed around my neck, tightening. *Air.* Liquid copper filled my mouth. From somewhere I heard the puppy whimpering again, only to realize it wasn't the dog at all, but me. I had bitten through the gummy inside of my cheek. The hand around my neck loosened, allowing me to gasp once before tightening again. The man lifted me off the ground by the throat and slammed me back down. The whimpering ceased. I felt my eyes bulge, my vision blurring, wetness spilling down my cheeks. I wanted desperately to cough. I gurgled short, desperate little sounds. *Lamb.* The thought was bigger than fear, filling up my chest like water. *He doesn't even know where you are.* The hand at my neck dropped away. I opened my mouth to scream.

I saw his fist an instant before it exploded into my face.

1

Let me tell you about desert people.

26

I came to under the sandman's heavy weight crushing my chest. *Air.* He moved his right hand back around my throat and spider-walked it to my cheek, pressing my face into the gravel. I gave in to a wild urge to laugh, sucking sand into my mouth, the gravel cutting a million tiny lacerations into the side of my face, already a raw wound. A warm breeze licked across my bare stomach. The sandman spread a warm, rough hand across my waist, unbuttoning the waistband of my jeans. I bucked underneath him, sucking in more sand, and managed to twist my face around, the tiny rocks digging into the back of my skull. His face shimmered above me behind a veil of tears. Above his sand-colored head the sky was black as velvet, a spattering of white specks that shimmered into focus and dissolved with each blink. The sandman pushed down my jeans, his hand tangling in my underwear. He pushed two rough fingers inside me, where no man had ever been. My body flushed hot, my face filling with blood. The lower half of my body clenched as if it alone could stop time, freeze it until something more could be done. My ears were muffled, but I heard screams inside my head, my ragged gasp every time his fingers moved. I squeezed my eyes shut and tried to direct my will like a knife, sawing myself off at the belly. He removed his hand to fumble at his own clothing, the distinctive metallic jangle of his belt being undone. I was waking up to the sound, struggling underneath his weight with renewed vigor. He was breathing heavily, we both were, just animals scrambling in the dirt. He pulled something out of his pants and held it in his palm as if it were precious: an emerald, a peach. Someone was making sad, squeaking sounds. He leaned over, the tips of his sand-colored hair against my cheek sweet with some lingering smoke, his bare, soft stomach pressing into my own. He lowered his mouth to my neck and slid his rough, wet tongue against my throat. He was going to tell me what special thing he had brought me, all the gifts I would receive, again and again. He guided himself between my thighs and I looked to see a flash of something heavy rushing by his right ear, too fast to comprehend—

THWACK—

The sandman made an *umph*, lurching heavily atop me. Penny stood above us in the rim of shadow where our headlights met night, heaving a long, weighty object up behind her head. I tried to use my voice but found it misplaced, my mouth soundless. Penny brought it down again—*THWACK*—landing meatily on his shoulder. His whole body jerked, the mass pressed against my thigh softening, pouring liquid onto me, wetting my jeans.

THWACK—

He howled now, angry. I pushed against his shoulders, his heavy head dipping onto my chest. I struggled to wiggle myself free from underneath, my jeans tangling around my knees. I kicked back against the dirt, leveraging his weight.

THWACK—

Penny raised the tire iron again, *thwack*, his shoulder, *thwack*, his hip. He twisted, jerked, popped. A spasm electrified his leg. I kicked again, finally managing to get out from underneath him, trying to yank up the waistband of my pants. There was no feeling in my hands, they blundered uselessly, all ten fingers made of rubber. The man was on all fours now, grabbing for Penny's ankle. I scrambled across the distance and kicked out, connecting with his side as he reared up under the arc of Penny's swing, her arms bringing down the iron too fast—a crunch that made me want to hurl. He groaned and fell forward, curling onto his side, his belt still undone, his penis flopping free from the front of his jeans. He made a gesture as if gathering the strength to rise, and Penny pulled the iron back, suddenly *so strong*, so sure. It connected with his skull with a loud, wet CRACK. He went very still.

I scrambled to my feet, unsteady, and reached for Penny, surprised to find my hands grasping uselessly at air. She was staring at his immobile form, the tire iron hanging by her side. I was afraid to touch her. Penny, always so familiar, seemed altered—but we were both unrecognizable now, we would be unrecognizable forever. A part of me, afraid that if I disturbed her in this fervor, she might spin around and bring the tire iron down on me. I squeezed my hands together, willing them to return. I tried again and managed to brush the wilted appendage against Penny's bare arm. A heat was coming from her, as if a fire had been lit inside. She transferred the tire iron to her other hand. I tried pulling at her gently, but my hands, *my hands*. The man moaned in the dirt. I watched Penny watch him with an expression I couldn't bear, her arm stiffening. I tried to pull her.

"Look at me."

As soon as the words came out of my mouth, I regretted them. Her eyes were black, deep as oil wells. I swallowed. Penny seemed to understand, looking away. I took a step back toward the truck, then another, surprised that my legs still worked. I reversed slow and steady in the relative darkness until I was able to turn around, making for the truck's feeble headlights. It was exactly where we left it, the engine running, both doors open. My pants were slipping down again. I managed to hook my rubber thumbs in the belt loops and wiggle them up. I walked around to the driver's side of the truck and climbed in. There was no sense of how much time had passed, how much of it still could, what was real. I glanced down at the milk crate but couldn't make anything out. I leaned over so far in my seat that my nose nearly touched the puppy's small, dry snout. He was sitting up, his ears pricked forward, his eyes shining and alert. He no longer made any sound. This dog would never be a good dog in all its life. He already knew too much about people.

When I straightened, I saw Penny walking back toward the truck, the long, heavy object still in her hand. I waited while she climbed in. She laid the tire iron across her knees and I tried not to stare at the glossy slick on one end. She shut the door. The man was still lying on the ground, a dark shape at the edge of the boundary where light melted into dark. A minute passed, maybe an hour. My ears popped. Finally Penny picked up my right hand, laying it on the shift. It was as if my own hands had been surgically removed, and these sewn onto my wrists as replacements. I turned them over and found blood drying in their mounts and valleys, blood in the indentations, their braided lines. Had it really only been a few nights ago that Penny and I had sat on her bed among a pile of library books, the windows darkened outside? We lined up beer cans on the nightstand as we emptied them, flipping back and forth in the pages of the books for reference. She ran the tip of a sharpened pencil across the lines of my palm, articulating all we had learned. *This is your heart line. This is your fate.* My hands were stiff now, but they would obey. I leaned forward to shut my door, reaching for the wheel.

I drove us away from that place, heading back the way we came.

30

I woke up in the dark, gasping for air. *You're home.* I had a scream lodged in my throat and forced myself to swallow it. The telephone was ringing down the hall. I kicked free from the sheets; Wolf, snoring like deadweight across my ankles, snuffled in protest. I wanted to reach the phone before Lamb turned on all the lights and stood blinking in his doorway, looking wounded, but by the time I made it out of my room the ringing had stopped. I remained suspended in the hall, uncertain how to proceed. I reached up to feel the side of my face, the swollen cheek, the row of spiky stitches above my engorged eye. Nothing forgiven in sleep.

I felt for the banister in the dark and descended the stairs by feel alone. In the kitchen, the glowing numerals on the oven read half past three. The window above the sink was still black, the mountain an inky mass behind the fence. These were the quiet hours preceding the diner's morning rush; Penny's last chance to refill napkin dispensers and salt shakers, to place calls to anyone still awake. I knew it was Penny calling, and I was fairly certain she would try again. I turned on the kitchen light. The world outside the windows disappeared. I opened our freezer and took down the coffee, ladling out spoons of grounds, setting the machine to brew. I rooted around for one of

Lamb's ice packs. I wrapped it in a paper towel and held it gently against my face. When the phone rang again, I snatched it off the cradle on the first ring.

"Penny." I recognized the bustling diner sounds in the background, the overnight cook yelling an order. So there would be no quiet hour for either one of us. "I tried calling earlier." I tucked the phone into my shoulder, hesitating. "I wasn't sure how—"

"Cale?" In the quiet of our kitchen, Jake's voice boomed over the line. "We need you to cover down here. I've been here since midnight and if I don't get home soon, Ellen's going to have my ass."

"What? Where's Penny?"

"Never showed. Flat tire or something."

"She doesn't have a car!"

"Whatever it is, we need you."

"She actually said that? A flat tire?"

"She didn't say anything. Didn't show up and she's not answering her phone. We're getting backed up already. Clara can't make it in until lunch. You'll be on your own for a few hours."

I heard a noise behind me in our own kitchen and spun around. Wolf in the doorway, his ears pricked. I hadn't even heard him coming down the stairs.

"Jake, did you call a few minutes ago? Someone just called and hung up. I thought it was her."

"Wasn't me. Take that to table four," Jake's voice became muffled, already distracted by someone else. He came back on the line. "I've got to go. Hurry, would you?"

He hung up but I waited on the line, as if Jake might pick up again, or Penny, someone who might offer an explanation I could under-stand. I cleared the line and dialed her number, the rich, sharp smell of fresh coffee suffusing the kitchen. Why hadn't I bothered to leave her a message earlier, no matter how awkward it felt? I listened to her voicemail and waited for the beep.

"Penny. I'm going to the diner to cover for you. Where are you? Call me there." I held on to the receiver a moment more, trying to muster some arrangement of words to convey my growing unease. Wolf was still watching from the doorway. Since returning from Carr he had kept me close in his sights, vigilant to my new distress, the odd hours. I hung up the phone, staring back at him. I had learned early the rules of beasts; chief among them, to never look a dog in the eyes. But I did it anyway, searching Wolf's gaze for any animal wisdom he might be willing to share.

Wolf woofed softly, shook himself, and trotted down the hall to wait by the stairs. I couldn't tell if he understood or he was merely asking to be escorted back to our comfortable bed, our assured life—his eminent tenure in a formerly happy home.

What I mean to say is, I have tried to find my blame in this many times, and though some days it seems to be everywhere, other days it's difficult to locate the exact pieces, like a plane breaking apart over the ocean, the wreckage strewn and lost.

28

We stopped at a gas station in Nye, halfway back to Pomoc. A small, shuttered convenience stand with two pumps locked up for the night. I followed Penny to the back of the lot where a broken hook latch offered easy access to a dingy bathroom, the smell of sewage permeating the air. The toilet was leaking, leaving us to move through puddles in our boots. Penny tore off a handful of paper towels from a roll propped against the windowsill and ran them under the cold tap, wiping the soggy mass over flecks of dried blood on her bare arms. I watched our warped reflections in the mirror: one of us a blur of useful color, the other a static pillar, our faces and hands perverted in the tin.

Penny stepped in front of me with another handful of wet paper towels dripping on the floor. Up close, her forehead was damp, her breath irregular. She brought the towels to my face, dabbing my cheek. The water trickled down my neck, ice cold. Her eyes were still a sticky chasm.

"Should we call the cops?" My voice raw.

"Do you want to?"

"I don't know." I was surprised some portion of my brain was still sifting details, processing action. How had we gotten here? I rolled my eyes around the bathroom, gathering clues: the harsh light and stained paint, the familiar citrus scent of Penny's shampoo as she bent her head near mine, absorbed in the practical task of cleaning up blood. The entire right side of my face was throbbing, but Penny still looked beautiful; her exquisite face was unmarred. She bore no physical change from the events of the evening, no by-product of terror beyond the characteristic flush of her cheeks. Yet it was her beauty that had been the catalyst for all disaster. It worked on men like a disease.

"Why did you get out of the truck?"

Penny rubbed harder than necessary at a spot of blood on my arm. "You were right about that woman. She'll forget our names." She turned away to run the faucet, bringing a fresh handful of sopping towels to my brow, wincing as she laid it on the wound, working the towel gently against the crusting blood. I hissed, blinking through the pain. Underneath her hands, the right side of my face felt hot and tight. "And the—her son," Penny continued, "he might not remember us."

He might not remember anything ever again. He might not live to forget. I could still hear the wet crack of the tire iron connecting with his skull. I had been bounced around, too; my head felt like a broken sugar bowl, all the jumbled pieces tied together in a cloth napkin. But there were things I knew I would never forget—the heavy weight of his bones on top of mine, the contortion of his mouth. His eyes in the trailer the first time I saw them, that deep, piercing blue.

Penny folded a dry towel into a square and held it lightly to my brow, raising my hand to keep it in place. She threw the stained paper towels in the trash, pulled her mass of long hair high up on her head in a series of quick, deft movements. I leaned over the sink, trying to make out the wound in the mirror, but the image was too distorted; it was impossible to tell where my face ended and the damage began. A tepid exploration with my fingers revealed a sore, swollen protrusion. There was no way Lamb wouldn't notice.

We left the bathroom. Penny disappeared into the back of the lot by the air pressure machines. When she emerged, she was pulling a long green water hose. I took the tire iron from the front seat and held it out without a word, turning it in the spray. When it was done she aimed the nozzle at the truck, paying special attention to the undercarriage, the tires and bumpers. The iron was heavy in my hand; I imagined running with it as fast as Penny had, lifting it with her precision, bringing it down again and again. Penny was taller than me, stronger maybe, though not by much. At the diner we both carried the same number of plates and lifted heavy boxes of stock, stacked chairs and tables after closing. It was something else powering her through those moments, some incubating fury she had never shown.

Penny finished hosing off the truck and rinsed her shoes. Then she pointed the spray at me. I lifted one foot, then another, my boots soaked through. When Penny was satisfied she dragged the hose away, and I stepped over the rivulets of muddy water streaming from the truck's tires down the drive. I climbed in the driver's seat and replaced the tire iron behind the seat. The puppy had curled itself up into a tight ball at the bottom of the carton, his face hidden from view. Even when Penny returned and slammed her door shut, he refused to stir.

I swung the truck back around to the highway. With my eye swollen shut, my vision doubled from one moment to the next, the road shimmering under tenuous moonlight. I switched lanes, Penny checking the shoulder. There was a smear of blood on the steering wheel I hoped Penny wouldn't notice. But of course we would miss things all over. Penny reached over and laid a finger on my wrist.

"What?"

"You're shaking," she said.

I looked down at my hands. It was a small tremor, deepening under our fixed attention. I flexed both hands, tightening my grip on the wheel. Penny seemed to have relaxed a degree, though she kept close attention on the side mirrors, as if the zombie might return at any minute, rushing up behind us to light up the road. The whole way back to the Crossroads I watched the tremor in my hands, waiting for it to still. I didn't need to check Penny's to know that they were fine. Penny, who had shed her human skin and become, for an instant, towering and mythic.

When we finally reached the Crossroads, the park was quiet. I pulled up in front of Penny's unit, my foot keeping the brake. "Are you sure you don't want to stay at the house?"

"I told you, I'm fine." She unbuckled her seat belt and began collecting her things, retrieving the cellphone from where it landed in the console when she threw it. She pulled her purse into her lap, hesitating. "Will you be all right?"

"Will you?" I asked.

"We have to try to get some sleep."

"Okay," I said. Then, "How?"

She turned in her seat and covered her face with her hands. I waited for whatever came next: for Penny to change her mind, to talk me into the next unsavory thing we had to do. Instead she reached for me like a child, the way I had seen little boys and girls raise their arms for their parents, the way I had reached for mine. I hugged her gently, tucking my chin in the hollow of her shoulder, closing my eyes. When she finally let go, she didn't meet my eyes. She opened her door and lifted the milk crate out of the truck. I stayed until she made it up the stairs, balancing the crate between her hip and the ledge to unlock the door. She turned on the lights and looked back over her shoulder, her hands too full to wave. I flashed the brights once, twice, and drove away.

18

The burned-out house smelled like damp wood and mold, the rich, peaty smell of animal droppings. The animals themselves were long gone, abandoning this forlorn shelter for greener pastures. In the middle of the room was a picnic bench, stolen from the high school and mysteriously transported, tagged with Sharpied doodles, hearts carved into the resin, sheltering the initials of quixotic couples KH + PL, JP + RS, YUNG B LUVS GS 4EVER. One of the walls of the house had been broken through and a panel of corrugated roof lay propped against the studs, dragged in by one of the transients who sought temporary shelter; the hitchhikers who materialized when construction began on the freeway junction two years earlier, disappearing when it was done.

I lowered myself gingerly onto the bench. It rocked but held. Penny straddled the opposite side, her seat more secure or her balance superior. She grinned as if reading my mind. We set out our cans of soda, our sandwiches wrapped in paper.

"Next time we can ride bikes here," she said, trading out the second half of her sandwich with half of mine. "It's not so far."

"I don't know how to ride a bike," I said, shrugged at the look she gave me. "Lamb was always working. I tried to teach myself once. It didn't turn out well. Who taught you?"

"Who do you think?" she asked, and though I tried my best to conjure her family—the older brother I knew she had, the mother I remembered dimly—the picture was hazy in its particulars. The answer arrived in spontaneous image. A young Flaca pointing out the training wheels with militant focus, offering curt instructions. I had to laugh. Penny sighed.

"What else didn't Lamb teach you, nerd?"

"I don't know. I'm useless in a sword fight."

Penny dug in her purse and pulled out a marker. I recognized the fat white stem, swiped from the dry-erase board in the diner's back room. She smoothed a corner of her sandwich's butcher paper and drew a series of flat lines, then, leaving some space, sketched a long, narrow pole with a flat base; a hook at the pole's apex sturdy enough to hold the body that would swing if I proved unable to predict the occupations of her mind. This was a game that depended as much on what I knew about Penny as what I didn't, the memories she did or didn't have, the places and movies and flavors she preferred. She tapped the first blank space with the marker's cap, looking expectant.

"You're supposed to give me a category," I said, but I could feel the tide beginning to turn. I had fast-forwarded past this moment to the next, after this body hung and the keen, ruthless pole demanded another. When it would be my turn to string one up, I would draw a hand and hair and fingernails and pants, his shoes like two oblong shapes; a watch, a hat, an overcoat, gloves. I would create numerous, layered opportunities for his subsisting. I would make a man who lives forever.

"It's a place," Penny said, tapping the paper again, the first of three blank lines, followed by six lines, then five. She was watching me the way Trixie did in the mornings when Lamb sent her to my room to bring me down for breakfast, because I refused to appear for breakfast anymore. Trixie sat politely on the floor of my room to wait, tilting her head this way, then that, one gingerbread ear flopping forward. *Why don't you get out of bed*, she meant to say, but how could I explain that I seemed to have lost all desire? I couldn't do anything but stare at her with my arms and legs drawn up on the mattress. If I didn't move for a very long time, Trixie would begin to bark.

"Lourdes' rich tía got married there," Penny said. She was watching me, too, having grown familiar enough with my moods not to ask. Didn't Penny have moods of her own. One late morning, I arrived at the diner to find her sitting at a booth by the window, looking forlorn and adolescent in two French braids, her tips counted into a small, neat pile. I brought her a cup of coffee and a slice of pecan pie. I would let Penny tell me in her own time, the things that ate her up. I was already too full on anguish, the nebulous vapor creeping, creeping in.

"Just try," she said.

36

The day after I visited Flaca at the panadería, I went to work and came home to find Lamb's truck already in the drive. Inside the house felt muted, dogless; there was an abrupt, wretched feeling, as if *all the dogs* might have vanished along with Penny's. I walked through the kitchen calling their names until I noticed the back door propped open to the yard. Wolf was near the grade, sniffing at something unlucky in the brush. Trixie lolled in the dirt on her back, paws kicking at nothing. When I stepped outside Wolf looked up to check if I had brought him a treat. I called them firmly in a tone they couldn't refuse, their contracts stipulating a certain obedience. They trotted over, reluctant, and I took a seat on the ground, draping my arms around Wolf to pull him in for a hug. He resisted, panting a little. Trixie mistook the purpose of my visit altogether, splaying out, settling her head between her paws. It ruined the feeling a little, their disinclination, but they were only dogs, and it must have been exhausting for them to keep reminding me.

From inside the house came a muffled sound, Lamb hollering for the dogs, or for me. They heard it, too, their ears pricking up, but they didn't bother to move. I stood and went back inside, picking my way past the quiet kitchen and the front room with Lamb's empty reading chair, his wire-rimmed glasses folded neatly on the arm. At the bottom of the staircase I looked up, expecting to see him standing on the landing, wearing his new favorite expression of pinched consternation.

"Lamb?" I called out, but when no answer came I took the stairs two at a time, hesitating outside his closed door. I would like to say that after breaking into Penny's house, the density of all borders had become permeable, but the truth is I have never been any good at respecting boundaries. I have wanted things and hearts and people; I have always tried to make them mine.

Lamb was bent over his bureau in a cotton undershirt, clutching a fistful of loose denim at the waistband of his jeans, the sum total between his past and present selves. With his other hand he gripped the lip of the dresser, looking strained, a film of perspiration on his forehead. For the first time I noticed the stale air in the room, its odor of ointment, illness, dust. I went to the window and pushed the curtains aside, cracking it open. I returned to Lamb and flattened my hand against his damp back, his bones distinct ridges underneath my fingertips.

"Come sit down—"

"A shirt and a belt."

"I'll get it. Can you sit down?"

"A goddamn shirt!"

A beat went by, long enough for hope to wither. He remained stooped, adhered to the dresser, glaring at me as if I had grown a second head, as if I had made this all happen with my own carelessness, my slovenly negligence. And didn't I agree? I forced myself to walk to his closet and rifle through the familiar array of neatly pressed shirts on their hangers. My favorite, a green plaid with buttons like moonstone, the cotton worn at the tips of the collar, the edges of sleeve. *I will dress him as if he were my child, and he will flourish.* I undid the buttons and stepped up to him cautiously, holding the shirt open. He made no effort to straighten or raise an arm.

"You're going to have to let go of the dresser for a second. Put your hand on my shoulder."

"We're going to be late."

"Where are we going?"

"Your mother is waiting."

I folded the shirt over my shoulder. "What?"

"Find me a belt that fits."

I felt his back again, recognizing the heat of fever. I pressed my fingers against his forehead, his breath a papery wheeze. The only possible mother—two—Catherine, or Catherine's daughter. I had heard of the original father-daughter custom, the younger Lambert pair piling into the truck at every dusk to fetch Catherine from the telephone company in Noe where she logged customer complaints. I glanced at the clock above the dresser. It was already two hours, and twenty years, too late.

"Lamb. All your belts are too big now."

"Your mother's sick of your excuses." He spat it, his anger so savage that I had to look away, my eyes skimming over the scarred dresser and the full-length mirror angled in the corner, the reflection of a wizened old man and a young girl trapped inside. My skin was still bronzed from the mountain hike with Penny; his, never any shade deeper than pale. My resemblance to Lamb most evident in a scowl and a right-leaning stride, a penchant for simple things. It was in our blood, but it had skipped our faces. If I hadn't taken his name, would anyone even know I was his?

I left him then, and in the hall picked up the phone to call the doctor, scared of the ringing line and what to say in it. *Hello? I'd like to report an emergency. Everything, everything.*

When it was over, I went across the hall to my bedroom, kneeling in front of my dresser, tugging out the bottom drawer. I sifted through the remnants of a lucky life, picking up each object and laying them down on the floor. A miniature felt teddy bear from the Golden Bear Casino. A plastic charm bracelet from the pizza parlor's vending machine. A brontosaurus valentine constructed in fourth grade art class. Every one of Wolf's discarded leashes, the last one six feet long of sturdy braided nylon. I grabbed a pair of scissors and brought the leash across the hall to Lamb, displaying my find like a prize.

"Eleanor?" he said.

We fashioned the leash into a second life, double-knotted at the waist.

37

I rode in the back seat of the ambulance on a thinly padded bench. The EMT was a pale, frog-faced boy just a few years out of school. He crouched over Lamb, sticking electrodes on his exposed chest, calling to a second man who scribbled on a clipboard Lamb's pulse, Lamb's blood pressure, Lamb's rate of respiration, all numerical calculations of Lamb's subsistence. They pushed up his sleeve and one moonstone button popped free from a cuff, skittering across the floor. The boy inserted a needle into Lamb's vein, the second man holding a bladder of clear fluid above Lamb's head, the boy *click, click* on the drip. Beyond his shallow breath Lamb was treading a pool of morphine. The second man asked for a timeline of Lamb's last meals and medications, symptoms scaffolding a path to this misfortune.

"I don't know," I said, meaning *all of it.* For years, I'd washed Lamb's socks, made his coffee, polished his boots, pressed his clothes. I thought about him at every meal, as in *What did Lamb eat for lunch today? What would Lamb like for dinner?* But with his illness I was given no say. Even before the blood in the sink, hadn't I known something was wrong? Oh, I knew, I knew. I hung mantras of casualty in my mind like paper garlands. *Name the thing you fear the most, and it will never come to pass.* The line seemed like something plucked from the pages of a book. How many years with Lamb had I squandered to books, the unserviceable blank space between two lines?

"You okay?" The boy reached across Lamb, shaking my knee. "Hello? We can't have you passing out. Look away if you want."

"Where? There are no windows." We were in a metal box on wheels, a wailing canister of alarm. I didn't need a window to know where we were headed. I shut my eyes against the sirens echoing in my skull, the ambulance's jerky starts and stops over potholed freeway until we began picking our way through Tehacama's local roads in the direction of the hospital. Finally they cut the sirens, the boy pushed open the ambulance doors and hopped out into late afternoon, clattering Lamb's gurney onto the drive.

The hospital had aged poorly since the last time I'd seen it, the paint chipping off the stucco facade. We rattled Lamb's gurney through the front lobby, past cramped waiting rooms doused with the acrid scent of bleach. A coffee cart was parked near the elevator; a stooped old man with grizzled knots of hair shorn close to his scalp dispensed cups of pungent sludge to tired faces. There was a taut, transitional energy humming through the halls, a current of anguish moving from room to room.

On the fourth floor I followed the EMTs down an air-conditioned corridor to a petite nurse standing in wait, tapping a pen against the clipboard at her hip as if she were keeping time; as if we were wasting hers. She kicked the brake on Lamb's bed hard enough to make the gurney rattle.

"Watch it," I said, reaching out to steady the bed. She didn't seem to hear. Across the hall, another gurney was parked outside cardiology, an older man stretched under the white sheet, visible only in profile. His eyes were closed but his lips were moving. An older woman stood nearby; his wife, I assumed. She was dressed smartly in starched slacks and a square jacket, a low, sensible heel. I watched them for several minutes, their voices faint impressions across the distance. Whatever he said next, she threw her head back to laugh at his joke, her whole body relaxing as if she'd taken off her stiff clothes and shaken them out before climbing back into them again. I wished Catherine were here for Lamb, too, though in the end this place would come between the couple across the hall, it would divide us all. One of a pair, always left behind.

The nurse wheeled Lamb's bed through a labyrinth of hospital corridors until we came to an empty room. She raised the metal guardrails on his bed, connecting various tubes and wires to several nearby machines. My old affliction, a pre-Penny condition of invisibility, had returned. I stood in the corner of the room while the nurse switched on a small monitor by the bed. The reassuring, steady beep of Lamb's heartbeat filled the room. She left without asking my name.

There was a single hard chair by the wall. I took a seat on the doctor's stool instead, rolling over to the medical cabinet to paw through the glass jars of cotton balls, tongue depressors, and alcohol swabs, searching the drawers for lollipops. There was no candy to be found, only a weathered home decor magazine I flipped through in boredom. An hour ticked by before the baby-faced doctor finally arrived, the same mousy nurse in tow, bustling as if she'd just come from one emergency and was headed shortly to another. She pulled out a drawer underneath the sink and snapped open a folded gown.

"Fever's high," the doctor said, looking over Lamb's chart. "Likely an infection. We'll run some tests. You have to know he hasn't been taking his medication."

"He did. He was."

"I can tell from the bloodwork, Cale. If the cancer's spread, and I suspect it has, there's only so much we can do."

"What does that mean?"

"I suggested a more aggressive approach months ago."

"Suggested to whom? Lamb?" I gestured toward the bed, Lamb sleeping on, oblivious.

The doctor made a face, sympathy or something like it. I realized I was standing, that I had gotten to my feet when the doctor entered the room. I sat back down on the stool and arranged my hands in my lap like two limp, unfeeling animals. All the things they used to do! The person they had belonged to.

"We'll need to stabilize him before we try anything else, okay? One step at a time. We should get the results back tomorrow. Why don't you head home? He's probably going to sleep through most of this."

"I'll stay."

The nurse pressed a button on the side of Lamb's bed. The top half of his mattress rose steadily, bringing him up to a sitting position. His eyes fluttered open. I waited for him to take in the room, the nurse. For his lips to form the name of his favorite daughter, his second chance, the way he used to say it. *Cale.*

He coughed, a wet sound, followed by gasping, as if he were being strangled all by himself. It happened before I could look away—Lamb expelling yellow rivers down his chin and the front of his gown, hot, sour-smelling vomit pouring out, and it just kept coming. The nurse jumped back, crashing into Lamb's IV, his beeping machines. I reached over to steady the pole, brushing against her cool, fleshy arm. She moved toward the medical cabinet and knocked over a tray of kidney dishes in an attempt to grab one. The doctor seized a box of nitrile gloves from the counter and hollered for the nurses down the hall. I was amazed at the sheer volume of liquid Lamb was spewing forth; I tried to make myself small, afraid that if Lamb saw me, he would be embarrassed. But Lamb wasn't seeing anything; he was glassy-eyed, feverish. Strange faces crowded in the doorway, two more nurses and a stern, bespectacled resident in a white coat. They swarmed the room, wiping at Lamb, pulling the bedding, calling for a second gurney. Still the bile poured from his nose and mouth, and since he had eaten nothing, I could only imagine from where it came. The doctor's face had grown red. "Get her out! There's blood here. Don't lose the catheter."

A nurse jostled me toward the door, pushing me into the hall. I grabbed for the door as another nurse rushed in, shrinking from her petite features drawn tight and angry. "Go to the waiting room," she snapped. "Don't come in here."

How much more did I really need to see? I wanted them to take the broken parts of Lamb and give him back to me whole. I let the door close and stood alone in the empty hall.

48

After I hung up with Fischer I turned off all the lights in the diner and let myself out. The heat was like Vaseline, sticky and close. I was locking the door when I heard a sound behind me. I could just make out the thin shape of a woman smoking a cigarette in the corner of the porch, her figure illuminated by Christmas lights. If I hadn't seen Flaca in exactly the same spot so many evenings in a row, waiting for Penny, I wouldn't have recognized her now.

"Are you trying to give me a heart attack?"

She brought the cigarette to her lips and took a drag.

"Flaca!"

"Come with me," she said, "if you're looking for her."

"You don't know where she is."

"I know where she isn't." Flaca dropped her cigarette on the porch and crushed it out. I watch her bend down to pick up the butt. Instead she yanked the Christmas lights, plunging us into darkness. When my vision cleared she was standing closer than before, her features obscured in shadow. I felt her hand groping for my arm, squeezing tight. This close I could smell alcohol on her breath, but her grip was sharp. She had drunk just enough to lubricate herself for whatever she meant to say or do.

"You were supposed to help me," I said. "What did the sheriff say? *Christina Cruz. Hasn't seen your friend and has no idea where she might be.*"

"I already told you. No cops. You want to be Sherlock Nerd, come with me."

"Not a chance."

"Why not? You'd go anywhere with her."

"I actually like her!"

Flaca dropped my arm. For a moment I was certain she would leave. Then she said, "She told me all about it, Cale."

I felt my heart beat faster. "All about what?"

"She told me about Carr." She sighed, suddenly weary. "What did you think?"

"I *asked* you if you heard from her that night. You lied to me."

"Maybe I wanted to see if you would tell me yourself."

"Why would I!" I paused. "What did she say?"

She smiled. "You show me yours, and I'll show you mine."

"Flaca. The longer she's gone—"

"What? The more dead she gets? She either is or she isn't."

I brushed past her down the stairs, but I heard her following behind. Of course Penny told Flaca what happened. They had always been close; Flaca would always know Penny in a way I never could. Still, I had felt certain that Penny had been changing, growing into someone else. Yet if Penny was really gone, then all the girls we had been, or could have been, were gone, too.

"Come on!" Flaca called after me. "What else are you going to do?"

I had reached my truck in the back of the lot. Flaca had parked her beat-up gold hatchback next to it. What had Penny called this car? A deathtrap.

"What else am *I* going to do?" Flaca said behind me. When I turned around, she had stopped a couple feet away. "Do you know, since Penny's been gone, the thing I've felt most is bored? There's not one fucking person in this town even a little bit interesting."

"That's not true. What about Luz, and—"

"Lifeless! Penny was a disaster but at least she was always *fun*. At least until she started hanging out with you."

I couldn't make out her features clearly in the dark, why she kept using Penny's name in the past tense, Penny as a *was*. She had been gone only a week—or was it two?—but it felt longer, a lifetime.

"A few weeks ago she asked me to do her this favor," Flaca said. "You know Penny doesn't do that? She *suggests* things. She bosses people, which I taught her. But she *asked me a favor*. I put it off. Now she's gone, and I feel like shit that I never did it. I don't want to go by myself."

"Where?" I wished I could see her better, but even in the dark, I could feel her frustration. Penny, not the only one uncomfortable asking for help. Flaca didn't answer.

"Are you going to be a jerk the whole time?"

"No." Flaca said. "Maybe." After a minute, "I'll think about it. Just get in the car, Cale."

I did think about it, but eventually I walked the long way around the hood to wait for Flaca to climb in, sliding across to pop the lock. I bent into the deathtrap's low seat, trying to avoid crunching the soda cans underfoot. In the reflection of the headlights, Flaca's skin looked wan, as if she hadn't slept in days. She looked older than Penny. For all I knew, she was.

She patted around the console for a lighter and pulled a joint out of a hard pack of cigarettes and lit up, the skunky scent filling the car.

"What about Lourdes?" I asked her.

She rolled down her window and blew a supple coil of smoke, passing the joint to me.

"Got a kid now," she said. "Very annoying."

I sucked in too fast, as if the joint were a portal I might jump through to travel back in time, to find the precise moment when, as children ourselves, one of us might have offered the other a crayon or a push on the swings, some gesture that might have landed us here as something more like friends.

Flaca pulled out of the lot and headed down Main Street. For the first time, Pomoc felt unrecognizable, the road a long black strip with no sign of life in either direction. How different was Pomoc from Carr, really? I had no idea where we were headed, but if we never returned, there'd be no one left to notice I was missing. They would find out days later, when the dogs began to howl.

I handed Flaca back her joint. "Tell me," I said.

Flaca took another hit and held it for a moment before exhaling smoke through her nose. "I called her late Thursday afternoon and left a message. She must have still been with you. I wanted her to do a drop at the Tex. By the time she called back it must have been three, four in the morning. She knew I'd be awake; I never sleep. She sounded . . . bad. Said you guys went to Carr and some guy lit upon you when you were leaving."

I picked out the joint from between her fingers and took another hit to steady my nerves. "Is that it?"

"She said he grabbed you." Flaca looked over from the road. "Is that true?"

"Did Penny go to the Texaco?"

"No, that's what I'm saying. She wouldn't. She sounded upset."

"Could you tell if someone was with her?"

"No. Who would she have been with?" Flaca glanced over again, her attention diverted from the road. She was speeding now, heading toward the *palo*. Was this how Penny felt when I was careening through the desert, she stuck in the passenger seat next to me? Not entirely sure that the driver wouldn't kill her. We passed the thrift store, the drugstore, the windows dark, shuttered against the night.

"Flaca, the road."

"I got it." She wanted to ask me a second time, I knew. *She said he grabbed you. Is that true?* What would I have said? Yes. It is true. It can never be undone.

"I thought she just didn't want to do the drop," Flaca said. "But it sounded like maybe she didn't want to drop anymore, ever."

"Would that be such a big deal?"

"Are you kidding?" Flaca slit her eyes over to me. "She was making good money."

"Maybe the money didn't matter to her anymore."

Flaca snorted. "The money always matters," she said. "And she was saving for something. Penny—nunca es suficiente. She always wanted something."

"That's not true," I said. Penny never spoke of things, clothes, possessions. Despite the attention she always paid to her appearance, she shopped for her clothes at the thrift—like everyone else—she just put them together better than anyone could. And she had managed to save all that money rolled up in the coffee can. But maybe what Flaca meant was that Penny wanted something more, something intangible. Hadn't she suggested the same?

We were in the heart of the *palo* now, passing strips of familiar businesses and buildings turned vacant, a discount store, a dry cleaner gone bust. As we passed the panadería Flaca didn't even look up. Her mood seemed to be improving from the diner, the pot taking effect. I felt nothing. A few miles down the road she turned left, away from the Crossroads. We drove so long I thought about reclining the seat, but the minute I felt my eyes beginning to close, she veered off onto a dirt road and I clenched my hands around the seat, the tires bumping over rocky earth. I checked the side mirrors, expecting to find the zombie sneaking up behind. How easily the 4x4 would run us down! But there was no monstrous sound, no suped-up colossus lurking in the shadows, though in an instant I was transported there again; the sandman's indecipherable hollering, the flash of his pale hand gesturing in the window as he drove by. I tried steadying myself. Flaca was watching me again.

"Were you mad Penny didn't want to do the drop?" I asked.

"Not mad enough to kill her, if that's what you're getting at." Her eyebrows knotted in the backlight.

"Of course not," I said. But I wouldn't be as naïve as Flaca thought I was. I forced myself to consider it.

Flaca cut speed and we turned into an undeveloped plot, a single-wide mobile home parked next to a large truck. A sweep of Flaca's headlights across the cab illuminated the hunter-green logo of a pine tree on the door. *Your father runs the nursery in Noe.*

"He's always hated me," Flaca said, turning off the engine, the small car shuddering from the effort. "So you're going to have to ask the questions."

"Wait. What questions? Flaca?"

She was already getting out of the car. I followed her, hanging back as she climbed the steps and rapped on the flimsy front door. Before I had a chance to press her, the door cracked open and a chubby girl poked her head outside, her long black hair split into two braids. She could not have been older than ten or twelve, her features still soft, prepubescent. The heavy eyes were familiar, but where Penny had always been fit, mean in her lines and the economy of her movement, this girl moved slowly. She let out little puffs of breath from an open mouth. Penny's little sister? Adorable but inept. Her name something I had never been told.

"Guapa," Flaca said, "¿dónde está tu padre?"

"Aquí." The girl hesitated, her enormous eyes trained on me. I tried to say something, anything, but the longer I stared at her, the more unsettling her resemblance to Penny became. She grabbed Flaca with both hands, pulling her inside. Penny's father might have hated her, but the girl liked Flaca just fine.

"¿Quién es esta?" the girl asked, loud enough for me to hear. I let the door shut behind us. The room was an icebox, a large window unit blasting cold air with a clattering hum, bare walls made close quarters by several large stacks of boxes behind the long couch, another in a corner partially covered by an old sheet, the exposed cardboard sagging with age and the weight of its contents. An older man sat on the couch looking as if he had been waiting for someone to arrive, his age an indistinct figure between forty and sixty, impossible to pinpoint on the fleshy, broad planes of his face. Though his features had none of Penny's classic symmetry, I knew he must be her father. I scanned the room for whatever might have been holding his attention before we came in, but there was no TV, no book discarded on the couch. I had the feeling he could have been sitting in the exact same spot for five minutes or five years. The girl broke away from us and crawled up on the couch by her father, settling herself against his bulk.

"She asked you a question," the man said. His voice was resonant and firm. I had no trouble imagining it booming across a room. He turned to the girl, laying her bare cheek against his arm, and nudged her with his shoulder. "Again."

"¿Quién es esta?"

"A friend of Penny's," Flaca said, and I could tell whatever uplifting effect the pot had on her was suffering in this man's presence. Her voice shrank into something small. I felt a wild, desperate desire for Lamb's tall and steady presence, the checkered shirts I grabbed on to as a child whenever I felt shy or scared. The ease of being able to hide behind someone bigger who had always kept me safe.

"Cale," Flaca said, "meet Alvaro."

39

I rode the hospital elevator downstairs to the wide, dingy emergency room, the air-conditioning pumping in sweet, cold air. There were no mothers now, only more broken men. A beefy man in a soiled T-shirt held a blood-soaked handkerchief to the top of his head. A wan teenager expectorated into a handkerchief. In the far corner of the waiting room a weary, sunburned father allowed a young boy to lean drowsily against his arm. I watched the father and son until it got too cold, and then I walked outside into another torpid night, no hint of a breeze. A group of smokers was huddled in plain view of a no-smoking placard nailed to the stucco. I stood a few feet away and bent my face to the sky. Pinned underneath the sandman, the stars had seemed like shimmering flares winking code, astrological talismans capable of granting mercy. I wanted to visit them again, to ask what they had seen. I heard someone approaching and turned to find a vaguely familiar face: a tan boy no older than twenty, a black bandanna tying back riotous dark curls. He had broken away from the group of smokers and held out a single cigarette in offering. I took it, leaning in to share his light.

"I remembered you smoked," he said, and the longer I studied him the clearer his features became. A couple years older in school, friendly with the goths but too sociable to commit. It was on the tip of my tongue to ask why he was here, but I stopped short, lest he feel compelled to return the favor. He tilted his head up to the sky, where I had been looking.

"Do you know any constellations?" he asked.

"Not really. Do you?"

"All of them. But sometimes it's better if you just look." He dropped his gaze earthward and smiled. We smoked in companionable silence, his friends sending occasional furtive glances our way.

"How did you learn?"

"You know Mr. Rowlands?"

"The science teacher?"

His smile widened. "He's my uncle."

He finished his cigarette and threw the butt on the ground. A petite girl from his circle was glaring at me across the distance, twirling her parrot green hair. His girlfriend, I assumed, seeking reassurance, a signal that I knew what wasn't mine to take. But any desire I had to bend, to comfort, evaporated more each day.

"We're heading out," he said. "Are you staying?"

"I don't want to. I mean, I came in an ambulance. Are you heading back to town?"

"Yeah. You need a ride? Where do you live, exactly?"

I smiled, hoping it was enough of an answer. I felt the way Penny must have that first night she slept over. *I don't want to be dropped off anywhere.* He signaled to his girlfriend and she broke away from the pack, scowling as she came near.

"This is Leslie," he said, introducing her to me. Then, to my surprise, "This is Cale, from Vista. We're giving her a ride home."

I followed them through the parking lot to a charcoal two-door, the bumper covered in band decals. I climbed into the back seat. The girl leaned over and turned on the stereo to a trippy synth beat on loop. I could see them clearly now, they were ravers, not goths at all. But what were any of us, really? Once we were on the highway, the girl rolled down her window. The rush of air melted into the music, creating a soundtrack of white noise discouraging deep thought. The boy in the bandanna drove too fast. I found his eyes in the rearview.

"Drop me at the Texaco," I said.

42

We slept in Lamb's room, where the dogs most wanted to be. We piled on top of one another on the mattress in a heap of flesh and fur. Every now and again one of the dogs sighed and stirred, readjusting itself against an arm or a leg. Each snuffle, an inquiry: *Lamb? Lamb? Lamb?* A question I didn't know how to answer. I smoothed Trixie's soft ears and cupped her leathery paw in one hand. All of us, looking for comfort.

I woke to some sound—the foundation settling, a creak of the floorboards. I sat up in bed and listened for it, everything coming back at once; Lamb in the hospital, Penny gone. I forced myself to get up and walk to the bathroom, to peel off the shirt I had slept in. I stood under the shower's hot spray until the marbled window began to grow light. I toweled off and cracked the door, the house already growing warm. When the steam began to lift, a narrow, clean girl transpired by degrees, taking shape in the mirror. I leaned in to examine the pattern of discoloration marking the side of her face. At some point without my noticing, the bruising had begun to patch apart like the stippled, varied flesh of an Anjou pear. I rummaged through the medicine cabinet for a pair of cuticle scissors and pointed tweezers, snipping the sutures in my brow, tugging the stitches free. In my palm, the short, slimy threads looked like excised parasites, the rejoined flesh a tender pink ridge.

Finally, something beginning to heal.

47

The person I wanted to see most was Clara, lone, enigmatic Clara. When I arrived for my shift at the diner she was taking an order by the window, and the way the afternoon light hit her platinum hair and thin arms and legs, they filled up with light. I wanted to tell Penny, *We have mistaken her all this time.* She was a witch, or an angel. She headed to the counter carrying a stack of dirty plates and cups, and when she saw me standing with my apron dangling by the hand, she slowed, the expression on her face reminding me of one of the nurses in Lamb's hospital room. I had become something people were frightened to look upon.

After a few hours of slinging plates and taking orders, I remembered how it was done. I answered diner patrons who brightened when I served them their coffee and pie, as if I had been on a long journey and only just returned. No one mentioned Penny at all. Even the regulars who sat at the counter and spent each day asking Penny for ketchup or a refill, who knew her voice and hands and smile, who said her name three times every visit—even they didn't ask where she was. Maybe they were afraid to say her name out loud, to test the boundary of unknown space and tip the fates in either direction.

Other things were not altogether the same. Clara continued to search me for cracks in the molding, the fragile places where I might snap. Through the server window Rico moved quickly between the counter and stove. When he caught my eye he looked away, knowing words were needed and not knowing which ones to use. I was markedly slower than before, like someone redistributing weight around a phantom limb. Clara left at dusk and following her exit the narrow diner appeared to double in size, there were suddenly twice as many tables and chairs, the civilized patrons swallowing coffee and toast transformed into repellent maws masticating paste. The sight of them brought to mind Lamb vomiting his yellow bile. If anyone noticed when I sat a glass of Coke down with a shaky hand or took a few extra minutes to sort change from the register, they didn't say.

Until Penny returned or Jake hired a new waitress, the diner would close overnight. After we locked up, Rico scraped his knives against the stove, wiping down the griddles. I scrubbed the counters and swept the floors, transferring tubs of ice cream from the cold case to the backroom freezer. After I carried the last one inside, I shut the heavy door and turned over an empty mop bucket, taking a seat to collect myself, rubbing my bare arms to get the goosebumps to disappear. Rico materialized in the doorway, untying his apron. "Conejita, tengo que irme. Ven conmigo."

"You go. I'll stay and finish up."

He hesitated. I felt a small twinge of panic at the prospect of being left alone, but I forced a smile. Rico, a father, too.

"I'm okay. I promise."

Rico shook his head and gave me a long look as he gathered his things from his locker. How could I tell him I was afraid I'd never be comfortable in the dark again? Making him stay would only delay the inevitable. I heard him moving around the front of the diner, stacking chairs on tables before his keys rattled in the front door. After a few moments I forced myself to stand and turn over the mop bucket, rolling it over to the ground sink. I poured bleach into the bin and ran the hose. Even after I turned off the faucet, I could hear the water trickling from the pipe behind the hollow wall. A stream of cool air escaped the crack between two loose tiles, blowing gently against my cheek. I kept my eyes fixed resolutely on the mop bucket; I didn't want to see what else might lurk in the crawlspace—a man? A skeleton? I scanned the back room, the giant walk-in freezer and rows of shelving, boxes of stock stacked high enough to hide behind. From where I stood I couldn't quite see around the corner, the heavy emergency door Rico disabled so he could sneak out for a cigarette between customers. He was meant to lock the door after closing, but we never checked. Even Rico could have forgotten, tonight, a million other nights. I remembered the lie I fed to Fischer, how it might not have been a lie at all—a man Penny was afraid of, a man who frequented the diner and lingered outside, waiting for her to finish her shift. I could feel the formless vapor seeping in, settling in the dark corners of the room.

I pushed the mop bucket in a corner and wiped my hands on my apron, surprised to find them unsteady. There would never be a good time to come back here, not unless Penny came back, too. The phone rang as I was pulling off my apron. I grabbed the receiver and stood on my tiptoes in an effort to see around the corner of the room.

"Jake's."

"Cale, it's Fischer." Though his voice grew more familiar as he spoke, something kept me from feeling relief. "I just tried you at home. I want you to come down to the station when you can. We might have found something."

"What is it?" I twisted the phone cord tight around my finger, watching the tip of my finger turn pink, then red.

"It's hard to explain. Come by the station tomorrow. There's something I want you to take a look at."

The tip of my finger, purple now. I waited to feel it.

"Are you there?" he asked.

"Yes, I heard you."

"Isn't it a little early for you to be back at work?"

"What do you mean?"

"When I picked you up from the hospital you were . . . I thought you would take some time. I'm sure they'd understand."

"Picked me up when?" That inky vapor collecting in the corners of the room seemed to coalesce, lurching closer across the floor. Because here was a fragment of memory entirely lost, never to be recovered.

"Weren't you wondering how you got home?"

"No, I thought . . ." I unwrapped my finger from the cord. There it was, a sharp pain, running through to my wrist. Pinpricks.

"The doctor gave me something to relax," I said to him. "There was a resident there. I thought . . ." What had I thought? Stupid, stupid.

"I was looking for you—I remembered when you called before, you said you were at the hospital. The doctor explained. It's okay not to remember."

"No, it isn't." There were moments Lamb was in the hospital that I couldn't forget, no matter how much I longed to. But I also meant, *It's not okay that I don't remember you.* The idea that we shared an encounter I couldn't recall. Fischer wasn't anyone to be afraid of; he wasn't the sandman or a stranger, he wasn't like the men who lingered on the stools at the diner counter watching Penny move. But I recalled again his finger moving on my knuckle, the involuntary thrill; my hesitation, too. The weight of Fischer's hand on the back of my neck, his thumb moving down my spine. It was almost funny to recall my embarrassment, that white hot shame. It was almost entirely gone. It was as if the doctor had cut me open while I was sleeping and carved out all the useless feelings. I would have to search carefully to find out if anything remained.

"Are you all right?" Fischer asked.

"It's only—I'm surprised the dogs let you in."

"They nearly didn't."

"How did you convince them?"

"Cale. I had something they wanted. I had you."

43

It was still early when I returned to the hospital. I bypassed the emergency room where I'd seen the smokers the night before, and took the elevator down to the cafeteria for a cup of coffee, bringing it with me to the fourth floor. I walked the long, lonely waxed corridors of the oncology department and sat awhile in the cool, quiet waiting room. I stood in front of a large window overlooking the back lot, watching the sun wink off the hoods of parked cars. Behind it were a number of small laboratories, but only a little farther out everything disappeared, the morning light filigreed over a desert landscape that stretched for miles in every direction. I hoped Penny was out there somewhere, just waking up. Or, more likely, just turning in to bed.

I finished the coffee and left the paper cup on an end table piled with dog-eared magazines. There was a recent desire to litter detritus like a trail of bread crumbs back to my person, a physical history of coffee cups, crumpled receipts, chewed-up gum, and strands of hair as proof of life. I went back out to the hall and entered the oncology department through the back door. There was only one nurse frowning pointedly at me from her desk in wrinkled teal scrubs, but she didn't get up, continuing to talk on the phone tucked into her shoulder.

I found Lamb in his room propped up against the pillows, still asleep. I took a seat on the edge of the bed. There seemed even more space for me on the narrow mattress than the night before, as if Lamb had shrunk in the hours I was gone. He began to stir, sensing another body in the room. His machines were beeping steadily, two bags of fluid hanging from the IV pole, the tubes disappearing underneath his blanket. I dug around in the sheets, hunting for his leathery hand. His fingers, so often gnarled and dry, were swollen fat and tight with fluid. I unfurled them and laid his hand over my face, breathing the faintest trace of tobacco still lingering in the braided nooks and valleys. He struggled to get his bearings, to parse the morning and this strange, colorless room. His eyes had lost none of their depth, though in recent years they had begun to lighten from a deep, dark brown to the color of amber held up to the sun. Now they searched mine, seeking clarity, Lamb flipping through a mental catalog of all the faces he had ever known, comparing them against mine to see which one fit.

Beyond the door the phones were beginning to ring, the halls filling with the traffic of footfalls and loud snippets of conversation. Someone knocked on the door, and a nurse entered carrying a breakfast tray. She set it across Lamb's outstretched legs.

"Where's the coffee?" he asked, his voice granular, the feel of sandpaper rubbed against a thumb. He was coalescing before my eyes, reemerging into personhood. The nurse excused herself to fetch the doctor, leaving me to deliver the news.

"You're not allowed," I said.

"Then what's the point?" A lock of hair fell across his forehead. I resisted the urge to push it back, to soothe him as if he were a child. *The point is to survive. The point is me.* Instead I lifted the plastic cover from his meal to reveal a lump of scrambled eggs, a child's juice box, toast, and green Jell-O. Lamb looked it over, considering. I unwrapped his utensils and handed him the fork. He poked at the scrambled eggs. Once. Twice.

"Did you bring the book I wanted?"

"Of course. How were your tests?"

He set down his fork without bothering to bring any food to his mouth. I watched him take a sip of his juice. It took a minute for him to work the liquid around, to swallow. He set it back down on the tray.

"Not bad," he said.

"What is? The juice, or the tests? At least *try* the eggs."

"Not these. I like my eggs. Your eggs."

"I'll make some for you tonight. Every night."

"Cale—" He hesitated, a pause so pregnant, so cavernous, that it threatened to swallow us whole. Could I fit everything inside that I needed to say? The sandman, Penny—Lamb's heart and how I yearned to be the only thing in it. We were interrupted by another knock at the door. The nurse returned, the baby-faced doctor trailing behind. He, at least, looked healthy, though I was comparing him with the other faces in the room, we who had already relinquished vigor. The nurse carried another bladder of clear fluid.

"I'm glad you're here," the doctor said, and we watched the nurse begin to replace Lamb's IV. "We found an infection in the right lung. We'll run antibiotics every few hours. He can rest a bit in between. It should clear up in a few days."

Lamb settled himself back on the pillows, none of it seeming a surprise. At some point the night before, he had already heard the news. As before, I was the last to know. He closed his eyes, finished with his breakfast, the nurse, this conversation, me.

"Does he have to stay here? If you show me what to do, I could bring him home."

"It's just for a few days, Cale. I'm afraid I was right before, the cancer has spread. We'll wait until the infection clears, but moving forward, radiation is still the best option."

"What about surgery? Can't you cut the bad part out?" *Unless all the parts are bad parts.* But they didn't know about Lamb's startling adaptability, how he had learned to live without Catherine and his daughter, how he might be willing to live entirely without lungs. He could learn to breathe through his skin, the first man to ever do it. Lamb looked as if he were already falling asleep again.

"Can we get a more comfortable chair?" he said with his eyes still closed. "For Cale."

"I don't want a more comfortable chair," I said. I didn't want the nurses to get used to us, to expect that we would stay. The doctor redirected his clinical squint, reaching for my face. He turned my chin up in the light, grazing a light thumb over my remade brow, the fresh pink scar. I turned my face into his palm, but the nurse cleared her throat, redirecting the doctor's attention toward Lamb's chart. His hand fell away, and they began to consult with each other in hushed tones. I wanted to interrupt, to ask a million questions of my own, but I really only ever had one, and I didn't think the doctor's answer had changed.

I left them to walk down the hall to the bathroom and splash water on my face, just one more step in my new hospital routine. By the time I returned to the room, they were gone. Someone had, in fact, brought in a bigger chair. I sank into it and closed my eyes. I would synchronize my sleep with Lamb's, the way a new mother might doze and wake with her child. Only I couldn't get comfortable, no matter how I tried. Finally I gave up and dug in the overnight bag I had packed with Lamb's clothes and medications, the book he requested I bring. Milton's epic poem, with its clash of angels and demons, had always seemed too grand when Lamb used to read it out loud, the ornate language irreconcilable with our own modest lives. But hours later, when Lamb began to stir, I reclaimed my seat on the edge of his bed and, amid a tilting sense of déjà vu, began to read it to him. This time, the violence and chaos seemed infinitely more real.

Lamb listened faithfully, adjusting himself against his pillows, finding purchase with some invisible point on the ceiling. The sun moved higher in the sky, flooding the windows with bright light. The nurse brought in another covered tray and left it on the bedside table, where it remained for hours untouched. Wasn't this how prisoners marked time, counting every meal? I read until my voice had been rubbed rough and hollow, bearing up against those intricate, striated sentences built like ships out of sound. The nurse brought a pillow and a blanket and set them on the big chair, lingering, waiting for a break on the page.

"How about an intermission?" she suggested.

"I'm fine." My throat felt sore.

"Not for you." She pointed at Lamb, his eyes closed again. "He's been struggling to keep up."

In fact, Lamb's breath was beginning to rattle, to lengthen. He was a deep sea diver pushing into the dark leagues, and I was just a girl waiting on the shore. The poem was the only thing between us, a single thread tied to us at either end. The nurse clicked Lamb's morphine drip and smoothed the sheet across his chest. She was one of the good ones, I could tell, generous and kind. It wasn't enough to keep me from wanting her to disappear. She took a seat on the opposite side of the bed and pulled a package from the pocket of her gown. I watched her stretch out his arm, tying him off with a thick rubber tourniquet.

"Oh, please don't do that. You'll wake him up—"

She ripped open the package, unwinding a small butterfly needle to pierce him as she met my eyes. Lamb dripped out, ruby red, into one vial, then the next. The nurse's hands made quick magic of twisting stoppers and smoothing labels while they filled. She pulled out the needle with a delicate flourish, taping a bandage into the bend of his arm. When she left, the vials clinked together in the pocket of her gown. I imagined I heard them all the way down the hall.

49

Alvaro didn't move to get up, nor did he appear very surprised to see us. Either Flaca had already told him we were coming, or there was very little in the world that might startle him. The A/C unit continued its steady, audible drone and there was a tamped energy in the room, like a basement that had been shut up damp for months and was now hungry for light and air. Standing close to me, Flaca touched my wrist, the gesture too small for Alvaro to notice. "Relájate," she murmured. To Alvaro she said, "¿Tío, te acuerdas? Trabaja con Penelope."

Alvaro was studying me as one would an animal having wandered, lost, onto his land, his eyes as black as the curved backs of clown beetles that overran our yard. He draped an arm around the girl and she scooted closer, nestling against his bulk, her legs bare from shorts to ankle. She wore a pair of lavender bobby socks trimmed in faux lace, the kind sold at the swap meet in pale turquoise and banana yellow and cotton candy pink. We had all worn these socks, we loved them. I regretted the pot; it lent the evening a surreal quality. I was developing a paranoid suspicion that the rest of Penny's family might soon emerge from the carpeted hall one by one in funeral procession, a mother, the older brother she had mentioned once in passing.

Alvaro asked Flaca a question in Spanish I didn't catch, and Flaca

answered too quickly for me to follow. They had the shorthand of familial connection between them, the ability to transpose meaning in a
look, a gesture. Was this the moment Flaca meant for me to interrupt,
to ask a question about Penny and where she might have gone? I already knew she wasn't here. If I slipped out of the room and stole Flaca's
car, if I drove it back through the darkened streets to the familiar
warmth of our old house, was there a chance I might find Lamb reading Milton in his favorite chair? Bespectacled? Resurrected? Whole?

"Come on," Flaca said. She moved toward the carpeted hall, gesturing for me to follow.

I looked to Alvaro, but he had already turned his attention to the
daughter by his side, a girl who, if not as shrewd as her sister, seemed
infinitely more amenable. The hall was cluttered with sliding stacks
of magazines and rows of empty bottles: clear glass, sea green, beer
brown, indigo. At the end of the hall Flaca pushed open the door. In
the dark I could see a giant glowing rectangle, a fifty-gallon animal
tank illuminating a rocky habitat dotted with leaves and scrub. Flaca
hit the lights and the rest of the room jumped into focus, the perime-
ters of the room shifting as if we were standing in the center of an
erratic labyrinth. Like the hall, the room was crowded with magazines and bottles, a sprawling collection of plastic storage containers
in varying sizes atop one another in Tetris-like formation. A folded
playpen by the wall was gathering dust, a stationary bike shouldered
lidless shoeboxes overflowing with rubber-banded audiotapes. A bookcase in the corner was jammed full of videocassettes. We were standing at one end of a narrow pathway that cut through the chaos to
a queen-size bed, the edge of the mattress pressed flush against the
tank. A second path, less clearly defined, ran from the bed to the
room's only window, covered by a heavy blackout curtain. The south

wall was lined with more irregularly balanced storage containers, numbers scrawled along their sides in different colored markers; 4, 8, 16, 29, 45. Every free surface of the room was filled with more containers loaded into asymmetric piles.

"Flaca," I said, to make sure we were seeing the same thing. She pulled open the crumpled flaps of a nearby box, the cardboard sagging. She pulled out a dusty VHS tape—*Flashdance*—and handed it to me. She passed me an amputated G.I. Joe and several ribboned hair bows before lifting the box to set it on the ground, ripping open the one below. After a few minutes of digging she abandoned it for another, adding a pair of faux-cow print pants I remembered seeing Penny wear in middle school.

"I actually like those," I said, surprised to see them again.

"Right?"

"Are all these hers?" I asked.

"No way," Flaca said, holding up a football. "I don't remember half this crap." She punted the football to a corner of the room, where it landed behind another stack of containers.

"Flaca! Jesus."

"Look." Flaca drew out a soft, spiral bound notebook, flipping through to show off its contents. The pages were covered in disparate magazine clippings all pasted together. I set the items I was holding onto the carpet and took the notebook for a closer look. On one page, a shampoo model's perfect head was fused with the corner to the Hollywood sign, an image of a surfer partially overlaid. The cut edges of a red Cadillac convertible were curling up, the distinctively cheap paper I recognized from the Carson car dealership's circular. How easily those colors had bled when Lamb set his coffee cup on its pages.

"Her collages," Flaca said. "Remember?"

I was almost touched by the idea that Flaca had momentarily forgot—
we had not been friends then, I was still a year behind Penny in school.
But I felt something clicking together in my mind; Penny at the thrift,
her arms loaded down with magazines. And I remembered Mrs. Mason
in third grade, the art project explained to us in great detail. Penny
would have learned the technique first, and must have taken away
something essential. I touched the pages: a collage of boy band members, a pastiche of wildflowers. Hadn't I noticed piles of magazines on
her bookshelves gathering dust? Didn't I see a fashion glossy folded
into her tote at work? Yet I had never asked. I handed the notebook
back to Flaca, weary of this experiment, this evening, how often I was
meant to review the same lesson over and over again: I didn't know
Penny at all. Flaca was digging deep with her free hand, nearly tipping
over into the box's depths. She pulled back a moment later, trium-
phantly brandishing a Slinky.

I picked my way to the vivarium across the room, bending to examine the graded rock and saltbush habitat. What appeared so visceral
from the doorway was, up close, only a paper backdrop clinging to
the glass, the tactual contrast a trick of distance and light. A layer of
wood chips and sphagnum moss covered the bottom of the tank, the
cork hide and water bowl like miniature kiddie toys next to the large,
thick-bodied snake, his cedar and buff-colored scales camouflaged to
his surroundings. At the sight of it, I stiffened, a prickling sensation at
the base of my neck. I hadn't forgotten the half-moons Penny clawed
in my arm on our hike up the mountain, the gopher snake slithering
away from us in the brush. Though this snake lay coiled, his head and
tail hidden from view, there was no mistaking the distinctive dia-
monds patterning his spine. It was the kind, as children, we had all
been taught to avoid.

"Flaca. Please tell me this isn't what I think it is." On the opposite end of the tank a small white mouse was curled tightly in a ball, petrified or newly dead. I turned around to find the room empty, the box Flaca had been digging through abandoned, its flaps sticking up. Alvaro stood in the doorway, watching me. I had no sense of how long he might have been there or when Flaca had left. I waited for him to come forward, picking his way down the center of the room. He smiled, reaching over to rub my bare arms with his warm, calloused hands. At some point I had broken into gooseflesh without noticing.

"It's good that you came," he said.

44

Someone was shaking me awake in a room of halogen white to the sound of a shrill, mechanical wail. I had fallen asleep stretched in the margin of Lamb's gurney, my head tucked against his shoulder. Lamb would wake to find me having stolen, once again, across his boundaries. All my life, trying to crawl into his skin.

"We have to move you." It was the nurse who had taken Lamb's blood the night before. She stood at the edge of the bed next to the young resident in a white coat, his face stern as he bent over the screaming machine. He shut it down, then turned to the others one by one, their screens blinking off. I sat up on the bed to look at Lamb, my eyes still gritty. The nurse caught my face in her hand.

"Honey," she said.

With the final echoes of the machines fading, I realized some part of me had imagined their wailing originated inside myself. I pushed the nurse's hands away. Lamb still hadn't opened his eyes, immune to the commotion. I grabbed his hand. My stomach lurched. "Is he sleeping?"

"What did you say her name was?" the resident asked, impatient. "Cale? Cale, we need you to get down from there."

"Page the doctor," the nurse said.

"He's on his way." The resident took the nurse's place next to the bed, leaning over, his breath stale with coffee.

"No." I screwed my eyes shut, my heart hammering. "Please don't."

"I'm taking you. I'm taking her," he announced, scooping me up, hefting me close to his chest. "Where do we want her?"

I was made of lightness and terror, a child again. His coat felt stiff against my cheek, his arm hard underneath my knees. He crossed the room easily, unbothered by my weight. Strong and able-bodied, he carried me out of the room, down the long white hall, hitching me close to maneuver a doorknob. In the hush of an empty room, he laid me down on an exam table, the paper crinkling underneath. I watched him rearrange his features into the clinical approximation of concern. This boy had gone to medical school. There was nothing he couldn't fix. He was going to be a man someday. He thought he already was.

I rolled onto my side, the exam paper sticking to my face. Rocking back and forth on the paper, this green, dense boy trying to hedge me in with his hands.

"The doctor's coming. I'll tell him where you are." He hesitated, flattening his palm against my hot back. I was making a horrible, familiar sound, the one I heard so often on the mountain in the middle of the night; the neighbors' little dogs stolen from their yards, their forlorn cries as they were ripped apart by the coys.

"I know," he said.

45

The baby-faced doctor clicked on his penlight and pulled up my eyelid with his finger, shining the beam through the back of my skull. Another day I might have asked him what he saw there—if looking inside a person was like peeking inside a handmade pot, bumpy and cool with shadows, but nothing you could hold. The doctor's fingers probed the base of my ear.

"Cale?" He wanted me to speak, to make an effort signaling wellness. It felt as if a shroud had been lowered between this life and my feelings about it. I wanted to cry but if I started again, I wouldn't stop. It was an old affliction, an infirmity of my person. When I was little, I woke up crying every night with an intensity that frightened Lamb so much, he threatened to drop me at the hospital if I didn't quit. I wasn't afraid of any monster, or myself. It was sorrow cracking me open, a fissure I couldn't explain, a yearning for something or someone I didn't know. Can you tell me what a mother is? Nothing you can measure.

Though I cried every night, no woman ever came. When the tears lasted long enough, Lamb turned on the lights in the hall, trundling to my room in a drowse. His weight, when lowered onto the bed, tilted the mattress so far that I spilled onto him. He gathered me up in his

Barbasol night smell and squeezed me too hard, forgetting I was a girl. If the heaving cries persisted and nothing else would work, he asked, *Do you want me to tell you a story?* I did.

Lamb didn't know any traditional fables. He had forgotten the nursery rhymes meant for children: boys living in the moon, duplicitous wolves, princesses in tall castles lending their hair. To calm an inconsolable child, what he came up with in the middle of the night was *Once there were three monkeys.*

Once there were three monkeys, and one monkey said, I want to build a spaceship.

Once there were three monkeys, and one monkey said, I'm going to make some macaroni.

Once there were three monkeys, and one monkey said, I want to ride a carousel.

"I'm going to give you something to help you sleep," the doctor said.

50

Alvaro moved a fleshy palm in the air in front of me, as if to stroke the neck of an invisible cat. "Relájese. ¿Usted siempre se pone nerviosa?"

"That's a rattlesnake. And that mouse—"

"Mi amigo."

"The mouse?"

He laughed, thawing into life. "Solo a los ratones le gustan los ratones, entiendes?"

"Where did Flaca go?"

"Son como perros. They can sense your fear."

"I'm not afraid." *Penny was afraid.* Alvaro nodded along, his interest piqued. I hesitated, wondering if I'd made the wrong move. "Does it have a name?"

"You name dogs in this country, mascotas. Pero no nombras a los animales salvajes."

I looked back at the tank. The snake did not appear to be sensing my fear or anything else. He remained coiled, his head tucked from view.

"Is it sick?"

"A little moody. Not as social as his friends. Do you want to see something special?"

I looked around the room for anything that might explain the damp feeling still lingering in the room. The boxes and tapes and magazines must have taken a lifetime to acquire, but Penny hadn't grown up in this overcrowded trailer. Penny grew up in a house with her siblings in the *palo*, close enough to Flaca and Lourdes and Luz that they all walked home together after school. *So where am I?* And where was Flaca? If she had driven away and left me behind, I would kill her. But I would have heard the deathtrap's engine turning over. I hoped I would have heard it. I hesitated.

"I think Flaca—"

"Shhh." He held a finger to pursed lips, his resemblance to Penny suddenly made clear; the abundant mouth strangely out of place on a face otherwise so flatly masculine. He pulled a shoebox-size container from the nearby stack, a loopy number 8 scrawled on the opaque plastic in red marker. He pried off the lid, bulleted with holes. The nagging feeling returned, a formless vapor curling through the vents. He motioned me closer. I took a step forward and looked inside. On a bed of newspaper, two thin, flame-colored serpents stirred, disentangling as if incriminated by their embrace. Corn snakes, siblings, too, their saddle markings nearly identical.

"Not these," Alvaro set the container on the bed, offsetting the lid. "Just wait. There are a few you have to see."

He pulled another container and set it on the bed. I took a step back, scanning the room, trying to count all the containers lining the room from the ground up, the reason they were all stacked Mad Hatter askew. *Air holes.* My breath was coming out ragged; Lamb in the hospital room trying to clear his lungs. I had never been afraid of snakes, not the occasional gopher on the mountain or the ball pythons trapped behind glass at the pet store in Noe. But the rattlesnake in the tank was wild, and any one of the storage containers might contain another feral surprise. I counted more than thirty storage containers on the floor, straining to make out the numbers scrawled alongside: 78 on one, 52 on another. Some seemed to be missing numbers altogether, or had been stacked backward, their codes facing the wall. I counted another twenty containers lining the path to the door. How many were piled behind others out of view? Was the large plastic hamper I spied in a high corner set apart for a reason, or was it crowning another tower of containers, invisible from where I stood? Even if the majority of containers held single snakes and only some held doubles, there were easily more than a hundred snakes in the room.

Alvaro pried open another container and pulled out a thick white serpent, an indistinct pattern of cardamom-colored scales along its spine, fading into tail. He held her up for me to admire. I was reassessing the boxes and videocassettes, the playpen, all manner of chaos in the room and Alvaro blocking the path to the door. He let the white snake down on the bed where she lay still, cautious of her newfound freedom. He began moving other containers out of the way, amassing them into piles according to size, clearing his way to a large tub anchoring the stack. Before I could invent a reason to stop him, he was pulling off its lid, hauling from the plastic bin a heavy gray snake, one hand behind the snake's arrow-shaped head, another hooked under the body; five, six, seven feet of stone-colored scales and still coming. The animal didn't look thrilled about being handled, kinking his neck into a tight S, widening his mouth to hiss.

"This is a constrictor," Alvaro said. "Do you know what that means?"

"It doesn't bite?"

"They bite," Alvaro said, "and then they squeeze."

He draped the dense gray body around his shoulders. I'd never seen anything like it. How many more of these creatures were from our desert? How many had been bought and traded for, bred or captured on other lands? On the bed, one of the corn snakes poked his head over the lip of his container and seemed intent on slithering free.

"Alvaro," I said, intending to warn him. But Alvaro was still preoccupied with the constrictor. He came closer, offering me the animal's long body to touch, watching my expression closely. It was a test, or seemed like one. I ran my fingers obediently down the boa's dry scales. Alvaro was electrified, wholly transformed from the reticent man I had met a half hour earlier. I stroked the animal again, meeting Alvaro's eyes.

"I need to ask you about Penny."

"You have to be careful with snakes this big. They can kill a dog, a baby, just playing."

"Do snakes play?"

"Todos jugamos," he said.

"The police must have called you about Penny. I've spoken to them. They've called Flaca. They're just trying to understand where Penny might be. No one's seen her for over a week."

Alvaro lifted the animal, draping the snake's thick torso around my neck. It weighed heavily on my narrow shoulders, but I was grateful Alvaro hadn't bothered to lift my hair free, that I still had some boundary, however thin, against the powerful body pressing like one smooth, protracted muscle against my neck. Out of the corner of my eye I saw the snake curling back its tail, seeking balance. I was careful not to turn my head. The energy in the room was tightening; the boa forked the air with a black tongue. I felt a sharp kernel of ancient alarm. How long did snakes live? I realized I didn't know. On the mattress, one of the corn snakes had slithered free and was moving steadily across the bed. Alvaro wasn't paying any mind, shifting and restacking other containers, absorbed by all the mysteries coiled inside their plastic dens, awaiting their brief reprieve. I hesitated, determined to try again.

"If you could think of anything—"

"Tú no conoces a mi hija," Alvaro said, continuing his work. "Or you wouldn't worry. Piénsalo. These snakes, you can catch them in the wild. Put them in a box for a week, a month, a year," he looked up at me to make sure I was following. I pressed my lips together to keep from nodding. "We could go now," he said. "Drive twenty miles and drop them in the brush. What do you think would happen? All of a sudden they'd forget? No. They survive better than us."

I coughed, the snake around my neck freezing at the movement, forking his cautious tongue. "Penny isn't a snake."

But Alvaro had already turned away, squatting to open another container, then another, setting them down across the path, further obstructing the only exit from the room.

"When was the last time you saw her?"

He shrugged.

"Alvaro. Please, can you think of anywhere she might go?"

"Where could she go?" He seemed suddenly surprised by the idea, looking up from his hands and knees on the floor. He stopped to consider. "Not far."

Why had Flaca brought me here? Alvaro wouldn't help us, even if he could. But I forced myself to consider what he said. In my mind's eye I saw Penny raising the tire iron over her head and bringing it down again and again. As if on cue, there was a sharp, sudden *thwack* behind me, the boa stilling against my neck. I turned carefully and saw the corn snake, having slithered to the edge of the mattress, had struck the glass and was now hovering in front of the rattlesnake's tank, fixated on the mouse that had uncurled itself in the corner inside. The mouse was now scratching furiously against the glass. The mouse must have only been stunned before, or scared, trying to make himself as small as possible. Now he had come to understand the gravity of his situation, his whiskers twitching. Inside the tank, the rattlesnake was beginning to uncurl himself in languorous fashion.

"Alvaro—" We both heard the low, distinctive rattle at the same time. At the sight of the rattlesnake's narrow neck rising, my heart dropped. I looked away, to the chubby girl who reappeared in the doorway holding a half-eaten chocolate ice cream cone. She stepped carefully down the path of open storage containers in our direction, wearing most of the sticky dessert as a dark stain on her lips and chin. Something about the girl's manner, her interruption, made me long for a wet towel to wipe her mouth. I had a sense that if I ever got my hands on her, I would scrub forever, until her face was rubbed raw.

"Come here," I said to her. I longed to unload the beast from around my neck, but I had no idea how to speak to a fledgling girl. I tried to turn my voice into candy. She shot me a scathing look much too full of knowledge for someone still wearing lavender socks. Her attention was riveted on the tank behind me, the rattling crescendo; another sudden *thwack*.

The corn snake struck the glass again and unsteadily withdrew. Inside the tank, the mouse was still trying to scratch himself to freedom. Alvaro let out a cry but seemed frozen in place; too surprised to move, or too wedded to the intrinsic autonomy of wild things. Inside the tank, the rattlesnake had taken notice of his competition, kinking his neck into a tight S, loosing a spray of venom against the glass. His rattling was insistent, mid-tempo maracas picking up speed. Even the girl was transfixed, her ice cream melting into her tight, fat fist. *Thwack.* The corn snake's third strike left a bright smear of blood on the glass before the animal slipped, stunned, off the bed into a soft pile on the carpet. The rattlesnake, still hovering inside his tank, refocused his attention on the mouse scampering around in a burst of desperation. The strike was lightning fast—before I could think to close my eyes, it was over. The mouse lay twitching in the corner of the tank, a slow circle of urine coloring the glass. The little girl bent to the tank and tapped the glass, blowing her cheeks full of air. The boa around my neck raised his face near mine, tasting air.

I tried to imagine Penny in the little girl's place, Penny fascinated by the stalking death, Penny scooting closer to Alvaro on their couch. I could not. The girl finished her ice cream and stepped around the lifeless snake on the carpet, angling for a better view. The main event, the rattler's slow ingestion of the corpse, was yet to unfold. If the rattler had changed his mind and managed to thrust himself through the tank to latch on to her face, I wouldn't have blamed him.

Alvaro was still frozen, visibly distressed but unable to move—to believe that his snakes, like his daughters, might surprise him. I couldn't bring myself to look at the vivarium again, the soft sounds behind the glass, the corn snake's limp scales on the floor. I took a deep breath and reached up to grip the boa's heavy body, lifting him from my shoulders, ignoring the sharp hiss. I dropped him on the mattress and snatched back my hands, making a break for the doorway across the room, dodging Alvaro as he tried to stay me, squeezing past the open containers—*don't look down*—trying not to run. I hurried down the trailer's cold hall, calling for Flaca, and pushed open the trailer's front door, welcoming the heat on my skin, gulping in air.

The deathtrap was exactly where we left it, Flaca slouched behind the wheel, finishing her own ice cream cone, her attention focused on something in her lap. I came around the passenger side, half expecting to find the door locked and Flaca beginning to pull away, leaving me to chase her, pounding desperately on the glass. But when I yanked the door, it swung open in my hand. I nearly leapt inside. Flaca closed the spiral notebook of Penny's collages, dropping it in the clutter of her back seat. I sat on my hands to keep from wrapping them around her neck. She popped the last bite of her cone into her mouth and chewed. I willed for her to choke on it.

"Well?" she finally asked.

"You've been sitting out here the whole time?"

"Not the *whole* time," she said.

I hung on to my seat as she fired up the deathtrap and pulled a sharp U-turn in the dirt. *Hurry,* I wanted to say. But no one was chasing us. Alvaro, for all his deep and unsettling strangeness, had not actually been unkind. A knot of anxiety had taken up permanent residence in my chest, it would be there forever, loosening and tightening by degrees. When we were back on the dirt road heading away from Alvaro's property, I began to breathe normally again.

"Why did you take me there?"

"What did he say?"

"Nothing! Did you really think he would?"

"Maybe. He's not exactly predictable."

I punched her in the arm. Her mouth dropped open. We drove in silence, Flaca rubbing her shoulder. I was perched at the edge of my seat and forced myself to lean back. I wrapped my hands around my own shoulders to make sure the boa was no longer there.

"Did you know Lamb just died?"

Flaca glanced over. I wasn't entirely sure she knew who Lamb was, but she looked surprised. "When?" she asked.

"A few days ago."

We were silent for a moment, Flaca looking increasingly uncomfortable. "I didn't know." she said finally. Then, "Are you expecting me to say something? Life's a beautiful journey?" Flaca glanced at me again. "Because it's not."

"I know," I said. Then, "Look, when we got back from Carr I dropped Penny off. I didn't hear from her the next day. But the next morning someone called the house. Early—four, five a.m. I didn't get to the phone in time. It could have been her."

"What do you think she was going to say?"

"I have no idea. What if she was in trouble?"

We were back on the main road. I wanted my corner of the bed and the warm, heavy dogs pressed up against me. Flaca was driving too fast, leadfooting the gas.

"He said Penny wouldn't go far."

Flaca shook her head. "I'd go over to her place," she said. "Where they used to live. After her mother left, her brother ran off. Alvaro worked all the time, my parents, too. When he was home we sometimes forgot he was sleeping, we could get loud and wake him up. He didn't like that. He didn't like kids, I thought, but now look at Guapa, it wasn't kids—it was us he didn't like. He loved those fucking snakes, though. I get it, working all the time, your wife gone, a kid like Penny—she wasn't any help. We were just kids, we got loud, had fights, stupid stuff. When he wanted to punish us, he'd make us clean out the snake bins. Then he'd put the snakes in the bathtub one by one, you know, fill the tub up with a little water. Put us in there, too, to help soak them. Penny was always so scared, no matter what kind they were. I used to think, well, maybe he thought she'd get over it. But now I think you could tell she never would. When we were bad he'd make us get in with them and leave us there for hours."

I remembered Penny on the mountain, the expression on her face. My throat was closing up.

"Penny was punished a lot, Cale."

"Yes."

"I wasn't always with her. Do you understand?"

"I think so."

"He called a few weeks ago asking for money. Business was never great, except one year when we were freshmen. All those new businesses in Tehacama started using him, but when construction was over on the junction, all the people everyone thought would come just didn't. You know. They closed and the nursery started to tank again. He let the house go. She was furious! She thought one day she'd do well enough to make him sorry. I knew she was saving her money for something. What if she gave it to him? What if he took it?"

"Why would she?"

"I don't know. Guapa? She felt guilty. I feel guilty, now. No matter how we fought, whenever she had more money, she took care of me. When I was up, I got her. That's the way it goes, right? But it's been so busy. She kept asking me to go with her to get her things. Ugh. I hate him, he hates us—why bother? There's nothing there she could want. But she needed to see him, I think, to confront him. Maybe she got tired of waiting for me and went by herself."

"What are you saying?"

"He said she didn't go far. How would he know? You want to know where she is, I'm trying to tell you."

"Flaca—"

"Wherever he buried her," she said.

46

The dogs covered me with their warm, solemn bodies, packing themselves in as if I were an organ to be harvested, a heart in transit to some new, more capable vessel. Trixie's snout poked the hollow of my throat, her breath dampening my skin. Wolf curled up with his spine pressed against my low back, emitting a low, intermittent whine. Somewhere a phone was ringing again. I climbed off the bed slowly, a prolonged effort. All the muscles in my back felt stiff from sleeping in torqued positions in the big hospital chair, until the moment I had given up and crawled onto the edge of Lamb's gurney, his slim parenthesis. Only now I couldn't remember how long ago that had been. Three days ago? Yesterday? In the hall I fumbled for the receiver, pressing it to my ear.

"Cale? How're you doing, kid?" In the long, awkward pause that followed, I could tell Jake had heard the news. "What time is it?" My voice like I had gargled a whole glass of rubbing alcohol.

"Half past noon," he said. "Wednesday."

"Anything about Penny?"

"Nothing yet."

But when did Penny disappear? When did Lamb die? I remembered climbing out of bed to use the bathroom, gulping palmfuls of water at the faucet, walking downstairs at regular intervals to let the dogs in and out of the yard. Gone were the transitions from day to night, the reckoning of hours. I could hear Jake hesitating on the line. He seemed sympathetic, but I was sure this wasn't the only reason for his call. When did I begin to doubt all kindness offered? But Jake was never a friend, only an employer, and I was the second waitress to leave him in a month.

"You need me at the diner," I said.

"I called to see how you were feeling." He paused. "But if you want to get your mind off things, it's not the worst idea."

I was still wearing the shirt I had worn to the hospital. The faintly sour odor trailing me from the bed to the phone, I realized, was my own.

"You think you can come in tonight?" he asked.

"Maybe tomorrow," I said.

"How about the night shift? Rico will be here."

"Okay. Jake, who told you?"

"Sheriff came by," he said.

After I hung up I went downstairs, turning on the lights in the kitchen. Surprising, still, to find no tepid inch of coffee at the bottom of the pot, none of Lamb's toast crumbs scattered on the counter. Everything was exactly where I'd left it. I set the coffee to brew and walked onto the porch in the sun, the wood warming the soles of my feet. Jake said it was just past noon, but it was already too bright; the light sparkled against the pie tins Jackson hung on the new peach tree he'd planted near our fence in some paroxysm of faith, knowing full well that stone fruit wouldn't last a year in our soil. I searched the mountain for the large, flat boulder Penny and I had climbed on a few weeks earlier, a smooth island of stone amid the stretches of half-burnt brush, like battle scars on some great, injured beast. When summer was gone, townie volunteers would choose a single temperate afternoon to trudge up the mountain and cut back the scrub, clearing the mountain of charred leaves and stems.

The door rattled behind me, the dogs poking their noses in the screen, snuffling mightily. I held it open and they rushed out, pressing themselves against my legs like cats. These fifteen minutes, the longest we had been away from each other in days. I picked up the empty pack of cigarettes left discarded on Lamb's chair, though I hadn't bothered to light up since returning from the hospital. I had lived for days without cigarettes, food, friends. It was expected I would persist.

I was starting to remember snippets of conversation from the hospital, flashes of memory, the baby-faced doctor, the reason the time between then and now had been wiped clean: two white pills like candy submarines in a paper cup, an orange vial containing more of the same. Like Rena, I had taken all the pills too quickly, I had enjoyed their ability to free me of feeling. I tried probing my memory further—a warning given, the doctor's expression of concern. But there was no way to recall how I had arrived home, if the doctor had driven me, a beleaguered nurse.

The dogs wandered to the edge of the porch and looked back, unable to decide whether I might be left alone. How much did they know? Could they understand that Lamb was never coming back? There was a rustle in the weeds on the grade and Wolf took off like a shot across the yard. A small, reckless gopher scrambled across the dirt, disappearing into a snarl of brush too thorny for even Wolf to hazard. He crouched down and barked furiously, regretting his size.

Trixie remained poised on the edge of the porch, her ears drawn. She glanced over her shoulder, her eyes communicating all the gentle curiosity of an intelligent animal.

"Go," I said.

She leapt off the porch, hurrying to catch up.

51

I asked Flaca to drop me off at the Crossroads, night blanketing the warren of boxy mobile homes, their windows as we drove by black, black, black. The lawn in front of the park was vacant, the young girls I had seen tossing their plastic ball back and forth, gone, too. Did they live here? Were they sisters? I hoped they were sleeping soundly, tucked into their worn twin beds. They already shared an intimacy greater than Penny and her morbid little clone—or else why had I never heard of her? Flaca insisted Penny and her little sister weren't close—strangers, even—so why would Penny want to invest in the girl's care? The world of siblings was a mystery I couldn't fathom. Still, it was a relief to glimpse the inner workings of another family nearly as convoluted as mine.

Flaca pulled in front of Penny's unit, her headlights sweeping up the small exterior staircase, ribbons of yellow caution tape crossed over the landing.

"What the fuck?" Flaca asked.

"I guess the police came," I said, but I made no move to get out of the car. The tape was only a signifier, it didn't tell us anything we didn't already know. Penny was missing, and the police were supposed to be looking for her. Only it hadn't seemed like they were looking very hard. Maybe the caution tape meant Fischer was keeping his promise to do everything he could to find Penny. I had no intention of keeping mine.

"You really want to go in there again?"

"No," I said, but I still hoped I might find a new clue, something I had missed before. I was sure that if I tried to sleep, I would feel the boa's cool, dry skin under my fingertips and see the flash of a black tongue. I forced myself to get out of the car but held the door. Flaca was still leaning over the steering wheel, squinting at Penny's unit. She looked as if she were mulling over a question bigger than the yellow caution tape, bigger than I might know how to answer. Her high had long since faded, leaving behind someone I had only ever seen glimpses of, stripped of her loudmouth talk, the bullying swagger.

"You can come with me if you want," I said.

"What's the point?"

I hesitated. "I don't know."

She shook her head, shifting the car into reverse, her foot was keeping the brake. "But if you find something," she said, "call."

I shut the door and watched her pull away, the taillights flashing red as she turned at the end of the lane. Alone again, I waited for a neighbor's sleep-worn voice to yell out a window about the noise, but the only sound was the caution tape flickering in the breeze. The quarter moon offered just enough light to show me up the stairs. I ducked underneath the tape and looked under the pot of bee balm for Penny's extra key. It was missing too, but when I tried the door, it was open. I scooped up the pot of flowers and hit the lights. Letting the door rest against the latch, I moved past the TV and the futon, the mirrored table, my eyes adjusting to the room. A week had given the unit the stale, untouched quality of a mausoleum.

In the kitchen a fine black powder covered the countertops, the microwave, even the fridge where Lourdes' baby shower announcement still hung. I reached for the faucet and realized my hands were already covered with the same inky grain. The tap gurgled and spit before dribbling a tiny stream of water into the plant's soil. I set the pot on the counter, rubbing my damp fingers together. The black powder smeared between them, making the irregular whorls of each fingertip distinct. I had touched all of Penny's counters and door-knobs, I had been a part of her life. So if the police had lifted her prints from the kitchen, they also had mine, preserved in some lab in county.

Inside Penny's fridge someone had thrown out the Styrofoam container from the diner, but her bottle of ketchup and the carton of eggs remained. I opened the crisper, several cans of Budweiser rolling against each other. The freezer was the same, trays of ice, the coffee can cold to the touch. I took it down, prying off the lid, certain that if the police had found Penny's spare key, they had found her cash, too— but all the tightly rolled bills were there. I took the can with me down the hall to Penny's bathroom, setting it on the counter while I rifled through her medicine cabinet: toothpaste and floss, a half-empty box of Trojans, and a row of six pennies arranged on the bottom shelf, heads up. Useless objects that now carried the gravity of relics. I pulled back the shower curtain and took her shampoo off the shelf, flipping the cap to take a whiff of the bright scent she left behind on T-shirts and pillowcases.

They had been in Penny's bedroom, too. They had stripped her mattress of its sheets, revealing a rust-colored stain in its center—a spilled drink, a period bled through. One of my library books was still on the nightstand, overdue. The top drawer of the nightstand was ajar, Penny's fingertips trapped in print dust; I pulled it open and rifled past a silky lavender sleep mask and a pot of lip gloss, an array of loose bobby pins. I surveyed her bookcase and picked up a fashion magazine, flipping through its lacelike pages, gaping holes left where Penny had gone to work with her scissors. But though I searched the room high and low, I could find no subsequent pile of haphazard images, no notebooks of collage. Some of Penny's blouses and dresses were draped over the chair at her desk, others hung neatly in her closet, patiently awaiting her return. I grabbed one of the purses lined up on a shelf—tan, faux snakeskin—and transferred the cash from the coffee can inside, rolling the empty can under Penny's bed.

I paused in front of the white ceramic jewelry box on her bureau. I had teased her about the naïve, girlish quality of the trinket; heart-shaped, a slim ballerina pirouetting on the lid. *From my quinceañera*, she had explained, laughing, and then produced a large box from the depths of her closet, all the extra party favors she had saved without knowing why. Had I ever stopped to consider this Penny, who kept fifteen heart-shaped jewelry boxes in reserve, commemorating a single tender moment in her youth? She had said nothing of the party, or of Luz and Lourdes and Flaca, who had all assuredly been there, celebrating the milestone with cake and presents, watching Alvaro waltz her across the dance floor. Penny showed me a pair of snowy pearl studs tucked inside the box's velvet folds, a gift from her father that I never once saw her wear. It was the only time he was ever mentioned, and I hadn't known to study her face when she said it. There was nothing in this room to point to where she might have gone, or had been taken. *There's nothing there she could want.* Flaca was right. This was a life she could live without. And even though I had once been Penny's friend and stood in these rooms beside her, I was just another intruder now.

From the front of the unit came a heavy metallic squeak.

"Flaca?" I had both hoped and dreaded that she would appear. But the weighty footsteps pounding down the hall to Penny's room could not have been hers, and soon a broad-shouldered man in a uniform was filling the doorway, his gun drawn. He pointed it between my eyes. I concentrated on the hole at the end of the barrel, like a trap-door I might leap through.

"Hands up. Nice and slow."

I was still clutching Penny's jewelry box. I set it on the dresser and spread my hands, readying myself to jump.

79

52

Dale handcuffed me to a metal folding chair between two desks. The only other cop in the station was an aged, paunchy veteran who watched us with a smirk. I wanted to hate them both, but Dale, at least, had been decent, deciding not to shoot me between the eyes. Alone in Penny's dark bedroom, he had turned me around and cuffed my wrists with as much respect as I deserved. Now he took the purse I'd stolen from Penny's closet and turned it over on his desk, shaking out the rolls of cash atop the foraged contents of my pockets: Lamb's worn, repurposed leather wallet stuffed with tips, a canary yellow lighter, several pieces of lint, and a tube of red lipstick I'd swiped from Penny's bathroom, the sharp wax peak worn down from the pressure of her lips. The older cop picked up one of the rolls of cash and unwound the rubber band, counting the twenties with a low whistle. He had ideas, I could tell. He was of Lamb's generation but hadn't turned out quite as well. It was possible that one of these men had been the driver of the dark sedan parked behind the Texaco, the one Fischer had signaled to while dragging me out of the pancake house to his car. The older cop moved on to Penny's empty purse, turning it over before refocusing his attention on me, scrutinizing my face and hair, my old jeans and

T-shirt. I felt my face grow warm and shifted in the chair, the cuffs rattling.

"Your wife's bag match her outfit, Dale?"

Dale had uncapped the lipstick, was rolling it up as if to check the color. He looked up, embarrassed.

"This purse belong to you?" the older cop asked me.

"Yes," I said, and I knew then that whatever resistance I had to lying was gone now; it would take a long and concerted effort to repair. I cleared my throat. "Is Fischer here?"

"Who?" The older cop raised his eyebrows at Dale. *Look at her,* he seemed to say. *She asks for Fischer.* Dale unfolded Lamb's wallet, pulling out the cash. He counted the money in front of the older cop for confirmation, passing back the look he was given.

"I'm a waitress. Those are my tips. Penny and I worked together at the diner. I just went by her place to see if she came back home. I'm sorry I went inside, okay? You could just let me go."

"Nah," the older cop said.

I regretted letting Jake talk me into coming back to work and allowing Flaca to drag me to Alvaro's. I was turning barbed in my discontent, resentful. But after ignoring Penny's disappearance for weeks, now these cops wanted to know who touched Penny's countertops, who borrowed her things, who missed her? They still didn't have any idea where she might be.

"You know who you remind me of?" I asked. *"They pay you a hundred and sixty-two dollars and thirty-nine cents a week just to look at bodies—why can't you look at this one?"*

"Excuse me?" The paunchy veteran turned to look at me.

"Stop," Dale suggested.

"You never saw it? Come on. I bet you love old cop movies. You always wanted to cruise around, eating donuts."

He stared at me awhile, seeming to consider just how pissed he wanted to be. He shook his head. "You're Clinton's girl, all right."

Lamb's name was like a punch to the gut. I counted backward from ten to keep my eyes dry. But of course he knew Lamb, most townies did. Dale produced a pack of cigarettes from his desk and offered one to the older man. They lit up, the smell of smoke enough to make my mouth water. My shoulder was beginning to throb, the awkward angle of my wrist cuffed to the chair. I began the long, slow process of disappearing before their eyes.

When Dale finished his cigarette he began to type on his computer with two index fingers, henpecking at the keys. The older cop resumed his seat at a nearby desk and made a call, leaning back in his chair, propping his boots on the desk. "Charlie? Yeah, Sam here. We got him this morning, four ounces of bud. You called it. Want us to send him your way?"

There were no windows in the back room of the station, but the clock on the wall read a quarter past four. I began to nod off, waking each time my chin brushed against my chest. I wanted to lean my head against something; someone. Another hour dragged by before the back door opened at the end of the hall, a current of chilly air snaking in. Fischer stalked past, pausing briefly at the end of Dale's desk to look me over, his dark hair still wet from a shower, curling around the collar of his shirt, his mouth a firm line. A few seconds later, the door to his office slammed shut. I watched another twenty minutes tick by on the clock and wet my lips.

"I need to go to the bathroom."

"Shhh." Dale didn't look up from his computer. I waited and

drowsed, startling awake to Dale shaking my shoulder. I straightened as best as I could in the folding chair. Dale bent low over my cuffs, whispering in my ear. *Behave.*

He stood me up and walked me back to Fischer's office, pulling the door shut behind me. Fischer sat at his desk, sweeping the remains of a deli sandwich in crumpled wax paper into a trashcan. He opened a Coke and pulled a second can from a paper bag on his desk, setting it down across the desk. I took a seat and popped the soda. I took a very long drink before I dared look at him again. There was no softening around his eyes.

"I'm sorry," I lied.

"What did we talk about you not doing?" He looked worn down by his shortened night, a succession of them. I tried to imagine where he laid his head to rest, the kind of place he might live, the bachelor dinners he made in some too-small kitchen—Ava already out of the house, Ava's mother long since remarried. He was waiting for my response. I came up with a few, but when I tried to speak they floated away one by one, paper boats on a winding river. He rubbed a hand over his face. "I could throw you in jail. Do you understand?"

"That was fingerprint powder all over her place, wasn't it?"

Fischer was silent for a moment, studying me. He opened a drawer on the side of his desk and pulled out a yellow folder, opening it to a stack of printed photographs. He picked up the top sheet and laid it between us on the table. The image had been blown up so close it was grainy, though it was still clearly a man walking through pneumatic doors. Older than Penny but younger than Fischer, he was slender and pale with dark hair and a sharp chin, dressed in a pair of jeans. The camera zoomed in so close his eyes had become pixelated holes, a city haircut brushing the tops of his ears. I touched the photo, as if I might sift through all the men I had ever seen like tactile memories in order to place him.

"Who is he?"

"Do you recognize him?"

"I don't think so."

Fischer laid a second photo on the table, this camera directly above the man walking inside the doors. It showed an average span of shoulders, the full crown of his dark hair, the over-projected bridge of an aquiline nose.

"I've never seen him before."

"You're sure?"

"Yes." I heard the conviction in my voice, a certainty I didn't actually feel. I was trying to recall every man I'd ever seen come through the diner: the familiar faces of the regulars, fuzzier recollections of travelers just passing through. I wanted to believe this man would have stuck out to me, even in passing. But if I'd seen him before, I'd forgotten him just as quickly.

Fischer set a third photo on the table. It was a bird's-eye shot of a casino, people milling around a gaming floor. Fischer pointed to a craps table, where several men were bent over the green felt, the casino lights lengthening shadows at the edge of the frame. A dark-haired woman reached for a chip with a slim, tanned arm, a swatch of bright fabric visible on her side. It took a moment to reconcile the figure with Penny. The yellow sundress that made her look as if she was from the islands? Hadn't I seen it in her closet an hour ago, hanging up among her clothes? I couldn't be sure.

Another photograph, another angle: her face still pixelated, indistinct. Impossible to read her eyes or what was in them, fear or excitement. She was standing now, the photograph highlighting the familiar way she held her body, tilting her torso away from every speaker, as if she meant to take in the whole of them at once. It was most certainly that dress, and the thin red strap across her chest a heart-shaped purse I had seen her wear more than once, slinging it over her head on our way out the door. The man had his hand splayed across her lower back. It looked as if she was being escorted off the floor, their faces pointed toward an area of the casino just out of range. I pointed to the space we couldn't see.

"What's over there?"

"Elevators." He consulted the file. "They were taken a week ago, the night after you dropped her off."

A beat went by; long enough for the news to sink in. I shoved the photographs across the table, Fischer grabbing at them to keep them from falling to the ground. How could she do it? Run again, when we had just been granted reprieve. I saw the sandman in my mind—six inches from my face with those astonishing blue eyes, his mouth a grimace—the way he appeared every night in my dreams. The whole story was on the tip of my tongue. I wanted confession, absolution. I wanted to hurt Penny, othered by the image, made suddenly a stranger; I wanted to point a finger at the girl in the yellow dress being led handily off the page. *That girl* nearly got us killed, starting a chase that, to my mind, had never ended. But photographs couldn't tell the whole story. They couldn't fill in the gaps, the ruptures in thought where decisions were made. Had Penny gone to Alvaro's after I dropped her off, as Flaca thought? Had he said or done something to make her flee? A man enters a casino and meets a beautiful girl. What happens next? I picked up the last photograph again, studying the tables. The carpet a fuzzy indistinguishable pattern of red and blue splotches. It nagged some loose thread in my mind. All casino carpeting, more or less the same.

"All these big casinos are hours away. How'd she get there? And if you know where she is, why don't you just go get her? Why did you tape off her place?"

"County's been looking for this guy for a few months for running on his warrant. We received these photos a couple days ago, along with every other precinct in a hundred-mile radius. It was a lucky hit."

"Who is he? Why do they want him?"

Fischer didn't answer. I stood up, unable to sit still.

"You're not going to tell me?"

"I'm telling you what I can. We know he checked in to the hotel for one night. We know they were both there that night because we have her on the floor. Cameras show him checking out the next morning alone. Unless she used an alias, there are no records that your friend ever had a room of her own."

I realized I was pacing. I stopped. "You mean you found her, and then you lost her again. Who *is* he?"

"I was hoping you could tell me. If you can remember seeing him before, there might be reason to believe Penny went to the casino to meet him."

"He's not from the diner, not that I know. You have to ask someone else. You're not checking with her friends—"

"Cale, of all the friends we tried, there was only one"—he checked the file again—"Lourdes Hernandez? Who was willing to come in and look these over. She identified Penny as the girl in the photos. Said she'd never seen him before, either." He leaned back in his chair, spreading his hands. "You want to do something to help? Get her other friends to actually come in."

I picked up the photograph again, looking for everything that wasn't there. Between dropping Penny off at her place, and Penny arriving at the casino, she had spoken to Flaca; she might have gone to see Alvaro. I weighed telling Fischer about Alvaro myself. Maybe he already knew.

"What's this guy's warrant for?"

Fischer straightened the photos and shut the folder. It was his turn to stand. It seemed our time together, and my potential usefulness, had expired.

"Fischer. What did he do?"

Fischer came around the desk. *Allow me to escort you the fuck out of my office.* When he came near I grabbed his sleeve, pulling him toward me. He let himself get close, not nearly close enough. He ran warm, the first two buttons of his shirt were undone, his sleeves rolled up. I could feel the heat radiating from his core. He kept his eyes focused on my chin, the tail end of his breath tickling my cheek. He was just a father, and I had recently lost one. When he spoke his voice was low and even; it might have soothed me, if I didn't listen to his words. "Beat up an old girlfriend. Skipped his arraignment. A month later, another court date, neither party showed. Lawyer was worried. They sent officers to her house on a wellness check. She wasn't there."

"Missing? Just like Penny."

"The girl could just be lying low. Staying with a friend somewhere out of town, if she thought it was a better way to stay safe. Maybe she didn't want to risk seeing him in court. She'd be careful not to tell anyone where she was going."

"And him?"

"He was spotted in Noe the following week, alone. Then, nothing. Whatever he did or didn't do, he can't run forever. They'll get him."

"But they never sent out these photos because of Penny in the first place. She's just a way for you all to find him. We don't matter to you at all."

"That's not true." He was studying me with a curious expression. "Cale."

I released his sleeve. I couldn't bear to be there a minute longer. I opened the door to his office and walked into the main room of the station, past Dale, past the older vet's empty desk, pushing through the tarp and the empty waiting room with its bolted orange chairs, straight out through the front door. Outside, the morning was cool. The sky was a crisp blue. It was a ten-mile walk home. I heard the station door behind me and Dale's keys jangling on his duty belt as he came up beside me, clutching the snakeskin purse, its long strap trailing in the dirt.

"Want a ride?" he asked.

"Yeah," I said.

Dale held open the door to the back seat, dropped the bag on my lap, and shut the door. I checked the purse. All of my belongings and Penny's money had been replaced. If I had one friend left in the world, it was Dale. He obeyed the speed limit the whole way, taking the dirt roads at a slow crawl, passing the abandoned train depot, the remaining tracks half covered by earth. Pomoc's previous life and all the people who had lived it. Pomoc in all her colors. The neutral taupe and char, her eternal yawning sky.

20

Penny drove too fast, tearing it the whole way out of town. We flew down Main Street to the on-ramp and coasted down the empty highway with the windows rolled down. It was already ten degrees cooler than the mobile home, which seemed to incubate heat, absorbing sunlight all day and loath to ever let it go. Half an hour earlier we lay prone as starfish on the floor in front of the television, sweating under its shifting Technicolor glare. *Fix it,* I said, my voice lost against the sound of the box fan rattling in the window, making more noise than air.

Now neither one of us spoke on the drive, our silence grown easy. After twenty minutes she pulled off a familiar truck stop into a bright tourist bay lined with clusters of fast food joints, gas stations, and cheap motels. Even though I wasn't hungry the restaurants appealed, if only for the frosty air-conditioning pumping inside. But we had rolled out of Penny's still barefoot. I wore a pair of shorts and a T-shirt, no shoes. Penny wore the baggy nightshirt she slept in and little else.

She pulled around to the Skylark Lodge and cut our headlights, easing the truck up the rear drive. It was a two-level, multiunit stucco spread with a tremulous-looking staircase on either end. The original custard paint was flaking from the walls of the second floor, but the first boasted a fresh coat of jaunty tangerine. It was a bust motel, all the dirty channels free. I glanced toward the check-in window near the front drive. The room was lit up but the desk was empty, no one visible behind the bulletproof glass.

"Shhh," Penny said, meaning *don't look*. I began to feel a slight tingle of nerves. I had emptied my wallet of tips at home the night before, and there was only twenty dollars in the billfold I had shoved in the dash. These rooms might have air-conditioning, but I wasn't looking forward to breaking into one. Penny circled the lot around the blocks of guest rooms, pulling up to a metal gate surrounding the motel's modest pool, padlocked for the night. Penny turned off the engine but left the keys in the ignition. We eased open our doors, resting them gently against their frame. I followed Penny to the fence. The pool hours were posted clearly on a metal placard by the door, 11 A.M.–7 P.M., SKYLARK CUSTOMERS ONLY. I linked my hands to give her a boost. I kept watch while she climbed over, the gate squeaking loudly under her weight. She dropped to the other side and unlatched the door. It was still shackled to the fence, but she leaned against it with all her weight, and I wormed my way through the tight opening, scraping my elbow on the rusty mesh.

Once we were together we groped each other's arms and faces, blind as mice, seeking our boundaries in the moonlight, where one of us began and the other one ended. My fingers closed around the tip of her nose. I honked it.

"How'd I do?" she whispered.

We stripped down and eased ourselves into the pool. The water was cold, holy against my skin like every wish I ever made all coming true at once. I ducked my head underneath and opened my eyes, watching our weightless limbs tread water, luxuriating in the bodiless sensation. I resurfaced to take a breath. Penny pushed her long hair back from her forehead. We grinned at each other, our teeth flashing in the dark.

"On your mark—" she said, drawing an invisible gun from the water. She fired. We swam four laps back to back, her long, even strokes easily outpacing mine. After several more I swam to the edge and hauled myself out, beads of water clinging to my skin. I lay back on the warm concrete, watching Penny pirouette in the deep water.

"Water ballet," she said, raising her hands to fifth position. She shifted forward into an arabesque, kicking up a splash of water with her toe. "Didn't you want to be one?"

"No," I said, closing my eyes. "But I wanted to want to." After several minutes the water on my skin began to evaporate. The greedy heat returned, pressing close.

Some part of me must have heard the man's footsteps approaching, the rattling of the gate. Still it seemed to happen all at once, the sound of his keys turning in the padlock, my eyes flying open and hurrying to stand, the flood of dread as the metal door squealed. Panicking, I looked to Penny, but she had gone perfectly still in the water, hands clutching her breasts. I covered my slim chest and the mound between my legs just as the stranger crashed through, flourishing a beam of light across us both, his shape mostly hidden in shadows. He swept the flashlight up, shining it directly in my face. I squinted, automatically lifting my hands to shield my eyes. Penny made a small, surprised noise from the pool. I realized how quiet the motel was, the only sounds the trucks accelerating on the on-ramp in the distance, the crickets chirping nearby. At some point we had forgotten to whisper. Our giggling and splashing had brought him here—we, the trespassers—though it still seemed an invasion.

Slowly, I lowered my hands. He swept the flashlight over the bushes and the perimeter of the gate, our T-shirts and underwear balled on the concrete. A sound in the back of his throat. Displeasure, a hairball.

"Keep it down," he growled. He turned around, his flashlight lighting the way as he lumbered back the way he'd come, banging the metal gate behind him. We held ourselves frozen, fat as ticks with guilt, until the sound of his jingling keys faded away, both of us straining for any sound from the motel, the road; a truck laboring on bad brakes, the rusty gears carrying freight downhill. I took several steps backward and made a running leap into the deep end of the pool, the splash slapping water onto the concrete. Penny's laughter ringing out against the night.

53

After lunch I dressed in a pair of jeans and one of Lamb's old chambrays and took the walk over to Jackson's small single-story next door. His Chevrolet C1500 was parked in the drive, the aqua paint chipped off the driver's-side panel. A black Pontiac Bonneville sat marooned in the gravel with its hood ajar and, next to it, an Impala, her rear windows and long, sky-blue tail partially obscured by a car cover. As a young child, tripping up this car-littered yard after Lamb, Jackson had seemed the remainder between them, a grizzled old bachelor benefiting from all of Lamb's magnanimous kindness. But Jackson was several years younger than Lamb and never married, always seemingly content in his own company. He turned plenty of favors our way, watching the dogs when we drove to the casinos, mending the fence between our two houses when it rotted through, fixing Lamb's old truck for what I had come to understand was much too fair a price.

When Jackson opened the door now, he took his time on the threshold, drying his wrists with a flowered dishtowel, his eyes roving over my face with the same grave scrutiny he paid the truck's engine under a popped hood, cocking an attentive ear to the machine's low hum. It was clear I had never appreciated this man for his singular worth. Lamb had always overshadowed other men, he had long been my sole

reference for any other human being, the rogue variable in every equa-
tion I struggled to compute. *Solve for X. Solve for Lamb.*

Jackson slung the dishtowel over his shoulder and took a step back
into the room. I followed him to the L-shaped kitchen at the rear of
the house with its speckled yellow countertops, the teal-colored tiles
that Lamb had helped mortar onto the backsplash above the stove.
Didn't I wonder why Jackson's patience for me, like Cesar's, was always so easy to come by? Because I was an extension of Lamb? Because Lamb had lost more than they? Or because both men had deep,
whole hearts, like Lamb himself, indifferent to the deficits of an or-
phan and her unyielding famine of affection?

"Is it a good time?" I asked, but I was already walking toward the
table, pulling out my old seat near the window. Jackson turned into
the small kitchen and grabbed the kettle off the stove, filling it with
water, firing up the range. I should have offered to help; I was no longer a child who waited to be served. But death granted favors, and
Jackson, like Lamb, preferred minimal fuss. While we waited for the
water to boil I surveyed his backyard out the window, the earth
weeded over, the carcasses of several other cars in amputated disrepair: a busted Riviera and slick, purple Electra like fossils excavated
from bygone eras. Those that found a buyer, Jackson would mend.
Twice a year, he'd load one to the hitch of his Chevrolet and pull it
down our road in glorious, solo parade; these vintage cars meant for
new lives in Vegas or Reno, where they might sparkle among their
kind. How much easier for an object to inhabit a second life.

The kettle whistled and Jackson moved about in the kitchen, opening cabinets. "I've got a Nova out there," he said, knowing where I'd
been looking. "Want to try it on?"

"Wouldn't fit," I said. "My head would get too big. Wolf thanks you for all the small beasts nosing around that peach tree, by the way. He almost got a starling the other day, or at least he thinks so."

Jackson brought a pair of oversized mugs to the table, setting one down in front of me. I wrapped my hands around it, palms smarting from the heat. He took the seat across the table and raised his cup to his mouth, swallowing a mouthful of tea, impervious to the curls of steam rising from the surface. His tongue, like the rest of him, invulnerable to any mortal wound. Men like him, survivors of so much already. He watched me carefully over the rim.

"You're not so big I can't see how you're taking it."

"I'm tougher than I look," I said, and because I thought he might really worry, "I'm Lamb-made, remember? I'm jerky."

"How long have I known you?" he asked.

"Before I could count."

"Picking up my tools, following Lamb around that yard. If he fixed a fan belt, you wanted to fix one, too. He had a drink, you ripened a god-fearing thirst. Clinton over that sink, pouring apple juice into empty beer bottles."

Jackson took a sip, the creases pulling deep around his mouth. Still handsome in the forgotten way of old men, the solitary kind. Wolf and Trixie were the only creatures left in earnest competition for his heart, growing more attached each visit. But hadn't they become reluctant experts, in the shepherding of august men? From outside came a squeaking sound at the side of the yard. We watched together as the short, squat man waded into view, the tall weeds snapping against the calves of his cowboy boots as he navigated islands of patched tires and coupe skeletons.

"Last chance Nova. Rocky's not worried about his head fitting."

"I have the opposite problem. I came to ask about Lamb's truck. Would you take it? I don't need two."

"Is that all?"

"Also. I can't stay here."

Jackson's eyes, both easier and harder than Lamb's to lie to. "You want to sell?"

"Not right now. All his things are there."

"You don't have to go through them right away."

"When will ever be good? I need a break, maybe."

"You want to leave the dogs here."

"For a little while."

"They're going to want you back."

"I'm going to want them back, too."

He took another mouthful of tea. "You won't be gone too long."

"I don't expect it."

"You will take care."

"I will."

"You don't know how yet. You think you do."

I finally tried the tea, my eyes watering from the scald. "No. I know I don't."

Why had I always seen myself as so alone? When there was Jackson, Maria, Rico, Rena—a dozen faces Pomoc gifted me, to sew up holes inside myself I hadn't known existed?

"It's hard to learn," he said.

59

The sky above the Leaspoke Casino was on fire. Traffic on the freeway began bottlenecking two miles from the exit; we inched along faithfully, captive spectators to a violent, blood orange sunset. I took the off-ramp and was nearly clipped by a white sedan with a bad bumper, cutting me off with a millimeter to spare. We were all heading in the direction of a tall casino just visible from the freeway, its giant pink and blue feathers glittering in lights. Everyone eager to begin their debauch.

The Leaspoke was big enough to poach tourists on their way to Reno and small enough for locals to retain the sense of familial ownership. After a mile I pulled into a long wraparound drive, a giant asphalt lot bordering seventy thousand square feet of grimy ivory paint, a wooden mannequin in warbonnet and breechclouts pointing an outstretched hand down the center lane. I parked in the back of the lot, trailing a pale, swollen couple in Birkenstock sandals to the entrance. A gaunt, glass-eyed speed walker, obviously tweaking, overtook us all, only to stop and wait for us at the door, sucking intensely on his Slurpee. His eyes pinballed on the couple, turning sticky over my face and chest. I felt the ghost of Fischer's hands pressing into my shoulders, his scent lingering on my neck and hair. I was sorely aware of everything between my legs, its impractical value.

I had hoped that once I arrived, I'd be gifted with spontaneous intuition, that I might understand instantly the reason why Penny came. But crossing the casino's wide, tiled lobby under a frigid blast of air-conditioning, it was still difficult to imagine Penny here just hours after we'd escaped the desert; Penny milling among these strangers' faces, the stale cloud of cigarette smoke clinging to her yellow dress and long black hair. Had she come to meet the man in the photograph? Did they arrive together? Or had Penny come alone, without any intention at all? And if the real Penny traveled to out-of-the-way casinos to meet strangers in the middle of the night, was it also the real Penny I giggled with on weekends at the diner; Penny who danced banda with Rico between customers on slow summer afternoons? How could it have been Penny in the desert that night, raising the heavy weight of the tire iron in her hands?

The gaunt man brushed past with his Slurpee, and I stepped in the check-in line behind the pale couple from the parking lot, digging out a handful of twenties from the depths of Penny's purse. The man behind the counter took it and asked for ID. I slid him another wad of cash instead, waiting for him to object. I had two hundred dollars in tips and the sealed white envelope from Jackson as an advance on Lamb's truck, along with all the cash from Penny's coffee can—but no real sense of how long any of it might last. I wanted to embrace all of Penny's recklessness, her insensible disregard.

"Will two keys be enough?" The man's elfin face, and the wry expression he sent over the top of his plastic drugstore readers, conspired to make my skin crawl.

"Fine."

He slid a small cardboard envelope across the desk and I pocketed it without having to answer anything else. Our transaction complete, I followed the path of the Slurpee-toting stranger onto the escalator and began the slow descent into the pit of the casino, the beeping, whirring sounds of slot machines and quarters clinking in coin trays tugging the worn contour of memory. *Here is the moment Lamb would reach for my hand.*

I mapped the layout from my vantage point on the escalator: craps on the left, slot machines on the right, pennies on the periphery, quarters inside. A row of felt-covered tables housed twenty-one and three-card poker, hold 'em and fold 'em. I stepped off the escalator past the rackety whirl of a roulette wheel; it was late afternoon but the anticipation of the evening's big bets already thrummed in the air. I took a lap of the floor, ignoring the flat stares of local seniors glued to their slot machines, the out-of-towners easy to spot in their zip-up anoraks and cargo shorts. The serious gamblers were still ten miles down the road at the Triple Eagle, filling up on the early-bird buffet or warming up at home, testing their luck with rapid-fire rounds of online blackjack.

At the very back of the room was an area secluded by velvet rope and leafy faux ferns, where players cycled through day tournaments from brunch to dusk. After dark, the space transformed for private parties; a poker table was carried in like a palanquin by casino personnel, leather wing chairs lined up on either side. If Penny hadn't already met the man in the photograph, this might have been where their paths first crossed. The man with his city haircut flush enough to play a round, Penny's discerning ability to know a high roller when she saw one.

A beaky cocktail waitress walked by, offering fluorescent plastic cups for coins. I took one and sidled up to the cage, trading another one of Penny's twenties for rolls of quarters. I parked myself at a slot machine in the corner of the room with a clear view of the tables. The dealers were dressed in pressed white shirts, cheap black vests, and pink and blue bow ties, the former so bright and deep a shade it might be mistaken for red in an indistinct photograph. The colors echoed the sparkling feather motif outside, the patterned carpet that had first stirred my memory. I had a vague childhood recollection of the mannequin in the drive and the feather-shaped keychains sold in the gift shop, but I hoped more memories would surface. So far, they had remained buried, this casino just one indistinct evening in a succession of early impressions.

The pale couple from the parking lot reappeared at the blackjack table, the wife snagging a seat at third base. Closer to the slots, an older croupier spun the roulette wheel for a row of locals, her auburn hair shining brassy under the lights. After each spin she touched her face, adjusting large, red buttonlike earrings. She looked like one of the women who came into Jake's for a solitary booth and spent hours gazing out the window, requesting three refills of hot water on a single teabag. If Penny saw her, she might have thought the same.

I fed the slot machine a quarter and pulled the lever. Lemon, lemon . . . cherry. From the corner of my eye I spied a flash of long black hair and nearly spilled my coins turning to look. But it was only another cocktail waitress swooping by to collect the empty cups.

I played the slots for two hours, switching seats when prompted by a group of elderly women in matching lilac velour tracksuits with *The Max Betties* embroidered across their backs, fixated on an intrinsic pattern of musical chairs intended to court fortune. I watched them and tried to decipher their system, but gave up halfway through. At the roulette wheel, a small crowd gathered around a young woman in a short denim skirt placing her bet. A nondescript man in a football jersey placed a hand on her back as she bent over to roll the dice. Catching my stare, he grinned. It was as if, after living innocuously alongside men for years, I had woken up to their intense attention, or they had awoken to mine. Maybe they could sense an unconscious shift within me, a willingness to endanger myself. I left my empty cup on the table for the waitress to find and rode the escalator up to the lobby to the parking lot, needing air.

The evening had grown soft and damp, gray sheets of cloud hanging low. I spent several disoriented minutes walking around the parking lot, trying to locate my truck among all the cars. When I finally found it, I fished out the duffel bag from behind the seat and headed back toward the casino. Several yards out I spotted two women emerge from a back entrance, identifiable at a distance by their uniforms. One disappeared back inside while I was still too far away, but the other looked up as I approached. It was the roulette croupier, auburn hair from a bottle. She took a long drag on a cigarette, holding a paper coffee cup between two fingers, her red nails filed into long, polished ovals. I felt for my own pack in the front pocket of the duffel, stopping a few feet away. "Can I borrow a light?"

"Where's yours?" She wore a nametag, I had to squint to make it out. Norma.

"Somewhere in the bottom of this bag."

"You're too young to smoke. And you're too young to be here."

"I'm older than I look."

She snorted. "Bullshit."

We stood apart for a few moments until it was clear I wouldn't leave. Finally she reached into the pocket of her uniform and produced the lighter. I leaned in to the flame. The back of Norma's hand was dotted with sunspots.

"What kind of mess are you?" she asked, dropping her cigarette butt to the ground. She squashed it with an orthopedic loafer.

"I'm looking for a friend of mine. She disappeared from this casino weeks ago. It's the last place she was seen."

"That Mexican girl?" Norma looked skeptical. I offered her my pack. She kept her expression but picked out another cigarette with her nails, lighting up again.

"You know about it? Her name's Penny."

"The police were here a few days ago." She gestured with her coffee cup hand. "But where's her family? You're not in any shape."

"But I'm the one who came."

"Well, I don't know anything that can help you. She looked like a nice girl. Real pretty." Norma blew smoke over her shoulder.

"You actually saw her?"

"I've been here nineteen years. I see everything."

"How did she look? I mean, was she upset?"

"I don't think so. But I wouldn't know. She didn't play roulette. I told the police the same thing."

"What about the man she was with?"

"No man, not that I saw. They asked me that, too. Showed me a picture. But I've got to be honest with you, the older I get the less attention I pay to men altogether. Your friend I remember. She was hanging around the blackjack table. If she came with anyone, I didn't see."

"She could have met him here." I remembered I was holding a cigarette and forced myself to take a drag. "They think something terrible happened to her."

"Do they? Well, they have a habit of thinking the worst."

"But no one saw her leave," I said. "It's not on the cameras, her leaving."

"You know what people do sometimes? There's a continental breakfast in the morning, in the restaurant. People go by for coffee before they leave and butter up one of those muffins. You should try them if you get a chance. A woman from Sparks drives all the way out here with them. Then people leave out the restaurant way and forget to check out. Pisses the manager right off."

"Aren't there cameras in the restaurant?"

Norma shrugged. "If they work."

"Wouldn't they *check* all the cameras?"

"You don't know much about our boys in blue, do you? Lazy unless it comes to writing you a ticket." Norma threw the cigarette on the ground and let it smoke. She slipped a tube of lipstick from her pocket and applied it expertly to her thin lips, recapping it with one hand.

"Do the cops know about the restaurant exit?" I asked. I was sure Fischer would have checked all the cameras. But Fischer hadn't come to the Leaspoke, only the local cops had.

Norma tilted her head, considering. She smoothed down her uniform, tucking her lipstick back into her pocket. Break was over; our conversation was, too.

"I don't think they asked," she said.

54

There were two numbers listed on Fischer's card. The first I recognized as the station's; the second had the same local prefix. I dialed the latter and held the phone gingerly, prepared to hang up if confronted by an answering machine, or Dale. On the third ring someone answered, fumbling the receiver. A phone dropped and retrieved.

"What?" Fischer's groggy voice over the line.

"It's Cale Lambert."

"What time is it?" I heard something else tumble from a desk or table, a muffled curse. "It's one in the morning. Is everything all right?"

"I meant to come by the station earlier, but things took longer than I thought."

Fischer didn't answer for a long time. He was still trying to wake up, or else he'd already fallen back asleep.

"Hello?" I asked.

"What things?"

"I'm heading out of town tomorrow. I need to talk to you."

"Where are you going?"

"I'm not sure how long I'll be gone. I could come by the station."

"I'm already at home."

"Maybe I could just drop by."

"It's the middle of the night, Cale. You can't come to my house. What's so important you had to wake me up?"

"It is important."

"Did you remember someone else Penny was afraid of?"

His scorn was grating. I was meant to feel the weight of my own desire for a friend's return, to feel guilty for it. I was not owed back a friend. We were owed nothing.

"You're upset," I said. "I'm sorry I woke you. Still, I'd like to talk."

"I want to be clear. I'm not in the mood for dramatics."

"Tell me all the ways I can't comprehend seriousness."

"Cale. If you have something to say, just say it now."

There was another long silence on the line. I considered hanging up. But I had already walked the dogs over to Jackson's and handed him their leashes, hugged their necks, kissed their handsome, furred faces. I had gone home and packed a duffel and set it behind the truck's bench seat, my fingers brushing against Lamb's heavy gloves and the cold, solid weight of the tire iron. I hauled out the tool and balanced it in my hands, as if the object itself might indicate next steps, a direction in which to proceed. Of course we should have just thrown it away. We should have wrapped it in the newspaper we didn't have and tucked it in the dumpster behind the gas station. But wasn't concealment, in itself, an admission of guilt? Examining the bowed handle, I couldn't make out a single drop of blood, but the people who fingerprinted Penny's house had other ways of seeing, black lights and solutions, tiny fiber-grabbing brushes. Penny had washed the car, the tires, our shoes—yet she never suggested throwing the tire iron away. Neither one of us, ready to admit our crime.

"You're the only one I can tell," I said.

Fischer coughed, his voice returning to the line. "Five minutes. Okay? That's it. I'm over by the water tower. You have a pen?"

I didn't need to write down Fischer's address. I knew Pomoc well enough for that. I only needed to remember the number, 416, a small single-story on a gravel plot, surrounded by a chain-link fence. Fischer answered the door in dark jeans and a white collared shirt as if he had just come from the station, but his button-down was wrinkled, his hair mussed. Stepping into the light of the porch in his white shirt, he appeared an arbiter, someone capable of granting mercy. His bare feet on the unvarnished wood were tapered, nimble; his bearing agile. In all animal lives preceding this one, he had been predator, never prey.

He led me inside, down a short hall papered with yellow chrysanthemums, a feminine remnant from previous owners that stood in contrast to the rest of the austere, masculine decor: a worn leather couch, a dark coffee table covered in red and fluorescent yellow files, two empty bottles of beer. Fischer scooped up his shield and service holster from the arm of the couch, tucking the gun in his waistband. It wasn't difficult to infer the shape of this evening or a hundred others like it, Fischer reading files on the couch until exhaustion surpassed nobler intentions. He ran a hand through his hair, looking sheepish.

"There's a reason I never let anyone over," he said.

"But you let me."

The edges of his mouth tightened. His eyes traveled over my features, searching for clues. For someone who spent an entire career studying faces, he must have found mine wanting. I should have explained. The girl he was looking for was gone.

"Let me guess," I said. "No news?"

"Cale. The investigation—"

"—is ongoing," I finished for him, glancing over the coffee table and the yellow files. One or more of them had to be Penny's. I took a seat on the couch. He sat, too, leaving a respectable amount of space between us.

"What did you want to talk to me about?"

"Does it matter?"

He shrugged. "It seemed important on the phone."

But now that I was here, he didn't sound all that surprised. He expected very little of me, and I was happy to comply. I slid across the couch, moving laterally like only the craftiest of animals: crabs, sidewinders, children, murderers. Fischer, mistaking my intention, raised an arm to offer comfort, shelter—as if he had any to give. I brushed it aside, and before he could stop me I was straddling his lap. He brought both hands up in surprise, to ward me off, to push me. In the hesitation that followed, his character was revealed. Here was a man unused to pushing girls. Until that moment, I hadn't been sure.

"Hi," I said.

The corner of his left eye twitched.

"Right before she left, Penny and I had an accident."

"Cale." His Adam's apple bobbed in his throat.

"I want you to know, he tried to kill us first."

"What?"

I pushed down the pointy collar of his shirt with a single finger and leaned in, taking a deep breath. Cedarwood and soap. I pressed my lips against the base of his neck and felt his pulse jump. When I pulled away, his eyes were darkening with real anger and something else, too, something wet and tarry that stuck to the whorls of my fingertips when I spread them across his jaw.

What did I think the truth could do? No matter how much I wanted to believe these choices were mine to make, our futures had already been devised. *This is your heart line. This is your fate.* Fischer clenched his jaw under my hand. I leaned back as if to backbend over the coffee table. If I fell, I already knew he wouldn't catch me. I pulled myself back up by degrees and pressed my face into his cheek. He said my name again, the word lost in my hair. I turned my face to hunt it and found his mouth, warm and willing. How you learn to kiss a man without ever being taught. Fischer touched his tongue to mine, tightening his hands on my hips, lifting me with him as he stood. He made it one step, two, before stopping with a noise deep in his throat, dropping me as if I had become a fire that burned through his hands. I landed hard, half on the couch, half on the floor, gasping at impact. Fischer stood over me, furious.

"Get out," he said.

I sucked air into my lungs, propping myself up on an elbow, still dazed. Fischer adjusted his collar, looking away. As if I had flattened myself on his couch without any help from him, snuck in through the window, distilled into form from ether. As if he didn't know the entire spine-rubbing time that this was what we were working toward. His mouth looked soft and recently kissed, but the longer I stared at it the angrier he became. He grabbed my wrist and hauled me up.

"Ow!"

"Get out."

"You're hurting me!"

He tightened his grip, shaking my arm hard enough to rattle my bones. With his other hand he raised a finger and pointed it between my eyes. An image of Ava sprang to mind. How many times had she been on the other end of this pointed finger, the forthright tone she probably couldn't take seriously, even now.

"You need to leave," he said.

I yanked back my wrist. "I don't have anywhere to go."

We stared at each other for a moment, daring the other to make a move. Finally he pointed down the hall. "Down there. Take my bedroom and lock the door. Go to sleep. When you wake up in the morning, we're going to drive down to the station and you're going to tell me, very *carefully*, very *clearly*, whatever the hell you're trying to say now. You're going to write it down in a sworn statement. Because if I find out one single thing you're saying isn't true—"

"I can't—"

He raised a hand between us, strangling the air. It seemed to take all the effort he had to keep himself from doing it to me. "None of this is up for discussion. Pick up your bag."

I turned away, my legs shaky. Fischer was right; my duffel bag had appeared at the foot of the couch, though I had no memory of bringing it inside. Ever since I'd left the hospital, Lambless, my mind had taken to skipping large chunks of time, whole sections of day sucked into thin air. I came across the evidence when I brought a water glass to the sink and discovered a bouquet of violet penstemon on the countertop, its hairlike roots still muddy with soil; or carried my pajamas to the hamper, old photo albums weighing down the dirty clothes; or woke up in the middle of the night to find my fingers clenched around the handle of a kitchen knife I couldn't remember placing underneath the pillow. I picked up the duffel bag and made my way down Fischer's unlit hall. The first door opened to a white-tiled bath, the porcelain sink a ghostly protrusion in the dark. I backed out and made my way to the next door. When I looked over my shoulder Fischer was still standing at the end of the hall, his hands balled into fists. The distance between us was not so great that he couldn't cross. When I blinked, Fischer was gone.

60

On the twelfth floor of the Leaspoke, the elevator doors opened on to a long, carpeted hallway, eerily silent after the crash of coins and voices downstairs. At the end of the hall I inserted a card to unlock a single room furnished with a small television and a polished desk, a twin bed with a printed coverlet I was certain had never been washed. I checked the closet and dropped to my knees to peek under the bed. I turned on the light in the bathroom, waiting for it to flicker and hum before pulling back the shower curtain. The paint at the bottom of the tub was nicked.

I stretched out on the bed beside the duffel bag and closed my eyes. When I opened them again the room was cold, the windows dark. I was frightened by how deeply I had slept, how time had been eaten up. It felt like another blackout, another distressing lapse in memory. It was cold in the room; they had turned up the air-conditioning, which meant things must be getting warm downstairs. I opened my mouth wide, trying to pop my ears. An image flashed across my mind of Alvaro's rattlesnake preparing to swallow his limp mouse. I closed my mouth again very carefully.

In the bathroom I stripped off my shorts and Fischer's T-shirt and ran the shower, the water only available in two temperatures, freezing or scalding. I chose the latter and climbed into the spray. The pinpricks of water brought up flushed red constellations on my chest and belly. I had been a child in casino hotel rooms like this one; I had been allowed to order cheeseburgers from room service, take shampoo bubble baths, watch television for hours while waiting out Lamb downstairs. One evening, flipping the channels in search of cartoons, I found a popular, frosty-haired talk show host meandering thoughtfully up the aisles of his studio audience, turning to ask questions of several elegantly dressed women onstage. Under the studio lights, the women sat on high stools. They wore long skirts and pumps and guileless expressions. The host squinted in their direction, his wretchedly pale eyes peering out from behind large, bifocal lenses. *I'm not a psychiatrist,* he said, *but what are you punishing yourself for?*

One of these women had thrown herself off a bridge, only to land in a safety net installed to deter suicides. Another woman, her deep chestnut hair swept up in a sleek, high bun, outsized clip-on earrings like jade discs at her throat, admitted to regularly carving notches in her forearm, as if her flesh were a post she could use to mark off time. The third, a redhead with skin the color of cream, looked coolly into the audience, her features drained of all expression. The host listed her attempts: overdose, hanging, bungled wrist slitting, overdose. The host paused in his litany, stalking the carpeted steps of the studio, pushing the rim of his glasses up with a single finger. *What are you punishing yourself for?* Not one of the women spoke up, but even then I knew they harbored secret replies.

I uncapped a miniature bottle of shampoo and worked the suds through my hair, releasing the smell of oranges into the steam. If the police were right—if the cameras caught Penny entering this casino in a yellow sundress, and in all this time she had never left—then Penny was dead. In my nightmares, I imagined Penny strangled on a bed, stabbed on the floor, her body stuffed in a mechanical closet or crawl-space, stashed under a bed. But what if the man with the pixelated eyes had only used Penny in the spirit she desired to be used? What if Penny, after all that happened in the desert, felt the need to punish herself, too? What if, once the man excused himself to refill a bucket of ice or play a round of craps downstairs, he returned to the room to find Penny, having ingested a potent prescription cocktail, lying unresponsive on the bed; Penny, floating lifeless in the bathtub? What if then, and only then, did he dispose of her body?

What if the person who needed to punish herself was me?

I rinsed my hair, the suds skimming over the sharp planes of my hips, the elongated curve of my thighs. The water at the bottom of the tub rose a degree, lapping at my toes. The drain was clogged from an accumulation of skin cells shed from a thousand different bodies, all the women who had stood underneath the spray to wash their hair and hearts and limbs. On my waist was a small bruise in the shape of a thumb.

The water rose at the bottom of the tub, sloshing around my ankles. I soaped my hands and ran them over my face and neck. I allowed them to follow the path Fischer's had taken, rubbing the wound between my legs, inserting a finger where he had first introduced himself. I rest my forehead against the steamed tiles of the shower stall, desperate to reach deep enough inside to touch the center of all things, to tear out the new, thorny part of me that had taken me away from Pomoc, but kept me barreling toward some unknown culmination of grief, a shimmering, formless mirage.

55

Fischer's bedroom was dark, with just enough moonlight filtering in from the curtains to make out the shape of a bed, a nightstand, and the back of a chair. I shut the door and fumbled with the bedside lamp, dropping the duffel on the chair. From the front of the house came the faint sound of a refrigerator door opening and closing, the discordant crackling of ice cubes breaking apart in a tray.

I took a seat on Fischer's mattress and eased open the top drawer of the nightstand, disturbing a worn paperback thriller and a handheld flashlight, an inexplicable number of rubber bands, a pack of matches. I shut the drawer and went over to his closet, rolling the hollow door back on its track as quietly as possible. A row of collared shirts hung from evenly spaced wooden hangers. On the shelves his sweaters were folded into perfect squares, stacked neatly at their crease. A pair of broken-in bag gloves dangled from a coat hook. I stripped in the lamplight and pulled a T-shirt down from the shelf, slipping it over my head. It smelled like laundry detergent and faintly, in the collar, of Fischer. I crouched to examine his shoe rack and recognized the slim black case stacked between boxes. I slid it out carefully, straining for any sound of Fischer approaching, flipping the latches to reveal a short, neat Smith & Wesson. I had assumed that Fischer, like most townies, kept his guns in a locked display case or tucked away in the garage. For some reason this gun had been set aside; a spare forgotten or recently used, not yet returned to its proper place. It could have been Ava's, though I hadn't seen any other evidence of her in the house. I took the gun out of the case. It fit comfortably in my hand. Even Ava wouldn't have a problem handling a gun this simple. Despite all the years since Cesar's last shooting lesson, neither would I.

I checked the safety before replacing the empty case between the shoeboxes. I grabbed a pair of sweatpants off the shelf and rolled the gun inside, crossing the room to shove both in my duffel bag. I stood still in the middle of Fischer's bedroom, listening. The sounds from the kitchen had quieted, Fischer fallen asleep on the couch or returning to work on his files.

Fischer's bed was twice the size of my narrow twin at home, and when I climbed in, the sheets smelled of him, too. I turned off the lights and closed my eyes, hoping to override the ache in my chest and the strangeness of the room: the missing weight of a dog at the foot of the bed and Lamb's intermittent snore rattling faintly across the hall. The dogs, at least, would be fine. They would have eaten together, played together; they would lean into Jackson's home, confident in each other's company for a while yet. They trusted I would return to them. I rolled onto my side, reaching underneath the pillow for the kitchen knife that wasn't there. The moonlight through the curtains wasn't quite the same.

4

After several days of hard rain, the elementary school's field flooded. Every day that week we stared out classroom windows gray and dreary, gloomily receiving the morning's lesson. At third period, the fourth and fifth graders trekked to the locker rooms and lined up outside, shivering in our gym shorts in the February chill. The phys ed teacher, a sinewy, impatient woman with long, crimped hair that flew every which way in the wind, shuffled us to the stuffy auditorium, where we threw flattening dodgeballs at one another with growing ill will. By Friday, the bleak weather had lost all novelty, and the phys ed teacher had grown sick of our whining. She sent us to walk laps around the edge of the oblong field, still boggy from the rains. The moisture had unearthed the peaty smell of fertilizer in the air, and on the south end of the field where patches of yellow crabgrass sprouted, the stalks bent under the weight of stagnant water. The ground was still too sodden, with stretches of mud that sucked the bottoms of our sneakers, for anyone to attempt a jog.

We arranged ourselves in a single-file line and began to walk. I hung toward the back of the procession, an ideal position to keep watch on the other students. As we neared the end of our first lap, the line curved along the south bend so that as we moved the line it met

up behind the head, forming a closed loop of students moving along
the periphery like a bike chain turning around rusty gears. We com-
pleted three dutiful laps before the restless among us began looking
around for Ms. Price. She was spotted at the edge of the blacktop,
deep in conversation with the football coach, clutching his bare, hairy
arms. Both of their expressions partially obscured by sunglasses.

Farther up the line, a boy broke out in laughter, the sound distilled
in the cold. Some of the older students broke formation, sneaking up to
join their friends. After a little while other students followed suit, skipping forward or falling behind until the line disintegrated and the two
grades walked freely in pairs and clusters of their choosing. I spied
Penny several yards ahead, flanked by Luz and Lourdes, three dark
ponytails swinging in step. Luz kicked a rock, darting out of line to
find where it landed before punting it back to their route. After another
lap around the field, Penny began to fall behind the other girls. She
slowed way down, letting other students pass her. After a few moments,
she was closer than before, and she hung back again, until she was
walking only a few feet ahead of me. One of the most riotous boys, a
fifth grader, was telling an animated story to a group of girls nearby,
pitching his voice shrill and fractured. Every time he spoke I turned to
look at him, as if expecting to find a stranger in his place—someone
new—as if we hadn't all known for years that there would only be each
other.

Penny walked more slowly now. She was close enough that if I hurried ahead, I could reach out and tap her shoulder. There were only a
couple other students, and an entire world, between us. Far ahead,
Lourdes stepped out of line, turning back as if only just noticing Penny
was gone. Spotting her, she started walking back through the crowd in
our direction.

The sky was still cloudy; there was a clammy feeling in the air, signaling more rain. The traction from all our sneakers made a slick in the mud. To avoid it, some of the students began taking a shorter, circumscribed loop around the field. We were approaching the south bend, the early mist from another drizzle just beginning to form. After a while the puddles quivered under the first drops of real rain. How many more years would we circle this same invariable field? Finally Lourdes reached Penny and fell in step beside her. Out of the corner of my eye I saw Penny make a sudden, strong gesture, like sweeping crumbs off a tablecloth, or drawing aside a curtain. Someone let out a sharp gasp. I turned in time to see Lourdes landing with a hard, wet plop in a puddle of mud, muck splattering her face and hair. We stopped short behind her, a number of students nearly toppling into one another. All eyes were on Lourdes, who sat blinking in the puddle, looking stunned, her shorts growing more waterlogged by the minute. The chill of the water must have reached her, because her lower lip began to tremble. The riotous fifth grader stepped out from behind and offered her a hand, helping to pull her up. From somewhere in the growing huddle, a girl began to titter. Another joined in, and soon several students were laughing openly at the sight of Lourdes soggy and mud splattered, covering her face with her hands.

I searched for Penny in the crowd but couldn't find her. When we had all stopped short, Penny kept walking. I finally spotted her across the field, her long ponytail swinging as she passed students who were only just beginning to notice the commotion behind them and turning back to look. She passed the students at the front of the procession who had yet to realize anything had happened at all. Watching her, it was almost possible to believe she was one of them—that she had never noticed Lourdes fall. But there was a rigid determination to her stride as she passed Luz, who didn't even seem to notice, and as the head of the procession began looping around the far bend, Penny walked straight off the field altogether, onto the blacktop. She passed Ms. Price and the football coach, who seemed to know better than to stop her. I watched Penny cut across the asphalt in the direction of the locker rooms and our classrooms beyond, not bothering to slow down. It was almost as if she had decided to keep walking forever, as if she had decided just that minute, that she'd had enough of this school and everything in it, and she had to begin taking matters into her own hands. As if she already knew exactly where she was headed, and it didn't matter who or what she needed to leave behind.

56

I woke in the haze of morning light. Fischer stood by the bed in a pair of white shorts, his skin pale as tusk, his dark hair disheveled. In his left hand he rolled an empty glass along his fingertips; first this way, then that, as if it were a crystal or a rune, something with which to portend. This Fischer was otherworldly, different from other Fischers I had known. His face lacked accusation. I pulled myself up on his bed. The curtains covering his window stirred as if by an invisible hand. *When you wake up in the morning, we're going to drive down to the station and you're going to tell me, very carefully, very clearly, whatever the hell you're trying to say now.* But it was still too early, and that internal chord of alarm—struck first that night in the desert—was thrumming now. The chill in the room turned my bare arms to gooseflesh. Without noticing when or how it happened, summer was gone.

"Is something wrong?" I asked. Time rolled over and showed her belly, polished a fang. I pulled the bedsheets higher on my chest.

"You didn't lock the door," Fischer said.

He set the glass on the nightstand and turned down the covers on the opposite side of the bed. He climbed in, infinitely casual, as if we shared a familiar routine that spanned continuums. I felt his warm, muscled thigh come to press against my own. Across the room I spied my duffel bag slouched on the chair, his gun inside, unmolested.

"Wait—"

Fischer rolled over me in bed, tucking the length of my body under his. The heat and the weight of him, shockingly new.

"Fischer—" His name caught somewhere in my throat.

He lowered his mouth onto mine and kissed me, manipulating my chin with his hand at the base of my throat, showing me how to reciprocate. Was I pliable? I was. His mouth tasted sweet. I felt his wide, warm hands slipping up my thighs, under the T-shirt I had stolen, pulling down my underwear. I tucked my nose in the crook of his neck and tried to recall a line from Milton, the sound of Wolf's snuffle mid-sleep, any fragment from a life I would no longer inhabit. My underwear tangled around one ankle. He parted my legs with his hands and pushed himself inside. I cried out as he began to move. He pressed his hot, moist mouth against my ear.

"Tell me what you like." His fingers digging into my hips.

"I don't know." My breath belonged to someone drowning at sea. "This?"

I closed my eyes, opening them in time to catch a fleeting emotion cross his features; bewilderment, fear. He thrust himself deeper inside. I tilted my hips and watched his worry, and the last drops of my girlhood, disappear.

64

I sat in the truck in the parking lot of the Leaspoke, staring at the duffel bag with Fischer's gun in the next seat, the white paper bag of muffins bleeding clear spots of grease through the paper. If Penny left the Leaspoke alive, where would she go next? This was another game of hangman, a test of friendship that relied as much on my knowledge of the things Penny would do as the things she wouldn't. I remembered her as she was on the mountain, sitting on that flat boulder, her long, dark braid thick as a child's fist.

Are you sure you know what you're doing?

Not at all.

I started the truck. If Penny left the Leaspoke through the restaurant, she would need to hitch a ride. I backed out of the lot and pulled around the side entrance. There were several cars in the parking lot, and a spattering of semis. The closest road led to the freeway on-ramps, a gas station, and the Grindhouse Drive-In, the last chance for food or fuel for thirty miles. I drove to the gas station first. A handful of big rigs were parked along a wide pullout behind the diesel pumps. Their cabs were empty, their owners filling up on shakes and fries across the street.

Inside the gas station, the cashier looked up from behind the counter, tugging a long, skinny black goatee sectioned off with green rubber bands. The only customer was a middle-aged man in a bright knit poncho, his attention fixated on the hot dogs rolling on the grill, cradling a split bun in the center of his palm.

"Dude's waiting for a lucky one," the attendant said, following my gaze. "You filling up?"

"Twenty on three, please." I selected a map from the carousel by the register, a bag of red licorice. I pulled out the glossy page I'd torn from our senior yearbook before leaving Pomoc and unfolded it on the counter. Four rows of blithe and tender faces, Penny's ample grin.

"Can you tell me if you've seen this girl?"

He grabbed the bag of licorice, squinting at the page. "Nah. Cute though. Friend of yours?"

"You're sure?"

"I mean, would I put money on it? We get a lot of people passing through."

I hesitated before reaching into my purse for the mugshot I'd stolen from Fischer's file.

We flattened it on the countertop together, considering Lucas Driscoll in black and white. The mugshot was several years old, predating his city haircut. His hair was shaggy and he sported a thick beard, his eyes clear but no less black. His convictions were listed in ascending order: breaking and entering, resisting arrest, simple battery, domestic violence. What made one type of battery *simple*? The cashier tugged on his goatee.

"How about him?" I asked.

"Nah. I'd remember him."

"I need to make some copies. You know where I can find a copy machine around here?"

"There's one in the back. I can do it for you if you want to wait. Five cents each."

"That would be great. Could you blow hers up a little?" I counted the bills in my wallet. "I could get fifty each."

"Give me a minute. I gotta ring this guy up first."

I stepped back to wait for the man to select his hot dog and spread open my map on the flat surface of the ice cream cooler, tracing the highways with my fingertip, the varied paths they cut through the state. The options, as I saw them, were few. If Penny was looking to hitch a ride to Pomoc, she would head back on the highway the way I came. But Fischer, or any of the local precincts that received her photograph, should be watching those truck stops, and would hopefully spot her along the way. The other options were to head south to Vegas, or west to Reno, hitting smaller casinos on the way. Lastly, truckers from the Midwest hauling freight to California would take local freeways to the 80 before connecting to the I-5, taking the Grapevine that looped south, into California's gullet. If Penny was serious about Hollywood, I should follow her there, where even if her luck turned sour, she could push farther south to a cluster of Indian casinos a hundred miles from the border. Alvaro's words echoed in my mind, even though I wanted Penny to prove him wrong. *Where could she go? Not far.*

The clerk rang up the man's hot dog and disappeared in the back. I folded the map. There was a second, smaller rotary stand by the register bearing postcards with casino nightscapes; the Leaspoke's spread of electric feathers, the churning waterwheels of East River Mills, an aerial shot of the new, glittering Vegas, her sleek, modern lines lit up brighter than a nuclear test site. I grabbed one for Cesar and slipped it into Penny's purse. When the attendant returned I borrowed a marker and wrote Fischer's number across the top of one of the yearbook copies, sliding it back over.

"In case you see her," I said.

I watched him tape the flyer to the cash register. Penny's profuse grin would be the last thing customers would see when they checked out. It was a face I knew they wouldn't forget. I stopped myself from giving him a copy of Driscoll's mug shot to tape up alongside, as if by keeping their photos far apart, I might spare Penny his company in real life, too.

"Good luck," the cashier said.

57

Leaving Fischer's house, I took Main Street to the freeway, watching Pomoc grow smaller and smaller in the rearview until it finally disappeared. From here, anywhere was possible: Washoe, Tehacama, Reno, Carson, Carr. The freeways between these places were black and hungry, split open like rattlesnakes drying in the sun. With one hand on the wheel, I unzipped the duffel and shoved Penny's yellow folder inside. The radio was still set to her favorite oldies station; I forced myself to sing along. When I looked over, I could see Penny in the passenger seat, twisting a strand of dark hair around a finger, examining the exquisite angles of her face in the side mirror. Rubbing strawberry lip gloss on her fat bottom lip.

After an hour of driving, I took the detour through a series of old mountain roads, corkscrewing up one of the dry gravel faces, flattening down the opposite side into rock-strewn sand. After ten minutes the radio gave out, dwindling into buzz. I moved cautiously up another long, sharp bend, but when the road began to dip and level on the other side, I stepped on it to make up time, speeding too fast to avoid the great cloud of dust picking up a couple yards in the distance, coalescing into a funnel. There was no time to shut the windows before it swept down the road, heading directly for the truck. A

cacophony of sand and rock hit at once, pinging off the windshield
and doors, pelting the exposed flesh of my face and arms, obscuring
every mirror. I braked hard, a dry, earthy taste filled my nose and
mouth. This was what it felt like to be buried alive.

A few moments later, the noise began to drop away and the spray
eased. I opened my eyes to a mist of sand particles drifting past the
windshield, catching in the light. My hands were shaking, not from
the dust cloud, but from the truck's dead spin two weeks earlier, the
sandman parked just a little off the road to the right. I could already
feel how much of my life would be spent trying to recover a feeling of
carelessness I hadn't known to treasure.

When the last specks of grit fell away, the innocuous world reappeared; the sun bright, the sky clear. But it was almost too quiet; no
rustling brush, not a single bird. I was stopped in the middle of a road.
There were no cars behind and none ahead. I unzipped the duffel
again, digging deep for Fischer's gun. I closed my hand around its
solid weight and moved it to the truck's console within easy reach.

If this desert was a mother, she was the type to eat her young. I
didn't want to be alone when darkness fell and she let out her coyotes,
her cats, her men. A few feet ahead, another cyclone of dirt began to
lift and spin, taking thin form in the breeze.

61

Inside my room at the Leaspoke, I stood in front of the mirror naked and dripping wet, considering the narrow-hipped girl in the mirror, skin still tawny from her mountain hike. I took out Penny's lipstick from the front pocket of the duffel bag and applied it carefully to my open mouth. It looked like an accident, a gaping wound. The lipstick made it impossible to go unnoticed, but Penny had never wanted to be invisible, just the opposite. I pulled on a short jean skirt, the kind Penny would wear, and a black top. I slipped the hotel keys into Penny's purse along with a pair of twenties from the coffee can and the glossy page ripped from our high school yearbook, folded into fourths. When I was ready to leave I sat down on the edge of the bed. I could hear others in the hotel just checking in or returning from dinner, their luggage rolling down the hall, the sound of showers turned on and off, the thump of a suitcase dropped on the floor. I took the phone and dialed Fischer's number. On the second ring, he answered.

"Hi," I said.

"Cale? Are you all right?" At the sound of his voice, a liquid warmth suffused my extremities. "Where are you?"

"Not far."

"Where? I'll pick you up."

"I don't want to be picked up."

"I don't care what you want."

"I can describe your bedroom, the mole on your dick. The way you enjoy fucking young girls."

There was a long silence on the other end of the line.

"You don't know what you're doing," he said. "I want to help you. I drove by your place. I met your neighbor, Jackson?"

"Why did you do that?"

"Whatever you're thinking, it's the worst idea you've ever had. You shouldn't have taken that file."

"Did you see the dogs?"

"I can find you in about ten seconds if I want to."

"Yes, but only if you want to." From somewhere in the hall outside came a woman's laugh, a heavy hotel door slamming shut.

"I'm too old to play hide and seek, Cale. That's not what this is."

"What is it?" I forced myself, though I didn't drive all this way just to ask.

"I owe you an apology," Fischer said.

I laughed, a spontaneous, terrifying sound.

"Listen to me. I don't know what I was thinking. I thought you were—that you had—" He tried again. "Listen to me. I made a mistake."

Suddenly I couldn't remember why I'd called. The satisfaction of dialing a long distance number, the idea of connection. I wanted to tell Fischer about the restaurant, the second exit, the muffins made by a baking prodigy in Sparks. It had all seemed so important moments ago, but now nothing felt right. Did it matter whether Penny left from the restaurant, if Penny left at all? Penny was formless, Penny was vapor. Penny was too smart to ever end up on the other end of a phone call like this one. I remembered the women from the talk show all those years ago. *What are you punishing yourself for?*

"For Christ sakes. I'm forty-three years old." Fischer's voice was caught between degrees of apology, a grasp for authority. He sought to cling to it, recalling his badge, his career, his proficiency fielding questions from needling, concerned townspeople. *Your friend disappeared sometime between the hours of then and now. Your friend is nowhere and everywhere at once. I am forty-three years old. You might not have noticed when I was fucking your brains out, but just in case you didn't, let me tell you again. I am most certainly forty-three years old.*

I closed my eyes. When I opened them I saw Penny in the mirror, leaning back on an elbow on the bed, wrapping a long chunk of black hair around her index finger, rolling her eyes as Fischer prattled on. She was doing the thing she had begun to do in my dreams, speaking without even moving her mouth. Our brains had formed a psychic connection, the vibration between two allied souls.

Men, she seemed to say. *Am I right?*

"So right," I said.

Fischer stopped talking. Coughed into the line. "Cale? Is someone else with you?"

"No one you know."

"Listen to me. You've had a hard time. I understand. I just don't want you doing anything rash."

"So give me a novel idea."

But before he could answer, Penny stood up from the bed. She was giving me a look I had seen before. She took the receiver from my hand and set it down gently on the cradle.

We don't even need him, she seemed to say. *Do we? There are so many fun things we can do. I'll show you exactly where to look.*

80

A PRAYER FOR
TRAVELERS

May those you love be
near you in thoughts and
dreams.

May the business that
brought you our way
prosper.

May every call you
make and every message
you receive add to your
joy.

When you leave, may your
journey be safe.

We are all travelers. From
birth till death we travel
between the eternities.

27

We drove in silence, going slowly now, the zombie gone, every bump of tires on the gravel sending a new, uncomfortable awareness between my legs. I kept the brights on as we inched along, the challenge of finding the freeway in the dark made more difficult by a film of tears. I wasn't sure we were headed in the right direction until we came upon the fork in the road. I slammed the brakes, the truck shuddering, bisecting the lane. We were blocking any traffic that might come by, but let a car come now. Let it come.

"God, you're a mess," Penny said. She bent over in her seat and lifted the puppy from his crate. She held the noiseless animal underneath her chin. Penny, already recovered. Penny, battery-operated, a switch flipped from sanity to fervor and back again.

Was I hallucinating, or had the black outside our windows become infinitely more dark? We were in a hole. We were nowhere. At any moment we would hear the zombie again, the snare drum of his engine rumbling behind.

"Do we go left or right?" My voice was hoarse.

"You know."

I looked to the left, past her window, then right. Each seemingly a blank obsidian wall. Nothing revealed, nothing shared.

"I actually don't know," I said.

"We have to turn around. Go back."

"Are you crazy?"

She averted her face for a moment, replacing the puppy in his crate, before she looked at me. "What if he finds us?"

"He doesn't even know our names!"

"His mother does. We told his mother our names, where we were from."

I wiped the snot from my nose onto the leg of my jeans. The denim was still damp across the right thigh where the sandman had lost control of his bladder, the sharp smell permeating the cab's confined space. Was it him I smelled, or the new dog? I rolled with another wave of nausea. My head was pounding.

"Cale—"

"It's the stupidest thing I've ever heard."

"Do you want to keep wondering if he's going to find us? Our whole lives."

"You're talking about killing someone!" I screamed it, slammed the heel of my palm down into the steering wheel, the bleat of the horn echoing out across the desert. The words reverberated off the windows. I wrapped my hands around the wheel so tight I thought they might burst. If a car came now, Penny would see it first; it would barrel into my door, crushing us. I wanted the car to come.

"What do you think he was going to do to us? Walk us home?"

Without wanting to, I felt his warm hand spreading across my bare stomach, my body clenching in response, trying to shrink itself inside. Already I knew I would keep some part of that feeling forever, flinching at every creak in the floorboards.

"So his mother knows our names," I said. "And if he never makes it home, you don't think she's going to go looking for him? She isn't going to give the police our names?"

"She knows what he is."

"I can't."

"Turn the car around."

"I am pretty fucking sure I get a say in this! We're not turning around so you can murder him!"

She turned her face to the window, but not before I saw her grimace. Penny, unrecovered. Penny, only passing.

I took my foot off the brake. The fury split me open like a seed at the belly, sprouting a slippery green plumule hungry for light. Because I wanted to turn back, too. I was dying to.

"It's probably already too late," she said.

62

There was a bar at the Leaspoke but I knew, even without Penny to tell me, that it wasn't the bar she would have visited. Penny wanted to go to all the places she had not yet been, to traffic in new and varying kinds of danger that might differ from all manner of danger in which she already excelled. In the lobby, I snagged a laminated map of nearby attractions and headed out the door, bypassing the parking lot to the street. There was a gray, drizzling evening sky like a damp cloth laid over tired eyes. Cars and trucks sped by, a large, white paneled van honked, the blare fading down the road. I touched the corners of my mouth, conscious of the new lipstick spreading.

Half a mile from the Leaspoke, I stopped at the Lonestar Bar & Casino, passing a dozen mud-spattered Harleys parked outside. The rustic pioneer aesthetic was all too familiar, but the fraying mulberry carpets conveyed warmth, and the unfinished walls reminded me of our floors at home, the feel of bare wood worn smooth underfoot. There was a small crowd gathered inside, mostly men, a handful of couples, their attention absorbed by a flatscreen TV mounted in a high corner, a basketball game playing on low volume. I recognized the favorite jerseys, the leanly muscled sports star and his easy, backward lope across the court. I took a seat near a row of bikers who swelled the length of the bar, leaving only a few empty seats at the far end, the last one occupied by a tall, slim man in a baseball cap who hunched away from them as if guarding his stein of beer, glancing up occasionally to check the score on his screen, fingering the brim of his baseball cap. Imaginary Penny was gone, though I could have used her company, sidling up on a barstool nearby. Why had we never done anything so simple? Could we ever do something simple again?

The youngest of the bikers was at least five years my senior with thickset shoulders and dirty, shoulder-length hair he tucked behind his ears with studied disregard. He saw me looking and signaled the others before heading off in the opposite direction toward the bathrooms with a long, ropy walk, as if all the time he spent straddling a bike had permanently altered his gait. The farther I traveled this way, the more bikers I would find, buzzing in pocketed formations on the freeways like clouds of black bees, rushing down long mountain passes to split around a slow-moving car, streaming together in the distance to meet the bends. On the road they were mythic, but in the reclaimed setting of the bar they were simply men again: dethroned, unmasked. When the young biker returned from the bathrooms, patting his damp hands against his jeans, he loped over to where I sat, skittering his eyes over my own.

"Buy you a beer," he said.

Among the endless row of glass bottles and draft knobs, Lamb's brand was missing, the kind he drank his entire life, the one I wanted to taste again like a live memory. The bartender was polishing a rocks glass with a dishtowel, pretending not to notice I had come in and sat down, that I was too young to do either.

"I'll have what you're having," I said.

He grinned, revealing a chipped front tooth. I was saying all the right things, or else it was clear I was hopelessly out of depth. He leaned over my crossed legs to the bar to order, his shirt riding up to reveal an inch of his low, pale back, the dryer-eaten waistband of his briefs. I expected we might not be served, but the bartender didn't ask for ID. He grabbed a pair of pint glasses and filled them without a word, sliding them down the bar. How much easier it would have been if I could have done the same—avoided asking questions when I knew their answers would complicate my life.

The biker picked up his glass and waited for me to follow suit. I tasted the beer, peatier than Lamb's brand, more substantial than the watery cans Penny had brought to Rena's. I took a long drink and imagined I could already begin to feel the effects, a tingling in my hands and feet. And maybe I could. I had forgotten to eat again. My appetite had dwindled and my body was deteriorating right along with it, as if I could secret myself away pound by pound, coyly pursuing Penny into the ether. The biker took a sip of his own beer, preoccupied already, squinting at a spot on my throat. I touched my neck reflexively.

"What is it?"

"You have something. A hickey."

"Maybe it's a bug bite," I said.

He laughed, appreciative. "Maybe it's a rash," he said. "I'm PJ, by the way."

"I'm looking for a Lucas Driscoll. A Penny."

"You're too pretty to go looking for anyone, aren't you? Dudes should come looking for you."

I took another sip. "Sometimes they do."

"Really, what are you doing here by yourself?"

"Trying to find a friend."

"This guy Lucas?"

"No, a girl." I stood up and pulled out the glossy page I had torn out of our yearbook before leaving Pomoc, Penny's senior photo in a row with other boys and girls, their smooth cheeks and youthful smiles. I watched him unfold the paper on the bar. I had circled Penny's image with a casino pen again and again, manifesting an inky black orbit around her face. PJ glanced over at the other bikers, but they were paying us no mind. The bartender had already gone back to pretending I didn't exist. PJ looked at me.

"How old are you?"

"It's an old photograph."

He folded the sheet carefully, handing it back. "Haven't seen her. Sorry."

"It's important."

"Most people don't walk around bars carrying yearbook photos." He nodded as I put it away. "You want another drink?"

"No, not yet," I said, but when I looked back at the bar, my glass was already empty, froth sliding down the side. Behind us, a group of college boys slammed their bottles down on their table, the basketball star sinking a three-pointer. I noticed for the first time how many men were in the room, their incredible, heated focus as the game was beginning to turn. Only the lone, tall figure at the end of the bar seemed unmoved under his baseball cap, reaching up to scratch his stubbled jaw. As if he could feel my stare, he shot a look down the length of the bar. I froze. He froze, too. Slowly, the man returned his attention to the TV, and in the seconds that followed I classified symptoms of a body betrayed: heart pounding, palms damp. I considered excusing myself to find a phone and redialing Fischer's number. How could I be sure?

"Are you all right?" The biker clasped my thigh, keeping me from falling off the stool. I felt my face flush hot. I replayed my earlier call with Fischer in my mind, how casually I disconnected. Before I left the hotel room, I aimed his gun at my reflection. But when I imagined pulling the trigger, I hesitated. At the last minute, I had left the gun behind.

"I don't know," I said.

"Where are you staying?"

"Just down the street. The Leaspoke."

"Let's go there. I'll walk you."

Too late I realized I shouldn't have named the casino out loud, squandering my last margin of safety. I would have to remind myself not to smile at men in bars, not to look at them, not to wear skirts or tight jeans, not to accept drinks or refuse them, not to walk alone or alongside them, not to appear rude or too inviting. Tomorrow I'd buy a cell phone and keep it with me at all times. I'd never again drive so fast, and so far into the desert as to render it useless.

The biker turned away to confer with his friends, but kept hold of my hand. When he was ready, he walked me out through the main lobby of the casino, past the foyer cluttered with antique wooden benches. The front doors were propped open. We heard the rain before we saw it, crashing off the casino awning, pelting the windshields of cars and the gravel outside. Despite its fervor, it wouldn't last. It might pour through the night, but there would be nothing to keep me from the road in the morning. So I would leave again; so I had made the decision without conscious design. Maybe it had been the same with Penny. One drink with Lucas Driscoll, then another. Lamb's first lie, an omission, folding into the next.

I stood at the threshold of the casino's entrance, the mist dampening my skin, curling the fine strands of hair around my face. The biker came up beside me and bent his head to mine for a kiss. I turned so that his lips grazed my jaw, the marks on my neck. I cupped the back of his head, staring past him down the long hall of the casino where the tall man from the end of the bar was just stepping out onto the frayed carpet, looking first one way and then another, as if searching for the bathrooms, a friend, some mislaid purpose. Had Penny stood in this same spot a few weeks earlier? PJ sensed my distraction and pulled away, the movement catching the stranger's eye from the hall. The man stared, the distance between us still too far to make out his exact expression, his eyes obscured by the low brim of his hat. But I could sense the tension in his body, the angle of his jaw.

I stepped backward into the rain, the shock of cold rain dousing my hair, freezing the crown of my head, my bare arms and legs. I ran toward the Leaspoke, gasping at the thrill, my own miraculous speed. It felt like flying, like the slow soar from the highest swing of our grade school playground, until I crashed through the lobby of the Lea-spoke and slipped in my boots on the polished hall, shooting out a hand to steady myself against one of the casino columns. I hurried to the elevators and slammed the button again and again until it came, shivering the whole ride up to the twelfth floor.

Inside my room, I turned the duffel bag upside down on the mat-tress, sorting through the jeans and underwear and rolled-up socks to grab Fischer's bright yellow file and shake out his notes, the surveil-lance photos, Lucas Driscoll's mugshot and arrest record listed in black and white. Though several years old, the mug was clearer than any casino eye-in-the-sky. A drop of water from my nose landed smack on the page, bleeding the image, fuzzing a spot by his ear. The high, smooth cheekbones could have been the same, the dark hair sticking out the bottom of his baseball cap. In the photo the man's mouth was set on edge, as if biting his tongue. I understood how sleeplessness and hunger and grief could eat away at reality, bending experience into phantasm. Hadn't I imagined Penny on this selfsame bed only hours before, stretching on the coverlet like a lioness?

It was a question of possibilities. If the man in the photograph could have been the man at the Lonestar, if one person could be so brazen as to disappear and reappear consistently in your life, while others you longed for stayed gone, impervious to the depth of your yearning for their return. I walked away from the bed to the bathroom and turned on the light. I began to peel off my wet things, shucking my shorts in a corner. I arranged my T-shirt over the shower rod with cold hands, then sat down on the toilet seat, listening to rainwater drip from the hem.

58

The second time I drove to Carr, I was alone. In the midday light, the narrowing of freeways felt familiar, the fork in the road, the demarcation of the dirt road from gravel, the small metal mailboxes with their eager scarlet tongues. Only the distance remained unchanged, the feeling of time stretching across the miles. The gas cans I filled in Nye clattered in the truck bed with every bump of my tires. I didn't want to stop for any reason, or allow for the burden of unencumbered thought. I drove through the back of the hamlet and pulled the truck under a pine tree, the lower boughs partly obscuring the truck's windows, the rearmost portion of an abandoned Winnebago. From where I parked, I had a partial view of the peach trailer. If the zombie had been parked out front, I would have seen something of its monstrous girth when I entered the park and circled around. That it was missing probably meant the sandman was, too. Still it was a relief not to have to see it. That giant, hulking shape, the memory of its blinding light cage cutting through the dark.

I worried I'd fall asleep while waiting; that in a community as small as this one, some nosy neighbor would inevitably feel compelled to stop by the cab and knock insistently on my window, interrogating my purpose. Only after the minutes began to accumulate—twenty, thirty, an hour—did I realize how wrong I'd been. In a community as small as this one, there was a compound interest in minding one's business, in making peace with difficult neighbors, in living and letting live.

An hour later, a slim woman in a long printed dress ducked out from a vintage rollaway, a plastic hamper balanced on her hip. I watched her set the hamper on the ground and pull a wet sheet from the basket, shaking the twisted fabric free. She pinned a corner of the sheet to a clothesline with a wooden pin, then walked the sagging fabric along the length of the line, placing another in the middle of the sheet, a third at the opposite end. She returned to the hamper, bending to retrieve a clumped fitted sheet. Halfway through, she seemed to run out of clothespins. A moment of consideration, a breeze ruffling stray curls around her face, her hand seeking her hip's perch. Then she was moving again, draping the remaining pillowcases over the line unsecured. She picked up the basket and disappeared inside.

After she was gone I slipped out the passenger door and unbuttoned my pants, squatting by the back tires to relieve the pressure that had been building for miles. I climbed back inside the truck to wait, sweating again. I unlocked the glove box and fished through weathered copies of car insurance and old gas station receipts to find a handful of stale peanuts. More than three hours after I first arrived, the front door to the peach trailer opened and the rasp-voiced mother stepped out, her dark hair pulled into a messy ponytail. She spoke over her shoulder to someone still inside before letting the door slam shut behind her. She walked a few yards to a row of cars parked along the perimeter of the hamlet and unlocked the door of a red compact, the roof sunken in as if an asteroid had fallen from the sky years before and landed there, and no one had ever thought to fix it.

I felt a wave of nausea watching the woman start her car and back carefully out of the spot, a sparkling white hatred. Yet she had done nothing wrong. She had simply birthed a child, the same as Catherine's daughter, and Catherine before her. Children emerged in variability, for better or worse. When I felt certain she was really gone, I adjusted the strap of Penny's purse across my chest and forced myself to get out of the car, easing the door shut.

I had imagined a million different scenarios for this moment: a break-in, a holdup, a masked army flanking my back in solidarity, guns drawn. In reality, I simply knocked on the door. For a long while, nothing happened. Then the metal door screeched back on its hinges. The sandman stood in front of me, stooping as if under some psychic weight, white gauze wrapped around his skull like a cockeyed halo. He took me in slowly, his blue eyes limpid, uncertain, stripped of their once fierce, blazing intent. The longer I stared, the tighter the furrow between his brows became, as if he had an inkling of why I'd come and a storm was threatening to gather in response. Before his fury made it to the surface, he looked away and took a step back from the door. He wandered away as if he'd forgotten why he'd come at all. I was left alone at the threshold.

I stepped inside and pulled the door shut behind me. The baby gate was gone, the puppies, too, though the dank animal smell remained. Hank lay sprawled on the couch like a weary lion. He tucked his great furred head between his paws, watchful but silent. The sandman was ambling deeper inside the trailer, disappearing down the hall. I felt a sudden desperate thirst, as if I were the one who had been left in the desert for dead and only just crawled my way back, dusty and parched. I moved into the kitchen and took a jelly glass drying on the dishrack, filling it under the tap. I drank it down in three gulps and filled it again. When I was done I picked up the rubber gloves hanging over the

faucet and wriggled them on. I washed the glass. On the kitchen counter was a spice rack, an innocuous pair of faux crystal salt and pepper
shakers, a knife block. I dabbed the gloves on the dishtowel and pulled
out the chef's knife, examining the blade. Then the bread knife, the
blade long and serrated like alligator teeth. The paring knife fit in the
palm of my hand, easy to maneuver, probably the best for close work.
I slid it back in its slot. Wouldn't it be better to leave people and places
and things just as they were, to stop before sending more ripples into
a restilled pond?

From somewhere inside the trailer, a television turned on. I followed the noise down the hall until I came upon him in a small, claus-
trophobic bedroom in the back, propped up on a pile of pillows. He
was watching old cartoons on a small TV, Tom chasing Jerry all the
way up a long, winding staircase, then back down again. He made no
acknowledgment of me but reached for the nightstand. I lurched farther into the room, but it was only a bowl of cereal he wanted. He
picked it up, cradling the bowl in his giant palm, tucking it underneath his chin. He spooned soggy flakes into his mouth, chewed
slowly. Did I really know if he could speak?

"Look at me."

My hands were beginning to go numb again, but they had been
capable, they might still obey simple commands. I reached for the
purse, pulling out Fischer's gun. This weight was so unlike the tire
iron in the truck, so much easier to lift: one tool never meant for violence, the other made in its image. I moved deeper into the room and
came alongside the bed; I set a knee on the mattress and raised the
gun in my hands. I bent incrementally closer, until the tip of the gun
brushed past his bandage, sinking into his sand-colored hair, the
muzzle trembling against his skull. It would be just like shooting a

squirrel, like shooting a watermelon. It would be like none of those things.

"Do you know who I am?"

Still he didn't look up, his expression focused toward the television set, a lamblike unconcern.

"I'm going to tell you who I am," I said.

63

Early the next morning I checked out of the Leaspoke, then headed downstairs to the restaurant. A dishwater blonde with a lip piercing was laying out breakfast as Norma had promised, stacking cereal bowls and coffee cups on the tablecloth, overloading a plate with cinnamon rolls and bagels, a pyramid of bulbous muffins. The bar was already open, Bloody Marys on five-dollar special. In the corner of the room I saw the rear exit Norma had mentioned. It was early for breakfast; I had beaten the tourists, but there was already an elderly man at the bar nursing a beer, looking like he had yet to go to bed. A younger man in a casino uniform poured coffee from a carafe directly into his travel mug. I stepped up to the spread of pastries with Penny's yearbook photo in hand, holding it up for the blonde behind the table to see. She glanced at it warily, already annoyed.

"I'm wondering if you can help me," I said. "My friend stayed at this hotel a couple weeks ago and never came home. Can you tell me if you've seen her?"

The girl snapped her gum. "Isn't that the girl the police were here about?"

"Yes. No one's heard from her since."

"Are you here with some cops?" She took her time to blow a large pink bubble before snapping that, too. "Do I need to call security?"

"No! I'm just a friend of hers. I paid for my room. I'm leaving. Can you tell me if you've seen her?"

"Yeah," she said. "I saw her."

"When?"

"I don't know. A few days before the cops showed up. Pretty, right? I could have told them. They didn't ask me. They asked the dealers on the floor. The manager told us that."

"You really saw her?"

"She took a muffin and some coffee, yeah. Then she went back inside."

"She didn't leave through that back door?"

The girl swiveled around to look at the rear exit, as if just noticing it was there. When she turned back she was making a face, as if my question was a complication she hadn't bothered to consider.

"I don't think so. I'm pretty sure she was going back to her room. I guess if she came back later she could have left that way. Why? She's your friend?"

"Yes. And she's still missing."

"I mean, she's not a very good friend if she didn't call you."

"The police think something might have happened to her. If she came back later, could she have used that back door without you seeing?"

"If it's slow I'm in the back."

"Aren't there cameras in here?"

"Listen," the girl said, "this isn't the Venetian, okay? I mean, there are cameras in front, in the lobby. And the gaming floor, duh. I know because they arrested a grip of people for skimming the house. But

I've worked here for over a year and if there's a camera in here—first of all, that's super creepy, because they don't tell us shit, and second of all, the manager's a perv so I don't even want to know where he's got them going." She leaned in, close enough that I could smell the bubble gum on her breath. "What do they think happened to her?"

I folded up the yearbook photo, zipping it into the front compartment of the duffel. Like PJ the night before, the girl seemed to relax once the photo was put away. I picked up a muffin, pretending to be interested. "What is this, poppy? I heard some woman in Sparks makes these."

"You know she won some fair? The grocery store's going to start selling them."

"They look great." I set the muffin on a plate. "When you saw Penny, how did she seem? Did she look like she might be in trouble?"

"I don't know. She was wearing sunglasses. Big ones like . . ."

"Like a movie star."

"Hold on." The girl held up a finger, taken by a sudden idea. She disappeared into the back room. I waited for her to reemerge with a fresh clue, another employee, the Jake of this place who could explain the camera system, the tapes; how the world could lose a person and so few people could seem to care. Five minutes later the girl returned alone. She carried a white paper bag, bumpy and full.

"Oh," I said. "Thank you."

"Whatever," she said. "I hope you find your friend."

65

The rain stopped and left behind more temperate weather; supple, prolonged afternoons, sable evenings dipping into chill. I drove through Virginia City's downtown peppered with locals, through a series of back roads thronged by unkempt cottonwood trees. The hostel was a refurbished cabin painted an intrepid cornflower blue. I walked along the length of the building, scanning the dusty windows for some clue as to what lay inside. Near the front of the building I caught sight of a hollowed-out face in the reflection, sharp in the chin and cheeks. Striking, if only in the moment before I recognized it as my own, pared away from the previous life that marked it strange.

The interior of the Prickly Pine was quaint; a rose-patterned couch, a crowded array of porcelain squirrels suspended on the fireplace, a crocheted doily covering the TV stand, its black screen covered by an inch of dust. On the wall a corkboard was covered with pastel flyers advertising English lessons, AA meetings, paranormal support counselors, movers for hire. A hefty, straw-haired woman sat behind an inset counter with the type of pale, nondescript features that would be difficult to describe later if she ever disappeared. She worked on a book of crossword puzzles behind the desk, her mechanical pencil poised. When she looked up I met a pair of watery gray eyes trapped behind clear plastic frames.

"How much for a single night?"

She gestured to a blackboard behind the desk, the rates printed in chalk. "Fifteen. Cheaper if you stay awhile."

I dug into Penny's purse and slid her a twenty. She passed me the change and stood up, grabbing a key from a lockbox of hooks behind the desk.

"You don't have to tell me your name," she said, "but give me something to call you."

"Cale." *If something happens to me, tell them my name is Cale.*

"I'm Martha," she said, shuffling around the desk. Generous in the hips and thighs, a childbearer with a family somewhere to miss her. "Cale, I don't know how much you know about us out here in Virginia City, but we have lots to love and plenty to do. Have you been to the miner's museum? The opera house? We have a cultural center on R Street where you can take painting classes, ceramics, knitting. I do believe they offer glassblowing. Just ask if you want a brochure."

She stopped midway down the hall in front of a groove-paneled door and turned the key. The room was painted the same impossible blue as the cabin's exterior. Inside it felt like I was moving within an ocean or a tear, treading water through Poseidon's tumultuous feelings. There was a single set of bunk beds flanking either wall, boasting identical lapis-colored sheets pulled into tight hospital corners, thick navy fleeces folded down at the feet of the beds, a small square notecard propped on every pillow. I set my duffel bag on the bottom bunk closest to the door and picked up the prayer card, scanning its message. I stepped up the ladder to peek at the top mattress. They were all the same.

"Did you want a brochure?" Martha asked.

"No, thank you."

A set of steel lockers along the wall hung open, all the cubbies empty. There was no luggage in the room. It was off-season, and business was slow. I was surprised by my own disappointment. The longer I was away from Pomoc, the more I missed my childhood bedroom, the house I grew up in, the sanctuary of a family made up of even a single other person, and that, creating a world. I reached in the duffel bag and pulled out one of the gas station copies of Penny's yearbook photo, handing it to her. Martha unfolded it warily. "What's this?"

"Have you seen her? She's a friend of mine. She disappeared from home a few weeks ago. She might have passed through this area at some point."

"I don't think so. Who is she?"

"Just a friend. She's missing."

Martha's expression, not unlike that of casino personnel and waiters and gas station attendants and bus depot drivers from Pomoc to Virginia City and everywhere in between: bewilderment, distaste, a sudden desire to distance themselves from me and whatever tragedy I'd managed to court. She handed the flyer back, clapping her hands together when they were free.

"I didn't tell you about the movie theater!" she exclaimed. "And did you see the rotary out there in the main room, on the side table? Local calls are free. Long distance I've got to charge you a dollar a minute. When I'm not here you're on the honor system, just write down your calls on the pad by the phone."

She turned around to leave.

"You're going to want a brochure," she said.

66

The Twin Desert Cinemas played double features at midday, six bucks a pop. Even with matinee prices, I was the only one in line for the three o'clock show, peeling a bill from Penny's dwindling supply. I stood under the neon glow of the convenience stand and ordered a popcorn from the skinny teenage usher, his ruddy cheeks pockmarked with acne. I pegged him for a sophomore, the new school year only recently begun. He must have shot up several inches over the summer because his movements were jerky, spastic, an unoiled tin man growing into new arms and legs, the incalculable degree of power required to motor through a stride. He reached for a stack of flat popcorn boxes on a high shelf and brought the whole pile crashing down on his head. I watched him build them one by one, springing to life like cardboard castles in his hands.

I carried the popcorn through the carpeted halls, up an illuminated staircase to a row of seats in the middle of the theater. I leaned back, propping my feet on the back of a chair. When the lights dimmed I began the detailed work of scrutinizing the nameless faces studding club scenes and restaurant tables behind the famous actors, the kind of roles Penny the fledgling actress might one day score for her debut: a beautiful woman laughing in candlelight over a romantic table for

two; a pair of girlfriends at a mall, rifling carelessly through the clothing racks. The studied way one extra considered herself in front of a
mirror, pulling at her dress with two fingers, arranging the fabric
across her body. I watched the same movies again and again, determined not to miss a single anonymous face. Weren't people like this,
too? All of us moving through the peripheries of each other's lives until
the winds changed: an orphaned baby discovered on a hospital table,
a father answering the phone in the middle of an afternoon, a waitress
pouring coffee for a familiar face across the counter. One unsettled
man living apart in a desert township, returning from a routine errand
to find two young women manifested in his mother's home.

Toward the end of the film, a sliver of lemon-colored light sliced
across the dark. The usher's gangly shadow appeared at the side entrance, lurching along the front row to take a seat so close to the
screen he must have sprained his neck looking up. If I could have spoken to him, if I didn't feel that something had come in the night and
carried away all my words and the ability to use them, I would have
asked, *What is it about endings?* They compelled him, every day I had
come, to steal into the theater during the last twenty minutes of a film.
We both sat quietly, watching the pictures spin their artful fallacies,
their myths of resolution. I would have spoken to him if not for the
distance I would have had to travel across his apathy and my own,
trespassing into the secret, silent world he had taken such obvious
care to build. I could only imagine the manner of questions he might
turn back on me, the lengths I would go to to avoid them. *Who are
you? Why do you come here? What is it you're looking for?* And I
would only have been able to answer the last and most elusive, the
answer only recently made clear. *All the lives she should have had, all
the lives she could have, still.*

When the movie was over, we remained seated until the credits finished rolling and the overhead lights eased on. Leaving was the worst part, the drive back to the Prickly Pine never long enough to lift the weariness of repetition, weeks spent asking the same questions of different faces and learning nothing new. *Have you seen this girl?*

I gathered my popcorn and the sweater I'd peeled off mid-film, the days just turned cool enough to call for one. When I stood up, I heard the plastic crinkling from a bag of candy. I froze. The theater had been empty when I took my seat a couple hours before. Had I been so easily distracted by a familiar storyline that I hadn't noticed a person entering the theater behind me, settling in one of the nearby rows? I turned around and felt the blood leave my face. He walked down into the aisle between us, one hand in his pocket, the other clenched into a fist. He wore the same baseball cap I had seen him in at the Lonestar, but under the theater's full lights there wasn't any chance of mistaken identity. High cheekbones and dark hair, a peculiarly set mouth. He hadn't bothered to shave; his stubble filled in to a low beard. If he made a move in my direction, I would run. I felt a new, cold certainty staring at him across the aisle. He would never touch me. I would do anything to keep myself from being touched.

"I heard you're looking for me," he said.

67

Inside the Golden Bear, locals milled through a polished, wood-paneled foyer that fed into a cozy dining room bar, the walls studded with buck heads and mounted shotguns, a giant axe in a glass-paneled shadow box. I took a seat in a back booth under a large American flag and watched the fat, thin, dark, pale, strange, sad people arrive; the groups of men and women clutching at one another's hands and faces, raising their glasses as if revelry might insulate them from future harm. I scanned them for something or someone recognizable, as if Penny might spontaneously appear among them, prepared to console me through all manner of peril I had already experienced, the gamble I was taking now. I adjusted the long, thin strap of her purse between my breasts, kicking myself for not bringing Fischer's gun to the movie theater. But I couldn't pull a gun on Lucas Driscoll in a theater or a bar, no matter how much I might want to. If he was the kind of man Fischer said he was, I doubted it would make any difference.

Lucas had gone to the bar to place our order. I watched him move back through the crowd in my direction, slick as an eel. He returned with glasses aplenty; a beer for him, a Coke for me, waters for us both. A murderer with beautiful manners. He slid into a seat across the table. Even with his resuscitated beard and the baseball cap pulled low, the girls at the bar had tilted their bodies toward him at his approach. He didn't have any trouble. The only thing I felt in his presence was anxiety, an impulse to withdraw the minute he sat down, to chase my mind where it scrabbled down a million fathomless holes—what he might have done to Penny, to the other woman whose name I didn't know. *Focus.* I took a sip of soda, not daring anything stronger. I wanted my mind clear.

"Enough people for you?" He took a sip of his beer and set it down. He tugged on the brim of his baseball cap, the same reflexive gesture I recalled from the Lonestar. It hid his eyes, highlighting his prominent cheekbones and the strange, tense way he held his mouth.

"Not really, no."

Those lips curling into a sardonic smile. "Who's afraid of the big bad wolf?"

I studied the ochre of his skin, the hand gripping his glass. All parts of him a perverse marvel, conjured from an image into life.

"Should I prepare to be eaten?"

He looked away, in dismissal or boredom, a quality of restlessness I couldn't parse. "You're safe enough."

"How do I know?"

"You never know. Only people trust each other sometimes."

"Where did that get my friend?"

He shrugged. "She was fine when she left me."

"And then what? Where did she go?"

He leaned in suddenly, his face closer to mine across the table. "Didn't you say you had something to show me?"

I hesitated. Around us there was an uptick of noise, a swell of bodies pressing through the door. I opened the purse under the table and felt for the flyer. I slid it across the table, watching him open it up, studying her face as if he hadn't been the last person to see it alive. He stared at it a minute before crumpling the flyer into a tight paper ball. He dropped it in his beer. I watched it float.

"Do you know how I found you?" he asked.

I peeled my eyes away from the floating ball, back to him. "I saw you at the Lonestar."

"And how did I find you there?"

"I don't know."

He leaned back, smiling briefly, the flash of a gold canine tooth, the creases near his eyes folding up. "You've been talking," he said. "Yapping. You were yapping to that boy at the bar. I found you at the Leaspoke easy, just by asking around. Yap, yap, yap. Lucky for you, I can't go back there, the cops are still crawling all over."

"I wish that were true. I didn't see any."

"You wouldn't, would you? You'd need to open your eyes. Well, imagine my surprise when I decided to lay low for a few days and stopped for gas on my way out of town. Guess what happened?" He lay his hand over mine on the table before I could withdraw. I felt the rough calluses of his palm brushing against my knuckles, a gentle pressure. "Guy says, Hey man, haven't I seen you before? Some girl comes in showing flyers. Passing around my fucking record." He squeezed my hand. "Imagine that."

I reached my free hand toward my Coke and took a long sip, my mouth gone dry. "It's possible I shouldn't have done that," I said.

"No? I don't know. Because here we are." His smile tightened another inch. I glanced at the tables around us, the revelers deep in their own private worlds.

"You're going to stop showing my photo around," he said.

"I can," I said.

"You will."

"I just want to know where you met my friend."

"She was wandering around the poker tables, but she wasn't making any bets. That'll tell you. We struck up a conversation. I bought her a drink."

"At the Leaspoke?"

"Where else?"

"You'd never seen her before?"

"Never."

"But your story—"

He cut me off with another squeeze of his hand. The irony wasn't lost on me, my futile resolution to remain untouched. "Not a story," he said. "I didn't touch her. I bought her a couple drinks and we went up to my room. She was so quiet, I got comfortable. Rookie mistake. When I got out of the bathroom, she was already gone. So was my wallet. If someone got to her after that, I don't know anything about it."

"She didn't say anything about where she might be going?"

"She didn't have much to say, period. I wouldn't be surprised if she didn't know. There was something . . ." He licked his lips, trying for a word just out of grasp.

"How did she look? How did she seem?"

"How would I know? I'd never seen her before."

"How much did she get from you?"

"Sixty bucks? Eighty?" He shrugged, slipped his hand free from my own. "Swiped a candy bar, too. If she bothered to look in my bag she could have cleaned me out."

Why would Penny follow this man anywhere? He was handsome enough—even now, he exuded a moody, edgy intrigue—but the quickening of my pulse signaled only menace, my antennae fine-tuned to threat. Yet if my intuition had only recently sharpened, Penny's had long been a spike. The wheels in my mind, churning now.

"So you saw me at the Lonestar," I said. "You knew where I was staying. How did you find me here? I would have noticed someone following me."

"Would you? Let's just say if you look for something hard enough, you can find it."

"But that's not true. I've been looking for Penny for weeks. If you're so good at tracking people—if you really had nothing to do with her going missing—you could find her. You could clear your name."

He stared at me a moment, nodded. "You're crazy. You know that?"

"If I'm crazy—" I didn't finish the thought. *What are you?* I was running his rap sheet, his list of crimes. I wanted to ask about the un-named woman; I knew I shouldn't. He flashed another unfocused smile, aimed at the table, the glasses, the dark shape he saw moving around my mind.

"I've always had what my mother would call delicate skin," he said. "Do you know what that means?"

"No."

"I don't like people saying terrible things."

"I didn't say anything."

"But you're thinking it," he said. "And that's just as bad."

I looked down at the stained table, the pool of condensation under-neath my glass. "It's not just me showing your photo. The police must be doing the same thing."

"You'd be surprised."

"Penny doesn't have a car," I said. "How did she get to the Lea-spoke? You say you've never been to Pomoc."

"What's in Pomoc? It seems like everyone's trying to go the other way." He reached for my glass and removed the straw, laying it on the table. He tilted his head back to drain his glass, his Adam's apple leaping in his throat. He slammed the glass back down on the table and grinned. "Hold that thought."

He stood up, heading for the bathrooms through the hall. I felt a degree of hopefulness flicker. *If you look for something hard enough, you can find it.* There was something like grudging respect in the way he spoke about Penny taking off with his money. He thought about things the way Penny did, he had angles. If he hadn't hurt Penny, if I could convince him to try to find her, I was sure he could. But how? I felt uncomfortable enough in his proximity, and we were in a room full of people. A few minutes ticked by, and with them, a degree of my conviction. After a little while I stood up from the table, following the path he had taken past the bar, down the hall to the men's bathroom. There was no one waiting in line. I hesitated, hoping someone else would show, but when no one did, I pushed the door open a crack, calling his name. There were two narrow stalls, a urinal, and a single small sink, the tap dribbling. No one looked to be inside. I went in then and bent over the porcelain sink, unsure whether I was going to be sick. Of course any man who managed to evade the police for months was not dumb enough to get caught by me. And on some level, I was grateful. The nausea passed and I straightened slowly, tightening the faucet, stopping the slight dribble of water. I studied the girl in the mirror, her face finally healed. A small scar, mostly hidden by my brow, that would remain always.

71

DEAD
OR
ALIVE

68

Indistinct Martha was missing from her post behind the Prickly Pine's front desk. I came upon her reclining on the living room couch, watching the evening news. She held a cross-stitched pillow against her chest the way a child would embrace a doll. At the sound of my boots she sat up, glancing over her shoulder as if surprised I should appear, invading her domestic picture. But the Pine was only a hostel, and she worked the front counter in shifts. Martha lived elsewhere, she had an entire other life sacred from this.

"Oh," she said, "come sit." She patted the couch beside her. Only Martha knew how many hours I spent locked inside my very blue room, its lurid intensity evoking a submerged chamber, the interior of a tank or a pool, a vibrant ship's hold, a secret hollow for sequester. Who would paint such a room? I wasn't even sure the Pine had any other residents. The first night, I thought I heard someone moving through the walls, and the next day I found a slippery shower stall in the communal bathroom down the hall, a damp hand towel hung askew by the sink, an iridescent bubble clinging to the bar of gardenia soap in its porcelain dish. But I had heard no one since. It was only Martha and me, tiptoeing around each other for nearly a week. The first night I'd shown Martha Penny's flyer, she had declined to speak.

But we had been strangers then. Were we still strangers now? I had forgotten how other humans interacted, I had grown rusty with any socialization beyond the most transactional. *Have you seen this girl?*

"What are you thinking?" she asked.

I took a seat on the edge of the couch. Martha turned down the volume. On the screen, a petite blond anchorwoman in a navy skirt stood up behind the news desk and walked across the studio to deliver the weather report. Strong, shapely legs; a conciliatory smile. She stopped in front of a green screen layered with a topographical map of the state, replete with dips and valleys, and gestured toward towns and not-quite-towns littered over the display like so many impractical jewels. These temperatures indicated how our skin might feel in the wild. Pomoc was never listed on these maps, nor any place like it. When Lamb and I watched the news, we considered the forecast for the two cities nearest to Pomoc on either side and approximated the difference. How to locate legitimacy on a map, value.

A short wand coalesced in the anchor's hand. She circled a churning white mass over Reno, drawing arrows pointing east. A cold jet stream reversing direction. The temperatures dipped for tomorrow's forecast, a blue cartoon thermostat shivering on the screen under several falling snowflakes.

"That's impossible. Snow?"

"It won't stick," Martha said, but she didn't sound surprised, either. Summer was long gone and I was the only one who couldn't quite grasp its passing. I needed a long and lingering autumn, a tenure with which to ease into another state of being.

"It's only a flurry," she said, reaching for the remote to lower the volume. "It'll blow in and blow out, like you. Which reminds me, tomorrow's payday if you're staying."

"I don't think I am."

"Why am I not surprised?"

"You've been very kind," I said.

"Did you at least get to the cultural center?"

"I've been taking classes."

"No! Glassblowing!" Martha nearly jumped out of her seat. I had never seen a woman so excited. I had robbed her of this capacity in my mind, I had shortchanged her pleasure. I was surprised enough to smile. On the television screen, they had cut to a dark-haired newscaster in a yellow rain slicker standing under Reno's distinctive lighted arch, the man's expression solemn in the downpour, tiny drops of water clinging to his glasses.

"Ceramics," I told her. Then, hesitating, "I don't know why. I've been wondering what other people feel when they make things. Why do they do it?"

Martha looked deflated.

"It's supposed to be fun, honey," she said. "Aren't you having any fun?"

I stood up then, making my apologies. Martha grabbed the remote and turned the volume back up, the man's voice exactly as monotonous as I'd imagined, the droning nature of desert news. *Employees reported the abandoned vehicle after guests of the casino complained it hadn't been moved for several days. Police believe it belongs to this man*—I made my way down the hall to the room with the groove-paneled door and pushed it in, realizing only a moment too late that the door was already a millimeter ajar, that I hadn't needed my key. Before I could move, Lucas grabbed me roughly by the arm, yanking me inside. He clamped a hand over my mouth, pulling me tight with an arm over my chest, his mouth at my ear. Martha hollered from the front room, her voice barely discernible over the blare of the TV.

"Snow's coming!" she called, "I hope you're ready!"

Lucas kicked the door shut. The duffel bag had been turned over on the bed, my clothes strewn across the mattress, a corner of Penny's bright yellow folder sticking out from underneath a pair of jeans. I looked around the room, frantic, hoping Lucas had somehow missed Fischer's gun.

"I don't want to hurt you," Lucas said quietly, "but I will."

77

I cut a piece of clay from the hunk and hold the wet weight in my palm, liquid trickling down my wrist. In the first moments of squeezing and stressing the clay, digging my fingers into the testy mass, all manner of possibilities are still available. Even after I throw the clay on the wheel, offering it the shelter of my palms, when I begin to beg something of its nature with fingers and knuckles and thumbs, there is still room to change, to go back, to erase, to begin again. Inevitably there comes a time when the object must begin to take shape and a decision must be made—to guide it long and lean or short and fat—to make, in short, a bowl or a cup or a spoon or a vase, to author it out of the myriad of viable shapes into one solitary article.

In the moments before the kiln, even if I could still take this cup or spoon or bowl and reduce it again, it would already be too late. The clay has been formed, it has memory; it has been made into a shape with all the promise and intention in the world. No matter how I try to reduce the mass to its original form, it will never be nothing again.

69

Lucas relaxed his grip over my mouth but kept his hand close, ready the minute I tried to scream. What had he said earlier, at the bar? *You're safe enough.* A person, proclaiming themselves a harbor. He took a step back and I punched him in the chest, hard enough for him to suck air. He looked surprised, even before I rammed my heel down on his foot. In an instant his hand was around my throat. He slammed my head back into the door, making my teeth click. It didn't hurt as much as it could have. It hurt just enough.

He rubbed his chest with his free hand. "You want to get that nice old woman involved in this?"

I tried, unsuccessfully, to shake my head. He dropped his grip on my neck. For all of it, he appeared only mildly annoyed. He wasn't taking me seriously, still confident he had the upper hand. With his size and strength and his willingness to use them, he did. Only now I was beginning to understand why Lucas surprised me in the movie theater in the first place—because he had yet to learn where I was staying. Not until I was stupid enough to lead him here myself.

"I'll take the photos and be gone," he said. He kept his voice low.

"They're in the folder."

"I found those. I want all the copies."

"Those are all the copies." I stepped away from him, sinking onto the bottom bunk to sort through my strewn possessions, the tank tops and underwear, the yellow folder already emptied of its contents. Penny's tube of lipstick rolled around on the coverlet. I turned over the empty duffel bag, yanking the pillows from the bed.

"Looking for this?" Lucas lifted his shirt to reveal his tight, trim stomach, the butt of Fischer's gun sticking up from his belt. He pulled it out, palming it from one hand to the other. I had no sense of how much noise we were making, whether Martha was already on her way down the hall. I lowered my own voice, conscious of what Lucas might do to anyone who tried to enter the room.

"You don't want that. It belongs to a cop."

"Funny."

"It belongs to a police officer, and it's empty now. Check the magazine."

I could feel him hesitating. But he already had what he came for. He pointed the gun and pulled out the magazine. Whistled.

"Why would a cop give you his gun?"

"Why would you give Penny the money in your wallet?"

We stared at each other. Lucas was beginning to look troubled. He set the gun carefully on the top of the bureau near the door. Still within his reach, though it wouldn't do either one of us any good.

"You really are crazy," he said. "Both of you."

"Are we?" I asked. "Tell me what happened. Really." The words popped out; I was already embarrassed by them. What was truth, to a man like him? "Did you hurt her?"

He shook his head, his hand on the door. "They'll never believe me." He adjusted his strange mouth. "What did you say she does for work?"

"We were waitresses together."

"Try that."

"You mean to find her?" I could have laughed. "You think Penny's going to waitress now? When she can get more than a day's tips from a guy's wallet?"

The grimace again. "People don't change that fast."

"Do you know something?"

"I told you, she was wandering around the tables, looking lost. Before that, I saw her pull up outside the Leaspoke. She got out of a guy's truck and he drove off. I asked her about it before we went upstairs. The last thing I need, some angry boyfriend showing up."

"She didn't have a boyfriend." Even I was impressed by the conviction in my tone, as if I still believed I was an authority on anything Penny might say or do. As if I ever was.

"That's what she said. Said he was just her ride."

"Did you see him?"

"Not really. White kid. She said he worked construction back home. Nice truck."

Lucas opened the door carefully, holding it ajar. The sound of Martha's television filtered down the hall. I wanted to tell him to go quickly out the back, to leave Martha absorbed by her nightly news and crossword puzzles, her small, devout pleasures. But he knew, better than any of us, how to disappear. I watched him go, thinking of the first time Penny showed me her place, the mud-spattered Timberlands by her front door. I spoke to his shadow already slipping down the hall, to Penny, wherever she was.

"His name is Eric," I said.

70

The café at the Golden Bear was cheaper than the restaurant, so more people went. After checking out of the Prickly Pine, I loaded my duffel bag in the back seat and drove there for one last meal: a way to allocate time, to break up the day into manageable chunks. I was already too late for both breakfast and lunch, but it meant the crowds were gone, that I was free to linger over a cup of coffee for as long as I liked. I had become the old vet I used to wonder about, who showed up at Jake's every week and ordered scrambled eggs only to sit and stare out the window. A person as calendar, marking time.

I took my usual seat by the window, facing the parking lot. The desire remained to watch the hopeful way people walked into restaurants, as if the right meal could solve all their problems, or at least temporarily alleviate them. The waitress was one I knew from earlier visits, Bea, a Virginia City native and old town historian, as adept at reading people as the three-card tarot spreads she laid across the back counter after her shift: past, present, future; mind, body, spirit. It lessened the sting of her scrupulous appraisal.

She came by with a fresh pot and started pouring me a warmup, then stopped, the pot aloft. I followed her gaze to the television screen mounted above the counter. The tall, grim newscaster was rigid right

up to his immovably gelled hair. He was not the same man Martha and
I had watched the night before, but he, too, was solemn as he reported
under Reno's arch, its bright lights dimmed for the day. After the
night's rains, the sky had softened to oyster. The camera cut to a shot
of a big red truck in a familiar casino parking lot, the area cordoned
off with yellow tape. At the sight of it, a sour taste filled my mouth.
Eric's greatest wish, *a real cherry red screamer*.

Across the aisle, a small child stood up in her booth, all plump
cheeks and squat limbs. She began jumping up and down on the seat,
her ringlets bouncing. When I glanced back at the TV, the truck's
glossy paint seemed to shimmer.

"Do you hate children," Bea murmured, resuming her pour, "or is
it just me?"

Across the table, Penny's double materialized again, patiently
awaiting acknowledgment. Like an old married couple with all conversation spent between us, I didn't bother asking why she was there.
She pulled a marker from the air and drew four flat black lines on the
Formica tabletop, then a space, then two, then five, followed by a long
skinny pole.

Bea returned with a plate of eggs and two slices of toast. I shook
the ketchup bottle and asked for hot. Two men entered the café and
took seats by the door. Across the aisle, the little girl's mother reached
for a fork and stabbed it into her bowl of chili fries. The girl stopped
jumping and opened her cupid's mouth to let out a bloodcurdling
scream. Here was a spoiled child, reckless, she had been given things;
she was yet unaware of loss, accommodation, the way people in the
world would hollow her out.

"K," I said.

Imaginary Penny smiled. She uncapped the marker and began to draw a skull.

Bea brought the hot sauce but lingered by the table. A black sedan was pulling into the parking lot, and the sight of it spiked the anxiety already tingling down my spine. We watched the driver's-side door open and a man unfold himself from the car. Fischer's tall gait was instantly familiar, his brown hair ruffling in the breeze. But I had imagined Penny; I could be imagining him, too.

"P," I said.

Penny began to fill in a long, hefty torso, the hangman's solid core. I still hadn't solved Penny's first riddle from that summer afternoon when we traded sandwiches in Pomoc's abandoned, burnt-out house, and I had a feeling my game hadn't much improved. We had abandoned that game halfway through, the house grown too hot, and drove down the street to the ice cream parlor for cones. We stood in the sun licking lemon and black cherry scoops, milky pink rivers running down our wrists.

"E," I said.

Penny bent her head to fill in the letters. One on the top row, one on the last.

Bea distributed menus to the two men at the table by the door. They looked to have casual business between them; easygoing men who didn't demand favorite tables or memorized orders, who asked for nothing beyond a hot plate. Bea kept looking from the television to the window, as if something about the black sedan was nagging her, too, or she had been expecting its return. I tried to recall how many times I had come here in recent days; how presumptive my visits had become. It *was* Fischer walking toward the café. He had a determined stride and a firm set to his jaw, as if he had precise news to deliver, something I would never be able to unhear. I watched him until he disappeared around a corner, heading for the entrance.

On the other side of the table, phantom Penny was growing visibly more distraught, tapping the hangman's blank lines with her marker cap, the way she used to click her nails on the passenger window to tell me when to turn. It didn't really matter where we went or how far we drove, we were always going to end up here. There was a clatter from the men's table, a coffee cup knocked over, a river of hot black liquid puddling onto the floor. The men grabbed napkins to stem the flow, the little girl at the nearby booth began to cry. Bea stood unmoved, her attention fixed on the television screen and the new white ribbon of text ticking across the bottom of the screen.

POLICE INVESTIGATION: UNIDENTIFIED BODY FOUND.

Pick a letter, Penny said. That way she had of speaking without even moving her mouth, the sinuous conventions of her illusory world. She tapped the hangman on the table again, insistent. If Fischer had his way, he would take us both back to Pomoc, where for different reasons we had really never, but somehow always, belonged.

We have to go back, Penny had said.

Solve for Penny, she said now. *Solve for Cale*.

I stood up too quickly, knocking over my chair, and ran into the café's kitchen toward the rear exit I knew I'd find there, past the surprised shouts of servers and fry cooks who instinctively moved out of my way, wanting no part of the trouble I couldn't shake.

72

I drove down C Street, past the Comstock-era saloons and the restored Washoe Club, the old hotels leveled by fire and rebuilt again, their displaced ghosts left to rendezvous in parking lots like wasps flirting in the glare of old-fashioned streetlamps. I glanced at the passenger seat, but there was no Penny sitting beside, imaginary or otherwise; no phantom hiding behind the slim storage space where the tire iron still lay safely tucked. I bore east past the buildings that petered out, past the high metal fence lettered BLESSED ARE THE DEAD, bordering the cemetery of buried miners and assorted other dreamers, chasing gold and a better life. I picked up speed until the last of the downtown lights extinguished in the rearview and I was in the desert again. With no one chasing behind and seemingly nothing ahead, I pressed on until the first glimmer appeared like a comic trick of light, the giant horseshoe taking shape out of nothingness, glowing phosphorescent in the dark.

I eased up on the gas a few yards out, coasting toward a squat, square building with a covered awning, a white swing gate blocking the entry. There were several cars parked in a neat row in the dirt while others had been abandoned at wild angles, as if their drivers had leapt from their seats with their motors still running. I parked alongside an SUV several yards from the entrance and cut the engine.

The eerie light of the horseshoe flooded the truck's interior, making me feel as if I was caught inside a spaceship. I wrapped my small hands around the wheel. They were numb no longer. I traced the center of the steering wheel where the smudge of blood that had appeared that night and had long since been worn away. At the time I was certain it belonged to the sandman, but it could have just as easily been mine. After dropping Penny off that night, the shock wore off on the drive home, the right side of my face waking into a throbbing constellation of agony, my nose beginning to bleed again. I found the blood everywhere later; crusted around my nostrils like cuprite, smeared on my chin and the backs of my hands, on my shirt, smudged across the thighs of my jeans. Penny had to have known, even as she hosed down the wheels on the truck, how impossible it would be to remove all trace of our crime. Some things could never be washed away.

Outside, a car door slammed. A few minutes later a cluster of girls wobbled past the windshield, their arms linked, all three of them in short skirts and heels. One wore a cowboy hat over her dark hair; another was slim and indistinct, the third blond and buxom, an all-American wet dream. I watched them clicking toward the awning in their high heels, holding each other up. As they approached the entrance a mountainous shadow stepped aside, waving the girls through. I opened the door and climbed out into the sharp nip. I walked toward the Golden Horseshoe under light so bright it seemed to erase the lines of my body so that I was only glow, a charged electrical field. The enormous shape moved behind the gate, but when I came upon him I saw it was only a man, taller than any had a right to be, broad across the chest, dressed sharply in a black suit and a black shirt that melted into the night, his patent shoes winking in step.

I could hear the thrum of music and raucous laughter inside, purple strobe lights blinking against the glass. I was reaching for Penny's purse when I heard a low, distinctive growl. The man uncrossed his arms in warning, turning to look. "Quit," he said, and only then did I sense movement, the dog splayed off to the side of the entrance, his leash tied to a post, the silver glint of a water bowl. The dog's fur was as black as the man's suit, indecipherable as silhouette. I tried to angle for a better look past the man's sizable girth, venturing two steps before the man shot a firm arm across my chest. Unyielding, but not unkind.

"Nope. He ain't for petting."

"I just want to see him," I said, straining my neck. The dog seemed to sense our conflict and climbed to his feet, his growl deepening. He'd grown a little taller, a little longer; he had gained some weight, too. One ear now stood upright of its own accord. But his fur was still sticking up all around him like adolescent down, his paws still too big for him yet.

"Hi you," I said to the dog, trying in vain to push past the man. He looked at me askance, straining against his arm, as if I had recently misplaced my mind.

"I know him!" I finally said. "I know Penny, too."

"Who?" he said, but he relaxed his arm a little, close enough to block me if needed. "Dog's mine now." He was studying me up close, his eyes moving curiously over my face and hair.

"What about the girl who gave him to you?"

"She worked here. For a split second."

I nodded, trying to ignore the flood of disappointment that threatened to drown me. Must Penny always be smarter, faster, one step ahead? I took another step toward the dog, who let loose with a couple of barks. The man reached for my hip to keep me back. I covered his giant hand with my own. He allowed me to gently pull it free.

"If he bites you," he said, "don't blame me."

I stopped a foot away and squatted in the dirt. I didn't disbelieve either of them, especially not the dog, growling still. But I held out my hand, keeping a wide distance between us. The dog retreated, holding himself tense against the gate. He looked away, beginning to whine.

"What's his name?"

"No name," the man said.

A mismatched couple approached the gate, seeking entry. An older man in a collared shirt, the top three buttons undone to reveal a shaved, sunburned chest. The leggy showgirl in a jean skirt, hair teased to Texas. The older man passed the bouncer a handful of bills, and he waved them inside.

"He's been going around without a name?" I asked once they were gone. "All this time?"

"Wasn't her thing," he said, with a carelessness I could well imagine, coming from Penny. I crabwalked toward the dog. He stopped whining but still held himself rigid. I inched close enough for him to point his snout in my direction. He sniffed delicately, then, picking up the scent, came forward to sniff with more interest, growing excited, the old memory stirring. He rushed me then, working his snout under my palm, pushing my hand up once, twice, three times. *Hi. Hi. Hi.*

I reached for him with both hands, stroking his soft crown, kissing his grown ear in apology for the early tumult of his young life. He set his front paws on my thigh, the way his brother had set his paws on Penny in the trailer. I had already been wrong about this dog once, betting against his generous heart, the propensity of animals to forgive. The man watched us for several minutes, fascinated or annoyed, I couldn't tell.

"Don't steal him from me now."

"You'll give him a great name, won't you?"

"I guess I'll try."

"The girl who gave him to you. She must have trusted you. You have to know where she is."

"Do I?"

"Please tell me."

"I'm not sure I know what you mean," the man said. "Who are you, anyway? You want to tell me what brought you here?"

I smoothed the dog's face one last time, then forced myself to stand, brushing the dirt from my legs.

"I wouldn't know where to begin," I said.

I reached for the flap on Penny's purse and pulled out the last of Penny's twenties from the coffee can. The man let the money hang between us, his arms still crossed.

"Maybe you know something about the boy she came here with? Eric Spears?" I asked. "Tall, blond—kind of a jerk? He was a bouncer, too, back home. Anyway, I saw the news this morning. I'm not sure he's doing much of that anymore."

The money hung between us for a moment. Finally the bouncer took it, tucking the bills deep inside his jacket. I felt something wet land square on my nose and brushed it away, only to feel something else landing on my bare arm, the back of my other hand. The man in black emerged from underneath the awning and looked up at the sky. I followed suit, stepping into the flurry to crane my neck, recalling the gangly usher at the movie theater and how close he always sat to the screen. I would go back and find him someday, I would tell him he was right. This was the best way to observe spectacle. The man beside me laughed, a rumbling sound that felt like joy. I stuck out my tongue and tasted snow.

19

THE
AZTLÁN
HOTEL

73

It was a forty-minute drive from the Golden Horseshoe to Reno, and even before I saw the casinos rising in the distance like a mythical cosmopolis, I could tell that this place, despite being the opposite of Pomoc in so many ways, was still also exactly the same. In the dark the Sierra Nevadas were mostly obscured, but I could still make out their irregular shape from their shadow, like a piece of construction paper ripped across the bottom of the sky. Driving through the center of town the casino lights reflected on the wet streets, washing the city in vivid color. The snow dissolved as soon as it touched our skin, but a lingering chill remained. The girls on the sidewalks remained defiant in skirts and shorts, loath to submit to the season. Unique amid the city's angular skyline was the Silver Legacy's ivory dome; in the northeast corner of the city, a two-hundred-thousand-square-foot double pyramid peaked above the fray. The last time I'd been here with Lamb, the Aztlán hadn't yet broken ground, and Reno was still the old west's antidote to Vegas in every way. But time had changed things, people, too; an influx of businesses had moved west, driving up development. As I drove closer, I circled the first large pyramid, following the arrows pointing to the second. It was a sprawling, multi-tiered garage. I took the last empty spot on the top floor. The long walk to the elevator didn't feel unlike arriving at the Leaspoke only a few weeks earlier, save for the luxury cars I passed on the way, the high-tech camera system clearly marked every fifteen feet, a dozen lime-green sensors, blinking.

Lourdes' rich tía got married there.

All of life a repetition, the details slightly changed.

I took the elevator to the ground floor, where the doors opened onto a nascent passage marked with tōnalpōhualli symbols. I followed as it fed into a grand lobby where guests milled across an enormous sunstone. A small family was huddled by one of the engraved columns, each of them loaded with backpacks and camera equipment, the father directing his lens to a vaulted skylight projecting a vast and shifting cosmos. At the front desk, women in long, rust-colored tunics watched coolly over the crowd. I was absorbed by the momentum of tourists cycling through the floor around discreet bars and restaurants. I stepped inside a gift shop, thinking of Lamb, a decade's worth of miniature teddy bears and feather keychains collecting dust in my bedroom dresser at home. But this store was all sharp, polished corners; silk scarves in glass cases, gold jewelry, rich textiles hanging from tall fabric racks. The woman behind the counter ran her eyes over my shorts and tank top, a reminder of my appearance and its devolvement over weeks on the road. As I edged out of the store, I saw her reaching for the phone on her desk. I hadn't forgotten the look on Fischer's face as he approached the Golden Bear's café, or my own narrow escape.

I crossed the lobby to the main elevator bay and ducked onto the next lift, heading up. A ruddy-faced businessman stepped on, too, adjusting his disheveled suit, loosening the tie around his neck, enveloping us both in the fumes of his alcohol consumption and bluegrass

cologne. I recalled Fischer's words about Penny at the Leaspoke—
they show her getting on the elevator. So these cameras would capture
me, too, for better or worse. The man produced a cardboard envelope
of keycards and pressed a button for the twenty-sixth floor, swiping
the card through a slim reader protruding from the door. He leaned
against the mirror as the lift closed and we began to rise, his face
slackening in repose. I simply took the envelope from between his
fingers—they tightened slightly as I pulled, then they released—and I
removed one of the cards before replacing the envelope in his hand.
He said nothing to me, just watched with calm, bloodshot eyes. When
the doors reopened on his floor, he heaved himself away from the
mirror.

"Be good," he said, the doors closing behind him. I punched another
button and went down one floor, walking the hushed, labyrinthine
hallway from end to end, then stepped back on the elevator to repeat
the exercise on every subsequent floor. Somewhere inside this casino,
Fischer was being called, or had already arrived; I felt time slipping by.
On the nineteenth floor, I passed service trays piled in the hall, the
murmurs of televisions trapped behind heavy doors. On the fifteenth,
at the end of the hall, voices were pitched in anger. On the thirteenth, I
followed the hall to a glass-paneled fitness center and swiped the card
again to enter a room lined with aerodynamic treadmills and rows of
free weights, all four walls embedded with full-screen TVs.

I couldn't bear another headline, but these televisions were playing
a national news network with broader concerns; a kohl-eyed reporter
spoke seriously from the middle of a Marrakech souk, passing mer-
chants vying to bogart the lens. On the other end of the gym was another darkened glass door flanked by card readers and a second
tōnalpōhualli symbol I couldn't read, but was sure corresponded to

the hotel map I had passed in the elevator bay. I swiped the key and stepped into a large, open-air courtyard, shivering from the chill.

This high up, the breeze was sharp and cold, rustling the dark green shrubs that lined the planters, the huddle of patio umbrellas lashed in anticipation of the next warm day. The beach chairs, too, had been stacked in a corner, save for one chaise dragged away from the others, draped by a towel. In the center of the courtyard an enormous hourglass pool changed colors from a deep turquoise to an uncanny, kryptonite green. The woman crossing its surface took long, smooth strokes, impervious to the weather or the minuscule black bikini I wouldn't have been surprised to learn had been purchased by the disheveled businessman I had just left—or by any number of men foolish enough to believe her affections might be bought. I walked over to the chaise and picked up the towel, weighing damp and heavy in my hands.

I stripped off Penny's purse, my tank top and shorts, and left them in a pile on the concrete, easing into the shallow edge of the pool. It was ice cold, freezing my feet, legs, belly, breasts. I dunked my head under and screamed at the feeling, the water eating up the sound. The pool changed colors again, our bodies moving through the deep, vibrant red of languid magma. I came to float on the surface. When I looked down, I could see gooseflesh rippling my skin, my nipples poking through my thin cotton bra. Above us the sky was jet black, the pyramids' lights eclipsing the stars. I closed my eyes and tried to focus on my breath, the sounds of splashing. I was waiting for hotel security to crash through the doors at any minute, for Fischer's angry voice to crack across the courtyard—but the longer the silence lasted, the deeper I slipped into a strange inertia, the water lapping at my ears. I might have fallen asleep if not for the acute cold, the uneasy knowledge that the splashing had stopped, the water's equilibrium slowly shifting, and going still. I opened my eyes to find her sunk in the water not two feet away, only her eyes and nose breaking the surface. The first pyramid's wide, candy-colored peak soared up behind her. She tilted her head back, clearing her mouth from the water to speak.

"Surprise," Penny said.

74

I waited for Penny to swim closer, realizing, as she did, that I had entirely forgotten the small second mole on her chin, how maddening she was in the flesh. She leaned back into the water, coming to float nearby. We stayed like that for some time, suspended on our backs within arm's length of each other. I shivered again, a deep, emergent chill.

"Your cop's been snooping around," she said.

"Mine?" I made a strangled sound at the back of my throat. "He's been looking *for you*."

"You believe that? He told the front desk manager you emptied a magazine into that boy's headboard."

"He's hardly a boy."

"But that's what your cop said. He's going to be a boy now, forever."

I closed my eyes. "Isn't that what you wanted?"

"In the moment."

I sank my legs down in the water, turning to face her. She kept her eyes closed, her arms stretched out, palms to the sky, the same as Lamb had when I came upon him in the doctor's exam room weeks before, chasing grace in his darkest hour. Yet I had never thought of

Penny as someone who received; she was the one who meted out judg-
ment, who acted upon the world. The pool changed colors again. We
were drifting in a frigid amethyst sea, and I was beginning to lose
feeling in my legs. I reached out and pinched her arm. Her skin was
rubbery. Still real.

"I didn't suggest you try to kill him, Cale. I said *I* wanted to."

"I wasn't trying to kill him."

"Then what were you doing?"

I shoved her then, hard enough to upset her balance. Her eyes fluttered open, she backstroked to keep afloat.

"He doesn't remember us! He doesn't remember anything!"

Penny sank down legs first, then waist, ribs, chest and neck, gathering speed to pike underwater. The pool turned green again, lighting up her sinuous shape from below. I kept treading water, though I
sensed her an instant before her hand closed around my ankle, yanking me under. The icy water rushed over my head. All at once I remembered Alvaro, Flaca, the bathtub full of snakes, and Penny among
them. I sucked in cold water, kicking my free leg in an attempt to stay
close to the surface. I felt her hands climbing up my calf, trying to secure a firmer grip. I kicked again and connected with her shoulder,
then lunged forward and kicked a third time, harder than necessary.
Wanting to bruise her.

She released me, and I propelled myself back to the surface, cough-
ing, gasping, my eyes stinging with chlorine. I swallowed, my throat
sore. She slipped up to the surface only a few feet away, keeping low
and partially hidden, only her eyes above the water, watching my reaction. I was hurt and felt dumb for it.

"Fuck you!"

When the water had settled, she tilted her head above the water to speak.

"He's never going to remember anything again. We did that."

"I know." My face ached from the cold, my lips and nose beginning to turn numb. "I needed to see him."

She was nodding. "But now you've pissed off a cop."

"He's just pissed I stole his gun."

She laughed, a genuine, sparkling sound. The pool changed colors again, hemorrhaging a deep, dark sapphire. We could have been in the ocean, how far away everything seemed. She caught my eyes. I watched her mirth slowly dissolve. I remembered the look on the bouncer's face when I mentioned Eric's name, a similar leaching of sentiment. I hesitated, cautious now.

"Where *did* Fischer go? This the floor manager . . . ?"

Her smirk, familiar still. "Relax. She just redirected him a bit. He'll be here soon."

"Penny. Do you understand? I thought something happened to you."

"Something did," she said. She rolled facedown in the water, her hips and legs coming up to float. She let herself drift like that for a second, a corpse in the water, her hair fanning out before she sank her legs back down to tread. Her hair was sticking to her face like a dark spider web. When she reached up to push it away, I realized she had cut it. I hadn't noticed when it was slicked back from her forehead, hidden behind her shoulders, but now the ends were clinging to her collarbone. I felt an air bubble growing inside my chest, threatening to pop.

"Penny," I said. "I don't think you understand. I thought you were dead."

"Not me."

I watched her face for some crack of emotion, the tremor of remorse she would never allow herself to show.

"Eric?" I paused, but she said nothing. "I'm going to guess he deserved it."

"That's a good guess." She spit water. "Define deserve."

"If you had just told me you were going, I would have come with you."

"I know."

"It makes no difference, you mean."

"I mean I didn't know how far I would go. I mean I didn't mean for any of this. But it makes no difference now."

"What will you do?"

"I don't know." She said it simply, as if we might be discussing the weather, the latest customer to come into Jake's, their strange and incongruous food pairings. "Any ideas?"

"I thought you were the one with all the good ideas."

She considered this. "Maybe the aliens will come get me."

She dunked her head, disappearing under the water. I waited for her to return. When she did, she was closer, only a few inches away. Another breeze blew across the patio, causing us both to shiver. I waited for whatever terrible thing she might do. But she only took my hand out of the water and pressed it, briefly, to her chest. Her skin, exposed above the water, was just as cold as mine. When she met my eyes, I saw her. Just Penny. Not terrible, not mythic. Not particularly good, for long periods of time, at passing as someone who was. My shivers were turning into shakes, the icy feeling penetrating my bones. I would need to lie in front of a fire to get rid of it, I would need to climb into one. Penny lowered my hand back into the water, squeezing it briefly before letting go.

A shudder overtook me, my body rejecting the chill. "I'm so *cold*."

"I know. We both have to get out soon."

"Where can we go?"

She shook her head. "You go."

"Penny—"

She shook her head. "He's okay. Leave me here. Let him come."

"Why?"

She looked at me then, her eyelashes wet and stuck together, her eyes enormous. I saw in them all the banked fear Wolf and Trixie had around the brush fires; the idea that something existed in nature more unpredictable and ferocious than themselves. Something that would, if they weren't careful, eventually eat them alive.

"We always do what I want," she said.

75

There were only three pay phones left in Reno. I was still shivering when I dropped my quarter into the coin slot outside the Diamond Aces Motel & RV Park, my damp underwear like something dead between my legs, though I had wrung them out at the Aztlán before wriggling them back on. I knew I should have thrown away my wet things, but I couldn't bear to leave anything else behind. I worried a scale of paint from the booth with my fingernail while I listened to the phone ring, the flaking Pepto pink a local prank or somber attempt to compliment the Aces' flickering neon sign, I didn't know. On the other side of the phone, no one spoke, but the ringing stopped. I couldn't tell if the call had dropped, my heart prepared to follow. I was all out of change. Eventually I discerned the sound of someone breathing.

"Hello?"

"What," Flaca's voice was still thick with sleep, "the fuck?"

"I thought you never slept," I said. But I did feel bad. I was forever disturbing people's rest. I no longer obeyed the boundaries of night and day, I couldn't seem to remember why others did. A moment passed, the yawn that followed only a degree less hostile. Languorous, like any creature roused in the middle of the night, waiting for the shape in the brush to emerge. I could hear some other noise in the background on Flaca's end; a fan running, a stranger's snore. I waited for wakefulness to dawn, for her to realize the time, my voice, the reason I might be calling. I gave her a minute, though there was hardly any left to spare.

"Flaca?" I said finally. "It's Cale."

"I know it's you, dummy."

"Are you still bored?"

"Why?" she asked. "Whatever it is, just tell me. You've got to be in some deep shit, if you're calling me."

"Actually, my shit is medium," I said. "Thanks for asking. Although, who better to call? But it's our friend who has bigger problems."

It took a moment for her to sink in. Her exhalation was slow and steady, a pressure valve releasing steam. The background noise faded as she got out of bed and moved to somewhere else in the room.

"Where are you?" she asked finally. "Where is she?"

"Do you remember the Aztlán in Reno? Where Lourdes' tía—"

"Yes."

"Drive south from all the lights. It'll seem like you're driving into nothing. About ten miles out, there's an old petroleum factory. Pull around the back. About a quarter mile down the road, there are a couple big trees—alders, I think—you'll see where the fence has been cut. You'll have to get out and walk to the warehouse on foot. There are three doors on the side of the right building. The last one, the one closest to the street, we broke the lock."

"Jesus, Cale." I could hear the sound of a door squeaking, drawers opening and closing. "You can't just drop a pin?"

"No phones," I said. "You should leave yours behind." I paused. I could feel a wave of something hot and ugly coming on, everything I had been driving away from for several weeks, all speeding now to catch up. I squeezed my eyes shut, banging my head gently against the pay phone's plastic shield. "I hope your piece of shit car makes it."

"You know what? This must be your white side talking."

"Can you hurry?"

"I'm coming, I'm coming. Will I see you there?"

"No. You're free of me now."

"Good," she said. "Great. Finally."

But neither one of us hung up the phone.

For the first time ever, I heard her hesitating. "Is she okay?" Flaca asked.

"I don't know," I said. "No."

"Are you?"

"No." I said. "But we have to go, anyway. You'll be safe." I said it firmly, like I could will it for them both. "Flaca? You will. You're going to make it."

The sound of something in the background—a duffel bag, a suitcase—zipping up.

"I always make it," Flaca said.

76

I crossed over at Verdi, heading south through Mystic, the descent through the Sierra Nevadas obscured by low morning light and an evanescent fog like dispersed crystal clinging to the pines. The mist filled the ravine over the Truckee River so that the sound of rushing water seemed to come from an invisible place in the distance. Climbing the mountains' steep elevation, the truck's red temperature needle spiked over Floriston and Hinton, then leveled over Donner Pass, as if in reverence to those famished pioneers made so desperate by snow.

I pulled off the freeway into the woods, parking under a thicket of incense cedars to let the engine cool. I hiked to the white elders peppering Secret Ravine and tramped the slippery banks before returning to the road, my boots slickened by a fresh layer of mud, cupping my hand against the truck's hood, hot as a sick dog's belly. When I started her up, the red marker had barely moved. I drove cautiously past Colfax's railroad depot, recalling Rhyolite and Gold Butte and Lucky Jim, all of Nevada's ghost towns long since gone bust.

By noon the overcast burnt off or I had descended the mountains far enough to escape it. I kept a steady crawl through Concord until hitting the 101, praying the engine would hold. It did, past Santa Clara

County and Gilroy, but by the time I spotted the sign for Monterey whorls of thick white smoke were twisting free from the hood, fogging up the windshield. I coasted into the nearest gas station and killed the engine, the cab filling with the odor of rotten eggs. This, too, Lamb had predicted, warning me not to travel too far on the old truck's last legs. I hadn't listened—not to him or to Jackson, who, had I let him, would have had me coasting along in the refurbished Nova. I got out of the truck and pulled my long shirtsleeves over my fingers before popping the hood, hiding my face from the plumes of steam that rolled free. The radiator looked too hot to touch.

It had warmed up some outside, a bright sun filtering through the clouds. There was a supple brine to the air that clung to my skin, kinking my hair. Funny how, having never smelled the ocean before, I knew it all the same. But for all I knew, Catherine's daughter had been here before; maybe I had, too. I left the truck and made for the station. Inside I was soothed by the endless rows of packaged nuts and cough drops, the cold cases full of beer; the unrelenting human drive to categorize objects, as if doing so might begin to clarify the chaos within ourselves. I swiped a bag of gummy bears off a low shelf and wandered over to the soda machine, where a redhead was playing the dispensers like piano keys, mixing sodas into her Big Gulp with a chemist's singular focus. She wore a robe of patchworked velvet, her pale, elegant hand made remarkable by an assortment of cumbrous silver rings: carnelian and moonstone and blue lace agate, malachite bright as a parakeet's feather. She glanced over at me, a feather earring brushing her shoulder.

"What?" she asked.

"I've just never seen a hippie before," I said. I left her there, looking offended. In the next aisle I grabbed coolant and a gallon of water, trying to recall Jackson's technical sermons. At the cash register I fondled packets of gum to avoid small talk with the toothless man who rang me up. There was no longer any need to reach into my purse for Penny's flyer or unfold it on the counter between us, to mine strangers' depths for sympathy. Penny had already been lost and found. I was the only one left to seek.

Outside, the redhead was smoking near the truck and sipping her Big Gulp, walking around to peer curiously under the hood at the truck's splayed guts. She backed off as I approached, but stopped a few feet away, watching as I set the coolant on the ground. I unscrewed the radiator's cap with my sleeve, feeding coolant and water in slow increments, pausing in between. I sensed the hippie's scrutiny, her bangles clinking with every drag.

"I'm actually not a hippie," she said, as if reading my mind. "Who even still uses that word?"

"Me, I guess."

"Yeah? Where are you from?"

"Not here."

"Oh, obvious and friendly. Do you know what you're doing to your car?"

"Kind of. I'm not sure it's going to help." I added more water and walked around to try the engine. The needle popped right back up the dash, well into red. With the hood up I could now discern a distinct plastic rattle—cracked flexplate? Loose drive belt? I killed the engine and grabbed the duffel bag before climbing out again, locking the door.

"You fucked?" she asked.

I gave her a sidelong glance. "I didn't think hippies smoked."

"I quit," she said. I stared at her cigarette another second. She waved it impatiently. "E-cig," she explained. Nodding at the truck, "Maybe it's like a computer—you know, turn it off and on again."

I screwed the radiator cap back on and lowered the hood. "It's not. Which way are you headed? Could I bum a ride?"

"Sorry. I'd love to help, but that's a lie. I have to get back to L.A. tonight."

"Los Angeles?"

She snorted. Then, sensing I was serious, tilted her head, Trixie-like. "No one calls it that."

"I thought you wanted to be friendly?"

She gestured with her e-cig. "It's a smoke-chat," she said.

"But that's where I'm headed. There's a new restaurant looking for waitresses." I unzipped the duffel and pulled a crinkled sheet of paper from the pocket, offering it to her. She transferred her cigarette to her other hand and reached for it, glancing up at me. Her pale green eyes keenly focused. She scanned the paper. "This is on Melrose," she said. "That's *L.A.*, L.A. Have you been there?"

"No."

"Well, they dress better than you. Where'd you get this?"

"The internet. I already called. They said I could come by." I took the advertisement back from her, trying not to snatch it. "I can pay for gas." I dug in my duffel for Jackson's white envelope and pulled out a twenty. She bypassed the proffered cash and reached for the envelope, slipping her nail under the ragged edge I had ripped open in front of Penny at the old petroleum factory, our fingers still pruned from the pool. The hippie removed the contents, counting out twenties. When she finished, she gave me an exasperated look and replaced the cash, looking as if she had aged ten years.

"You cannot move to L.A. with a hundred and sixty dollars," she said flatly. "Are you serious?"

"I had to repay a friend."

"My god." She gave me back the envelope. "They're going to eat you alive."

"Look," I tried again. But I didn't have anything else to show her.

"You can tell me about it on the way," she said.

"I don't think I can. Not for a long time."

She rolled her eyes, motioning for me to follow. "I can already tell you're going to make me want to start drinking again," she said.

I trailed her to the other side of the station, past a row of cars, stopping in front of the kind of calypso green convertible Jackson wouldn't even start working on without clearing a deposit. I slowed at the sight of it, ready to plead my case all over again. She removed the duffel from my hands and settled it in her back seat without a word. I went around the passenger side and climbed in, sitting on my hands to keep my nerves from taking over. There was something too heavy about being in a stranger's car, leaving the old truck behind. *This is your heart line. This is your fate.* She started the engine, turned up the radio to the sound of old rock 'n' roll—road songs with their insistent, pounding beat. We pulled out of the station and down the street toward the winding 101, picking up speed until the wind was whipping our hair from our faces. She grabbed an elastic band from the dash and tied back her wild curls. I held my hair with one hand, watching the coast open up along our side like a vast blue mystery. She reached for the radio and changed the station once, twice. I tensed—but desert news wouldn't reach us here, not until it was too late to change. After some time, I twisted around in my seat to watch the long strip of tar fading behind us. Her eyes, when she glanced over, were impossible to read behind the dark glasses she had pulled on. I could hardly hear her in the wind.

"Don't look now," she said.

ACKNOWLEDGMENTS

I would like to thank The Center for Fiction, Vermont Studio Center, the MacDowell Colony, and the Creative Writing Department at Stanford University for their support. Thank you to Ashlee Miller and Mark Rodriguez for research assistance, and to early readers Katherine, Anya, Lulu, Hilary, Taryn, Danny, Sam G, and Callan for their valuable feedback. Thank you Elizabeth Tallent, Adam Johnson, and Chang-rae Lee. And thank you, finally, to Joy Harris and Cal Morgan for supporting all the women of this novel, including me.

The line "The sea is smooth. It is a flat stone without any scratches" appears originally in *The Island of Blue Dolphins* by Scott O'Dell.